PRAISE FOR C. S. HA... ...YSTERIES

"Sebastian St. Cyr is everything you could want in a Regency-era nobleman-turned–death investigator: uncannily clever, unwaveringly reserved, and irresistibly sexy. The entire series is simply elegant."
—Lisa Gardner, #1 *New York Times* bestselling author of *Still See You Everywhere*

"Thoroughly enjoyable . . . moody and atmospheric, exposing the dark underside of Regency London."
—Deanna Raybourn, *New York Times* bestselling author of *Kills Well with Others*

"This riveting historical tale of tragedy and triumph, with its sly nods to Jane Austen and her characters, will enthrall you."
—Sabrina Jeffries, *New York Times* bestselling author of *Accidentally His*

"Filled with suspense, intrigue, and plot twists galore."
—Victoria Thompson, *USA Today* bestselling author of the Gaslight Mysteries

"St. Cyr is a brawler and his tough sleuthing is admirable. . . . This series is a favorite."
—*The New York Times Book Review*

"Harris is a master of the genre."
—*Historical Novels Review*

"With such well-developed characters, intriguing plotlines, graceful prose, and keen sense of time and place based on solid research, this is historical mystery at its best."
—*Booklist* (starred review)

WHAT CANNOT BE SAID

A Sebastian St. Cyr Mystery

⁓

C. S. HARRIS

BERKLEY
New York

BERKLEY
An imprint of Penguin Random House LLC
1745 Broadway, New York, NY 10019
penguinrandomhouse.com

ISBN: 9780593639207

The Library of Congress has cataloged the
Berkley hardcover edition of this book as follows:

Names: Harris, C. S., author.
Title: What cannot be said / C.S. Harris.
Description: New York: Berkley, 2024. | Series: A Sebastian St. Cyr mystery
Identifiers: LCCN 2023032411 (print) | LCCN 2023032412 (ebook) |
ISBN 9780593639184 (hardcover) | ISBN 9780593639191 (ebook)
Subjects: LCSH: Saint Cyr, Sebastian (Fictitious character)—Fiction. |
Murder—Investigation—Fiction. | LCGFT: Detective and mystery fiction. | Novels.
Classification: LCC PS3566.R5877 W53 2024 (print) |
LCC PS3566.R5877 (ebook) | DDC 813/.54—dc23/eng/20230717
LC record available at https://lccn.loc.gov/2023032411
LC ebook record available at https://lccn.loc.gov/2023032412

Berkley hardcover edition / April 2024
Berkley trade paperback edition / March 2025

Printed in the United States of America
1st Printing

The authorized representative in the EU for product safety and compliance
is Penguin Random House Ireland, Morrison Chambers, 32 Nassau Street,
Dublin D02 YH68, Ireland, https://eu-contact.penguin.ie.

For Whiskies

4 August 2009–1 November 2022

What cannot be said must be wept.

—Sappho

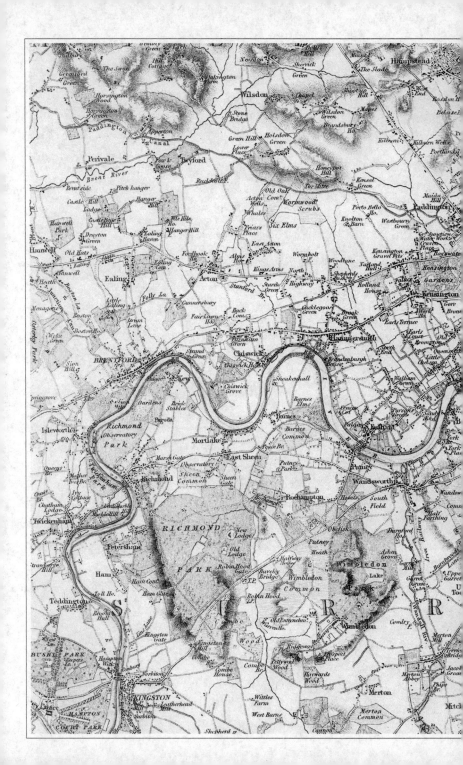

WHAT CANNOT BE SAID

Chapter 1

Richmond Park: Sunday, 23 July 1815

"I've figured out what's wrong with women," declared Ben. He lay on his back on the grassy hillside, his face lifted to the wide blue sky, his cheeks ruddy from a heady combination of sunshine, fresh air, and a bota of cheap red wine.

Harry swiveled his head to look at his brother. "So what is it?"

"They're *women*!"

The observation struck both young gentlemen as uproariously funny, and they rolled about in the sun-warmed grass, eyes squeezing shut, bodies convulsing with laughter. Separated in age by only two years, the sons of Thomas Barrows, Esquire, had retreated to Richmond Park on this glorious July afternoon to escape the hubbub surrounding their elder sister's wedding, which was scheduled to take place in three days' time.

"I think," said Ben, "that—" He broke off, his jaw going slack as a loud *cr-rack* echoed across the park.

"What was that?" said Harry, jerking upright.

Ben sat up beside him. "Sounded like a pistol shot."

Cr-rack.

At the second shot, the brothers looked at each other. "Reckon it's a duel?"

Harry pushed to his feet. "Let's go see!"

Snagging the straps of their leather wineskins, the brothers sprinted up the hill. From the top they could look out over the vast royal park's rolling vista of lush green grass and leafy woodland; London was a dirty smudge in the distance.

"Don't see anyone," said Ben.

Harry nodded to the stretch of oak mingled with chestnut near the base of the hill. "Bet it came from there."

They ran down the daisy-strewn grassy slope, laughing as they gained momentum, arms flung wide for balance, botas bouncing against hips. Then they slowed, breath catching as they stumbled to a halt. Harry felt the sun hot on his back, felt his stomach clench and his mouth go dry.

A woman and a girl lay on their backs in the grass beside a picnic rug scattered with sturdy white ironstone plates and the remnants of a genteel nuncheon. Dressed in fine gowns of delicate white muslin, they lay not side by side but in a line, so that the soles of the woman's shoes almost touched the girl's. Their hands were brought together at their chests as if in prayer, their silent faces turned to the sky, the bodices of their gowns shiny red. The stench of freshly spilled blood hung thick in the air, along with the lingering sulfuric stench of burnt gunpowder.

"*Oh, my God,*" whispered Ben.

His breath now coming in gasping pants, the blood rushing in his ears, Harry heard a child's lighthearted trill of laughter.

He wrenched his gaze away from that bloody horror to see a

young girl and boy coming up the path that wound along a small stream, the girl golden haired and rosy cheeked, the boy younger and even fairer. Her arms were filled with a cheerful rainbow of flowers—cornflowers and lilies, daisies and sunflowers, tansy and field poppies—that tumbled to the ground as she drew up, her eyes going wide.

For a long moment she stood rigid, her throat working soundlessly. Then she opened her mouth and Harry tensed, waiting for her scream.

But she simply stood there, her chest shuddering with her ragged breaths, her nostrils flaring and the color draining from her face.

Chapter 2

*S*ir Henry Lovejoy, one of Bow Street Public Office's three stipendiary magistrates, stood at the base of the grassy hill, his hands tucked up under his armpits, his chin resting against his chest as he gazed at the scene before him. He was a slight, thin man in his late fifties, barely five feet tall and quite bald. After fourteen years as a magistrate, he should have become inured to the sight of violent death. But *these* deaths . . .

God help him, these deaths.

Swallowing hard, he turned to the full-faced, corpulent squire who stood to one side, the wind ruffling his unruly head of thick ginger hair. "No one's touched anything?"

Squire Adams, the local magistrate, shook his head. When called to the scene by the park's keepers, he'd taken one look at the murdered woman and girl and sent word straightaway to Bow Street. "No, sir. Made sure of that, I did."

"And we're certain of the victims' identities?"

"Aye, no doubt about that. It's Lady McInnis, all right—wife of Sir Ivo himself. And Miss Emma, one of his daughters."

"How old is she?" *Was she,* thought Lovejoy, mentally correcting himself.

"Sixteen, according to her young cousins. The wife of one of the keepers has them at her cottage—the children, I mean. Seemed best to get them away from here."

"Quite right." Lovejoy felt his throat thicken as he stared down at the winsome young girl. Her dark hair was fashionably cropped to curl around her face, her features even, her nose small and almost childlike, her mouth wide. The shot that killed the girl had been fired so close to her chest that the cloth of her muslin gown was charred.

Lovejoy glanced over to where the two young gentlemen who'd found the bodies now sat in the grass, their forearms resting on bent knees, their heads bowed. The younger lad, Ben, had been sick several times. His older brother was thus far managing to keep down his wine, although he kept puffing up his cheeks and then blowing out his breath, hard.

"You say the brothers just happened upon this?"

"Well, they heard the shots and came to investigate."

"But saw no one?"

"Only Lady McInnis's young niece and nephew, who came along right afterward."

"Those poor children."

"Aye."

Drawing a deep breath, Lovejoy forced himself to look again at the bodies before him. The mother and her daughter hadn't died this way; they'd been posed—carefully, deliberately posed by their killer. Lovejoy had seen such a thing only once before, fourteen years ago.

Oh, Julia, Julia, Julia, he thought. *How can it be? How can it possibly be?*

His head jerked around at the sound of rapid hoofbeats. A gentleman's curricle was approaching at a spanking pace, drawn by a splendidly matched pair of fine chestnuts and driven by a rakish-looking man in a lightweight summer duster with shoulder capes and a stylish beaver hat set at a reckless angle. He drew up where the narrow lane began to curve away again and handed the reins to his young groom, or tiger, before hopping down to the road. He said something to the boy, then turned to walk toward them, his gait slightly marred by the leg wound from which he was still recovering.

A tall, lean man in his early thirties with dark hair, fine features, and the strangest feral-looking yellow eyes Lovejoy had ever seen, Sebastian St. Cyr, Viscount Devlin, was the only surviving son and heir of the powerful Earl of Hendon. He'd returned to England some four or five years before, after serving as a cavalry officer in the wars. There'd been a time when his lordship had been accused of murder and Lovejoy assigned the task of bringing him to justice. But in the years since, the two men had forged a strong friendship, and as soon as Lovejoy heard the identities of today's victims, he had sent for Devlin. Murder investigations involving the aristocracy were always delicate. And this murder . . . Ah, this murder.

"Sir Henry," said Devlin, walking up to him. Then his gaze fell on the dead mother and girl and he said, *"Christ."*

"Did you know Lady McInnis?"

"Not well, although I have met her. She's a friend of Lady Devlin."

"Ah. I am sorry."

Devlin's brows drew together in a disturbed frown. "They were found like this?"

"They were, yes." Lovejoy cleared his throat. "You should know that two other women were killed here in the park fourteen years ago—a woman in her early forties and her young daughter, both shot in the chest and their bodies deliberately positioned exactly like this: feet to feet, hands brought together as if in prayer."

"Good God. Do you know who they were?"

"Oh, yes," said Lovejoy in a voice that sounded strange even to his own ears. "Julia and Madeline Lovejoy." He paused, then somehow managed to add, "My wife and seventeen-year-old daughter."

Chapter 3

Sebastian drew a slow, even breath as he studied the magistrate's tightly held features. He'd known this man for four years. Over the course of more murder investigations than he liked to think about, the two men had talked for endless hours, sharing some of their deepest thoughts and secrets. Sebastian knew Lovejoy's wife and daughter had died suddenly; knew that those deaths had altered the path of his life and profoundly impacted his spiritual beliefs. So how could he not have known *this*?

For a moment, he found himself at a loss for words.

Lovejoy said, "It can't be a coincidence."

"No." Sebastian gazed down at the oddly posed bodies. Their postures reminded him of the stone effigies one often saw atop medieval tombs, and he wondered if the echo was deliberate. "No one was ever arrested for their murders?"

"Oh, yes; someone was arrested—a one-armed ex-soldier named Daniel O'Toole who'd been menacing other people in the area. He was remanded into custody, tried, convicted, and hanged."

Sebastian glanced over at his friend. "You're thinking they hanged the wrong man?"

Lovejoy's small, dark eyes were filled with silent anguish. "What else can one think? The man did die shouting his innocence from the scaffold."

"Someone could have learned the details of the previous murders and patterned this after them. We've seen it before."

Lovejoy considered this. "I suppose. But . . . why would he?"

It was a question for which Sebastian had no answer.

He hunkered down beside the still, lifeless husk of what was once Laura McInnis. She'd been an attractive woman, probably somewhere in her late thirties, still youthful and slim, with honey-colored hair and delicate features. In death she looked peaceful, serene.

He hoped she was.

"What time did this happen?" he asked. Flies were buzzing around her open mouth and blood-soaked chest, and he batted them away in a spurt of useless rage.

"Half past one or thereabouts, we believe."

It had taken time for the brothers to summon one of the park's keepers, more time for the keepers to call in the local magistrate, and more time still for word to be sent to London some eight miles away. By now, Lady McInnis and her daughter had been dead at least four or five hours.

Sebastian picked up one of her ladyship's limp, still vaguely warm hands and turned it over. The edge of her fine kid glove was stained bright red from where it had rested against the blood-drenched cloth of her bodice. He could see no sign that she had attempted to fight off their attacker. But then, how could a couple of gentlewomen grapple with an armed man?

He shifted to where her daughter lay in a similar pose. Unlike her mother, Emma McInnis's soft brown eyes were open and staring, and she looked so young and innocent that it tore at his heart. He said, "*Christ,*" again and pushed to his feet.

He was intensely aware of a woodlark singing sweetly from the top of a nearby oak, of the restless sighing of the breeze through the leafy branches of the adjacent wood and the late-afternoon sun drenching the long summer grass with a deep golden light. Turning, he let his gaze drift over the nearby picnic rug and hamper. The cheese, bread, and chicken that remained from the women's nun-cheon were now dried and crawling with ants.

He said, "Has anyone told Sir Ivo?"

"One of my colleagues has undertaken the task of breaking the news to him, as well as carrying word of the situation to the surviving children's father. But it's difficult to say if he's managed to do so yet."

Sebastian's gaze shifted to where the brothers still sat. "What do we know about those two?"

"Their father is a prosperous barrister—has a small estate not far from Richmond. They say they came here today to escape a house filled with relatives for their sister's wedding."

"And they neither saw nor heard anything?"

"Nothing beyond the pistol shots," said Lovejoy, just as the younger brother pushed to his feet, whirled, and was sick again.

Harry Barrows was twenty years old, with lanky brown hair, a thin face, and a long, narrow nose. He sat now with his arms wrapped around his bent knees, his hands locked together so tightly his knuckles were turning white. His face was pale, and a muscle kept twitching beneath his right eye, but Sebastian could tell the young man was gamely fighting to maintain his composure.

"I hear you're down from Cambridge for the summer," said Se-bastian, settling in the grass beside him.

Harry nodded. "Yes, sir. Magdalene College."

"I'm an Oxford man, myself."

A faint smile touched Harry's face, then was gone. "Sir Henry said you'd be wanting to talk to us, but I don't know how much we can tell you."

"Where were you when you heard the first shot?"

Harry nodded toward the top of the nearby hill. "Just over there, sir."

"How many shots did you hear?"

"Only two, sir."

"Sir Henry says you think it was a pistol?"

"Yes, sir. No doubt about that. Ben and I've been going shooting with our father since we were breeched."

"Do you remember how much time there was between the first and second shot?"

Harry was silent, as if mentally reconstructing the moment. "Only seconds, sir. I figure it had to have been a double-barreled pistol—there wasn't enough time in between for anyone to reload. Ben thinks so, too." He turned his head to look at his brother, who was now lying on his back in the grass with his eyes closed. "Is he going to be all right? He's been awfully unwell."

"It will pass. How long was it between the last shot and the time you and your brother arrived here?"

"Not long, sir. Not long at all."

"Yet you didn't see anyone running away?"

"No, sir. But then we wouldn't, would we? I mean, not if whoever did that had headed straight into the wood."

"And you didn't hear anything besides the pistol shots?"

"No, sir."

"No voices? No screams?"

The young man pressed his lips together and shook his head.

There was a bleakness to his expression that Sebastian had seen before, the look of someone whose safe, predictable existence has suddenly been touched by evil and horror. The world would never be quite the same for him again.

Harry said, "That girl—the one who'd been picking flowers down by the stream with her little brother. She didn't scream. She opened her mouth, and I kept waiting and waiting for her to scream. But she never did." He swallowed. "In a way, it was almost worse than if she had screamed."

"I suspect she was in shock."

"I should have tried to stop her from seeing it—the bodies and all that blood, I mean. I didn't even think of it."

"Not your fault," said Sebastian, although he knew it would do no good, that this burden of guilt and regret, once picked up, would niggle at Harry Barrows forever. "Had you seen anyone else in the park before you heard the shots?"

Harry stared at him blankly. "I suppose we must have, but I don't recall anyone in particular, if that's what you're asking. We weren't really paying attention, if you know what I mean?"

"I understand."

Harry stared off across the park, the westering sun shining through the branches overhead to dance a pattern of light and shadow across his face. "Who would do something like that? Shoot a woman and girl having themselves a picnic? And then do that weird thing with their bodies? It makes no sense."

"No," said Sebastian. "No, it doesn't."

Miss Arabella Priestly was seated on a bench beside the sunny, whitewashed stone walls of the keeper's cottage when Sebastian walked up to her some time later. She had her head bowed, one hand moving rhythmically over the purring gray-and-white kitten in her lap. She looked younger than her fifteen years, small and boyishly slim, with long golden hair, a thin face, and large gray eyes. According to Lovejoy, she was the second child and only daughter of Miles Priestly, Viscount Salinger, Lady McInnis's brother, and she was holding herself together with a composure Sebastian found both awe-inspiring and worrisome.

"Do you mind if I ask you some questions?" he said after the keeper's middle-aged wife had introduced them and then quietly withdrawn.

Arabella drew a ragged breath that shuddered her thin chest. "No, sir; I understand you need to. But I don't really know anything."

Sebastian gazed across the nearby duck pond to where her thirteen-year-old little brother, Percy, was chasing frogs. He hated like hell having to ask this young girl to relive the horror of what she'd been through. He said, "Did you hear the shots?"

She nodded. "We didn't think anything of it, though."

"You'd gone to pick flowers?"

"Yes, sir." She hesitated, then added, "Well, I was picking flowers. Percy was looking for tadpoles."

"How long would you say it was between when you left your aunt and when you heard the shots?"

"I don't know. Not that long. Maybe ten or fifteen minutes?"

"Did you see anyone?"

"No, sir. No one except the two brothers."

"Had you seen them before? Before you went to pick flowers, I mean."

"No, sir."

"How did your aunt seem before you and your brother left her?"

She stared at him, her eyes wide and still. He had the impression she was tamping down so many emotions right now that she was numb. She said, "What do you mean?"

"Did she seem nervous? Afraid? Worried in any way?"

She thought about it a moment. "I guess she seemed pretty much the way she always did, sir."

"What about your cousin Emma?"

Arabella twitched one shoulder. "She was just . . . Emma."

"Can you think of anyone who might have wanted to hurt either your aunt or your cousin?"

"Hurt them? No, sir." She glanced toward the lane, where Lady McInnis's carriage stood waiting. "Will we be able to go home soon, sir?"

"Soon," said Sebastian. It was an hour's drive back to London, and the light would be fading from the day before long. If neither Sir Ivo nor Viscount Salinger arrived soon, the keeper's wife had volunteered to accompany the children back to London in Lady McInnis's carriage, with Lovejoy following behind in a hackney.

Arabella sucked in a deep breath that flared her nostrils, her gaze dropping to the kitten now sleeping in her lap. "What about Aunt Laura and Emma?"

"Sir Henry—the magistrate from Bow Street—is taking care of that." The bodies were being sent to a surgeon named Paul Gibson for autopsy, but Sebastian saw no reason to burden this young girl with that knowledge.

"What—" Arabella broke off, her throat working as she swallowed, then tried again. "What do you think would've happened if Percy and I hadn't gone off like that? Do you think Aunt Laura and Emma would still be alive? Or would Percy and I be dead, too?"

She was looking up at him with liquid, pleading eyes, and he understood only too well the anguish that was tormenting her, that would probably always torment her. He'd seen it too many times in war—the guilt that bedevils the lucky ones who are inexplicably left alive when those near to them die. He wanted to say, *Don't ask yourself that, don't even think it.* But all he could say was, "I'm not sure we'll ever know. But I do know that your aunt and cousin would be very thankful that you're here now, safe. You and Percy."

She nodded, her face tightening in a way that told him she was fighting back tears. And all he could think was, *Where is their damned father?*

Chapter 4

Sir Ivo McInnis arrived just as they were preparing to load the children into their dead aunt's landau.

He swept up before the simple thatched keeper's cottage in a black barouche drawn by a team of black horses driven by a liveried coachman. "Uncle Ivo!" called Arabella, darting forward to throw herself against the Baronet's chest as soon as he descended his carriage's steps.

A big, thickset man in his late forties with a full face, small pale eyes, and thick dark hair, he had a reputation as a sporting man—a bruising rider to hounds, a member of the Four-in-Hand Club, a regular at such places as Jackson's Boxing Saloon and Angelo's Fencing Academy. His estates were in the northwest of England, in Cumberland, although he also kept a hunting lodge near Melton Mowbray in Leicestershire and spent much of his time there or in London. He might be only a baronet, but his family was ancient, wealthy, and powerful. Even as he clasped his niece to his broad chest, his gaze went beyond her to where Sebastian and Lovejoy stood in conversation beside Lovejoy's gig.

"You're Sir Henry?" said McInnis, setting his niece aside and walking toward them.

Lovejoy stepped forward. "I am, yes, sir. My sincere condolences on the—"

"Where are they?"

Lovejoy paused. "Lady McInnis and your daughter, you mean?"

"Yes, yes," said McInnis impatiently.

"On their way to London."

"To Grosvenor Square?"

"No, sir." Lovejoy threw a cautioning glance in the direction of the children. Percy had crept up to his sister's side, and the two were now holding hands, watching and obviously listening intently. The magistrate lowered his voice. "To the surgery of Paul Gibson, in Tower Hill. For a postmortem."

"What the devil?" the Baronet's voice boomed. "I've authorized no such thing."

"I'm afraid it is necessary, sir."

"Why? I'm told they were shot. Why the blazes do you need a postmortem?"

Lovejoy glanced again toward the children, who were silently staring at them, their faces lacking any emotion in a way Sebastian found profoundly troubling. "It may tell us something, sir. Something that could help us catch the killer."

McInnis's jaw hardened, his eyes narrowing as he shifted his attention to Sebastian. "You're Devlin, aren't you?"

Sebastian knew the man, but only vaguely. "I am, yes."

"What the blazes are you doing here?"

It was Lovejoy who answered. "I have asked Lord Devlin for his assistance."

McInnis stared at Sebastian, his nostrils flaring. "I've heard you do this sort of thing. Queer start, for a peer's son."

"True," said Sebastian, and left it at that.

McInnis's frown deepened. And it struck Sebastian that the man appeared far more annoyed than grief-stricken.

Sebastian said, "How many people knew that Lady McInnis was planning an expedition to Richmond Park today?"

"I've no idea."

"You never had any intention of joining the picnic yourself?"

"Me? Hardly. Why do you ask?"

"Simply trying to understand what happened here and why. Did Lady McInnis have any enemies?"

"Not to my knowledge. But then, I'm not particularly familiar with my wife's circle." He glanced again at Lovejoy. "When will the bodies be released from this blasted surgeon you've sent them to?"

"Hopefully by tomorrow evening, sir. The inquest will in all likelihood be scheduled for Tuesday morning."

"Bloody impudence," McInnis muttered only half to himself as he started to turn away.

"Will you be taking your niece and nephew back to London with you, Sir Ivo?" said Lovejoy, raising his voice.

McInnis paused. It was obvious he hadn't given the children a second thought. "I suppose I could." He glanced at his wife's landau. "Where was Lady McInnis's coachman while all this was happening?"

"At the Blue Boar in Richmond," said Lovejoy. "Resting and feeding the horses. Lady McInnis had asked him to return at four."

"Huh," McInnis grunted, and walked away toward the children.

"How well do you know Sir Ivo?" Lovejoy asked Sebastian quietly as they watched the Baronet confer with his wife's coachman, then shepherd his niece and nephew toward his own waiting barouche.

"Not all that well."

"Does he strike you as . . . grieving?"

"No," said Sebastian. "But then, I'm told some men find it difficult to express any emotion other than anger."

"Perhaps that's it."

But Sebastian didn't need to see the pained, puzzled expression in the magistrate's eyes to know that Lovejoy was remembering his own reaction to the deaths of his wife and daughter fourteen years before. It would have been a hideous, soul-destroying time in Lovejoy's life, and for him to be forced to revisit it now, in this way, was beyond brutal. Sebastian watched the magistrate take off his glasses and clean them with his handkerchief, his movements painfully slow and deliberate.

And he found himself aching for the somber, rigidly controlled, and profoundly shaken man beside him.

"Why would anybody want t' shoot a gentlewoman and 'er daughter when they was just 'avin' themselves a picnic?"

The question came from Sebastian's young tiger as they bowled through the park toward London, the boy perched on his seat at the curricle's rear. Tom had been with Sebastian ever since the dark days when Sebastian had been on the run from the law and Tom a scruffy pickpocket with a strange affinity for horses and the courage to risk his own life to save a man he barely knew. The boy was still small and sharp faced, his hair a nondescript brown, his features usefully forgettable. He'd always taken an interest in Sebastian's investigations, and it had recently become his ambition to someday serve as a Bow Street Runner.

Sebastian said, "It certainly wasn't done in the heat of passion. Whoever shot that woman and her daughter deliberately came here to the park today carrying a double-barreled pistol."

"I 'adn't thought about that." The boy was silent for a moment, then added, "I talked to Lady McInnis's coachman and footman, like ye asked."

Sebastian glanced back at his tiger. "And?"

"The coachman didn't 'ave much t' say, but it still weren't hard to tell that both 'e and the footman liked their mistress a whole heap better'n they like the Baronet."

"Oh? Did they say anything about how Sir Ivo and his wife got along?"

Tom nodded. "Not weery well, accordin' to Jem—Jem's the footman, ye know. From what 'e said, it sounds like Sir Ivo 'as the devil's own temper."

"That I can believe."

"'Andy wit 'is fives, too, says Jem."

"Oh? Likes to knock the servants around, does he?"

"Aye."

"And does Jem have any idea who might've been interested in murdering his mistress?"

"Nobody other than Sir Ivo 'isself."

"He said that?"

"Yup."

"Interesting. Did either Jem or the coachman happen to notice anyone in the area when they dropped off Lady McInnis and the children?"

"Nobody 'cept some old codger walkin' 'is dog."

"And what time was that?"

"Jist after eleven, Jem reckons."

"Did they have anything else to say?"

"Well, Jem in particular don't think much o' young Master Percy. Says the lad's a real handful. Never know what 'e's gonna do next."

Sebastian guided his horses through the park's gate. "It can be a difficult age, thirteen. I suspect what happened today will sober the lad considerably."

Tom was silent, his face expressionless as he stared out over the fields of ripe wheat flashing past, lit now by the rich light of approaching evening. "Why would somebody do that? Lay them out like they was statues on some old tombs in a church?"

"That I can't begin to explain."

"Seems to me, whoever done it ain't right in the 'ead."

The same thought had occurred to Sebastian, and he found it a disquieting possibility. What if there was no logical, discernible link between Lady McInnis or her daughter and whoever had shot them dead? What if the link was the park itself?

The park, and the mother-daughter relationship that helped tie this killing to that of Julia and Madeline Lovejoy fourteen years before.

Chapter 5

*A*nd I want a grand display of fireworks," announced George Augustus Frederick, Prince of Wales and—thanks to the ever-deepening madness of his father, King George III—Regent of the United Kingdom of Great Britain and Ireland. "At least two hours' worth."

The remark was addressed to Charles, Lord Jarvis, the King's powerful cousin and the acknowledged stabilizing force behind the Prince's fragile regency. The two men were in the Prince's porcelain room, Jarvis standing with his shoulders propped against a silk-hung wall while the Prince looked over a new shipment of Ming vases and jade carvings laid out on a long table for his inspection. The skinny, nervous dealer hovered nearby.

"Two hours, sir? You don't think that might be . . . excessive?" said Jarvis. He was a man in his early sixties, still strong and healthy. His physical appetites were robust but, unlike his cousin the Prince, he managed to carry his added pounds without drifting into the realm of obesity. He also still preserved a measure of his good looks, with fine, piercing gray eyes, an aquiline nose, and a surprisingly charming smile he could use to both cajole and deceive. He was a complex man, brilliant, uncannily prescient, utterly ruthless, and feared throughout the land. But he was also genuinely devoted to the preservation and the aggrandizement of both Great Britain and its monarchy. Without his wisdom and guidance, the Hanovers would in all likelihood have lost their heads along with the Bourbons across the Channel.

They certainly wouldn't be celebrating the one hundred and first anniversary of their accession to the throne.

"Excessive?" The Regent turned up his nose at a copper red bowl and set it aside, his corset creaking with each movement. Once, he had been beloved by his people and cheered wherever he went; once, he had been handsome, with thick auburn hair, a fine figure, and pleasing features. Now, weeks shy of his fifty-third birthday, his hair was gray, his body fat and bloated, his good looks lost long ago to rampant pleasure seeking. As for his once-adoring subjects, they'd come to hate him, both for his expensive self-indulgence and for the petty cruelty with which he treated his wife and daughter. Now, whenever they saw him, they booed.

"Excessive?" he said again. "Hardly. It isn't every day a country is given the opportunity to celebrate the one hundred and first anniversary of the accession of their monarch's family to the throne *and* a crushing victory over a monster like Napoléon. I'd say the people deserve an extravaganza befitting the occasion."

"Some are suggesting it might be prudent to wait and celebrate after we're certain that Napoléon is securely in our hands—or dead," said Jarvis.

The Prince's lip thrust out in a pout. "But if we wait, then we won't be able to combine the two celebrations, each one enhancing and emphasizing the other."

With falling wages, spiraling food prices, and the gloomy shadow cast by a decades-long war that had recently ended so spectacularly at Waterloo, Jarvis suspected "the people" were in little mood to celebrate the accession of the Hanovers. In fact, the previous year's ruinously expensive extravaganza—which included not only a massive fireworks display but also a mock naval battle staged on the Serpentine and a fanciful Temple of Victory erected in the park—had ended in a riot. But all he said was, "Then two hours it must be." Chewing the inside of his cheek to hide a vaguely malicious smile, Jarvis shifted his shoulders against the wall. "I hear the people are expecting to see Princess Charlotte in London for the festivities."

The Regent's nostrils flared in annoyance. Nineteen-year-old Charlotte might be his only legitimate child and the heir presumptive to the throne, but he viewed her more as a rival and a source of aggravation than as a daughter to be loved and cherished. The previous summer he had forced upon her an unwanted betrothal to the Prince of Orange as part of a nasty scheme to get her out of the country. When she ultimately rebelled, the Regent reacted by flying into a frothing rage, dismissing her entire household, and banishing the disgraced Princess to a damp, cramped, unpleasant house deep in the woods of Windsor Castle.

And he was still furious with her.

"Ungrateful brat," muttered the Prince, frowning down at a fifteenth-century Dehua piece. "What the bloody hell does she have to do with anything?"

What indeed? thought Jarvis. *She's only the future of the House of Hanover and the people love her.* But Jarvis knew his prince, so he didn't say it, for the Regent was as jealous and vindictive as he was vain and selfish, and the knowledge that his daughter was beloved while he himself was universally reviled ate at him.

The Prince's corset creaked again in protest as he leaned over to study the pattern on the side of a particularly large vase. "I'll never understand why Our Heavenly Father should have seen fit to bless me with some half dozen fine bastard sons and yet make my only legitimate offspring a headstrong, willful female totally lacking in any sense of what is owed either to her sire or to her royal house."

Given her parentage and the way she'd been raised, those who knew the Princess tended to be amazed she'd turned out as well as she had. That she existed at all was something of a miracle, given that the Prince had spent one night in his wife's bed and then never returned. Rumor had it the newly wed Princess of Wales had criticized both her drunken bridegroom's performance and his anatomy, with disastrous results.

Carefully keeping his features utterly bland, Jarvis said, "Lord Liverpool has suggested it might be appropriate to invite Her Highness the Princess of Wales to return to England and attend the festivities."

The Prince straightened with a jerk, his eyes bulging, his full, florid face darkening to an angry crimson. "Good God! Whatever can the man be thinking? *Caroline?*"

"I told him I didn't think it would be necessary."

"It's beyond unnecessary; it's madness!" The Prince stepped back from the table and waved a languid hand over the array of exquisite pieces, the cost of which would no doubt feed the poor of England for quite some time. "I'll take them all—except for the red bowl."

The dealer executed a deep bow. "Yes, Your Highness."

Jarvis pushed away from the wall. "Liverpool also expressed a desire to meet with you to discuss what he and Sidmouth believe is a growing threat posed by the Spenceans." As followers of the late Thomas Spence, the Spenceans were an annoying group of radicals who not only opposed the ongoing enclosure of traditional common lands but also advocated for any number of shockingly revolution-ary concepts, from equal rights for all to universal suffrage.

"Damn rabble-rousing insurrectionists," muttered the Regent. "What is there to discuss? Simply find something to charge the ras-cals with and hang them. How difficult can it be?"

Once again Jarvis hid a private smile, and bowed. "As you wish, sir."

Chapter 6

The sun was hovering low in the summer sky by the time Sebastian made it back to his house on Brook Street, in the district of London known as Mayfair.

He paused at the base of the steps leading up to the shiny black front door, his gaze drawn to the distant swath of green that was Grosvenor Square. The light was fading fast from the day, the shadows in the narrow, affluent street deepening, the air heavy with the scents of delicate dinners being concocted by expensive French chefs up and down the street. He could hear the laughing shouts of children mingling with the clear, sweet notes of a swift singing somewhere out of sight. Normally the simple beauty of the moment would have filled him with quiet joy. Now he found it served only to accentuate the disquieting ache in his heart.

The image of the dead mother and daughter—the woman cut down in the prime of life, the girl only just emerging from childhood—tore at him. He'd spent six years at war, yet he still found violent death disturbing and the senseless loss of the young particularly so. But there was something about the careful posing of those two innocent victims that transcended both tragedy and loss, that hinted at a level of human malevolence that reached beyond hate, beyond revenge, to something he could only understand as evil.

He was not a religious man. He'd lost his belief in the teachings of his youth long ago in the smoke-obscured charnel house of some half-forgotten battlefield. And yet he believed in good. And while he rejected the idea of evil as a personified external force, he knew it when he saw it. Still felt the intensity of its animus when he was in its presence.

And he'd felt it today, like a breathless chill lingering in that sun-warmed glade.

The two little boys sat side by side on the rug before the drawing room's empty hearth, trying to arouse the attention of the big, long-haired black cat that lay curled up on a nearby chair, pretending to ignore them. Both boys were tall for their ages, tall and unusually lean, with their fathers' almost black hair and strange yellow eyes. Except for a slight difference in their heights, they looked enough alike to be twins, although they were not even brothers. Only Simon, now two and a half, was Sebastian's own son; Patrick, slightly older, was the orphaned child of a man who'd looked enough like Sebastian to be his brother—and died because of it.

"Papa!" the boys cried in unison, bounding up to run toward Sebastian when he walked into the room.

"I didn't expect to find you two still up," said Sebastian, hunkering down to wrap his arms around both boys and hold them tight.

"They wheedled me into letting them stay up a few more minutes in the hopes you might come," said his wife, Hero, rising from one of the chairs near the room's bow window. Like her son, she was tall—almost as tall as Sebastian, with warm brown hair and Jarvis's aquiline nose, piercing gray eyes, and extraordinary intelligence. She was now nearly six months pregnant with their second child, and Sebastian had passed many a sleepless night worrying about the dangers to come, for Simon's delivery had not been easy. When he'd first met her, Sebastian had thought her as cold, hard, and enigmatic as her father. Now he couldn't imagine living without her.

"I think I hear Claire coming," said Sebastian, and laughed when both boys chorused, "*No!*"

He gave them another hug, then rose and said to Hero, "Morey tells me you've pushed back dinner, as well. I fear Madame LeClerc may never forgive me."

Hero's eyes crinkled with a smile. "Praise her trout meunière effusively enough and she'll forgive you." The smile faded. "Was it Laura?"

"It was, yes. I'm sorry. And her daughter Emma."

"Dear God," whispered Hero. "Were they—"

She broke off as the boys' nurse, a Frenchwoman named Claire, appeared in the doorway, and Simon set up a howl.

"Hush, *mon petit*," said Claire, scooping the little boy up into her arms and holding out a hand to Patrick. "You're tired. Come now, say good night to *Maman* and *Papa*."

After the children and their nurse had gone, Hero said quietly, "Were they both shot?"

"Yes," said Sebastian, going to pour himself a brandy. "How well did you know Laura McInnis?"

"I've known her for years. I admired her immensely, but I also *liked* her. She was an extraordinary person, so giving and caring, so passionate about helping others, so determined to make the world a better place for those in need."

Sebastian paused, the carafe in hand, to look over at her. "You said she was involved with the Foundling Hospital?"

Hero nodded. "She's the one who suggested I write the article I'm doing on the mistreatment of apprentices." For several years now Hero had been writing a series of articles for the *Morning Chronicle* on London's working poor. The endeavor was an endless source of rage for her father, Lord Jarvis. But she simply smiled and kept writing.

"What can you tell me about her marriage?"

Hero looked thoughtful. "Very little, actually. I could be wrong, but I wouldn't say she and Sir Ivo were what you might call 'close.' I had the impression he disapproved of her work with poor children, with the result that she kept much of what she did as quiet as possible. Probably the only exception to that is the work she did for the Foundling Hospital. But then, that's something that's seen as socially acceptable, even laudatory, isn't it?"

"Are there other children besides Emma?"

Hero nodded. "Yes, there's McInnis's heir, Malcolm—he's either seventeen or eighteen—and a younger girl, Thisbe. She's eleven or twelve."

"I wonder why she wasn't at the picnic."

"Thank goodness she was not." Rising to her feet, Hero went to stand at the window, one hand resting curled on the sill, her gaze on the darkening street below. After a moment, she said, "There's no chance it could have been an accident?"

"No. Whoever killed them then deliberately posed the bodies—moved them so that their hands were together at their chests as if in prayer, with the soles of the mother's shoes touching Emma's."

Hero's lips parted, a frown drawing two thoughtful lines between her eyebrows. "I remember hearing about something similar that happened out at Richmond Park once before, although it's been many years. I think I was still a child."

Sebastian took a long, slow swallow of his brandy and nodded. "Fourteen years ago a woman and her daughter were shot while picnicking in Richmond Park, their bodies posed in the exact same way."

"The killer was never captured?"

"Oh, someone was hanged for it, all right. But you and I both know how fallible our justice system is." He took another deep drink. "What I didn't know until today was the identity of the earlier victims: Madeline and Julia Lovejoy."

Hero stared at him. "Not . . ."

He nodded. "Sir Henry's wife and daughter."

"Oh, no. The poor man. How is he taking this?"

"About as well as one might expect—which is to say, not well at all. Although he's trying his damnedest not to show it."

"Where does one even begin with a killing like this?"

Sebastian brought up a hand to rub the back of his neck. "God knows. As far as we can tell, there were no witnesses beyond the two young men who found them, and they didn't really see anything. Gibson might be able to tell us something after the postmortems, but I'll be surprised."

Hero said, "I have an interview scheduled with the director of the Foundling Hospital tomorrow morning to talk to him about their apprenticeships. I can see if he knows anything useful."

"That might help. Thank you."

Setting aside his glass, he went to stand behind her, his arms around her waist to draw her body back against his, his head resting against hers. For a long moment, he held her. Then he said quietly, "Why would someone do something like that? Pose their bodies like effigies atop medieval tombs?"

"The man they executed for the murder of Lovejoy's family—did he ever explain it?"

"No. According to Lovejoy, the man maintained his innocence until the very end."

"So perhaps he was innocent."

"Perhaps. Although, if this is the work of the same killer, why the gap of fourteen years?"

"He could have been away."

"He could have. Or perhaps there was something we can't yet begin to imagine that drove him to it—then and now."

"What could possibly motivate someone to do something so . . . hideous?"

He met her gaze and saw there a horror and fear that mirrored his own. "The only thing I can think of is madness," he said, tightening his arms around her and burying his face in the soft fragrance of her hair. "You will be careful tomorrow, won't you?"

"Why? Was there a connection between Julia Lovejoy and the Foundling Hospital?"

"Not to my knowledge. But then, I didn't want to question Sir Henry too closely about his wife. I wasn't sure he could take it."

"What if—" Hero broke off, then said, "Dear God, what if the killer chose Laura and Emma at random and deliberately posed their bodies like that in order to torment Sir Henry?"

"That's a frightful thought."

"But it is possible, isn't it?"

Sebastian felt his stomach roil at the idea. "Yes, it is."

Chapter 7

That night Sir Henry Lovejoy sat alone beside his open parlor window, his gaze fixed unseeingly on the shadowy street below, the room in darkness around him.

He was a simple man and he lived simply, in a modest row house in Bloomsbury. Once, he had been a relatively successful merchant, obsessed with worldly things. But the cruel, senseless deaths of Julia and Madeline had changed all that. Withdrawing from commerce, he'd dedicated the remainder of his life to public service, becoming a magistrate first at Queen's Square in Westminster, then at Bow Street. The loss of his family had also had a profound effect on his religious beliefs, shifting what had been a largely unthinking adherence to the Church of England into something more closely akin to the stern teachings of sixteenth-century Calvinism. There were times when he could find a measure of comfort in those austere religious beliefs.

This was not one of those times.

His hands tightening around the arms of his chair, he drew a deep breath, his senses filling with all the scents of the city on a warm summer's evening, the smell of roasting meat and the streetlamps' hot oil mingling with the more rural odors of horse droppings and hay drifting from the livery stables at the end of the street.

"Ah, Julia," he whispered aloud to the darkness. "Did I make a mistake all those years ago? Did I in my mindless grief and hubris help kill an innocent man, leaving the one who did take your life still walking this earth to kill again?"

There'd been a time, not so long ago, when he used to talk to Julia like this often. When had he stopped? he wondered. Had he simply moved on with his life? Some might say that after fourteen years it was right that the burden of his grief should have begun to ease, even if only by a little.

And yet not a day went by when he didn't think of both Julia and Madeline at some point, and usually more than once. Sometimes the memories would come with a fleeting, bittersweet smile, as when he'd hear a child's joyous laughter or catch sight of a little girl with long dark curls playing in the square. But such moments always carried with them, inevitably, a pang of grief and useless guilt that tore at his insides. It never goes away, the pain of missing those we loved and lost, he knew that. In time the pain of grief might become less onerous, less overwhelming. But it never goes away. And neither does the guilt.

Julia and Madeline had both asked him to go with them that sunny spring day, to join their picnic to Richmond Park. He could have gone. But it had struck him as a frivolous waste of time, somehow not quite proper for a man of business. And so he'd kissed them goodbye, wished them a good time, waved them off, and then turned back to the important letter he'd been writing.

He had never seen them alive again.

Would they have died, he often wondered, if he'd gone with

them? Could he have saved them if he'd been there? Or would he have died with them? Impossible to know. There'd been a time when he'd told himself he'd been spared for a reason, so that he might avenge their deaths and make life safer for others. There'd been a time when he'd comforted himself with the belief that he had done so, that the man who'd taken their lives had forfeited his own, justly and righteously.

But what if . . . what if he'd been wrong? What if he'd helped kill an innocent man? What if the real killer was still out there, living and laughing, while Julia and Madeline turned to dust in their graves?

Pushing to his feet, Lovejoy felt so overwhelmed by doubt and rage that for a moment he staggered, one hand flinging out as he steadied himself against the windowsill.

"Who did this, Julia?" he said, almost shouting it this time, so that the words seemed to echo in the room's empty silence. "Who did it to you, and who is doing this now, again? *Who?*"

He paused, then said more quietly as he turned away from the window, "If only you could tell me."

Chapter 8

*E*arly the next morning, the rising sun was only beginning to cast long, cool shadows down the streets of the slowly awakening city when Sebastian drove east, to the Tower Hill surgery of the anatomist Paul Gibson.

This was an old part of London, its narrow cobbled lanes dominated by the massive looming presence of the grim eleventh-century Norman fortress on the banks of the river. Gibson's surgery and the small, low-roofed stone house beside it both dated back to medieval times.

Leaving the chestnuts in Tom's care, Sebastian cut through the narrow passage that ran along the side of the ancient house to a warped wooden gate set in the high wall that enclosed the old yard. Once, this had been little more than a weed-choked wasteland. But for several years now Alexi Sauvage—the Frenchwoman who shared Gibson's house and bed but not his name—had been turning the space into a garden. At the base of the garden stood the high-windowed stone outbuilding that Gibson used for both his postmortems and the surreptitious dissections he performed on cadavers filched by gangs of body snatchers from the city's overflowing churchyards on dark, moonless nights.

"You're early," said Gibson, looking up from doing something Sebastian didn't want to think about to the body of a woman lying on the high stone slab that stood in the center of the room. Sebastian glanced at her once, then looked away.

It was Laura McInnis.

"Too early?" said Sebastian, pausing outside the dank building's low doorway.

"Not really. I couldn't sleep, so I figured I might as well get started." Gibson set aside his scalpel and reached for a rag to wipe his hands. Irish by birth, he was in his mid-thirties, although he looked older. The lingering pains from the loss of part of his leg to a French cannonball—and the ever-increasing doses of opium he used to control those pains—had left his frame gaunt, threaded his once-dark hair with silver, and dug deep grooves on either side of his nose and mouth.

But this morning he looked even worse than usual, his face haggard with fatigue, his eyes bloodshot and deep in shadow. It had been weeks since he'd promised to let Alexi—who'd trained as a physician in Italy—try to do something about his leg's phantom pains. But so far he'd kept finding one excuse after another to put her off, and Sebastian was beginning to wonder if it was ever going to happen.

"When was the last time you slept?" said Sebastian. "You look like hell."

Gibson's eyes crinkled with his smile. "Why, thank you."

The friendship between the anatomist and the heir to an earldom dated back more than a decade, to the days when Sebastian had been a cavalry captain and Gibson his regimental surgeon. For years the two men had laughed and drunk, fought and bled and faced death together, forging the kinds of bonds that are rarely broken. Seeing his old friend slowly kill himself like this, one grain of opium at a time, was tearing Sebastian apart.

"I might not be finished," said Gibson, tossing the rag aside, "but the truth is, I doubt I'm going to find anything that will help you. The mother did have some blood smears on both her arms, here"— he touched one of the dead woman's pale, delicate wrists—"and there, on her stockings at the ankles. I noticed them when she was still in the wagon that brought her. Do you know how the constables lifted her into it out at Richmond?"

"Yes, I watched them. One slid his hands beneath her shoulders while the other grabbed her legs—but he had her skirts wrapped tight around her, so even if he had blood on his hands, he couldn't have smeared it on her stockings."

Gibson nodded. "So it was probably left by the killer. I suspect he posed the girl first and got her blood on his hands, then inadvertently smeared it on the mother's body when he grabbed her arms and legs to drag her over into position by her daughter."

"Jesus," whispered Sebastian. The mental image of the killer calmly positioning his victim's bodies somehow made the act seem even more revolting.

"What do you know about the husband?" said Gibson.

"Sir Ivo? Why do you ask?"

"Mainly because of this." Gibson pointed to a large, yellowing bruise on Lady McInnis's left side. "And these—" He touched first one shoulder, then the other, where Sebastian could see dark purple bruises in a distinct pattern that could only have been left by a man's heavy hands, the fingers digging in deep. "Whoever did that grabbed her by the shoulders and shook her, hard, maybe three or four days ago. The bruise on her ribs is older, probably a week old or more at this point, and made by a fist. That time he punched her."

"The bloody son of a bitch," whispered Sebastian. "McInnis's servants told Tom that Sir Ivo is 'handy with his fives,' but I assumed they meant the bastard had a habit of striking his servants. It never occurred to me that he might also beat his wife."

"Men who start out beating their wives frequently end up killing them. Far more often than most people like to admit."

Sebastian stared at the dead woman's calm, pale profile. *I could be wrong, but I wouldn't say she and Sir Ivo were what you might call "close,"* Hero had said. Did she know about this aspect of Laura McInnis's marriage? Somehow, he doubted it.

Aloud, he said, "I can see Sir Ivo maybe killing his wife. But his own daughter? Why would he do that?"

"Perhaps the girl was hit by mistake. He takes aim at his wife, except then, just as he's pulling the trigger, the girl throws herself forward, trying to protect her mother."

"And then, having accidently killed his own daughter, he turns and shoots his wife next?" Sebastian thought about it a moment. "That might make sense if he'd then run into the woods. But why pose the bodies like that? And if he were going to kill his wife, why do it someplace public like the park, with his daughter as a witness?"

Gibson gave a faint shake of his head. "That I can't begin to answer. Have you spoken to him yet?"

"Briefly, yesterday evening out at Richmond. I'll admit his reaction to the deaths of his wife and daughter struck me as odd. But that doesn't mean he's the killer."

"Huh. My money's still on him," said Gibson. "But then, I have a significant prejudice against men who hit women."

"You have to be a special kind of bastard, there's no doubt about that." Turning, Sebastian let his gaze rove over Alexi's garden, awash with color now in the waning days of July. In the strengthening morning light, the dew on the bright green leaves of the roses and honeysuckle, hollyhocks and daisies, glistened like diamonds. "The thing is, fourteen years ago, another woman and her daughter were shot in Richmond Park, and their bodies posed in the same way."

"Good God. So it's happened before?"

"At least once that I know of."

Gibson blew out a long, slow breath. "So maybe not the husband . . . unless there's some connection between the two families?"

Sebastian shook his head. "The earlier victims were Julia and Madeline Lovejoy—Sir Henry's wife and daughter."

Gibson's eyes widened. "I don't like the sound of that."

"Hero thinks the killer could be someone deliberately echoing the first killings to torment Sir Henry."

"Now, there's a chilling thought. Magistrates must rack up an ungodly number of enemies. How long has Lovejoy been a magistrate?"

"Ever since his family was killed—fourteen years."

"In other words, your pool of suspects might as well be infinite."

Sebastian met his friend's worried gaze. "Exactly."

Chapter 9

The sprawling redbrick complex known as the Foundling Hospital lay in Bloomsbury, just north of Guilford Street. Dating back some seventy years to the mid-eighteenth century, it was a hospital only in the word's original sense of a charitable institution offering "hospitality." It owed its existence to the efforts of a retired sea captain named Thomas Coram, who had been so horrified on his return to England by the number of dead and dying infants he saw abandoned in the streets of London that he decided to do something about it.

It hadn't been easy, for the stern moralists of Coram's day argued that saving the lives of illegitimate children would serve to encourage the sin and debauchery against which they railed endlessly. But he persisted, and in the end managed to secure a royal charter. A number of aristocratic ladies convinced their lords to lend their respectability to the scheme, while artists and musicians such as Hogarth and Handel helped raise the necessary funds.

Yet despite its name, the institution no longer actually took in foundlings. In the first years of its existence it had been so inundated with babies—fifteen thousand in four years—that it now received only infants surrendered by known mothers who could successfully prove they had been of "good character" before their fall. And there were still so many of those applicants that the few babies lucky enough to be taken in had to be selected by a lottery system.

The children who made it past those hurdles lived in a three-story brick building that included two dormitory wings fronted by long arcades, a large chapel in which Handel had once staged yearly performances of his *Messiah*, and an impressive art gallery that helped fund the hospital by attracting patrons who then made donations. Hero had visited the institution before, in the course of research for a different article, and the impressive financial gift she'd given at that time brought the Foundling Hospital's chaplain, the Reverend Reginald Kay, bustling out to meet her when she arrived there that morning.

They exchanged the usual polite pleasantries and then, at Hero's suggestion, turned to stroll along the institution's famous art gallery. "I fear you find us all at sixes and sevens today," said the Reverend with a sigh. A small white-haired man with pale blue eyes and a pink, unlined face, he was visibly shaken, and kept bringing up one plump white hand to swipe down over his nose and mouth. "You've heard the dreadful news about Lady McInnis?"

"I have, yes. It's beyond horrid." Hero made a show of pausing before a canvas depicting the story of Moses brought before the Pharaoh's daughter and tried to make her next question sound as casual as possible. "When was the last time you saw her?"

The Reverend Kay looked thoughtful. "Let's see . . . It must have been last Tuesday, I believe. Yes, Tuesday. She is—or I suppose I should say *was*—organizing a benefit concert for the foundlings and had come to look at some details of the layout of the chapel."

"Did she say anything while she was here to suggest that she felt in any kind of danger?"

"Danger? Good heavens, no. She was quite cheerful—you know what she was like."

"Yes," said Hero, surprised to find herself suddenly blinking away the sting of threatening tears. She had to swallow hard before she could go on. "Tell me about this benefit concert she was organizing."

"It's scheduled for next month, although I don't suppose it will happen now. She organized a concert of operatic selections last year, but she wanted something different this time. I understand she was putting together a collection of popular stage songs—pieces from Shield and Dibdin and the like—along with some Scottish and Irish airs arranged by Haydn and Beethoven . . . that sort of thing. She hoped it might attract some new, younger audience members. Her thinking was that we need fresh blood if we're to keep the donations coming . . ." His voice trailed away, his face blanching as if he'd suddenly remembered the circumstances of her death and feared his use of the word "blood" might be considered inappropriate.

Hero said, "Was anyone working on the concert with her?"

"Yes, Mrs. Veronica Goodlakes. You know her?"

"I do, yes." Veronica Goodlakes was a wealthy widow in her late thirties who, unlike Laura, was not especially known for her devotion to philanthropy and benevolent works. "Is Mrs. Goodlakes an active supporter of the Foundling Hospital, as well?"

"Not exactly," said the Reverend hesitantly. "But she has been quite keen to help Lady McInnis with this year's benefit concert."

"Perhaps she'll be able to keep it going."

"Perhaps," said the Reverend, although he didn't sound convinced.

"What about Lady McInnis's efforts to convince Parliament to improve the current laws regulating apprenticeships? Do you know if she'd made any enemies in her work on that?"

"Enemies? I don't know if I'd go so far as to use that word, but there's no denying she definitely ruffled a few feathers." He paused, his face looking pinched. "You can't think that's why she was killed?"

"No, of course not," said Hero mendaciously. She moved on to the next painting, this one a pastoral scene with a young shepherd holding a lamb. "When you say she ruffled a few feathers, precisely whose feathers are we talking about?"

The Reverend's watery blue eyes drifted sideways. "Well . . . I believe she tangled with the director of more than one of the workhouses. The Foundling Hospital learned long ago the importance of screening the tradespeople who take our children. But I fear the workhouses bind their children out to virtually anyone who will have them, and I understand Lady McInnis didn't hesitate to voice her disapproval to some of the directors."

Of course, the reason the Foundling Hospital had learned long ago the importance of screening the tradespeople who took their children was because they'd once apprenticed a young girl to a midwife who was ultimately hanged for torturing the poor child to death. But all Hero said was, "Do you know precisely which workhouse directors?"

The Reverend glanced away and cleared his throat. "I can't say that I recall, sorry."

Which was not, Hero noticed, exactly the same thing as saying that he could not recall. But all she said was, "Before she died, Lady McInnis was arranging for me to interview several children who'd been bound out by the workhouses to masters and mistresses that had abused them terribly."

Kay nodded. "Yes, I remember her telling me about one case involving a cheesemonger that was beyond shameful. The poor child had been bound out terribly young—at eleven, I believe. We typically apprentice our boys at fourteen, for seven years, and the girls at sixteen, for five years. But the workhouses will bind out both boys and girls much younger, and into some of the least desirable and most dangerous trades. They even sell their children to chimney sweeps when the poor tykes are scarcely four or five years old. I know people say the sweeps need them small so they'll fit up the chimneys, but the wretches beat their charges horribly. The little ones are so terrified, it's the only way to make them climb up such hot, dark, narrow spaces. It was one of the things Lady McInnis was particularly anxious to see changed, but I don't believe she was getting very far."

"Was Mrs. Goodlakes working with her on that, as well?"

"I don't believe so, no. Organizing a benefit concert is one thing, but I fear dealing with the likes of grubby little climbing boys is something else again." Then he colored, embarrassment flooding his cheeks as he rushed to say, "How terribly ungracious of me that was. Please forget I ever said it."

"It's forgotten," said Hero with a sympathetic smile. She glanced around as the tall, ornate clock at the far end of the gallery began to strike the hour. She had originally planned to come here today to ask the Reverend some searching and probably uncomfortable questions about the Foundling Hospital's own apprentice program, but that no longer seemed appropriate. "Goodness, I'd no idea it was so late. I've taken up far too much of your time. I know how busy you are."

"Always happy to help, Lady Devlin," he said, turning to walk with her toward the hospital's ornate eighteenth-century entrance hall. "If we can be of any further assistance, please don't hesitate to let us know."

"That is very kind of you. Thank you."

She was aware of him watching her as she walked away down the institution's forecourt, with its two long flanking ropewalk arcades. The day was warm without being unpleasantly hot, the morning breeze balmy. But the boys working beneath the arcades to twist the massive piles of hemp into long, thick cords were largely silent, for it was difficult, unpleasant work. They ranged in age from twelve or thirteen down to five or six, for this was the way of their world: Poor children were put to work as young as possible, either by their parents or by whatever officials found themselves saddled with their care. Somewhere out of sight behind the brick walls of the Foundling Hospital, the little girls who were these boys' female counterparts would likewise be busy cleaning, cooking, and sewing. But at least these children were given a few hours of education a day, sufficient food, and warm clothes and shoes to wear in winter. Most of the children taken into London's workhouses died, usually of malnutrition, disease, neglect, or simple despair. There were so many ways for a child to die.

As she let herself out the hospital's massive iron front gates, Hero couldn't help but wonder what had driven Laura McInnis to devote so much of her time to bettering the lives of the city's wretched poor children. As the Reverend Kay had so bluntly observed, it was one thing to organize a prestigious benefit concert in the Foundling Hospital's grand, illustrious chapel, but something else entirely to risk alienating one's peers—and one's own husband— by working to save the likes of grubby little climbing boys.

And yet Laura had been undeterred. What had drawn her to dedicate her life to such an admirable but unfashionable undertaking? It was something Hero had never thought to ask her friend while Laura still lived. Now it was too late.

Chapter 10

Sebastian left Gibson's surgery on Tower Hill and went looking for Lovejoy.

According to the Bow Street magistrate's clerk, Sir Henry had planned to leave early that morning for Surrey in order to consult the records of the trial of the man who'd been convicted and hanged for the murder of Lovejoy's family. "I offered to do it for him," said the clerk, a plump, bespectacled man named Collins. "But he insisted on going himself. After that I believe he intended to visit the Old Bailey to look at something there, so that's probably where he is now."

Sebastian could see his own worry reflected in the other man's eyes, but all he could do was nod and say, "Thank you."

Out of respect for Tom—whose memories of Newgate were painful—Sebastian left the boy with the horses at a watering trough by St. Paul's Cathedral and walked up the street to the court. The criminal court known as the Old Bailey stood at the intersection of the streets of Newgate and Old Bailey, right beside the grim, hulking prison of Newgate. There'd been a time when condemned prisoners had been trundled through the streets from here to execution on the gallows at Tyburn, near Hyde Park. But when that area became fashionable with the wealthy, the hangings were transferred here, to a scaffold erected outside one of the doors of Newgate prison. As Sebastian walked up Old Bailey, he could see men working to erect the scaffold now, their hammering reverberating down the ancient narrow street. And standing to one side, quietly watching them, was the small, solitary figure of the magistrate.

He nodded a greeting at Sebastian's approach, his gaze still on the scaffold. "They've four thieves scheduled to hang tomorrow," he said as Sebastian drew nearer. "I'm told the youngest are nine and twelve."

"*Hell*," Sebastian said softly.

The two men turned to walk together toward Ludgate. "Learn anything?" Sebastian asked after a moment.

Lovejoy shook his head. "There have been no other even vaguely similar incidents in the area. And as for O'Toole, his case seems as straightforward to me today as it did fourteen years ago. The man was never right in the head after he was wounded in Ireland—used to roam the hills around Richmond dressed like a scarecrow, his hair and beard wild, shouting angry nonsense at anyone he chanced to come upon. People were afraid of him."

"Did you or your wife know him?"

"No. I'd never even heard of him until . . ." The magistrate's voice trailed away, and he drew a deep, shuddering breath.

"So how did O'Toole come to be suspected?" said Sebastian as they turned toward the cathedral.

"He was found standing over the bodies, covered in their blood."

"I thought they'd been shot."

"They had. But he'd taken and literally *painted* his face with their blood, as if it were war paint. It was quite horrible."

"He still had the gun on him?"

"No. That's the one problematic aspect of the case. The gun was never found, and there was no evidence that he'd ever owned one."

"But he had been a soldier."

"Oh, yes. And a spinster named Miss Carter who was walking in the park with her young nephews had seen him shouting at Julia— my wife—shortly before the murders."

"Did she say what about?"

"She said it was all nonsense—something about women and children being burned alive in churches and kings doing the devil's work."

"Did she hear the shots?"

"No; no one did. A couple of bricklayers who'd been working on repairs to the park's wall came upon the scene quite by chance. O'Toole ran away when he saw them, but they chased him down and caught him. It was assumed he must have thrown away the gun while in flight—although, as I said, it was never found."

"And O'Toole continued to insist he was innocent?"

"He did, yes. To the end. Claimed they were already dead when he'd come upon them."

"Did he say why he'd painted his face with their blood?"

"He said—" Lovejoy's voice broke, and he swallowed, hard. "He said he hadn't meant to, that he must have somehow got their blood on his hands and then touched his face."

Sebastian was silent for a moment, his gaze on the soot-streaked walls of St. Paul's rising up before them. "There were no other suspects?"

"Not really. Just a fellow who lived in a cottage not far from one of the park gates who was seen having words with Julia earlier."

"Words about what?"

"He claimed Madeline threw rocks at his dog—which is rank nonsense. Madeline loved dogs."

"And that was it? No other suspects?"

"No."

"Was your wife involved in any way with the Foundling Hospital?"

"No. Not at all."

"What about Sir Ivo or Lady McInnis? Did she have any contact with them?"

"Not to my knowledge, no." They'd almost reached the steps of the cathedral, and Lovejoy paused to look back down the hill toward Temple Bar. "I spoke to him again this morning—Sir Ivo, I mean. He says he still has no idea who could have killed his wife and daughter, or why. Seems his son and Salinger's heir recently left for a fishing trip in the Highlands with friends. He's sent after them, but he's concerned the lads might not make it back in time for the funeral. In this heat, it can't be put off for too long."

"When's the inquest?"

"Tomorrow at eleven. Gibson assures me the postmortems will be completed by this evening."

Sebastian nodded. "He'd almost finished with Lady McInnis when I saw him earlier."

"Anything?"

"Not really. Just some older bruises—two sets, actually. Evidently Sir Ivo was in the habit of brutalizing his wife."

"Good heavens," said Lovejoy, looking distressed. "Not what one would have expected, is it?"

"I doubt it means anything, although it might explain his hostility to the postmortems."

"Yes, I can see that. If it weren't for the death of young Miss Emma McInnis, such a history would be more than suggestive. But I can't see Sir Ivo murdering both his wife *and* his daughter—quite apart from the matter of the killer's strange positioning of the bodies."

Sebastian studied the magistrate's drawn features. "Have you considered that someone could have committed these murders and staged his victims' bodies in a way that echoes the deaths of your family in order to cause you grief?"

Lovejoy's eyes widened. "What a chilling thought."

"Is there anyone you can think of who might hate you enough to do something like that?"

The magistrate was silent for a moment, his lips pressing into a thin line. Then he let out his breath in a long sigh and shook his head. "I suppose there must be any number of people who hold me responsible for the execution or transportation of someone they loved. But to do something so diabolical, so *evil*, as to kill two innocent women to torment me?" He shook his head. "No, I can't think of anyone like that. Not anyone recent, at any rate. But perhaps if I give it some thought . . ."

Sebastian hesitated. He wanted to say, *Don't put yourself through this, my friend. Let one of the other Bow Street magistrates take the lead on the case. You can't bring to this ugly crime the kind of detached objectivity it requires, and the memories you're forcing yourself to revisit are too painful, too raw. You're going to destroy yourself.*

Except of course he couldn't say any of those things. And so he said instead, "This fellow you mentioned with a cottage near one of the park gates—is he still alive?"

"I'm told he is, yes. Coldfield is his name. Cato Coldfield."

"I was thinking I might drive out to Richmond to have another look around, and I might as well talk to him while I'm at it." Sebastian started to turn toward where he'd left Tom with the curricle, then paused. "Was there a particular reason Coldfield was eliminated as a suspect?"

"No," said Lovejoy, looking more distraught than ever. "Only that O'Toole seemed the obvious culprit. I mean, he didn't simply have their blood on his face; he was covered in it. What other explanation could there be?"

Sebastian thought about how a damaged young ex-soldier, traumatized by having repeatedly witnessed his government's indiscriminate slaughter of innocent Irish women and children, might react were he to stumble upon the brutal murder of a mother and her daughter.

But he kept that theory to himself.

Chapter 11

$\mathcal{T}$he sky was a crystal clear blue, the air sweet and fresh, the fields of ripening grain dancing gently in a soft breeze as Sebastian left behind London's dirty, crowded streets and turned toward Richmond. Once a royal retreat beloved of the likes of Henry VII and Queen Elizabeth, what was now Richmond Park had long ago been thrown open to the general public. On such a balmy, sunshiny summer's day, the rolling green hills and open woods of the park would normally be filled with everything from boys playing cricket to birdwatchers and picnicking families.

Not today.

"Why we stoppin' 'ere?" asked Tom when Sebastian drew up before the honeysuckle-draped thatched cottage of the keeper he'd met briefly the evening before.

"Reconnaissance," said Sebastian, handing the boy the reins.

The keeper himself was off looking at a downed tree on the far side of the park, but his wife was home and more than willing to talk.

Her name was Sally Hammond, and she was a plump, good-natured, sandy-haired woman somewhere in her forties. "People are staying away from the park," she said as they walked along the reedy banks of the pond beside her cottage. "Reckon they're scared, and I can't say I blame them. Anybody in their right mind would be scared."

"Who do people suspect might be responsible for the killings?"

She gave a faint snort. "Some folks are saying it must be the ghost of the ex-soldier they hanged after the last time something like this happened around here. It's nonsense, of course. But when did that ever stop people?"

"And the others?"

"Well, some reckon it might be a French prisoner of war, although I don't think they've let them go yet, have they? Others are sayin' it must be some ex-soldier returning home from the wars who ain't quite right in his head, same as they said last time."

Something about the way she phrased it caught Sebastian's attention. "Do you think he was responsible? Daniel O'Toole, I mean."

Sally Hammond paused beside the trunk of an old willow, her gaze on the ducks paddling lazily out on the sun-spangled pond, a frown pinching her forehead as her arms came up to cross over her apron. "No, I never did. There's no denying he weren't right in his head when he came home, poor Danny. But he was a gentle soul. Always had been, even as a boy. That's why the things they made him do and the things he saw in Ireland bothered him the way they did."

"You knew him?"

"I did, yes. His mother and mine were cousins."

Sebastian kept his gaze on her half-averted face. "So who do you think was responsible for the killings fourteen years ago?"

She pressed her lips into a tight line. "It's not my place to say, now, is it? Idle speculation can hurt people."

"What about Cato Coldfield? What can you tell me about him?"

He saw something flash in her eyes, something she hid quickly by looking away as she shook her head. "Let's just say I don't reckon anybody would ever call Cato Coldfield a 'gentle soul.'"

"I'm told he was seen arguing with Mrs. Lovejoy and her daughter earlier in the afternoon they were murdered. Is that true?"

"He was, yes. He had a dog back then—a big brown thing he called Chester. He has a different dog now—a little mutt named Bounder. Now, Bounder, he's as sweet as he can be. But Chester? That dog was impossible. Always going after the ducks and deer in the park, he was. Brought down at least one fawn every spring. My Richard—that's my husband, you know—he was always threatening to shoot that dog if Cato didn't keep him out of the park. But Richard never could bring himself to do it. He's a soft touch like that. Always said it weren't the dog's fault that Cato let him run like that."

"And Coldfield accused Madeline Lovejoy of throwing rocks at his dog?"

Mrs. Hammond nodded. "Chester was going after a fawn, you see. That's why the girl was shouting and throwing rocks—to try to get that danged dog to leave off. Put Cato in a rage, it did."

"Someone saw them arguing?"

She nodded. "I did. I caught Chester by his collar and told Cato to leave off shouting at the girl and take his dog home."

"Did he?"

"He did, yes. Muttering all the while, of course. But he left."

"I understand his cottage is near the park?"

"Yes, just outside the Petersham Gate. He shouldn't be coming in here all the time without a ticket the way he does, but there's no keeping him out."

Sebastian turned to gaze off across the vast park. "Where exactly in the park were Julia and Madeline Lovejoy killed?"

"By Sidmouth Wood, that was," she said. "Near what happened yesterday."

"And how far is that from the Petersham Gate?"

Mrs. Hammond's features contorted with a spasm of silent, unstated worry. "Not far. Not far at all."

Cato Coldfield's small, whitewashed cottage stood on a narrow lane near the southern edge of the park. The house's long-straw thatched roof was new and masterfully done, with an elaborate ridge pattern using cross spar work. But the cottage's walls were in serious need of whitewashing, and what must once have been a charming cottage garden was now an overgrown mess, with a broken front gate that hung open. As Sebastian drew up and hopped down to the lane, a black-and-white dog came bounding out to greet him, all wagging tail and wiggling hind end and happily lolling tongue.

"Look who's a good boy, then," said Sebastian softly, reaching down to scratch behind the dog's ears as he cavorted around Sebastian's legs. "Only, mind you don't scuff the shine on my boots or Calhoun will have your hide."

"Bounder! Git away from him!" shouted a man coming around the side of the cottage. He was a big, burly man probably somewhere in his fifties, his thickly curling dark hair threaded with gray, his full-cheeked face weather-beaten and sunbrowned. He had a bulbous nose and wide mouth and heavy dark brows that drew together now in a frown as he paused before the house's closed front door. "Wot you want with me?"

Sebastian gave the dog one last pat and straightened. "You're Cato Coldfield?"

"I am." He sniffed. "Know who you are, too. You're that fancy London lord they brung out here yesterday evenin' to help with them new killings."

"How do you know that?"

"Saw you, I did. See things, I do."

"Did you see anything yesterday that might explain what happened to that woman and her daughter?"

"Wot? Me? No." He raised one hand to point a thick, blunt finger at Sebastian. "That ain't got nothin' t' do with me, you hear? Just like I didn't have nothin' t' do with them other killings fourteen years ago."

"Where were you yesterday at midday?"

"Me? I was right here. Feelin' poorly, I was. Was supposed to start top dressin' Jake Dempsey's roof, but I musta ate something that was off. Hit me hard, it did. So I stayed home. You can ask Jake if you don't believe me. He'll tell you."

"And yet you saw me."

Something flared in the other man's eyes. "That was later. Feelin' better by then, I was, so I went out t' see what was goin' on. But earlier in the day, when folks say them two was shot, I was here. Sick." He stared at Sebastian, eyes wide and belligerent, as if daring him to doubt him.

"Can anyone vouch for that?"

Coldfield showed his crooked yellow teeth in a nasty grin. "Well, I reckon Bounder here could."

At the sound of his name, the dog looked up, wagged his tail, and gave a soft *whoof.*

Sebastian let his gaze rove over the jumble of objects near the cottage door: the piles of split hazel spars; the long pole ladder splayed at its base; the biddles, legget, shearing hook, and thatch rake. Unlike the garden and cottage, the thatcher's tools were well tended, with the metal blades of the shearing hook, eaves hook, and long eaves knife all carefully honed to a gleaming edge.

A tin pail filled with white ironstone soaking in soapy water stood nearby.

Sebastian said, "Where were you fourteen years ago when Julia and Madeline Lovejoy were shot in the park?"

"I was here then, too. Mindin' me own business, like I always do."

Sebastian nodded to the pail of ironstone. "I see you've acquired some new dishes."

Coldfield's jaw jutted out. "They was just left there in the park. Why shouldn't I pick 'em up? Why leave 'em there to be ruined?"

"No reason I can think of," said Sebastian, bringing his gaze back to the man's sun-darkened face. "Who do you think killed that woman and her daughter yesterday?"

"How would I know?"

"You've no ideas at all?"

"Nope."

"Seen any strangers hanging around here lately?"

"Nope."

"Did you see the woman and her daughter earlier on Sunday, before they were shot?"

"Nope. Told you I was here sick, remember?"

"So you did." Sebastian let his gaze drift, again, around the overgrown jumble of lavender and hollyhocks, stinging nettles and rampant ivy. "Thank you for your time," he said, and turned toward where he'd left Tom with the curricle.

The thatcher sucked in a deep breath that flared his nostrils, but said nothing. He was still standing there beside his broken gate, the dog at his side, when Sebastian swung the curricle around and drove back toward the main road.

"I reckon 'e's hiding somethin'," said Tom as Sebastian turned toward the park again.

Sebastian glanced back at his tiger. "I agree. But what makes you think so?"

Tom shrugged. "Just somethin' about the way 'e was standin' there. So what ye reckon he's hidin'?"

"I have no idea. But I think I'd like to take another look at that meadow by the wood."

Chapter 12

*I*t was an idyllic spot, this sunny, daisy-strewn meadow at the edge of a shady stand of chestnuts and oaks.

Pulling his curricle off to the side of the lane, Sebastian handed the reins to Tom and hopped down. The picnic hamper and rug he'd noticed the previous evening were now gone, doubtless carried off by the same man who'd helped himself to the white ironstone dishes. All that remained to mark what had happened here were the faint impressions left in the grass by the picnic rug and the bodies of the two dead women who'd been posed beside it.

That, and the dried splashes of blood still visible on scattered clumps of grass and patches of bare earth.

Walking to the center of the meadow, Sebastian turned in a slow circle, taking in the lay of the land: the open wood, the narrow brook with the path running beside it, the slope down which the two brothers had run after hearing the shots. A gentle breeze brought him the lowing of distant cows, the chatter of an unseen squirrel, the purling of the nearby brook.

It should have been a peaceful moment, but it was not. When he closed his eyes, it was as if the air here still hummed with a violent swirl of emotions—bewilderment, shock, horror, and a numbing grief, all tangled together with a strange aura of exhilaration tinged with what he thought might well be triumph. It was surely no coincidence, Sebastian thought, that the creatures of the wood were avoiding this place.

Taking a deep breath, he began to walk in ever-widening circles around the site. Lovejoy's constables had searched the area the previous afternoon, but Sebastian wanted to get a feel for the place himself. He found the bundle of flowers Arabella Priestly had been gathering, now lying wilted and forgotten where she'd dropped them. Perhaps ten or fifteen feet farther upstream, where the broad grassy bank of the brook curved away from the path, he spotted a white ironstone cup that her brother Percy had doubtless been using to catch tadpoles. It lay on its side in the shallows of a pool teeming with tiny, darting black shadows. Reaching down, Sebastian picked it up, turning the cup upside down to let the water run out.

So far he'd seen few flowers here besides the inevitable scattering of daisies, which meant that the sunflowers, poppies, and cornflowers in Arabella's bouquet must have come from farther upstream. Had young Percy stayed here, scooping up tadpoles in this shallow pool, while his sister ventured farther afield in search of her flowers? If so, the boy could conceivably have seen or heard something that Arabella had not.

Sebastian turned to look back toward the meadow. A clump of brambles hid the fatal picnic site from his view. But the boy had been close enough that he might have heard something. And if the man who shot Laura and Emma McInnis had then ducked into the wood, the young lad might even have seen him.

It was a worrisome thought, for more than one reason. It had been unfortunate enough to have to question Arabella, to ask a girl of fifteen to relive the horrors of that afternoon. But a child of thirteen? Sebastian wondered if the boy's father would even agree to it.

Still carrying the forgotten ironstone cup, Sebastian turned back to where he had left Tom with the curricle. He had only a passing acquaintance with the children's father, Miles Priestly, Viscount Salinger. A widower now for some years, he was, like Sir Ivo, a sporting man ten to fifteen years older than Sebastian, with an estate in Leicestershire. Beyond that, Sebastian knew little of the man.

"That's what ye found?" said Tom when Sebastian walked back to the curricle. "A cup?"

Sebastian leapt up to the high seat and took the reins. "Just a cup."

It was midafternoon by the time Sebastian arrived back in London.

Leaving his tired horses in Brook Street in Tom's care, Sebastian walked the short distance to the relatively modest town house of Viscount Salinger in Down Street, off Piccadilly. He wouldn't have been surprised to be told that the dead woman's grieving brother was not at home to visitors. But Salinger's butler, a stately, prim man in his early sixties, bowed deeply and said, "Ah, yes; Lord Devlin. Lord Salinger warned us to expect you. If you'll come this way?"

Escorting Sebastian upstairs to the drawing room, the butler promised to send a footman with a pitcher of ale, then went off to apprise Salinger of his lordship's arrival.

Sebastian was standing at the front window, watching the shadows lengthen in the street below, when he became aware of the sensation of being watched. Turning, he found a fair-haired boy he recognized as Percy peeking around the doorjamb at him.

"Hullo there," said Sebastian.

Casting a furtive glance over his shoulder toward the stairs, the boy scooted into the room. He was small for his age and slight, with thin straight hair, delicate features, and a sprinkling of faint freckles across the bridge of his short nose. "You're Lord Devlin, aren't you?" said Percy, his pale gray eyes wide, his face aglow with barely suppressed excitement. "I saw you yesterday at the keeper's cottage, but we weren't formally introduced. I'm Percy." The boy flashed a quick, impish grin. "My brother Duncan is the heir, you know. I'm just the spare."

Sebastian smiled. "Well, how do you do, Master Percy the Spare? It's a pleasure to meet you."

The boy's grin widened, then collapsed. "You're here to talk to Papa about what happened out at Richmond Park, are you? I heard Uncle Ivo telling Papa that Bow Street has asked for your help. You do this a lot, don't you? Solve murders, I mean."

"I help when I can," said Sebastian, choosing his words carefully. However anxious he might be to question the boy, he had no intention of doing so without the father's permission.

"It must be great fun," said young Master Percy with all of a schoolboy's enthusiasm, "chasing after murderers and such."

"I don't know that I'd describe it as 'fun.'"

"You wouldn't? I think it'd be grand. Do you reckon the killer might try to murder us next? Arabella and me, I mean." Sebastian had the distinct impression the boy found the possibility far more exciting than frightening.

"I don't see why he would," said Sebastian, although it was a blatant lie. Because if the killer thought the children had seen or heard something that might help identify him . . .

"Arabella says—" Percy began, only to break off when a man's tread sounded on the stairs.

"Oh, drat," said the boy under his breath as Lord Salinger appeared at the entrance to the drawing room.

He was a tall man in his late forties, still strong and vigorous, although he was beginning to thicken around the middle, and his once-dark hair was now graying. His dress was neat rather than fashionable, more country gentleman than man-about-town, the points of his shirt collar and his cravat both modest, his coat cut loose enough that he would have no need of assistance easing into it. The resemblance between brother and sister was slight but there, mainly around the chin, which was square.

He drew up abruptly at the sight of his son, then came forward, saying to Sebastian, "Lord Devlin; I thought you might come." To Percy, he said, "Off you go now, lad."

"But, Papa—"

"No buts. Make your bow and then go."

The boy executed a reluctant bow, then turned slowly away, dragging his feet.

Salinger watched him go, his face pinched with a father's worry and haggard with a brother's grief. Then he turned to Sebastian and said gruffly, "I see James has brought us a pitcher of ale. I had a barrel delivered fresh from the brewery just this morning, you know. May I pour you a tankard? It's devilish hot out there."

"Yes, please."

"Is it too much to hope that you're here because Bow Street has caught this mad killer?" said Salinger, going to the tray.

Sebastian shook his head. "If they have, I'm unaware of it."

Salinger sighed and reached for the pitcher. "I knew it unlikely. But still . . ."

"It's early days yet," said Sebastian.

"Yes, I suppose . . ."

"Do you know of anyone who might have wanted to harm either your sister or your niece?" asked Sebastian, accepting the tankard held out to him.

"Me?" Salinger turned back to pour himself some ale. "No, sorry. My sister and I held each other in affection, but I'm afraid we were never very close. The differences in our ages and interests were too great. Our brother Alfred is between us, you know, and we had a brother named John who died while still up at Oxford."

"What were your sister's interests, if you don't mind my asking?"

A gleam of gentle amusement showed in the other man's eyes, then faded away to something sad and hurting. "Everything I consider a dead bore: literature, art, music, good works—that sort of thing. She thought hunting cruel and boxing savage, and while she liked dogs well enough, she never had much use for my hounds since she associated them with hunting and, well, you wouldn't have wanted to get her started on *that*."

Sebastian took a slow swallow of his ale. "Is there someone who might know more about her?"

Salinger thought for a moment, then shook his head. "Sorry. She must have had friends, but I'll be damned if I could name any of them. Alfred's now a vicar up in Leicestershire, so I doubt he could tell you anything useful, either." He rubbed a hand across his forehead and down over his eyes. "I know it sounds like I'm being uncooperative, but I really don't know anything that would be of much use to you. And the truth is, I'm so bloody worried about my children that I'm finding it difficult to think straight."

"Have the children said anything to you about yesterday?"

"Not really. I know they saw Laura and Emma's bodies from a distance, but, thankfully, those two lads had the sense to keep the children from getting too close."

"And neither Percy nor Arabella saw or heard anything that might help explain what happened?"

"I don't think so, no."

"Would you mind if I talked to young Percy?"

Salinger stared at him a moment, then shook his head. "Sorry, but no; I don't think that would be a good idea. I want the lad to forget what happened yesterday, not dwell on it."

"Sometimes talking about things is the best way to move past them."

Salinger's face hardened. "Not this time."

"If they know something that could help identify the killer—"

"They don't. And I won't have them upset further by being forced to relive the horror of what happened."

Sebastian took a deep drink of ale and tried to swallow his frustration with it. "How well do you know your brother-in-law?"

"Ivo? I've known him most of my life. We were at Harrow and Cambridge together. Laura actually met him through me. Why do you ask?"

"Did you know he used to hit your sister? Hit her hard enough to leave bruises?"

Salinger's eyes narrowed, his nostrils flaring. "That's ridiculous. I don't know where you got that, but whoever told you that should be hauled into court for slander."

"The bruises were discovered during the postmortem examination. You didn't know that he hit her?"

"No, and I don't believe it. If she had bruises, she must have fallen."

"Perhaps," said Sebastian, and let it go.

Salinger drank deeply of his own ale. "If you ask me, what you ought to be doing is looking into all the bloody undesirables with whom she came into contact at that Foundling Hospital or as a result of this newest start of hers—apprentices or some such thing."

"Did she talk to you about that?"

"No. She knew how I felt about it."

"How many people knew about yesterday's expedition to Richmond Park?"

"The servants, I suppose—mine and Ivo's. But beyond that, I couldn't say." He paused. "Laura was always so good about taking Arabella and Percy—and Duncan, too, of course, when he was younger—on picnics and such. It hasn't been easy for me, raising the three of them without a mother. I don't know what I'd have done without Laura." He glanced away, and although he didn't say it, the words *I don't know what I'm going to do now without her* hung unvoiced in the air. Then he swallowed and said, "It's going to be hard on the children, losing their aunt and their cousin, too."

"Yes, I can see that. I'm sorry." Sebastian drained his tankard and set it aside. "Please accept my condolences on the loss of your sister and niece, and my apologies for having to disturb you at such a painful time."

"I appreciate your coming," said Salinger, walking with him to the top of the stairs. "You'll let me know if you learn anything?"

"Yes, of course."

Salinger nodded. "Thank you."

He stayed there, at the top of the stairs, watching as the footman in the entry hall below leapt to open the front door for Sebastian. He was still there when the footman closed the door behind Sebastian.

Glancing back at the house, Sebastian could see Percy's frustrated face peering down at him from one of the second-floor windows. Then the boy jerked around, as if someone had called his name, and all that was left was the swaying curtain where he had been.

Chapter 13

Amongst London's upper classes, it was considered rude and déclassé to make social calls before three o'clock, which was why Hero waited until that magic hour to pay a visit to the sprawling St. James's Square mansion of Laura McInnis's friend Veronica Goodlakes.

Hero found the wealthy widow dressed in an elegant high-waisted gown of pale pink silk and seated at a delicate inlaid Italian writing table positioned so that it overlooked the lush private rear gardens. By birth, Veronica was a Trent, from a proud old family connected to some of the grandest houses in Britain. But her father, the late tenth Baron Trent of Mollis, had gambled away most of his substantial inheritance by the age of thirty, then spent the next several decades plunging deeper and deeper into debt. Faced with the prospect of either eating the muzzle of his pistol or dying in debtors' prison, his lordship had chosen instead to auction off his only daughter to the highest bidder. A socially ambitious Bristol shipbuilder named Nathan Goodlakes coughed up a small fortune for the privilege of joining his plebeian blood to that of the nobility. But in the end Goodlakes's gambit failed, for despite eighteen years of trying, the union produced no offspring. When he succumbed to a nasty case of influenza at the age of sixty-nine, he left Veronica a very wealthy young widow.

"Lady Devlin," she said now, rising quickly to come forward with both hands outstretched. "I was just writing to you."

"Were you?" said Hero, taking the widow's small, slim hands in hers. Now in her late thirties, Veronica was still a nice-looking woman with a headful of bright guinea-gold curls and a delicately curved mouth that smiled with gentle amiability. But unlike most people, Hero had long ago noticed the gleam of cold steel that could sometimes glitter in the woman's pale gray eyes before being quickly hidden by lowered lashes. It was said that, at Nathan Goodlakes's insistence, she had remained on easy terms with both her father and elder brother throughout her marriage. But she publicly cut both men immediately after Goodlakes's funeral and had never spoken to either one since. And although Hero knew that Lord Trent had recently died, Veronica was obviously refusing to go into mourning for him.

"Do I take it you know why I'm here?" said Hero as the widow drew her over to sit on a blue silk–covered settee beside one of the cavernous room's empty marble-framed fireplaces.

"I think I can guess. Laura McInnis was my dearest friend since we were in school together, and it's not exactly a secret that Bow Street has involved Lord Devlin in their attempts to catch whoever is responsible for these shocking murders. I'd like to help in any way I can."

"You know something that could explain what happened?"

"I might," said Veronica, her hands coming up together, palm pressed to palm as she leaned forward. "Are you aware of Laura's clashes with a certain master sweep?"

"You mean a chimney sweep?"

Veronica nodded. "Dobbs is his name; Hiram Dobbs. Sir Ivo brought the fellow in to sweep the chimneys in McInnis House this last spring, and Laura came upon him deliberately burning the bare feet of one of his little apprentices to make him go up the chimney! The poor child couldn't have been more than four or five, and was so afraid of the chimneys that he wouldn't go up them otherwise. Laura was horrified; she tried to get the authorities to take the boy away from the man, but they refused to interfere. And then a week or two later she discovered that the child had died. Laura was shattered—blamed herself for not having tried harder. She thought the sweep would be taken up for murder—or at least manslaughter. But he managed to convince the authorities the child had died of the flux, and the workhouse gave him another little boy."

"Good heavens."

"Shocking, isn't it? Needless to say, Laura was in a rage about it. And when he found out she was trying to get his other apprentices taken away from him, Dobbs walked right up to her in the street one day and told her to her face that if she didn't leave him alone, she'd regret it."

"In those exact words?"

"Yes."

"So did she? Leave him alone, I mean."

"Oh, no. She truly was determined, even though he tried his best to intimidate her."

"In what way?"

"Following her . . . watching her. That sort of thing."

"Was Laura afraid of him?"

"I don't know if I'd say she was *afraid*, exactly. But she was definitely concerned, yes. That's why I was writing to you, because it seemed to me that Lord Devlin ought to know about this fellow."

"You say his name is Dobbs? Where does he live?"

"Some mean court off St. Martin's Lane, I believe."

"Is he the only person you know of who might have wished her harm?"

Veronica thought about it a moment, then shook her head. "If there was anyone else, she never mentioned them to me."

"Was she happy in her marriage, do you think?"

The widow dropped her gaze to her now-clenched hands and bit her lower lip. When she looked up again, her face was strained. She said, "How much do you know about Laura's marriage?"

"Very little. Why?"

"Sir Ivo was essentially her father's choice. If it had been up to Laura, she would have married a young officer she'd known most of her life." A faint, wistful smile touched her lips. "I remember him quite well. Very tall and handsome he was, and quite dashing in his new regimentals. But he was a younger son of a younger son, with his way still to make in the world, and her father refused to agree to the match. Laura swore she'd wait for him and marry him as soon as she came of age, whether her father gave them his blessing or not. But then the young man went off to war, and she heard he'd been killed. She married Sir Ivo two or three years later."

"Was she happy with him, do you think?"

Veronica gave a strange, hollow-sounding laugh. "How many women of our station are truly 'happy' in the marriages their parents arrange for them?"

It was a telling statement. "Content, then," said Hero. "Do you think she was content?"

The widow gave a vague, dismissive jerk of one shoulder. "She didn't seek to escape it, if that's what you're asking." She hesitated, then added, "At least, not to my knowledge."

"Would you know?"

Veronica's brows drew together in a frown. "Honestly? Perhaps not. Laura kept a great deal to herself."

"Did she ever tell you that Sir Ivo hit her?"

Veronica stared at her. "Good heavens, no. Did he?"

"So it appears, yes."

"No, she never said anything to me about it. Oh, poor Laura. If only—" She broke off as her stout, middle-aged butler appeared carrying a heavy silver tray with tea things and a plate of small cakes, which he set with a flourish on the table before them.

Hero waited until he had withdrawn, then said, "When was the last time you saw Laura?"

Veronica reached for the teapot and began to pour. "Last week. It was either Tuesday or Wednesday, although I can't recall precisely which."

"How did she seem? Troubled in any way? Worried?"

"I wouldn't have said so, no. I've been helping her to organize a benefit concert for the Foundling Hospital, you see, so that's mainly what we discussed. She was telling me about the musicians and singers she'd convinced to volunteer their time; that sort of thing."

Hero took the teacup held out by her hostess. "Have you always helped her with the concerts?"

"No, this was the first time; I was still in half mourning for Mr. Goodlakes last year. She'd been coaxing me to do it for years, but Mr. Goodlakes refused to countenance it. He used to say that while a nobleman's wife could enhance her image as Lady Bountiful by lending her prestige to such an institution, a shipbuilder's wife needed to take extra care never to be seen consorting with the low born."

Even when the shipbuilder's wife is herself a nobleman's daughter? thought Hero. *Interesting.* She took a slow sip of her tea. "What about Laura's efforts to convince Parliament to change the laws regarding apprenticeships? Were you involved in that?"

The widow had the grace to look vaguely discomfited and glanced away. "No. Given the circumstances, it didn't seem wise."

Hero was itching to ask *What circumstances?* but refrained. Instead she said, "I'm told Laura had run-ins with the directors of some of the parish workhouses. Would you happen to know which ones?"

"No, but if I had to guess, I'd say St. Martin's was one of them. I mean, they're the ones who apprenticed that poor little boy to Dobbs in the first place, then turned around and gave him another child when the first one died."

"Yes, that makes sense."

Veronica was silent for a moment, her tea forgotten in her hands, her gaze fixed unseeingly on something in the distance. Then she gave herself a little shake that was more like a shiver and looked over at Hero again. "I still can't believe this happened. Laura was always so full of energy, so determined, so full of *life*. And now she's . . . dead. And in such a senseless, frightening way."

"You said you'd known her since you were at school together. Do you know if she ever had anything to do with a woman named Julia Lovejoy?"

"The woman who was killed in a similar way out at Richmond years ago, you mean? I don't *think* she knew her, but obviously I could be wrong. It was so long ago now."

"Fourteen years," said Hero. "At the time, Laura would have been—what? Twenty-four or twenty-five?"

Veronica nodded. "Yes. Why?"

"Do you have any idea how old this fellow Dobbs is?"

"Forty or fifty, I'd say; something like that. He's a short, stocky man with graying dark hair and a crooked nose."

"You've seen him?"

"Oh, yes. I was with Laura one time when he confronted her.

We were coming out of Hatchards in Piccadilly, and he walked right up to her and said—" Veronica broke off, her eyes widening.

"And said—what?"

Veronica swallowed hard. "He said he'd given her a chance to back off and she'd refused to do it. So now she was going to pay."

It was an hour or so later that Hero received an unexpected visit from her father, Charles, Lord Jarvis.

She was seated on the flagged terrace at the rear of the Brook Street house, enjoying the first stirrings of a cool evening breeze and watching the two little boys prowl through the shrubbery of the garden in pursuit of their long-haired black cat, when their major-domo, Morey, showed the Baron out to her.

"*Grandpapa! Grandpapa!*" shouted Simon, pushing himself up from beneath a holly bush to run up the broad, shallow steps to the terrace and fling himself against his grandfather's legs.

"*Simon! Simon!*" mocked Jarvis with a laugh, catching the sweaty, dirty little boy around the waist and holding him at arm's length. "Good heavens, how grubby you are. Vegetation in your hair"—he raked a twig from the boy's dark curls—"and what, if I'm not mistaken, is mud ground into the knees of your dress." He glanced over at Hero as he set the boy back on his feet. "You're going to need to breech him, you know."

"Yes, both of them. Very soon," agreed Hero. She was aware of Patrick coming slowly up the stairs to stand quietly at a distance, watching them. Jarvis adored his grandson and now had his head bent, studying the caterpillar Simon held cradled in one grimy palm for his inspection. But as far as his lordship was concerned, Patrick didn't exist.

"A lovely specimen," Jarvis told Simon. "But I suggest you put him back where you found him while I talk to your mother."

Simon gently closed his fist around his treasure with a laugh.

Jarvis stood for a moment, watching the boys run off together, then he tossed his hat on the glass-topped terrace table and settled in the chair opposite Hero. "I can only stay a moment," he told her. "But I thought you'd like to know we've received confirmation that Napoléon did indeed surrender to the captain of one of our ships last week—the *Bellerophon*, off the western French port of Rochefort. They reached Devon this morning—Torbay, to be exact. One of the captain's lieutenants has arrived at the Admiralty with dispatches and a letter from Napoléon for the Prince Regent."

Hero was aware of a strange sense of light-headedness, so that for a moment she could only breathe. "So," she said at last. "It truly is over. What will be done with him?"

"For the time being, he'll be held on the ship, although I'd like to see the *Bellerophon* moved as soon as possible to Plymouth. It's a much safer harbor, and the presence of the Navy there should preclude any possibility of him being rescued—or seized. But what happens to him after that has yet to be decided. According to his letter, Napoléon is seeking political asylum and wants nothing so much as to buy a small estate somewhere in England and settle down to the quiet life of a country gentleman."

"Seriously?"

"Seriously. Needless to say, there are more than a few who'd like to see him turned over to the Bourbons to be hanged."

Hero studied her father's impassive features. "But not you?"

Jarvis pressed his lips into a tight line and shook his head. "It sets a dangerous precedent, executing a deposed head of state. And even if one sees Bonaparte as a general and not as an emperor, the fact remains that he wasn't captured. He surrendered to us voluntarily, and one does not execute generals who surrender." He paused, then added, "Or at least, one should not."

Hero said, "Apart from the stain it would be on our honor, it's also basically a bad idea."

"Undoubtedly. If the last hundred days have shown us nothing else, it's how popular Bonaparte still is with the people of France and how unpopular King Louis XVIII and his family are. I can't think of a better way to make Napoléon a martyr than for the Bourbons to hang him—especially if he were turned over to them by the very nation the French people have been fighting off and on for the last century and more."

"So you favor—what? Sending him into exile again? Where?"

"A number of places have been suggested, from Malta and Gibraltar to the Cape of Good Hope. Personally, I favor St. Helena. The disgrace of exile—at a safe distance from Europe this time—would make him a far less dangerous figure than one who found glory in death. Thank God he didn't die at Waterloo. They say he tried to poison himself at Fontainebleau after he was defeated last year, but the poison was old and only made him ill. I'm surprised he didn't try again after Waterloo."

"That might have been better."

"Perhaps." Jarvis heaved himself to his feet with a grunt. "At least he didn't manage to escape to the United States, which we're told was his plan. Ironically, if he'd set off for the coast immediately after he abdicated, rather than dithering at Malmaison for the better part of a month the way he did, he probably would have made it."

Hero rose with him. "When will it be in the papers?"

"Tomorrow morning. Needless to say, the Prince is pleased. He can now go ahead with his plans for another grand celebration on the anniversary of the accession of the Hanovers to the throne of Britain."

"Another one?"

"Another one. Combined with a celebration of our recent victory at Waterloo and the final defeat of Napoléon." Jarvis reached for his hat, then paused. "I'm told Devlin has involved himself in these ghastly murders out at Richmond Park."

"Did you think he would not?"

She was surprised to see a shadow of concern flit across Jarvis's normally controlled, impassive features. "It's disquieting, someone going around killing mothers and their children."

"It is disquieting, yes. Which is why Devlin is determined to see whoever is responsible brought to justice."

Jarvis fixed her with a steady look. "You will be careful." It was not a question.

Hero smiled at him. "Of course. I'm always careful."

Jarvis sighed and turned away. "No, you're not."

Chapter 14

*L*ater that night, after dinner, Sebastian stood before the open windows in the drawing room, a glass of port cradled in one hand, his gaze on the moonlit street below.

"What is it?" asked Hero, coming to stand beside him.

He turned to face her. "I'm trying to absorb the fact that out there right now, off the coast of Devon, Napoléon Bonaparte is pacing back and forth on the deck of a British warship. *A British warship.*"

"It does seem unreal, doesn't it? Do you think Jarvis will prevail?"

"In preventing the more vindictive souls amongst us from letting Prinny hand Napoléon over to the Bourbons to be hanged, you mean?" Sebastian drained his glass. "I sincerely hope so. That's the last thing the world needs at the moment."

"What is Hendon's position? Do you know?"

He went to pour himself more wine. "No, but I imagine it's much the same as Jarvis's."

She was silent for a moment, her gaze on a dowager's aged carriage rolling slowly up the street. "It all seems so . . . useless. Untold millions of lives disrupted or destroyed by twenty-five years of revolution and war, and for what? So that everything can be put back the way it was before? I keep thinking about the tragedy of Laura's life—separated from the man she loved by the war and her father's greed, forced to marry to please her family, then finding herself at the mercy of a cold, brutal man who used his fists on her."

"Did you ever see bruises on her?"

"No. He must have been careful to hit her where it wouldn't show." She paused. "I'm not sure why that makes it seem worse, but somehow it does. I suppose because it's so . . . calculated."

Sebastian took a slow sip of his wine. "If Laura McInnis were the only victim of this murder, Sir Ivo would be at the top of my list of suspects. But any man calculating enough to hit his wife only where the bruises won't show isn't going to lose his temper and shoot her in front of their young daughter—whom he hits by mistake."

Hero looked thoughtful. "What if it wasn't a mistake? What if he was angry at both his wife *and* his daughter?"

"And followed them out to Richmond with the intent of killing both and then posing their bodies in a way designed to make everyone think it the work of whoever killed Lovejoy's family fourteen years ago?"

"It's possible, isn't it?"

"I suppose it is, yes. In which case the question becomes, Why would a man be so filled with rage at his sixteen-year-old daughter as to want to kill her?"

Hero gave a faint shake of her head. "I can't imagine. Emma wasn't out yet, so it isn't as if she could have been refusing an advantageous match he'd arranged for her. Has anyone from Bow Street interviewed the girl's governess?"

"I don't know, but it would definitely be worth hearing what she has to say. Did Emma join her mother in her work with the Foundling Hospital?"

"No, she didn't. I remember Laura saying something once to the effect that Emma was upset because she wanted to, but Sir Ivo refused to allow her to involve herself in 'all that nonsense.' He was afraid it would hurt her chances on the Marriage Mart."

"I suppose it could—with a certain kind of man."

"A man like her father, you mean." Hero turned her head, her gaze caught by something in the street below. She said, "There's a hackney stopping before the house. And unless I'm mistaken, the man getting out of it is one of Sir Henry's constables."

Sebastian swore softly as the man rang a peal at the bell below. They heard the exchange of voices in the entrance hall; then a stocky man in a buff-colored coat whom Sebastian recognized as Constable Higgins labored up the stairs in Morey's wake.

"Message from Sir Henry, my lord," said Higgins with a jerky bow, holding out a twisted note.

"What is it?" asked Hero as Sebastian spread it open.

Sebastian ran his gaze down the magistrate's quickly scrawled message, then crumpled the paper in his hand. "There's been another murder—this time in St. James's churchyard, Piccadilly."

Chapter 15

The girl looked as if she couldn't have been more than thirteen or fourteen, her face thin and pale, her hair the color of corn silk. She lay on her back in the rank grass that grew between two crumbling old tombs not far from the gates of the churchyard, her arms crossed over the bodice of her gown in the manner of a corpse laid out for burial. A plain wooden tray lay upended beside her, with chocolate-covered fruits scattered about in the weeds. Someone had set a couple of horn lanterns atop one of the nearby tombs; more lanterns glinted in the darkness around them as Lovejoy's constables worked their way between the graveyard's tightly packed headstones and tombs, searching for whatever they could find.

Lovejoy himself stood beside the dead girl's body, his chin resting on his chest as he stared down at her, his hands thrust deep into the pockets of his coat although it was not cold.

"*Jesus,*" whispered Sebastian as he let his gaze drift over the girl's small, blood-drenched form. "Who is she?"

"A chocolatier's apprentice named Gilly. Gilly Harper."

Sebastian hunkered down beside the dead girl, his heart heavy in his chest. Her lips were gently parted, her thick dark lashes resting against the alabaster flesh of her cheeks. Judging by the bloody, slashed bodice of her plain stuff gown, she'd been stabbed, probably five or six times. He looked up at the silent magistrate. "What makes you think her death is connected to what happened out at Richmond Park?"

Sir Henry cleared his throat. "It might not be, of course. There's only the one victim; the method of killing—stabbing, rather than shooting—is different; and the body isn't posed in precisely the same manner. But according to the girl's mistress, Gilly met with Lady McInnis a few days before she was killed. And the killer has taken the time to lay the girl out and cross her arms at her chest."

Sebastian looked over to where a simply dressed woman in her forties stood beside the churchyard gates. Her plump, haggard face was blotched and wet with tears, and she had her arms wrapped around her waist, hugging herself. "That's the girl's mistress?"

"Yes. A Mrs. Monroe. She says Gilly left the shop before six to make a delivery and never came back."

"Who found the body?"

"A carpenter cutting through the churchyard on his way home. He recognized her and went to tell her mistress."

The woman was swaying back and forth, her tear-filled eyes unfocused, her voice a broken whisper as she said over and over, "That poor child. The poor, poor child."

Pushing to his feet, Sebastian walked over to introduce himself to her, offered the woman his handkerchief, and said gently, "Do you think you could answer a few questions, Mrs. Monroe?"

She blotted her plump face with the handkerchief and nodded. "I can try, my lord."

"I'm told Gilly was your apprentice. How long was she with you?"

Mrs. Monroe dabbed at the corners of her eyes. "Nearly six months, my lord."

"Her parents apprenticed her to you?"

"No, my lord. She's been an orphan for years. Came to me out of the St. Martin's workhouse, she did."

"How old was she?"

"Sixteen, my lord. She looks younger, I know, but I reckon it's from all those years of not getting enough to eat. Her parents died when she was eleven."

"Yet she's been with you only six months? I was under the impression the workhouses typically apprenticed out their orphans much younger."

Mrs. Monroe nodded and swallowed hard. "That they do, my lord. Gilly was with a cheesemonger before me. The woman abused the poor child horribly—beat her bloody with a nasty whip. It was Lady McInnis who convinced the authorities to take the girl away from the brute and assign her to me instead."

Sebastian watched the bobbing line of lanterns glimmer over the crowded rows of ghostly tombstones as Lovejoy's constables reached the far end of the churchyard and turned to work their way back. "I understand Gilly saw Lady McInnis last week?"

"She did, yes, my lord. Lady McInnis wanted to know if Gilly would mind talking to a lady who's writing an article on the mistreatment of apprentices."

Hero, thought Sebastian. Aloud, he said, "And did Gilly agree?"

"Yes, of course, my lord. But Lady McInnis was killed before it could all be arranged."

Sebastian was aware of the men from the deadhouse arriving with a shell to carry the girl's body to Gibson. He shifted his position slightly to draw the woman's focus away from the sight. "I understand Gilly left your shop around six?"

The chocolatier nodded. "She was supposed to take a tray of dipped fresh fruit to the Dowager Countess of Schomberg. But she never came back. And then around seven, the Dowager's cook sent one of their footmen to the shop, wanting to know why they hadn't received the delivery." A tear rolled down the woman's cheek, and she swiped at it with the handkerchief. "I was that put out with Gilly for going off like that and not doing what she was supposed to be doing. And here the poor child was lying dead the whole time—" Her voice cracked, and she pressed her trembling lips together and mutely shook her head.

Sebastian said, "Do you have any idea who might have done this to her?"

"No," sobbed the woman. "Who would want to kill a sweet little girl like Gilly?"

"Did she have a beau? Or perhaps someone who was interested in her even if she wasn't interested in him?"

The woman sucked in a deep, steadying breath. "No. Can't say she was really interested in boys, my lord. She was very young for her age, you see—and I don't mean only in size."

The men from the deadhouse were lifting the girl into their shell now. Sebastian said, "When Gilly was talking to Lady McInnis last week, were you with them?"

"Only part of the time, my lord. I was mainly minding the shop, you see."

"But Gilly told you afterward what they talked about?"

"Well, Lady McInnis herself told me she wanted to ask Gilly about doing the interview. And afterward, Gilly said as how she was fine with that."

"Did she say anything else about their meeting?"

"Well, let's see . . . I know Lady McInnis asked Gilly how she was getting on. She was like that, you know. She was such a fine, grand lady, and yet she somehow made Gilly feel that she was special, if you know what I mean?"

"I think I do, yes," said Sebastian, trying not to watch the men from the deadhouse lift the shell to their shoulders.

"There was one other thing," said Mrs. Monroe suddenly, her fist tightening around Sebastian's handkerchief. "I don't recall precisely how it came up, but I remember Lady McInnis saying something about how she was going to take her daughters and their cousins to Richmond Park on Sunday. Gilly said it sounded like a wonderful place, and I told her I'd see if I could get my brother Ned to drive us out there one day in his gig."

The woman's use of the word "daughters," plural, caught Sebastian's attention. If Laura McInnis had been originally intending to take both Emma and her younger sister, Thisbe, on the picnic with their cousins, then why had Thisbe stayed home? Because she was ill? No one had ever said.

"Was there anyone else in the shop at the time who might have overheard the conversation?"

"Not so's I recall, my lord. But there might have been."

"Could Gilly have told someone about it?"

"Well, I suppose she could've, my lord, but not that I know of." Her brows drew together in an uneasy frown. "You're thinking that's why Gilly was killed, my lord? That it's got something to do with what happened out at Richmond Park yesterday?"

"It might not," said Sebastian.

But he wasn't sure he believed it.

Chapter 16

*E*arly the next morning, Sebastian entered a mean, decaying court off St. Martin's Lane to find three filthy, ragged, barefoot little boys loading piles of empty soot sacks, cloths, brushes, and poles into their master's handcart.

"If'n you pack of lazy thatch-gallows don't want t' feel the weight of me hand on the back of yer heads, you'll step on it," said the chimney sweep, still buttoning his rough coat against the morning chill as he came through an open doorway in one corner of the court. He was a short, thickset man with a bony face, protruding ears, and skin so coated with soot and grime as to appear black. At the sight of Sebastian he drew up sharp, his nostrils flaring on a quickly indrawn breath.

"You're Hiram Dobbs?" said Sebastian.

"Aye," said the sweep warily. "Wot you want wit me?"

"I understand you knew Lady McInnis."

"Knew her?" Dobbs gave a harsh, ringing laugh. "That's rich. And how would the likes o' me come t' know a fine lady like herself?"

"Oh, you knew her, all right. You swept the chimneys of her town house in Grosvenor Square. And when she saw you lighting a fire under the feet of one of your apprentices to force him up a chimney and realized how bruised and battered he was, she tried to have the child taken away from you."

Dobbs's lips twisted into a sneer. "You think she's the first o' her kind I've had to deal with?" He turned his head to spit a mouthful of phlegm at a rat creeping through the rubbish at their feet. "They're all the same, them softhearted, sentimental ladies, bleating endlessly about the *'poor, poor little climbing boys.'"* As he said it, his voice rose in a vicious parody of a gentlewoman's tones, then dropped again. "But I'll tell you a secret: Them kind, they're always the first to call us when the soot builds up in their flues and their fireplaces start fillin' their rooms with smoke and nasty fumes. Once they start worryin' their chimneys might catch fire and burn down their houses, it's amazin' how somehow they no longer give a tinker's damn about the poor climbing boys. Not then. They're all the same."

Sebastian glanced at the three children, who now stood shivering, silent, and watchful beside their master's cart, their faces blank with numb acceptance, their eyes red and swollen, and every visible inch of their skin black with soot. In age, they probably ranged from five or six to nine or ten. They didn't live long, climbing boys. If they weren't burned alive in a chimney fire, they often fell to their deaths or got stuck in a narrow flue and suffocated, or succumbed to a lung infection caused by constantly inhaling soot. Those who didn't die often went blind thanks to their endlessly inflamed eyes. And if by chance they survived to reach puberty, they invariably fell victim to what they called "soot warts," a cancer that began by eating at their genitals before spreading out to consume their entire deformed, wasted bodies.

It was one of the reasons climbing boys and girls were always young—that, and because they needed to be small to fit through the labyrinth flues of London's chimneys, which were often as narrow as nine by nine inches. The boys climbed the flues by shimmying up like caterpillars, using their backs and knees and elbows. To toughen up the skin on a new boy's knees and elbows, the sweeps would rub brine into the child's flesh every night with a brush until it ceased to bleed and hardened up.

"They're all the same," Dobbs muttered again.

Sebastian set his jaw against the upswelling of rage that threatened to consume him. "Not quite all. Lady McInnis tried to get your boys taken away from you. That's when you started harassing her and threatening her—threatening to make her 'regret it', was one of the expressions I believe you used. And threatening to make her pay."

An angry light blazed in the man's beady gray eyes, and Sebastian noticed the three boys take a wary step back. "Jist givin' her her own back again, I was. Figured she deserved it. But I didn't do her no real harm. And as God is me witness, I didn't kill her."

The phrase struck Sebastian as both telling and chilling, given the way this murderer liked to pose his victims' bodies. He said, "Do I take it you're a religious man, Mr. Dobbs?"

"'Course I am. Me parents raised me to fear the Lord and keep to His path. As the Bible says, 'Gather the people together so's they can learn to fear me all the days of their lives, and teach their children, too.'"

"Or something like that," said Sebastian.

Hiram Dobbs glowered at him. "I'm a good, God-fearin' man, you hear me? I work hard and pray hard, and I keep these here children on the path of the straight and narrow. That woman—that *lady*—she messed with the wrong man. I jist wanted to make sure she knew that."

"The climbing boy who died—the one Lady McInnis tried to have taken away from you; what was his name?"

For a moment Sebastian didn't think the man would answer. Then he sniffed and said, "Robby."

"Robby what?"

"He didn't have no other name that I ever heard of. He was jist Robby."

"How old was he?"

"Danged if I know. He was always a sore trial to me, that one. Forever cryin' for his mama, gettin' stuck in the flues, afraid of everything from rats and fires to the fallin' soot."

My God, thought Sebastian. *That poor child.* Aloud he said, "Where were you last Sunday, Mr. Dobbs?"

The sweep sniffed again, then wiped the back of one hand across his crooked nose, smearing away some of the soot. "Keep the Lord's Day, I do."

"You do?" Most sweeps and their climbing boys worked seven days a week, with only one day a year—May Day—off. Sebastian glanced again at the silently waiting boys, but all three were now staring at their feet. "Commendable, I'm sure."

Hiram Dobbs gave a snort and slung his broom up to his shoulder. "You might not understand it, you being a fine lord an' all, but you're stoppin' us from gettin' to work, keepin' us standin' around jawin' like this."

"Oh? And how do you happen to know I'm a lord?"

"Heard Bow Street had asked some viscount to help 'em look into them murders out at Richmond Park. Must be nice t' have nothin' t' do all day but stick your nose where it don't belong."

"'And what doth the Lord require of thee but to do justice?'" quoted Sebastian.

The sweep's eyes narrowed. "Who said that?"

"Obviously not anyone you know," said Sebastian, nodding to the three watching boys. "We can talk more later."

"We ain't got nothin' t' talk about," shouted the sweep as Sebastian walked away. "Ye hear me? Nothin'."

But Sebastian just kept walking.

Chapter 17

Shortly before nine o'clock that morning, Sir Henry Lovejoy was preparing to leave for the inquest into the deaths of Laura and Emma McInnis when he received a report from the constable he'd assigned to make certain inquiries into Cato Coldfield.

After the man left, Lovejoy sat at his desk for some minutes, his gaze fixed unseeingly on the far wall. Then he drew a deep, steadying breath, pushed to his feet, and reached for his hat.

He rode out to Richmond in a hired hackney. Lord Devlin had offered to take the magistrate up in his carriage, but Lovejoy had declined, partially because he had several other matters to attend to while in the area and partially because he knew his lordship would much prefer to drive himself in his curricle. The surgeon Paul Gibson had also declined his lordship's offer, for reasons Lovejoy found less clear.

The inquest was being held in the Bedford Arms, the same

sprawling eighteenth-century inn that had housed the inquest into the deaths of Julia and Madeline Lovejoy fourteen years before. Even the coroner—a frock-coated relic named Horace Niblett—was the same. The man's once-smart new gray wig was now moth-eaten and dusty, the creases in his parchment-like pale face dug ever deeper, the rasp in his voice more pronounced. But if Lovejoy allowed his eyes to go slightly out of focus, he might easily have imagined himself hurtled back in time to an occasion he could only remember with a pain so intense it threatened to steal his breath and double him over in agony.

He was careful not to allow his attention to drift.

Sir Ivo was there, a black mourning riband tied around one arm, his manner rigid with a self-control that could have concealed anything.

Lord Salinger was also in attendance, his face haggard with grief for his dead sister and niece, and pinched with concern for his two children, who were required to testify. Although only fifteen, Miss Arabella answered the questions addressed to her with sad, quiet poise, while young Master Percy's hushed, halting responses moved more than one member of the assembled spectators to sympathetic tears.

Their testimony was followed by that of Paul Gibson. The surgeon's appearance was a shock, his face gaunt and ashen, his eyes bloodshot, his disheveled clothes hanging on his underweight frame. But his voice was firm and authoritative, his evidence succinctly delivered. After giving his testimony, he walked over to lean down and whisper something in Devlin's ear, then left.

Lovejoy hadn't expected to learn anything new from the inquest, and he did not. The inevitable verdict of homicide by shooting by party or parties unknown was returned by the coroner's jury within minutes.

Afterward, Lovejoy walked with Devlin along the side of Richmond's sunny, expansive green, where some half-grown lads were playing cricket, their voices and joyous, carefree laughter carrying softly on the warm summer breeze.

"I fear it was a waste of your time, my lord," said Lovejoy. "Driving all the way out here for this."

"I was interested to hear what Percy had to say. Salinger has been unwilling to let him talk to me."

"But neither child added anything to what was already known."

"No. And while that's unfortunate in some respects, it will hopefully help keep them safe."

Lovejoy glanced over at him. "You think the killer could have been amongst today's spectators?"

"It's possible. Although I'll admit most of those who've attracted my attention weren't there. Have you by chance come across a chimney sweep by the name of Hiram Dobbs in the course of your investigations?"

Lovejoy frowned. "I don't believe so, no. Dobbs, you say?"

Devlin nodded. "Lives in a mean court off St. Martin's Lane. I'm told Lady McInnis was trying to convince the authorities to take the man's apprentices away from him after she observed him mistreating a little boy who later died. Dobbs was heard on more than one occasion threatening her over it. He claims he observes the Lord's Day, so has no real alibi for that afternoon, but his neighbors might be able to tell us something about his movements."

"I'll set one of the lads to looking into it."

They paused at the kerb as a dray loaded with roughly hewn building stones lumbered past. "I've also been wondering if it's possible Lady McInnis was not the main target of the shootings," said Devlin. "What do we know about Emma McInnis?"

Lovejoy thought about it a moment. "Not a great deal. The girl wasn't out yet."

"No. But it might be worth interviewing her governess and abigail."

"Yes, I can see that—especially now, with the death of young Gilly Harper. The girls might have come from radically different backgrounds, but they were of much the same age—something I hadn't considered before. I've also set one of the lads to looking for the cheesemonger to whom Gilly was once apprenticed. One never knows." He was silent for a moment, his gaze on the sun-sparkled river now visible at the base of the hill. "It's peculiar, isn't it, how one's understanding of a murder can alter with a slight shift in perspective?"

"I suspect the same could be said of much of life."

Lovejoy let out a long, slow breath, his voice suddenly unsteady as he said, "How very true."

After that, Lovejoy took a hackney out to the dilapidated cottage of Cato Coldfield, near the Petersham Gate of Richmond Park.

He found the thatcher stripped down to his shirt and rough breeches and chopping kindling in the dappled shade of a big, half-dead elm that grew to one side of the house. Coldfield watched Lovejoy approach, then turned away to set a length of wood up on his block and let fly with his ax. "Wot ye want with me?" he demanded without looking around.

"You know who I am?" said Lovejoy, drawing up a healthy distance away from the man.

Coldfield snorted and reached for another piece of wood. "What ye think?"

Lovejoy watched the man position the wood on his block. "You lied to my constables."

Coldfield glanced at him sideways. "Don't know wot yer talkin' about."

"You told us you were ill on Sunday; that you didn't leave your cottage until late that afternoon. Except we've since discovered you were seen in Richmond High Street that morning."

"So? Ducked out to buy me a loaf of bread, I did. Didn't have nothin' in the house to eat. A man needs to eat even when he's sick, ye know."

"So why lie about it?"

"Why? Ye think I don't know what folks was sayin' about me fourteen years ago? Ye think I want t' help you lot hang these new murders around me neck? Of course I lied. Anybody with any sense would lie. But I only went to the baker's, ye hear? I got me bread, then I come right back home. Ye won't find nobody who'll tell ye different."

A black-and-white dog that had been sleeping nearby pushed up, shook himself, then turned around three times and lay back down again. Lovejoy watched the mutt stretch his head out on his paws and sigh. "Lady McInnis's coachman and footman reported seeing an older man with a dog in the park earlier that day. That wasn't you, was it?"

Coldfield reached for another block of wood. "Nope."

Lovejoy watched the man's massive shoulders flex as he drew back his ax. "When was the last time you were in London?"

Whack. The pieces of kindling went flying, and Coldfield turned to stare at Lovejoy through narrowed eyes. "London? I dunno. Been years, I s'pose. Why ye askin'?"

"Do you know a young girl named Gilly Harper?"

"Who?"

"Gilly Harper. Sixteen years old but looks much younger. Apprenticed to a Piccadilly chocolatier."

"Never heard o' her. Wot ye askin' me about her for? Wot's she got to do with anything?"

"Possibly nothing," said Lovejoy.

"Then why ye askin' about her?"

"Someone murdered her last night."

"In London? An' ye come all the way out here, worryin' me over it? Ain't ye got enough riffraff in London t' bother wit this nonsense?" Coldfield swung his ax, the blade digging deep into the wood of the stump before him, then turned to point one meaty finger at Lovejoy. "I didn't have nothin' to do wit them two women who was killed out here Sunday, ye hear? Nothin'. An' I didn't have nothin' to do wit whatever yer sayin' happened in London yesterday. Ain't nobody can tell ye nothin' different. Ye hear? Nobody."

With a rude snort, the thatcher turned away, the muscles of his broad shoulders working beneath the worn cloth of his shirt as he swooped up an armload of kindling. Watching him, Lovejoy felt the gentle breeze caress his face, heard it lifting the leaves of the dying elm beside them. For fourteen years now he had found a measure of solace in the thought that the man who had killed his Julia and Madeline had paid the ultimate price for what he'd done. But that faint comfort, as pitiful as it might have been, was gone now. He felt a cold rage sweep through him, curling his hands into fists at his sides and twisting at something deep inside him. He wanted to seize this crude man by his thick arms and spin him around to slam him back against the elm and make him—*make* him—tell the truth. Not only about these new deaths but about what had happened fourteen years ago.

Except that Lovejoy knew only too well that he was an old man, barely five feet tall, and never, even in his youth, either strong or pugnacious. Trembling beneath the onslaught of unwanted and unfamiliar emotions, he swiped the back of one hand across his lips, swallowed hard, and forced himself to turn and walk away.

Lovejoy's next stop was a small whitewashed cottage on the banks of the river Thames.

"I shan't be long," he told the driver as he stepped down into the dusty lane. He was only dimly aware of the jarvey nodding in response, for Lovejoy's attention was all for the older woman he could see bent over pulling weeds near the cottage's door.

It had been fourteen years since he'd last been here, but the cottage still looked much the same, its windowsills painted a jaunty yellow, the climbing rose rioting around the front door thick with fat pink blooms, the small garden a well-tended jumble of honeysuckle and jasmine, hollyhocks and daisies. He wasn't certain that the woman he could see weeding and the woman he had come here to speak to were one and the same. But as he walked toward the garden gate, she straightened, her eyes narrowing as she recognized him, and he was surprised to realize that he'd been secretly hoping he wouldn't find her still here.

He supposed she must be in her sixties or seventies by now, Mrs. Mattie O'Toole. Her hair was iron gray and thinning, her face deeply lined, her dark eyes cloudy and nearly lashless. But she was still sturdy, her back still straight, her expression still closed and guarded. Once, she'd had four sons and a daughter. But her youngest boy drowned in the Thames when he was only eight; one of his brothers had been impressed and died in the Battle of the Nile; another succumbed to fever while in the West Indies with the Army. Her last surviving son, Daniel, had lost an arm and suffered a debilitating head wound fighting for the Crown in the Irish Rebellion of

1798. The Crown had expressed its gratitude for his service by hanging him for the murder of Julia and Madeline Lovejoy.

Lovejoy paused at the gate, his hand on the latch, as the woman continued to stare at him. He wondered how she recognized him, for he himself had changed much in the last fourteen years. He wondered if she'd been there in the crowd outside the Old Bailey when they hanged her son for a crime he died insisting he hadn't committed. He wondered if she still believed her son innocent; if she still wept for him the way Lovejoy still wept for Madeline and Julia. He figured she probably did.

He cleared his throat. "Mrs. O'Toole?"

Her nostrils flared as she sucked in a deep breath. "And what would you be wantin' from me, then?" She might have lived in England for decades, but her accent was still very much that of the Emerald Isle.

"May I come in?"

She shrugged and went back to her weeding. "Suit yourself."

He pushed open the gate and closed it carefully behind him. But he made no attempt to approach any closer.

Her attention still on her weeding, she said, "I heard about them new killings in Richmond Park. That's why you're here, ain't it? You're thinkin' maybe you made a mistake all them years ago? You're thinkin' maybe you should've believed my boy Danny when he told you he didn't do nothin' to nobody?" She tilted her head, looking up at him sideways. "Hmm?"

Lovejoy found himself at a loss for words, unsure precisely why he had come. "I frankly don't know what to think," he said, surprised by his own honesty.

She huffed a mirthless laugh. "Is that a fact? Well, I've no more boys for you to be hanging for somethin' they didn't do. Unless maybe you're thinkin' about hanging me?" Straightening, she reached for the cane he now noticed leaning against the cottage wall beside her. Her green-stained, gnarled hand tightened around the stick's curved handle as she limped toward him, not stopping until she was only a few feet from him. "Now, why would I be killin' some woman and her child I never met?"

He could think of one very good reason why she would do such a thing, but it was obvious that the murders in Richmond Park were physically beyond her. She might have been able to shoot Lady McInnis and her daughter, but she was obviously too crippled to have staged the bodies and then escaped quickly enough to avoid being seen by the Barrows brothers.

When he remained silent, her face creased in a faint, derisive smile. "I see what you're graspin' at. You're thinkin' maybe I shot that woman and girl so's everyone would think my boy must've been innocent of those other killings." She gave a faint shake of her head. "But if I was gonna do somethin' like that, why would I wait fourteen years? Why not do it when it might've helped my Danny?"

"I'm not here to accuse you."

"No? Then who are you accusin'? My girl Bridget? She died six months ago, you know. Her widower and my three grandbabies live all the way down in Plymouth now."

"I'm sorry."

"No, you aren't. You couldn't give a rat's arse about either me or mine."

He wanted to protest, to let her know that he did indeed care. What decent man would not? Instead he said, "Is there anyone else? Anyone you can think of who might have done such a thing?"

"You think I would give you their names if there were? So's you could hang them, too?" She snorted. "Not likely. But the truth is, there ain't nobody. Nobody but me and"—she nodded to the gray striped cat with white paws stretched out asleep on a nearby sunny windowsill—"maybe old Toby Cat there."

Lovejoy kept his gaze on the woman's wrinkled, broad-nosed face. "Fourteen years ago, at the time of the first killings in Richmond Park, who did you think was responsible?"

"Me? I'd no idea. How could I? Never met your wife and girl; never even been in Richmond Park, meself. Only thing I know is, my boy Danny didn't do it. Oh, I'm no' denying he weren't right in the head after what happened to him in Ireland in the 'Ninety-Eight. But he would never have hurt nobody, man nor beast. He was a gentle soul and he hated the things he saw done in Ireland. Hated doin' what he was ordered to do—herding innocent women and children into churches and barns and setting fire to them, then listenin' to 'em scream and watchin' till every last one of 'em was burned alive. What kind of officer orders his soldiers to do something like that? Them's monsters, anyone who orders that. But ain't nobody hanged those officers for murder. Oh, no; their kind get promotions and is called heroes."

She turned her head and spat, then brought her hard gaze back to Lovejoy's face. She was silent for so long that he wondered what she saw there.

He said, "You didn't know either Lady McInnis or her daughter?"

"Me? How could a simple woman such as myself ever meet such a grand lady? Reckon you're gonna have to look elsewhere to find somebody to blame for the killings this time." She paused a moment, then said, "And if you discover you were wrong about my Danny, will you admit it, I wonder? Even to yourself?"

"Yes."

"Huh. I'll believe it when I see it. Come on, Toby."

As she turned away, the gray cat stood up, arched his back in a stretch, then leapt down off the windowsill to follow the old woman into the cottage. Without looking back, she shut the door behind them with a snap. But for a long time Lovejoy stayed where he was, standing on the flagged path of her garden, surrounded by a jumble of sun-dappled roses and tansy and comfrey, and prey to an unsettling combination of sadness and uncertainty tinged, undeniably, with shame.

Chapter 18

The director of the St. Martin's workhouse was an officious little man named Felix Fry. Short-legged and pudgy, he had slicked-back black hair and a small, pointed nose and soft white hands he fluttered through the air when he spoke. Confronted with Lady Devlin, daughter of the King's powerful cousin Lord Jarvis and daughter-in-law to the Earl of Hendon, Fry was all bowing civility and obsequious smiles as he ushered Hero into his comfortable office near the grim brick building's front entrance.

But his smile froze when Hero settled in the seat indicated by him and brought his pleasantries to an end by saying briskly, "Thank you, Mr. Fry. I'm here because I'm interested in hearing about your recent interactions with Lady McInnis."

"Ah. Um, yes, Lady McInnis." He sank into the wooden chair behind his broad, lovingly polished desk. "It's beyond shocking, what happened. I fear the crime in our streets grows worse every day. The end of the war has emboldened the criminal classes, wouldn't you say? All this—"

"The murders are indeed shocking," said Hero, cutting him off. "So do tell me, please, precisely when was the last time you saw Lady McInnis?"

"Me?" Fry's eyes widened, then darted away. "Oh, it's been weeks now. Weeks."

"Sometime in early July, would you say?"

He swallowed. "Something like that, yes."

"She came here?"

Fry straightened the already neat pile of papers at the corner of his desk. "She did, yes."

"And why was that?"

The treacly smile was back in place. "Lady McInnis's interest in the children of the poor was . . . intense."

"It was, indeed. I'm told she was concerned about the manner in which the workhouse handles its apprenticeships, particularly your practice of selling very young orphans to chimney sweeps. Is that why she came?"

Mr. Fry gave a faint titter. "I wouldn't say we *sell* them, precisely. This isn't America, you know."

"No? I've heard the going rate is four shillings."

He was no longer smiling. "As your ladyship is doubtless aware, it is the duty of every Poor Law guardian to keep the parish rates as low as possible. Obviously, one way to do so is by apprenticing out as many of the workhouse children as we can."

"Tell me about the little boy named Robby."

"Robby?"

"The orphan who was apprenticed as a climbing boy to a chimney sweep named Hiram Dobbs. The little boy died, so you gave Dobbs another."

"Ah, yes; Robby Coker, or Cooper, or some such thing. His mother came to us last year. I believe the father was killed fighting the French."

"Is she still with you?"

"Oh, no. She died not long after they arrived."

"And that's when you apprenticed her little boy to Dobbs?"

"No; we found the position for Robby before she died."

"She didn't object?"

"She did, yes. But we explained that it was necessary."

"And she accepted that?"

"Not exactly. I fear she became hysterical. Uncontrollable, actually."

Hero thought about how she would react if someone were to tear Simon or Patrick—or the child now growing in her womb—from her arms and condemn them to the short, brutal, terrifying life of a climbing boy. And for one piercing moment the fear, pain, and rage that shot through her made it impossible for her to even breathe. Her fists spasmed around the strings of her reticule, and she had to consciously relax them.

She said, "How old was Robby?"

Fry shifted uncomfortably in his chair. According to the 1788 Chimney Sweepers Act, sweeps were not allowed to take apprentices younger than eight. The rule was never enforced, of course, but it was still the law. Which meant that if Laura McInnis had wanted to make trouble for Mr. Felix Fry, she might have been able to.

Except that with both Robby and his mother dead, how could anyone prove the child's age?

Fry spread his fluttery hands wide. "It's often difficult to say precisely how old these orphans are, you know. They frequently look much younger than their actual ages, and all too often they are old beyond their years. Like so many of the gentler sex, Lady McInnis was charmingly softhearted. As a result, I fear she sometimes failed to appreciate the extent to which the members of the lower orders are different from their betters. The poor are a deeply flawed lot, you know—their passions raw, their morals corrupt, their offspring tainted. What might be tragic in a different situation . . ."

He stumbled to a halt at the sight of the furious outrage flaring in Hero's eyes. "You don't find the death of an innocent five-year-old child tragic?" she said. "A child orphaned because his father was killed fighting for his country?"

"Yes, yes; of course, of course," he said hastily. "But if you knew the extent to which all the workhouses have been overwhelmed by the influx of widows and orphans because of the number of men killed in the wars! And now, with so many returning veterans unable to find work and also thrown onto relief, I don't know what we're to do."

"Oh? And do you consider our returning veterans 'tainted' and 'flawed,' as well?"

Fry's voice turned whiny. "We do what we can, my lady. If Parliament were to allocate funds to help the parishes cope, it might be different. But as it is, the maintenance of the poor is too much for local ratepayers to bear, and that is something Lady McInnis refused to comprehend. Why, I heard this last week that she'd been harassing one of the countrywomen who cares for the parish's infants."

By law, all workhouses were required to place their orphaned or foundling babies in homes at least three miles from London. As conceived, the law was admirable, since the thinking was that the infants would have a greater chance of survival away from the unhealthy city. But in practice the law was a disaster, for the workhouses tended to dump their infants on unscrupulous foster mothers who could generally be relied upon to kill the infants left in their charge within a very short time.

"What countrywoman?" said Hero.

"A most excellent, motherly woman named Prudence Blackadder. She and her husband care for a number of our infants at their farm—a lovely place not far from Richmond."

"And how do you come to know that Lady McInnis had a conflict with this woman?"

"Because I had Mrs. Blackadder here in my office, defending herself against Lady McInnis's attacks."

"What kind of attacks?"

The nostrils of his pointed little nose flared with indignation. "Frankly, I don't think I should even repeat them. The fact is that infants die all the time. To accuse Mrs. Blackadder and her husband, Joseph, of neglect—or worse—is beyond unconscionable."

"Oh? And what percentage of the babies left in this woman's care die?"

Fry looked Hero straight in the eye and said, "I've no idea."

"Really? One would think that is precisely the sort of information you should have."

A muscle jumped along Fry's suddenly clenched jaw. He glanced pointedly at the clock on the nearby mantel and pushed to his feet. "Dear me, look at the time. I fear you must excuse me, Lady Devlin; I am overdue for an appointment with our chaplain."

"Of course," said Hero, smiling as she rose with him. "Thank you so much for your time. And don't worry; if I need anything more, I shall simply come back."

Chapter 19

*N*estled in a pretty hollow just off the main road between London and Richmond, Pleasant Farm was small but prosperous-looking, with tidy fields bordered by neat hedgerows and a sprawling, slate-roofed stone farmhouse that showed signs of having been considerably expanded in recent years.

When Hero's yellow-bodied carriage drew up in the farm's cobbled quadrangle, she could see a half-grown girl in a plain round gown and sunbonnet feeding geese down by a small pond. Another child, this one no more than two or three, sat in a patch of shade near the open kitchen door, playing with a kitten. As Hero watched, a short, stout woman with a clean white apron pinned to her gray stuff gown came bustling through the doorway, one hand raised to shade her eyes from the sun as the team of fine black carriage horses came to a halt and one of Hero's liveried footmen jumped to open the coach door and put down the steps.

The woman let her hand fall to her side, her features settling into an expression of sympathetic concern. She looked to be perhaps forty-five, although the dark hair beneath her starched white cap was little touched by gray and her plump face showed few lines. She stood watching as Hero, dressed in a carriage gown of moss green and a shako-style hat adorned with a single artfully curling plume, descended the steps. Then the woman stepped forward and dropped a quick curtsy. "Good morning, and welcome to Pleasant Farm. I'm Prudence Blackadder. May I help you?"

"How do you do, Mrs. Blackadder?" said Hero, settling her skirts around her. "I'm Lady—"

"Oh, no need to be giving us your name, my lady," said the woman in a rush. "That is, unless you's wanting to, of course. Been doing this now for going on twelve years, I have, which means I know how to be discreet, I do. If you're wishful of having a look around, you're more than welcome. But if not, I'll understand that, too. There's many who'd as soon make their arrangements and then be on their way, never to look back."

Hero stared at the woman, puzzlement giving way to under-standing as it dawned on her that Prudence Blackadder had leapt to the inevitable conclusion that Hero was here to make arrangements to abandon some unwanted infant into the woman's care. The result of an illicit affair, presumably—either her own or some relative's or dear friend's.

"Well," said Hero, her gaze drifting around the quadrangle's cluster of neat stone-walled barns and sheds, "I would like to see where you keep the little ones you're currently caring for."

"Of course, my lady," said Mrs. Blackadder, extending a hand to-ward the flight of shallow steps that led up to the house's main front door. "Right this way, if you please. I've told my Lucy to put the kettle on, so's after you've had a good look around we can go into the parlor and have us a nice cup of tea while we take care of details."

"Thank you," said Hero as the woman ushered her into a picturesque, low-ceiled entry hall that probably dated back a hundred years or more, with flagstone flooring and a large fieldstone fireplace that ranged across most of one wall. The newer part of the house stretched away to the left, but the woman led Hero down an old corridor to an oak-wainscoted room with heavy dark beams overhead that was probably the original house's sitting room.

"We've not too many of the wee ones at this moment," said the woman as she stood back to allow Hero to enter the room first. Drawing up inside the doorway, Hero counted eight baskets and several larger cots. The cots and two of the baskets were empty; the rest contained tightly swaddled infants, none of whom looked older than three or four months. All were sleeping soundly.

Hero looked around. "And where are the older children?"

"Older children?" Prudence Blackadder's small, nearly lashless gray eyes widened. "Well, you may've seen little Eliza there by the kitchen door when you drove up, while I sent Jane off to feed the geese before you came. And of course the boys are down at the barn with my Joseph, putting up the hay."

"Oh? How many older boys do you have?"

"Two."

Hero felt her stomach tighten. The woman was currently looking after six tiny infants. But despite having been—as she herself said—taking in babies for nearly twelve years, she currently had only one toddler and three half-grown older children. By law, the parishes were required to leave their foundlings and orphaned infants in the country until they turned four. So then why, with the exception of the one- or two-year-old child in the yard, were all her babies so small?

"Now, if you'll step into the parlor, my lady," Prudence Blackadder was saying, "we can have a nice little chat."

The parlor was new and spacious and expensively if garishly

decorated, with thick, vividly colored Turkey carpets on the floor and a superabundance of heavily carved chairs and settees opulently covered in red damask. Yards and yards of the same damask covered the walls and hung at the windows, while a pair of large, rather hideous Sèvres vases graced a marble mantelpiece. Fostering infants was obviously a lucrative business—particularly if the infants left in one's care could be kept liberally dosed with opium to dull their appetites and make them sleep. And when no one cared or even noticed if they quietly died.

"My, what an . . . extraordinary room," said Hero. "Have you recently had it redone?"

"Last spring," said the woman, smiling proudly as she led the way to a grouping of chairs gathered around a table loaded down with a tray bearing a heavy silver tea set and delicate china cups and saucers. "Do have a seat, my lady, and we can get comfortable."

Hero chose a chair that put her back to the windows. "Thank you."

"Just so you know," said Prudence, settling herself before reaching for the teapot provided by the unseen Lucy, "this can be handled in one of two ways. There's some who like to pay by the month and come every now and then to visit their little ones, like Eliza and Jane. But most prefer to make one up-front payment and then leave the child in our loving care. That way they can put it all behind them and leave the past in the past, as the saying goes. Frankly, we've found it to be by far the best option for everyone involved."

Hero yanked off her gloves and set them aside. "Yes, I can see how that would be more convenient. For everyone."

Prudence smiled and handed her a cup of tea. "And when should we be expecting this infant you've decided to entrust to our loving care?"

"Well, before we get to that, I did have one or two questions."

Prudence Blackadder looked up from pouring her own tea. "Oh?"

"Your name was given to me by several different sources, obviously. But I must admit to being a trifle concerned about some of the things I'm told Lady McInnis was recently heard saying."

"Oh, that woman!" Rearing back, Prudence Blackadder threw both hands up into the air, then let them fall to her lap. "She was a foolish woman—foolish to the point of being demented, that one. Came here a week or two ago, she did—on fire, like some demon-possessed madwoman. Accused us of all sorts of unchristian evils. But it's the outside of enough to hear she was spreading her malicious lies all around, too. I'm sure I've no need to tell you, my lady, that there's not a morsel of truth in any of the wicked things she was saying. The thing is, you see, a good many of our babies come to us from St. Martin's workhouse. The Lord knows we do our best with them, but the sad truth is they're a weak, sickly lot. I fear most are born in sin and abandoned by their unnatural mothers." She gave a sad sigh. "Unfortunately they are not long for this world."

"Is that why Lady McInnis came here? To accuse you of neglecting the babies given into your care?" Hero almost said *killing them*, but caught herself in time.

"Who knows why she came?" said Prudence, setting the creamer down with a thump. "I tell you, the woman was mad."

"Do so many of your babies die?"

Prudence touched the corner of her apron to one eye, as if wiping away a tear. "There's no denying we always lose some, I'm afraid. Many of the ones who come from the workhouse are in their last days before they reach us. But it still breaks my heart every time." She sighed again. "Although our good reverend, he's always telling me not to take it too hard, for he says he has no doubt most would only have grown up to be hanged anyway." She leaned forward to whisper, as if imparting a dread secret. "It's in the blood, you know."

"So I've heard." Hero took a slow sip of her tea. "I must say, I'm impressed with how quiet your babies are. No one would guess you've six just down the corridor. I haven't heard a peep out of any of them. However do you manage to keep them sleeping so soundly?"

"It's the fresh air, my lady. Nothing like fresh country air and food to keep the little ones healthy."

"And yet so many of them still die. How . . . tragic." Hero took another sip of her tea. "There is one other thing I'm curious about."

"Yes?"

"The ones that die. What do you do with them?"

"Oh, they're given a good Christian burial, my lady. No need to worry about that."

"You relieve my mind, Mrs. Blackadder."

The woman smiled. "Now, when did you say we could be expecting our new wee one?"

Hero set aside her teacup. "I fear you've been laboring under something of a misapprehension, Mrs. Blackadder. I'm not here to make arrangements to abandon some poor child to your care. You see, your name came up in connection with the recent deaths of Laura and Emma McInnis."

For a long moment, the woman stared at her, her face going blank with confusion. "You're not here to make arrangements for a child?"

"No. But I would like to hear more about your visit from Laura McInnis. You never did say what had made her suspect that you were basically killing the children left in your care."

A deep crimson color rushed into the woman's face. "I think you should leave," she said, pushing back her chair.

"Do I take it you find the subject uncomfortable?" said Hero, reaching for her gloves as she rose to her feet. "Why is that, I wonder?"

Prudence's mouth tightened into a thin line that swallowed her lips. "I tell you, the woman was mad. I take good care of my babies. All of them. Always have, always will. Anybody who says otherwise either doesn't know what they're talking about or is mad."

"That is certainly one explanation," said Hero, walking toward the front door.

She was pausing at the base of the front steps to jerk on her gloves when a man came at a trot from around the corner of one of the stone-walled sheds. He looked to be somewhere in his fifties, with thick graying hair and a jowly face darkened by his years in the sun. His clothes were those of someone who was not afraid of working, but his air was that of a man accustomed to being in control of those around him, and Hero didn't need to see the look that passed between him and Prudence to know that this was the owner of Pleasant Farm.

"Lucy come t' tell me we had a fine lady here," said Joseph Blackadder, his eyes lighting up as he took in the glories of Hero's yellowbodied barouche and team of well-bred horses.

"The lady was just leaving," snapped his wife. "She only came to ask some downright nasty questions about Lady McInnis's visit."

The avaricious gleam died. "Oh?"

His wife drew a deep, angry breath that swelled her shelflike bosom. "Why, she all but came out and accused me of killing my babies!"

The farmer's eyes narrowed. Joseph Blackadder might be less educated than his wife, but he was obviously considerably shrewder. For while Prudence's reaction to Hero's questions had focused entirely on the woman's reputation as a foster mother, her husband was smart enough to see the danger of having it known that they'd quarreled with a murder victim days before her killing.

"We read about what happened out at Richmond Park," he said, his tongue darting out to lick his lips. "Told Prue here I wouldn't be surprised to hear Bow Street is lookin' into Basil Rhodes himself for it. Didn't I tell you, Prue?"

"*Basil Rhodes?*" said Hero. "You can't be serious." Basil Rhodes was a flamboyant, well-known personality. Boisterous and loud, with a reputation as a wit and *bonhomme*, he was a popular figure in the ballrooms and gentlemen's clubs of Mayfair. Ostensibly the son of the late Peter K. Rhodes, a onetime boon companion of the Prince of Wales, Basil was actually one of the Prince's favorite by-blows. Anyone who doubted the relationship had only to see Rhodes's curly auburn hair, full face, feminine lips, and stocky Hanoverian build to know the truth.

"Saw him arguing with her just last Saturday, I did," Joseph Blackadder was saying. "Right in the middle of Bond Street. Everyone could see he was mad as fire at the woman, shakin' his fist at her and yellin' till he was as red in the face as a man can be."

"Yelling about what?"

"Couldn't hear it all. Somethin' about her needin' to mind her own business, and how if she didn't shut her mouth, he was gonna shut it for her."

"Indeed," said Hero. "And how do you happen to know Mr. Basil Rhodes?"

"Brung us one o' his by-blows, he did. A few months back."

So much for the couple's famous discretion, thought Hero with a wry glance at Prudence Blackadder's closed, angry face. Aloud, she said, "You have his child here now?"

"Unfortunately, no," said Prudence with a warning glance at her husband. "The poor wee thing was never well."

"Ah. Mr. Rhodes paid an up-front sum, did he?"

The insinuation was not lost on Joseph Blackadder. Swearing under his breath, he took an aggressive step toward Hero, but drew up sharply when one of her waiting footmen moved to close the distance between them. The farmer might be big and brawny, but Devlin's footmen were all tall, broad shouldered, and in the prime of life. Blackadder eyed the man thoughtfully, then brought his gaze back to Hero. "I think it's past time you was leavin'."

Hero let her gaze drift around the sun-filled, idyllic-looking farmyard with its tidy stone-built outbuildings and sweetly scented tumbles of climbing roses and honeysuckle and jasmine. "Yes, I've seen more than enough. We'll let you know if we have any further questions."

"'We'?"

"Didn't I say? My husband, Viscount Devlin, is assisting Bow Street in their investigation of the recent murders. Exactly how far are you from Richmond Park, by the way?"

"Two miles," growled Joseph Blackadder. "Or thereabouts."

"Interesting," said Hero, carefully lifting her skirts as she turned toward the steps of the waiting carriage.

"We didn't have nothin' to do with what happened out there," the farmer shouted after her. "You hear me? Nothin'."

Hero paused at the top of the steps to look back at him. "I don't recall suggesting that you did," she said, and watched the color drain from the big man's face.

Chapter 20

That afternoon, Sebastian drove over to Tower Hill to find the door to Gibson's old stone outbuilding thrown open to the afternoon breeze and Gilly Harper's small, pallid body lying on the raised stone slab in the center of the room. But it was Alexi Sauvage, not Gibson, who set aside her scalpel with a clatter as Sebastian crossed the garden toward her.

A Frenchwoman in her thirties, she was built small and thin, with a head of untamable fiery hair and a fine-boned face with pale, almost translucent skin. Her relationship with Sebastian was complicated. Once, years before in the mountains of Portugal, he had killed the French lieutenant who was her lover and she had promised to take his life in revenge.

"I have not finished quite yet," she said now, a lock of her hair falling into her eyes as she looked up so that she had to brush it back with the swipe of one curled wrist. "But I think there is not much else to be learned."

"Where's Gibson?"

Her normally expressive features flattened, became unreadable. "I don't know. Down by the river, perhaps? Prostrate before one of the ancient altars in St. Katharine's? His leg is hurting and he keeps refusing to take anything for it—even a small dose. Except of course it will reach the point where he won't be able to bear either the pain or his opium cravings any longer, and then he'll take more than he should."

"Why?"

A muscle jumped along her tight jaw. "Why do you think?"

"I don't know what to think," said Sebastian with more emotion than he'd intended. "He looks worse now than he ever did. I thought he'd agreed to let you try to help him. So why hasn't it happened?"

"You're a man; can't you guess?"

"No, damn it!"

She looked at him with still, solemn brown eyes swimming with scorn and something else he couldn't quite read. "He is as afraid the sessions I want to try with him will work as he is afraid they won't. Because if they work, he'll have no excuse to keep taking the opium, and he's afraid he won't be able to stop. So he wants to get off the opium before we even try."

"Bloody idiot," said Sebastian, slapping one palm against the doorframe beside him. "It would be a hell of a lot easier for him to resist the opium if he weren't in pain!"

"I know that. You know that. Even he knows that. But for a sex that prides itself on logical thinking, you lot have a bad habit of letting pride and stubbornness and what you English like to call 'sheer bloody-mindedness' get in the way of sensible behavior."

That wasn't something Sebastian wanted to argue. He said instead, "What can I do?"

"I don't know. Try talking to him? Perhaps you can get through to him. I can't."

Sebastian nodded, his gaze dropping to the dead girl on the slab between them. After a moment, he said, "Have you learned anything at all?"

"Nothing beyond the basics. She was stabbed five times by someone who was probably holding the knife in an overhand position, so that he was striking down, not up."

"So not a professional."

"Not unless he was deliberately trying to disguise his skill. The weapon was also larger than a dagger. Whoever he—or, I suppose, she—was, they can't have escaped being covered in blood. Although if they were wearing a coat or cloak, obviously they could have thrown that away."

Sebastian was silent, his gaze on the dead girl's thin face, the corn silk–fine hair that framed it fluttering in the breeze that wafted in through the open door.

Alexi said, "You knew the girl was abused by someone at one time? She has . . . many scars."

Sebastian nodded. "Yes, she was originally apprenticed to a cheesemonger who was extraordinarily cruel to her. It was Lady McInnis who fought to have her removed from the woman and given to a new mistress."

"Interesting. So what do you know about this cheesemonger?"

Sebastian looked up to meet her hard gaze. "Not enough."

Chapter 21

$\mathcal{S}$ ebastian spent the next hour or two combing the Tower Hamlets and surrounding area, from St. Katharine's and Tower Wharf to St. Dunstan's and a certain ancient Tudor pub, looking for Gibson. In the end, frustrated, he returned to his friend's surgery to find Gibson sprawled in one of the overstuffed chairs beside the parlor's cold hearth, his sweat-stained cravat askew, his head lolling to one side, the pupils of his eyes tiny, telltale pinpricks.

"Devlin," he said, looking up with a hazy smile. "You back? Alexi said you'd been here looking for me. Pour yourself a drink and have a seat. You don't mind if I don't get up, do you?"

Sebastian stayed where he was, one hand curling around the edge of the door beside him, torn between a raging desire to pull the surgeon up out of that damned chair and shake him, and the equally powerful urge to wrap his arms around his friend and weep. His voice cracked as he said, "Leg hurting, is it?"

"Not so much anymore."

"That's good." Sebastian drew a deep breath. "Where's Alexi?"

"I don't know. She went out. Said she told you about . . . the girl. Can't remember her name."

"Gilly Harper."

"That's right. Gilly." Gibson gave a faint shake of his head. "Need to stop whoever's doing this, Devlin. Before he kills again. Wish . . . wish . . ." His chest lifted with his breath, and whatever he'd been about to say was lost as his eyes slid out of focus.

Walking over to him, Sebastian rested one hand, gently, on his friend's thin shoulder. "Don't worry about it," he said quietly. "You just take care of yourself. You hear me? Please take care of yourself."

Then he turned and left, his heart heavy in his chest and his eyes stinging with what he realized were unshed tears.

"He's going to kill himself if he keeps this up, isn't he?" said Hero as they took the boys for a walk later in Grosvenor Square. The day was still warm and sunny, the soft breeze sweetly scented by roses and damp earth, the boys shouting cheerfully as they raced ahead along the winding gravel paths.

"Yes," said Sebastian. "But if Alexi can't make him see sense, I'll be damned if I know how to do it."

Hero was silent for a moment, her gaze on the laughing boys, and he knew by her stricken expression that her thoughts were drifting back, inevitably, to the foster mother she'd interviewed near Richmond Park. He said, "You really think this Prudence Blackadder has been killing the babies left in her care?"

"She either kills them or she deliberately lets them die. I don't see how there can be an innocent explanation. I mean, I know foundlings and orphans put out to foster do die at an alarming rate, but that woman cheerfully oozed evil. What I don't understand is how she can have been allowed to get away with such a thing for so long."

Reaching out, he took her hand in his and felt her fingers tighten around his. "She gets away with it because no one cares," he said. "The workhouses assume most of the infants they send out into the country will die, so why would anyone be suspicious when they do? In fact, I wouldn't be surprised if your Mr. Fry is less than pleased whenever any of the parish's infants somehow manage to survive to the age of four and come back to the workhouse."

"The local vicar must surely realize what she's been doing—or at least guess."

"Perhaps—if she was telling the truth when she said they give all the children a 'good Christian burial.' But they do live on a farm, and the river is not far away."

"What a horrid thought." She paused, her brows drawing together in a frown as she watched the boys hunker down to examine a dandelion growing beside the path. "As a motive for murder, having someone accuse you of regularly killing the children left in your care must surely rank right up there near the top."

"I'd say so, yes—as would being a society darling threatened with having it known that you abandoned one of your own by-blows to such a fate."

She turned her head to look at him. "You think Blackadder was telling the truth about Basil Rhodes?"

"It seems rather too fantastical of a lie for the man to have invented on the spur of the moment, wouldn't you say?"

"There is that. I wonder how Laura came to know of it."

"It is curious. It's not as if McInnis and Rhodes run in the same set. Not only is Rhodes about as far from a sporting man as you can get, but he's a good ten to fifteen years younger than either Laura's brother or her husband. He's my age."

"You know him?"

"Oh, I know him. We were at Eton together."

Her eyes crinkled with a smile at whatever she heard in his voice. "Ah. Not one of your favorite people, I take it?"

"He's the sort of man who's always smiling, who works hard to make everyone like him and comes across as enthusiastic and full of good cheer. But—at least as a boy—he had a nasty tendency to turn churlish when he felt he wasn't being given special treatment. I used to wonder if he really was the natural son of the Prince of Wales or simply expected people to behave as if he were."

"Oh, he's one of the Prince's bastards, all right. Prinny is extraordinarily proud of him."

"He certainly looks like Prinny—and to a certain extent acts like him, too. As much as he likes to play the bouncing, exuberant buffoon, I've always suspected that beneath it all is someone with an outsize sense of entitlement and a grudge against the world for not giving him everything he wants and thinks he deserves."

"Could he kill?"

Sebastian met her gaze. "I've heard him boasting of what he called the 'delectation' of bedding women who have to do whatever he tells them to do because he owns them. Of holding the lives of men and women in his hands. So I'd say yes, I think he could kill."

That evening, Sebastian trolled the pleasure haunts popular with the men of the Upper Ten Thousand, from Cribb's Parlour and Limmer's to Covent Garden and Drury Lane, looking for Mr. Basil Rhodes. He finally came upon the Regent's natural son in the vestibule of White's, surrounded by a circle of cronies listening to his humorous account of a recent encounter with a Devonshire bull.

"So what did you do then, Rhodes?" said one of the men, laughing.

"Do?" said Basil Rhodes, his lips curling into an imp's smile, his unruly auburn hair falling into his eyes as he turned to face his questioner. "I quitted the field of honor in my opponent's favor—which translates into: I ran like hell! Personally, I'm all with Falstaff on this. Discretion is definitely the better part of valor."

The group around him laughed, and someone slapped him on his rounded back. But even as he fielded his friends' ribald jests, it was obvious the man was aware of Sebastian leaning against a nearby doorframe, watching him. After a moment he detached himself from his circle and walked over to where Sebastian was standing.

"Haven't seen you here in a while, Devlin. Why do I get the distinct impression you're looking for me?"

"Acute of you," said Sebastian, pushing away from the doorframe.

Rhodes looked startled for a moment, then let loose one of his braying laughs. "Well, I must admit that's not something I hear very often."

A full-faced, short-necked bear of a man with the Regent's slightly protuberant blue eyes and fleshy build, Rhodes habitually kept his flyaway auburn hair too long and combed forward, so that it was always falling into his eyes. His evening coat and pantaloons were expertly tailored, but he wore them negligently, so that he gave off a rumpled appearance that belied his considerable wealth. The late Peter K. Rhodes—a tall, thin, dark-haired man who looked nothing like his purported son—had died a rich man, having turned the simple Jamaican estate given to him as a wedding gift by the Prince of Wales into a vast sugar empire.

"There's a reason I didn't join the rest of you lot up at Cambridge and Oxford, remember?" Rhodes said, his smile widening.

"As I recall, that was because you thought your time would be better spent out in Jamaica learning how to run your father's plantations."

Rhodes laughed again, although less heartily this time. "That, too; that, too. It's a different world out there, you know."

"So it is," said Sebastian. "Walk with me a ways? There's something I'd like to discuss with you."

"Of course," said Rhodes, his genial smile firmly in place as the two men turned down St. James's Street, toward the old Tudor palace. "I was forgetting, you were in the West Indies yourself, weren't you?"

"For a time. With the Army."

"Beautiful, isn't it? Paradise on earth."

"For some, I suppose. Although not for the tens of thousands of enslaved men and women whose backbreaking labor makes it a paradise for those who keep them like animals. For them, it's a brutal life of cruelty and exploitation that ends all too often in an early, unmarked grave."

Rhodes slewed around to look at him. "Ah, I remember now. How passionate you were on the subject of slavery and the slave trade when we were lads! Still haven't got past it, have you?"

"Did you think I was likely to?"

"When you put it that way, I suppose not." His eyes narrowed as he squinted up at a streetlamp sputtering beside them. "But I presume you haven't sought me out to pontificate on the evils of bondage."

"Actually, I'm here because I'm told you knew Lady McInnis."

The other man's habitual half smile froze. "Not well, no."

"But you did know her?"

"I suppose you could say I did—the way one knows all the people one is forever meeting at balls and routs and dinners and such. But she wasn't exactly in my style, if you know what I mean?"

"Not really. Exactly what do you mean?"

Rhodes pulled a comic face. "Never did have much patience for women who devote themselves to 'good works.' They make for bloody uncomfortable company, if you ask me."

"Is that why you quarreled with her last Saturday in Bond Street?"

Rhodes sucked in a quick breath, then let out a startled bark of laughter, his soft blue eyes widening. "Heard about that, did you? Someone's been busy."

"So what was the quarrel about?"

"Damned if I can recall," he said heartily. "Bloody restless woman, she was. Always going on about something unpleasant—foundlings and climbing boys and all sorts of other societal ills one would really rather not think about."

"I'm told she accused you of abandoning one of your by-blows to a farm out near Richmond with a reputation for killing the infants left in their care."

Rhodes drew up abruptly and swung to face him. "Where the bloody hell did you get that?"

"Are you saying it's not true?"

"Of course it's not true!"

"You never had anything to do with Prudence and Joseph Blackadder?"

Rhodes raised one meaty fist to jab a shaky finger at Sebastian. "I see what you're trying to do here, my friend. But let me tell you right now, that's a cock that won't fight. Laura McInnis was an interfering, sanctimonious bloody pain in the ass who obviously made the mistake of pestering someone she shouldn't have. But I had nothing to do with what happened to her. You hear me? Nothing."

"So where were you Sunday afternoon?"

"Not that it's any of your bloody business, but as a matter of fact I was attending a pugilistic match that day."

"A mill?" said Sebastian, smiling. "I'd no idea you'd developed an interest in the Fancy."

Rhodes had half turned away, but at that he swung back with a huff of laughter. "I can't believe you," he said, one hand coming up to press against his forehead. "You really think I'd shoot a woman—a woman and her daughter!—because she found out I was less than excited that some stupid wench presented me with a baseborn brat she claimed was mine? Even if it were true—which it is not!—why would I care? And if you don't mind my saying so, you're a fine one to talk."

"What's that supposed to mean?"

Rhodes let out another snort of laughter. "You think we haven't all seen that boy you've taken into your household? Cheeky, that—foisting one of your bastards onto your own wife."

Sebastian had heard the whispers, of course. He supposed they were inevitable, given the resemblance between Patrick and Simon. But all he said was, "Patrick is the orphaned son of a man to whom I owe my life. That is all."

Basil Rhodes smiled, poked his tongue into his cheek, and winked. "Of course."

Sebastian forced himself to take a deep, steadying breath and let it out slowly. "Be that as it may, you never did tell me how you came to know Lady McInnis well enough to engage in an argument with her in the middle of Bond Street."

The other man waved one languid hand through the air in a vague gesture. "I suppose she must have been introduced to me by a mutual friend."

"But you've no recollection of the subject of the argument?"

"To be honest, I barely recall having encountered the blasted women. But she was damned opinionated, you know. Opinionated and nosy. From what we're hearing happened to her, one assumes she must have made the mistake of picking on the wrong person."

"You wouldn't have any idea who that person might be, would you?"

"Me? Good God, no." A burst of laughter and loud voices drew his attention to a group of men clustered at the door of one of the clubs down the street. "And now you really must excuse me. I see some friends I've been meaning to meet up with."

"Of course."

Sebastian stood for a moment, watching Rhodes walk toward his friends. As he drew nearer to them, he called out a greeting, threw his arms wide, and did a little dance step that drew another round of laughter.

Basil Rhodes might claim to have forgotten the subject of his disagreement with Laura McInnis, but he hadn't tried to deny that the argument in Bond Street had taken place—which told Sebastian it must have been spectacular enough to have drawn a significant crowd.

And that meant that someone, somewhere, might be able to recall its subject.

Chapter 22

$\mathcal{L}$ater that evening, Sir Henry Lovejoy sat in his parlor, drinking a cup of tea while he listened to Viscount Devlin detail one of the most bleak and profoundly disturbing tales he'd yet to hear.

"God save us," whispered Lovejoy when the Viscount had finished. "Babies? How could anyone kill innocent babies?"

"Evidently quite easily," said Devlin.

Setting aside his cup, Lovejoy rose and went to stand at the open window, his gaze on the darkened square below. A warm wind had come up, shifting the limbs of the plane trees against the black, starless sky and sending menacing shadows shivering across the lamplit pavement. So horrifying were the implications of what he'd just heard that it was a moment before he trusted himself to speak. "If this is true—and I see no reason to doubt it—it would certainly give both Basil Rhodes and these Blackadders a powerful motive for murder. I'll set one of the lads to looking into Rhodes first thing tomorrow morning, although it's going to need to be done delicately. Very delicately, indeed."

"No doubt. The instant the Palace gets wind of any such investigation, they'll shut it down."

Lovejoy nodded. "That's what I fear." He was silent for a moment as he considered the ramifications of the task that lay ahead. "As for this woman, Prudence Blackadder . . . I'm afraid the problem is going to be proving anything. People will say poor infants die all the time, particularly when they're orphaned or abandoned."

"Unfortunately that's all too true. Given that opium overdoses are impossible to prove, unless the Blackadders have simply been strangling some of the infants and then burying their bodies on the farm with whatever cord they used still wrapped around the babies' necks, we're probably out of luck. I suspect the most we can hope for is to force the parishes to stop sending Prudence any more infants. But if there's a way to keep people like Rhodes from handing the woman their unwanted side-slips, I don't know what it would be."

Lovejoy sighed. "No, that would be difficult." He came to sit again beside the table, started to pick up his tea, then set it aside untasted. "I personally interviewed Emma McInnis's governess and abigail this afternoon, by the way. The governess is an estimable woman named Miss Anne Braithwaite, who describes Emma as a bright, inquisitive child who was passionately interested in learning and never gave her parents any trouble. Neither she nor the abigail could think of anyone who might want to harm a girl still in the schoolroom." Lovejoy paused. "I also expressed an interest in speaking to the younger daughter, Thisbe, but Sir Ivo says she's already so upset by the deaths of her mother and sister that he doesn't wish to risk distressing her further."

"That's understandable, if unfortunate."

"Yes, although frankly I'd be surprised if the little girl knows anything. We can only be thankful she wasn't there."

"Did McInnis say why she wasn't included in the outing?"

"No. I had the distinct impression he generally had little to do with either of his daughters." Lovejoy rubbed his eyes with a splayed thumb and forefinger; it had been a long time since he'd felt this tired. "Beyond that, I fear we've learned little. I've yet to hear from the lad I have looking into the chimney sweep; nor are we having much luck locating the cheesemonger to whom Gilly Harper was once apprenticed. It seems the workhouses keep abominable records on those sorts of things, and all the chocolatier knows about the woman is that Gilly described her as 'large.'"

"Given Gilly's size, I suspect that would describe almost anyone."

"I thought the same." Lovejoy realized he was still rubbing his eyes and dropped his hand. "To be frank, I'm becoming more and more inclined to suspect that Cato Coldfield may be our man."

Devlin's face remained impassive. "Coldfield? Why?"

"Largely I suppose because he's the only conceivable suspect who ties back to Julia and Madeline. None of the others do. I thought at first he might be the 'old codger' with a dog Lady McInnis's coachman mentioned having noticed in the park earlier that morning, but it turns out the dog they saw was brown, while Coldfield's dog is black and white."

"Yes," said Devlin, his face still unreadable. He pushed to his feet. "It's getting late. You should try to get some sleep."

Lovejoy rose with him. "Sleep is proving . . . difficult."

"I know. But it's necessary."

Lovejoy walked with him to the stairs. "I am determined to be certain the right person is caught this time."

Devlin turned at the top of the stairs to look at him. "We don't know for certain the right person wasn't caught last time."

Lovejoy met the Viscount's worried gaze, then looked away, blinking. "Don't we?"

Chapter 23

$\mathcal{T}$he next day Sebastian joined Alistair St. Cyr, the Fifth Earl of Hendon and longtime Chancellor of the Exchequer, for an early-morning ride in Hyde Park.

The Earl was in his seventies now, his eyes the deep, unusual blue that characterized the St. Cyr family, his hair white, his body thick, and his face jowly. The two men were known to the world as father and son, although they were not. The painful revelations of the last few years had at one time strained their relationship nearly to the breaking point. But the affection they felt for each other was real, and they were slowly working their way toward a new understanding.

The morning had dawned sunny and pleasantly warm, and the two men posted along the Row in a companionable silence for some time. But after casting a few appraising glances at his heir, Hendon said, "That leg is still bothering you, isn't it?"

It had been some four months since Sebastian nearly lost his leg to a serious gunshot wound in Paris, and the truth was the wound still hurt more than he liked to admit. But all he said was, "Not too much."

"Bullocks," said Hendon, and Sebastian laughed.

After another pause, Hendon said, "I hear you've involved yourself in these murders out at Richmond Park. Is that wise?"

"You think I should sit at home nursing this damned leg while some madman roams the city killing women and girls, do you?"

"What I think," said Hendon with a low growl, "is that you should leave such matters to Bow Street."

"They're the ones who asked for my help."

Hendon growled again, louder this time.

"Enough about that," said Sebastian. "Tell me what's to be done with Napoléon."

"Ah. Well, at the moment, the ship carrying him is being transferred to Plymouth. But after that? It's still up in the air."

"Any chance he'll be allowed to buy a tidy estate in Devon or Cornwall and settle down to the life of a country gentleman?"

"Not bloody likely. Prinny's all for turning him over to the Bourbons to be boiled in oil, but hopefully wiser heads will prevail."

"So you're in agreement with Jarvis?"

"In this, yes. Marie-Thérèse and Artois are nasty, vindictive fools. And while the French King himself is neither nasty nor a fool, he's too weak and lazy to stand against his niece and brother. Between the two of them they're going to unleash a vengeful bloodbath on France—worse even than what King Ferdinand has been doing in Spain."

"Of course they will, and it's not going to end well. We might have succeeded in restoring that ugly, repressive collection of Continental monarchs to their thrones for now, but we're not going to be able to keep them there forever. Their people will eventually rise up to get rid of them again—whether it takes fifteen or a hundred and fifty years."

"Nonsense," said Hendon. "We've spent twenty-odd years and more lives than I like to think about to reach this point, but it's been worth it. Europe is more stable now than it's ever been."

"I hope you're right."

Hendon swung around in his saddle to stare at Sebastian, for the Earl was well aware of his heir's political philosophies. "Do you?"

Sebastian met Hendon's hard stare. "Of course I do. You think I want to see Simon marching off to war in another twenty years to save the Bourbons again?"

"Hopefully, Simon will have more regard for what is due his position as a future Earl of Hendon than to do any such thing. But I wouldn't put it past this next lad to be as army mad as you always were. When exactly is he due? December?"

"Early November. But this one is going to be my girl, remember?"

At that, Hendon simply shook his head and smiled.

An hour later, Sebastian and Hero were about to rise from their breakfast table when a messenger arrived from Lord Salinger. The liveried footman who delivered it was breathing hard, his face glazed with sweat and flushed, as if he had run the entire distance from Down Street.

"Bloody hell," whispered Sebastian as he broke the missive's seal and read through it.

"What is it?" asked Hero, watching him.

Sebastian looked up. "Someone attacked Percy and Arabella."

Chapter 24

Sebastian found the children's father pacing back and forth before the empty hearth in his library, his features grim and his hands clenched at his sides.

"Thank God you've come," said Salinger, turning as the butler ushered Sebastian into the room.

"I trust you've sent word to Bow Street?" said Sebastian.

"Yes, yes; in fact, they've only just left. But I've been thinking about what you said: how Laura and Emma's killer might worry the children know something that could identify him—something that would lead him to target the children next. God help me, if only I'd listened!"

"Can you tell me exactly what happened this morning?" Sebastian said calmly.

Salinger swiped a hand down over his face, sucked in a deep, steadying breath, and nodded. "Miss Oakley—that's the children's governess—typically takes them for a walk in the park every morning before breakfast. But she wasn't feeling well today, so she sent the children with Arabella's abigail, a girl named Cassy. They hadn't been in the park long at all when some blackguard jumped out and grabbed Percy. I get the impression he was trying to drag the boy off with him, except Percy bit and scratched and kicked him, and Arabella and the abigail started screaming, so in the end the fellow let Percy go and ran away."

"You were lucky."

Salinger swallowed hard. "I know. But it does sound as if the killer has reason to believe that Percy might have seen something—or possibly heard something—that could identify him. Something that Percy might not have thought to mention at the inquest because he didn't realize it was important." He looked at Sebastian with wild, haunted eyes. "Will you talk to him now? Talk to them both?"

Brother and sister sat side by side on a cream brocade–covered settee in the drawing room, with a gaunt middle-aged woman whom Sebastian took to be their governess quietly watching in the background from a straight-backed chair. The woman was pale from her recent illness, but her features were firmly set in the lines of one determined to do her duty. Arabella held her hands quietly folded together in her lap, her gaze focused unseeingly on one of the windows overlooking the street. But Percy squirmed restlessly, one stocking sagging down to his ankle, his nankeens smudged with what looked like grass stains at the knees, the collar of his frilled shirt awry. He leapt to his feet when his father and Sebastian entered the room.

"Lord Devlin! Did Papa tell you what happened?" said the boy, his cheeks flushed with excitement and his eyes bright.

"*Percy*," hissed the governess, leaning forward. "Apologize to his lordship, make your bow, sit down, and be patient."

The boy flashed his father and Sebastian a rueful grin, bowed, and plopped down on the settee again. "I beg your pardon. But . . . did he?"

"He told me, yes," said Sebastian, settling in a nearby chair. "But I'd like to hear it in more detail from you. I understand you make a habit of walking in the park every morning before breakfast?"

"Yes," said Arabella with her head turned in such a way that her grimace was hidden from her governess. "Miss Oakley calls it our 'daily constitutional,' and the world would need to end before we'd be allowed to miss it. So since she wasn't well this morning we went with Cassy."

"Where were you in the park when this man approached you?"

"By the spinney," said Percy, jumping in before his sister had a chance to answer. "I'd run ahead a bit—Cassy was dawdling so!— and then, just as I reached the grove, this fellow leaps out from behind a bush and grabs me!"

"What did he look like?"

"He was huge!" said Percy.

"He was not *huge*," said Arabella, frowning at him.

"Yes, he was!"

"No, he was not. He wasn't even as tall as Lord Devlin."

"Well, but almost," insisted Percy. "You know he was tall."

"Could you see his face?" said Sebastian.

"Not really," said Arabella. "He had a kerchief tied across his nose, like this—" She cupped a hand across her nose and mouth so that only her eyes showed.

"Did you get the impression he was young? Old? In between?"

"Young," said Percy, bouncing up and down on the settee's plump cushion. "And very strong."

This time Arabella nodded in agreement.

"How was he dressed?"

Brother and sister looked at each other. "Well . . ." said Arabella. "Definitely not in the first start of fashion."

"But not dressed rough, either," added Percy. "Sorta like Mr. Thompson."

"Mr. Thompson?" said Sebastian.

"My solicitor," supplied Salinger.

"Ah. Could you see his hair color?"

Percy nodded. "It was real dark. And so was his skin."

The children's father had been standing before the empty hearth, his hands clasped behind his back. But at that he took a quick step forward. This detail was obviously news to him.

"You mean he was browned by the sun?" said Sebastian.

"Maaaybeee," said Arabella, drawing out the word. "But not exactly." She hesitated, then said in a rush, "He reminded me of Malcolm's fencing master."

"Malcolm?" said Sebastian.

"Sir Ivo's son and heir," said Salinger. "He and my elder son left late last week for a fishing trip to Scotland with friends."

"What can you tell me about this fencing master?"

Salinger frowned. "I know that at one time Sir Ivo had engaged the services of Damion Pitcairn, but I don't know if he's still using him."

Sebastian knew a sense of deep foreboding. The son of a Scottish plantation owner and an enslaved woman, Damion Pitcairn gave fencing lessons to the sons of rich men to supplement his income as a violinist at the Opera. Brilliant and incredibly talented, he would have had a bright future ahead of him . . . were it not for his mixed heritage and the color of his skin.

Sebastian leaned forward, his hands clasped loosely between his knees. "I'd like to ask you a few questions about Sunday's picnic in Richmond Park, if you don't mind. Whose idea was the expedition?"

Again the children exchanged glances. Percy shrugged, while Arabella said slowly, "I think maybe it was Aunt Laura who came up with the idea, but I don't know for certain. It could have been Emma."

"How many people knew about the planned picnic?"

Another shrug, this time from Arabella. "Well, the servants did, of course. But beyond that?" She scrunched up her face in thought. "I don't think I told anyone, but Emma might have."

"Have either of you remembered anything—anything at all—that might shed some light on what happened to your aunt and cousin?"

Brother and sister shook their heads in unison. "No, sir," said Arabella. "I'm sorry."

Sebastian glanced at her brother. "Tell me this, Percy: Did you stay with your sister while she was picking wildflowers?"

The boy wrinkled his nose. "No, sir. I wanted to catch tadpoles. There's ever so many of them in that pool near where the path turns—you know the place where it's sandy? I nicked one of the teacups when Aunt Laura wasn't looking"—he cast a rueful glance at his frowning father—"and told Arabella to go on ahead."

"Did you see or hear anything while you were catching tadpoles?"

"No, sir. I mean, I heard a couple of shots, of course, but I figured maybe it was somebody shooting at wafers or some such thing. It wasn't until later that I realized no one would've been doing that in the park."

"You didn't hear any voices?"

"I may have," said the boy slowly. "But I wasn't really paying attention, if you know what I mean?" A ghost of a smile touched his lips, then was gone. "I was just . . . playing with the tadpoles."

"I understand," said Sebastian.

Percy looked at him with wide, solemn eyes. "You think that's why that fellow jumped me this morning? Because he killed Aunt Laura and Emma, and he thinks I saw or heard something?"

Sebastian threw a significant glance at the boy's father, who said, "We don't really know yet, Percy. Lord Devlin is simply trying to help us figure it all out."

"I wish I had paid more attention," said the boy with a frustrated sigh.

Sebastian pushed to his feet and reached out to rest a reassuring hand on the boy's small, thin shoulder. "Don't worry about it, lad."

The boy bit his lip and nodded, but his soft gray eyes were swimming with tears he refused to let fall.

"How long ago did your elder son and his cousin leave for Scotland?" Sebastian asked Lord Salinger as the two men walked down the stairs to the front door.

"Last Thursday. Why?"

"And for how long had the expedition to Richmond been planned?"

Salinger thought for a moment. "I suppose it's been two weeks or more since the children first started talking about it. Why?"

"So it's conceivable that one of the boys could have mentioned it to someone?" *Someone such as Malcolm's young fencing instructor,* Sebastian thought, but he didn't say it.

"I suppose so, yes. But why would they?"

Sebastian shook his head. "I have no idea. But I don't think we can discount it as a possibility."

Chapter 25

Sir Ivo McInnis was in the mews behind his house, hunched over with the hoof of one of his carriage horses between his knees, when Sebastian walked up to him.

"Someone attacked Percy and Arabella Priestly in Hyde Park this morning," Sebastian said quietly and without preamble. "Did you know that?"

Sir Ivo straightened abruptly, the horse's hoof settling back on the cobbles with a clatter. An expression Sebastian couldn't quite read flickered across the man's face, then was gone. "No. Good God. Why?"

"Presumably because whoever killed your wife and daughter is afraid the children might have seen or heard something that afternoon that could help identify him. Do you know if there were any threats against Emma? Was there someone she quarreled with, perhaps?"

"Emma? No, of course not." McInnis nodded to the groom silently standing nearby, then waited while the man reached out to take the horse's halter and led it back to its stall. "I went through all this with that magistrate from Bow Street. The girl only turned sixteen this past May; she was still in the schoolroom. What makes you even ask such a thing?"

"Two nights ago, a chocolatier's apprentice named Gilly Harper was murdered in Piccadilly and her body posed in a way that suggests her death might have been the work of the same killer. The girl was about the same age as Emma."

"A chocolatier's apprentice? You can't be serious. What could such a person possibly have to do with us?"

"Lady McInnis rescued Gilly from an abusive mistress some months ago and then met with the girl last week to ask if she was willing to be interviewed about the experience. Your wife didn't mention any of this to you?"

Sir Ivo snorted. "No. My wife knew exactly what I thought of her ridiculous obsession with foundlings and poorhouse children."

"You thought the work she did ridiculous?"

"Of course it was ridiculous. As far as I'm concerned, the sooner the wretched little brats all die, the better. They're nothing but a useless, costly burden on society, and most of them only grow up to be murderers and thieves anyway."

"Yes, I can see why your wife would refrain from discussing her work with you," Sebastian said dryly. "So tell me this: Do you know anything about her quarrel with Basil Rhodes?"

McInnis had walked to the open doors of the stables, but at that he drew up and whirled around. "*Basil Rhodes?* Are you telling me Laura quarreled with him? Of all the stupid, bloody-minded things to do! Quarrel with the Prince Regent's favorite bastard? God help us." His jaw tightened. "She's damned lucky I didn't know about it."

"Is Rhodes a close friend of yours?"

"I wouldn't call him a 'close' friend, no. But I'm friendly with him, of course. Who is not?"

Sebastian studied the man's tight, angry face. "According to the autopsy, your wife had days-old bruises on her shoulders and an even older bruise on her side. You wouldn't know anything about that, would you?"

"No, I would not." Sir Ivo stared back at him, as if daring Sebastian to contradict him. "I suppose she might have taken a fall, but if so, she never said anything to me about it. Laura had a tendency to be clumsy, and she bruised easily."

"Of course."

His brow darkened. "What does that mean?"

"Well, that is one explanation."

Sir Ivo grunted and turned back toward the door. "And now you really must excuse me."

"Just a few more things. I'm wondering, have you spoken to your younger daughter, Thisbe, about what happened to her mother and sister?"

"She's been told about it, obviously, although not in any detail. No point in that, is there? The girl is upset enough as it is."

"She didn't say anything that might explain what happened Sunday?"

"What could Thisbe possibly know about it? She wasn't there."

"Was she ill?"

"Ill? No. Not that I heard, anyway."

"I've been wondering why wasn't she on the picnic."

"Damned if I know. I left that sort of thing to my wife."

"Would it be possible for me to speak to her?"

Sir Ivo's lips tightened into a hard line, and he shook his head.

"No, I don't think so. The girl just lost her mother and sister. I already told Sir Henry I don't want her disturbed any more than she already is."

"I understand," said Sebastian as they watched a boy push a wheelbarrow piled high with fresh manure toward the mews' arch, the barrow's wooden wheel rattling over the cobblestones. "I believe your son, Malcolm, has a fencing master?"

"That's right; Damion Pitcairn. What could he possibly have to do with anything?"

"I don't think he does. But it's always possible he knows something he doesn't realize is relevant."

The Baronet shrugged. "I don't see how he could, but if you wish to waste your time chasing after that sort of nonsense, be my guest. And now you really must excuse me."

"Of course," said Sebastian. "My apologies again for intruding on what I know must be a difficult time for you."

McInnis gave a negligent nod and walked off toward the house.

Sebastian stayed where he was, aware of a deep sense of disquiet as he watched the Baronet stroll away. Some men were better than others, he knew, at disguising their grief, and the marriage between Sir Ivo McInnis and the former Miss Laura Priestly had reportedly never been a love match. But the man had also lost one of his own children, a beautiful, innocent girl of sixteen.

And yet his only response to the investigation into her murder was boredom and indifference bordering on irritation.

The violinist stood alone in the center of the darkened stage of the King's Theatre at the Haymarket, his instrument tucked between shoulder and chin, his fingers flying over the fingerboard, his body swaying with the music he conjured from the strings with his bow. His movements were supple and smooth, with the fluid grace of a dancer.

Or a master swordsman.

The lingering scents of oranges and greasepaint hung heavily in the air, but the pit before him was empty, as were the rows of gilded boxes hung with velvet curtains that arced high above. He was a young man, tall and slim, with tawny skin, thick dark curls that clustered close to his head, and a fine-boned face that exquisitely combined his Ethiopian, Arab, and European ancestry.

Slipping a coin to the attendant who made as if to stop him, Sebastian went to stand quietly before the stage. The violinist above was lost in his music, his eyes closed as he wove a melody of hopeless passion so piercingly sweet and sad that it tore at the heart and wounded the soul. Then he lowered his bow and opened his eyes, his chest heaving with emotion as he stared down at Sebastian.

"We're closed for the summer," said Damion Pitcairn hoarsely.

"I know," said Sebastian, his own voice coming out surprisingly husky. "That's a beautiful piece. Your own?" Pitcairn might be young, but Sebastian knew the man had already had several of his compositions publicly performed.

Damion Pitcairn lowered his violin. "Yes, but I'm still working on it."

Sebastian let his gaze drift thoughtfully around the darkened interior of the vast opera house before bringing his attention back to the young fencing master's face. "It's a rare man who is gifted by the gods with even one great talent. But you have been blessed with three."

"Perhaps," said Pitcairn, swiping a forearm across his sweating face. "Although some might call those gifts a mocking curse, joined as they are with a certain inescapable reality."

Sebastian gave a faint shake of his head—not in denial of the truth of what the man said, but in repudiation of the widespread ignorance and prejudice that made his words true.

"I know why you're here," said Pitcairn. He hesitated a moment, then added, "Lord Devlin."

"We've met?"

"Not exactly. You attended the exhibition fencing match between Henry Angelo and me arranged for the Prince Regent at Carlton House last year." A wry smile curled the other man's lips. "You were the only man there who backed me."

"And won handsomely because of it. But then, I'd seen you fence before."

"So had half the other men there."

Sebastian shrugged. "How long have you been Malcolm McInnis's fencing master?"

"Ever since that match, so . . . it would be eighteen months now. Sir Ivo engaged me immediately afterward."

"You must know Malcolm well, then."

"Well enough." The answer was guarded. Cautious.

"What about Lady McInnis? Did you know her?"

"Not really. She was always pleasant whenever I chanced to encounter her, although that wasn't often."

"And Malcolm's sister Emma?"

Something flickered in the younger man's eyes, something hidden by his thick, swiftly lowered lashes. He drew a deep breath before answering. "The violin concerto I was playing . . . it's dedicated to her."

"So you knew her?"

"How could I not, going to the house three times a week like that? She used to come and watch us fence. Sometimes—" he started to say, then broke off.

"Sometimes . . . ?" prompted Sebastian.

Pitcairn swallowed and gave a vague shake of his head. "I still can't believe she's dead. Who would kill someone like that—a beautiful, vibrant young girl of sixteen? For no reason. No reason at all."

"When was your last lesson with Malcolm?"

Pitcairn frowned in thought. "Last Wednesday. Why?"

"So, right before he and his cousin left for Scotland?"

He nodded. "I think they were planning to leave the next day."

"Did he say anything to you about his mother and sister's projected expedition to Richmond Park?"

"No. Why would he?"

"No reason that I can think of," said Sebastian as he watched Pitcairn crouch down to rest his violin and bow in the case that lay open at his feet. "Who do you think killed Lady McInnis and her daughter?"

Pitcairn closed the case, then buckled the straps. "You don't want to know."

"You underestimate me."

He looked up. "Do I? And if I said Sir Ivo? What then?"

Sebastian held himself very still. "What makes you suspect Sir Ivo?"

"Do you know he was accusing his wife of having an affair?"

Sebastian stared at him. "Lady McInnis was having an affair? With whom?"

Pitcairn shook his head. "I didn't say she *was* having an affair. I said McInnis *accused* her of it."

"How do you know this?"

"Emma told me."

Emma, Sebastian noticed. Not Miss McInnis, not Malcolm's sister, but Emma. Aloud, he said, "Why would she tell something so personal to her brother's fencing master?"

Pitcairn straightened. "Because I found her crying. It seems they'd had a big row about it right before I arrived at the house that day for Malcolm's lesson—Sir Ivo and Lady McInnis, I mean. Emma overheard it. She was upset and needed someone to talk to and . . . I was there."

"When was this?"

"The last lesson before Malcolm left for Scotland, so that Wednesday."

"Who was Sir Ivo accusing his wife of having an affair with?"

"If Emma knew, she didn't tell me."

Sebastian studied the younger man's carefully guarded face. "Sir Ivo would hardly be the first man to kill his wife because he thought she was having an affair. But why would he kill his own sixteen-year-old daughter?"

"I assume she was killed by accident."

It was the obvious explanation, of course. And it would make sense if it hadn't been for the surely premeditated way the killer had posed his victims' bodies. Sebastian was silent for a moment, then said, "Did you know a young girl named Gilly Harper?"

"You mean the apprentice who was killed the other night in Piccadilly? No. Surely you don't think the deaths are related?"

"They may not be," said Sebastian. "What about Basil Rhodes? Do you know him?"

A glint of something dangerous flashed in the other man's eyes. "Let's say I know *of* him—I'm from Jamaica, remember. Why? What does he have to do with anything?"

"I'm told he quarreled with Lady McInnis. Did Emma tell you about that?"

"No, but I'm not surprised. He's one of the biggest plantation owners in Jamaica, and Lady McInnis hated the institution of slavery. It's one of the things she was working the hardest to change."

"Was she? No one has mentioned it."

Pitcairn nodded. "Sir Ivo didn't like it, so she tried to keep it quiet."

"And yet you knew. Did Malcolm tell you about it?"

A faint flush rode high on the other man's cheekbones, and his eyes slid away. "I'm not sure where I heard it."

So that came from Emma, too, thought Sebastian with a deep sense of foreboding.

He didn't like where the implications of all this were leading.

Chapter 26

I'll walk when I leave here," Sebastian told his tiger as they drew up before an impressive Park Lane town house overlooking Hyde Park. "So go ahead and take the chestnuts home now. Then I want you to see what you can find out about Mr. Damion Pitcairn— who his friends are, whom he fences with, any secrets he might be hiding."

"Aye, gov'nor," said Tom with a grin, scrambling forward to take the reins.

Sebastian stood on the flagway as the tiger drove off, his eyes narrowing as he studied the familiar red barouche drawn up nearby. Then he turned to mount the steps to the house of the formidable woman he still called Aunt Henrietta, although he now knew she was not, in fact, his aunt.

Born Lady Henrietta St. Cyr, the Dowager Duchess of Claiborne was Hendon's elder sister. The sprawling mansion overlooking Hyde Park should by rights now be the residence of her eldest son, George, the current Duke of Claiborne. But George was no match for his awe-inspiring mother. On the death of his father, the amiable, middle-aged Duke had quietly elected to continue residing in the modest Half Moon Street establishment where he'd raised his family, rather than try to oust his widowed mother from the house to which she'd come as a bride more than fifty years before.

Now well into her seventies, the Duchess was one of the grandes dames of Society. She had a boundless curiosity about her fellow men and women, an inquisitive nature, and a flawless memory—all of which made her a particularly valuable source.

Sebastian was still on the second step when Her Grace's dignified butler opened the front door and a tall, slim woman in her midforties stepped out. "Thank you, Humphrey," she said to the butler with a smile. Then she turned, the smile fading from her lips at the sight of Sebastian.

"Good afternoon, Amanda," Sebastian said to his half sister.

Amanda stiffened, her nostrils flaring on a quickly indrawn breath. She was his elder by a dozen years, the first of four children born to the marriage of the Fifth Earl of Hendon and his beautiful, wayward Countess, Sophia. She had the late Countess's golden hair and elegant carriage, but facially she more closely resembled her father, Hendon, while her disposition had always reminded Sebastian of a vindictive, resentful wasp. As was her habit these days, she was dressed in an elegant, black-trimmed silver gown of half mourning, although her husband, Lord Wilcox, had been dead for well over four years—and she had heartily despised him for most of their married life.

"Devlin," she said now, and brushed past him without another word.

Sebastian watched her walk away, her head held high, her back rigid. Then he turned to the Duchess's now-frowning butler and said, "I take it Her Grace is in?"

Humphrey's frown deepened. "I believe she is on the verge of retiring to dress for dinner, my lord."

"Then I'm glad I caught her," said Sebastian, brushing past the stoic butler. "In the drawing room, is she?"

Humphrey sighed. "She is, my lord."

Sebastian found the Dowager seated beside the cold hearth, a half-empty glass of claret in her hand. "You timed that well," she said when he came to lean down and kiss her cheek. "Amanda just left."

"I know; we met on the front steps. She looked as if she would have loved nothing more than to rip into me about something, but the presence of Humphrey spoiled her sport. What have I done to earn her displeasure now?"

"Need you ask? She's in a pelter over your involvement in the investigation of these latest murders, of course."

"One would think she'd have grown accustomed to it by this point."

"Amanda? Resign herself to something she considers both an outrage and a personal affront to her dignity? Surely you know her better than that."

"True."

She nodded to the cluster of decanters and glasses on a nearby table. "Pour yourself a glass of wine and have a seat. Or there's brandy if you'd prefer."

He settled in a nearby chair. "Thank you, but I don't want to keep you too long."

The Duchess fixed him with a hard stare. "Why do I get the distinct impression you're here because of something to do with these ghastly murders?"

"Because you're a very clever woman," he said with a smile. "What can you tell me about Lady McInnis?"

"Laura?" Henrietta looked thoughtful for a moment. "Nothing to her discredit—at least, nothing beyond a somewhat lamentable tendency to prose on endlessly about the horrid treatment given the poor wretches in the city's workhouses or some such thing."

"Any chance she was having an affair?"

"Laura McInnis? I wouldn't have said so, no. If she was, she must have been extraordinarily discreet, for I've heard nothing of it."

"I'm told her marriage to Sir Ivo was no love match."

"No, not at all. My understanding is she married McInnis largely because he was her brother's best friend and her father pushed the match. Her father—the previous Viscount Salinger—was a hopeless gamester, you know. All done in. At one point Laura was set to marry a young cavalry lieutenant. He was the younger son of a younger son, but her portion was so small, Salinger was initially relieved to have someone take her off his hands. Then the old goat managed to catch a rich cit's daughter for his heir, Miles." The Duchess wrinkled her nose. "Septimus Bain was his name. Horrid, grasping little man. Bain balked at the idea of his daughter's sister-in-law becoming the wife of a mere army officer and following the drum, so old Salinger forbade the match."

"And Laura acquiesced?"

"She was underage at the time, so short of bolting for the border she didn't exactly have a choice, did she? The lieutenant went off to war while Laura promised to be faithful to him until she turned twenty-one and would be free to marry without her father's consent. Except the lieutenant hadn't been gone more than a few months when word came that he'd been killed."

"So she married Sir Ivo?"

"Not right away, but something like two or three years later."

"Do you recall the name of this lieutenant?"

"As it happens, I do. He's a major now—Major Zacchary Finch. I noticed he was mentioned in the dispatches from Waterloo."

"I thought you said he was dead?"

"No, only that Laura *heard* he was dead. As it turned out, he'd been wounded and captured. But that wasn't discovered until several months after she'd married McInnis."

"Tragic."

"It was, rather."

"I assume he's currently with the Army in France?"

"That I can't tell you. I believe he was wounded, so he may have been shipped home."

"Where is 'home'?"

"It was Leicestershire—his grandfather was the Earl of Arnesby, and I believe Finch's father was the vicar in a village not far from Priestly Priory. But if the father's dead, then the living will have gone to some other relative by now. The family has always bred prodigiously, and they have a tendency to run to boys."

"Good God. Where do you get all these details?"

She gave an elegant sniff and pushed to her feet. "People talk and I listen. And now you must excuse me; I'm having dinner with Hendon tonight." She watched him carefully stand up and said, "I see your leg is still bothering you."

"A bit."

"Somehow I suspect chasing a murderer halfway across London last month didn't help it."

He stared at her. "How did you hear about *that?*"

But she only smiled as she turned away.

"You think this Major Zacchary Finch could be the man Sir Ivo accused Laura of having an affair with?" said Hero later that evening when she and Sebastian retired to the drawing room after dinner. She was sitting beside the empty hearth, setting neat stitches into the hem of a gown she was making for the new baby, while Sebastian stood beside one of the open windows overlooking the street and sipped a glass of port.

"It seems possible—if he's back in London," said Sebastian, looking over at her.

She was silent for a moment, her attention seemingly all for her stitches. Then she said, "It strikes me as a strangely intimate thing for Emma to have told her brother's fencing master—even if he did chance to come upon her when she was upset and crying."

Sebastian took a slow swallow of his wine, his gaze shifting again to the darkened scene below. The night was warm and mostly clear, with a waning moon that was still nearly half-full and illuminated the few puffs of high clouds scuttling across the black sky in the balmy wind. The street was unusually quiet for the hour; he could see only a footman walking an aged pug and the half-obscured figure of a well-dressed man who'd been standing in the shadows near the corner for long enough to make Sebastian feel uneasy. He turned his head to look at Hero. "I could be wrong, but I have a worrying suspicion there was considerably more going on between the brilliant, handsome young fencing master and his student's pretty sister than he wants me to know about."

Hero looked up from her sewing. "That is worrying."

He glanced back out the window; the figure was still there. "I can't see a man of Sir Ivo's ilk taking that sort of development kindly."

"What are you looking at?" she asked.

Sebastian took another sip of his port. "There's a man across the street, near the corner. He's been standing there staring at the house since we came up from dinner."

"What man?"

"I don't know," said Sebastian, setting aside his drink and pushing away from the window. "But I think it's time I find out."

Chapter 27

The watcher took a step back when Sebastian slammed out of the house—a flintlock pistol held casually at his side—and strode across the street toward him. But the man did not run.

This was no ruffian. He wore buckskin breeches, Hessians, and a coat of superfine cut in a style favored by military men. Of above-average height, he looked to be in his late thirties, with broad shoulders and a strong frame obviously somewhat weakened by recent illness. His right arm rested in a sling, and his face bore the haggard look of a man who was still in some pain.

"Who the bloody hell are you?" demanded Sebastian, coming up to him. "And what are you doing out here staring at my house?"

The man looked sincerely chagrined. "I beg your pardon; I didn't expect you to see me. I've been standing here attempting to decide if I was being a fool even to think of trying to talk to you, and what in blazes I should say to you if I do."

"You're Finch?"

The man's eyes widened. "I am, yes. But how did you know?"

Sebastian eased the small flintlock pistol he'd been carrying into his pocket. "We need to talk."

They retreated to the Angel in Bond Street, where Sebastian bought a couple of pints and steered the Major to a table near the pub's old-fashioned massive stone fireplace.

"I still don't understand how you knew who I am," said Finch, settling across the table from Sebastian.

"Someone told me McInnis accused his wife of having an affair with you."

Finch stared at him. "Good God. When did he do that?"

"Laura never told you about it?"

"No. When did this happen?"

"The Wednesday before she was killed."

Finch wrapped both hands around his tankard and gazed down at it. "Bloody hell," he said softly.

"Were you?" asked Sebastian, watching him closely. "Having an affair with her, I mean."

Finch's head came up, his lips tightening into an angry line. "No!"

The man certainly looked sincere. But Sebastian had known too many accomplished liars to take him at his word. "How long have you been back in London?"

"A few weeks. I'm staying with one of my brothers—he's a barrister with chambers in Middle Temple."

"Had you seen Laura since your return?"

Finch drew a deep breath, pressed his lips together, and nodded.

"How did McInnis come to hear of it?"

Finch swallowed and looked away. "That I don't know."

Again Sebastian wasn't sure he believed him. "Were you in

London before? Between when Bonaparte first abdicated and his escape from Elba, I mean."

"Yes, for months. I was on extended leave, thinking of selling out. As far as I knew, the wars were over, and I figured it was time to move on with my life. But then word came that Napoléon was back in Paris, so I rejoined my old regiment."

"I take it you saw Laura then, too? When you were in London before, I mean."

Finch hesitated a moment, then nodded again. "Yes."

"Why?"

Finch looked at him. "What do you mean, why? We're old friends."

"You grew up near her in Leicestershire?"

"I did, yes. My father was the vicar of the village there. Laura's mother died when she was still a baby, you know, and the old Viscount never cared about much of anything besides his horses and his mistresses and the gaming tables. If it hadn't been for my mother stepping in and being there for Laura, I don't know what would have happened to her. We essentially grew up together. Why wouldn't I see her when I was in town?"

"So you also know her brother, Salinger."

"Yes, but not well. He was years older than we were."

"And Sir Ivo? You know him?"

Something hardened in the other man's face. "I used to run into him every now and then when he'd be at the Priory with Miles. And then of course he bought a hunting lodge nearby."

"How much did you see Laura when you were in London before Boney's escape from Elba?"

Finch gave a negligent shrug and looked away again. "I don't know. Some."

The artless evasion told Sebastian all he needed to know. "And how did Sir Ivo feel about his wife seeing her old childhood friend?"

This time Finch met Sebastian's hard gaze and held it. "I didn't think he knew." He paused, then said, "I know how that sounds, but Ivo's a nasty bastard and—" He broke off, then leaned back in his seat, his eyes widening. "*My God.* You think McInnis killed her because of *me?*"

"If his daughter hadn't also been murdered, he'd be my first suspect."

"Yes, of course." Finch scrubbed a shaky hand down over his face. "This is all so horrible, I still can't seem to take it in."

Sebastian watched the other man lift his tankard to take a long, slow drink. "When you heard Laura had been murdered, who did you think had done it?"

Finch lowered his tankard. "Honestly? My first thought was McInnis. But with Emma dead, too, I realized that couldn't be. . . ."

"Can you think of anyone else who might have wanted to kill her—kill them both?"

"No."

"What about a chimney sweep named Dobbs? Did Laura ever talk about him?"

"Hiram Dobbs? Yes, she told me about him. I know he threatened her. I was worried about her, but she wouldn't take him seriously. Are you suggesting he could have done this?"

"At this point, I'm not ruling out anything. What about a foster mother near Richmond that she tangled with? Did Lady McInnis tell you about that?"

He nodded. "She did, yes. It's beyond shocking, what she discovered about that place. Given how long they've been taking in infants, Laura suspected the Blackadders must have killed dozens of babies. *Dozens.* How is that even possible?"

"Do you know how she came to hear about the woman?"

The Major took another swallow of beer. "It was because of Rhodes."

"Basil Rhodes?"

He nodded again. "I know everyone thinks he's nothing more than an amiable, quick-witted buffoon, and God knows he plays the part well enough. But the truth is, he's a vile son of a bitch. He rapes his housemaids the same way he's always raped the slave girls on his Jamaican plantations. And then he dumps their babies on people like Prudence Blackadder, who can be relied upon to ensure the infants don't live long enough to bother him."

"Laura told you all this?"

"She did, yes. One of the women she dealt with at St. Martin's workhouse used to be his housemaid. Not only did Rhodes rape her, but when she fell pregnant, he accused her of trying to foist some other man's by-blow on him and then kicked her out without a reference after taking the baby from her. The poor girl couldn't have been more than fifteen or sixteen, and she was so debilitated from the pregnancy and delivery and grief that she couldn't work, which is how she ended up in the workhouse."

"And this girl told Laura that Rhodes had given her baby to Prudence Blackadder?"

"Yes. It wasn't the first time Laura had heard whispers about the Blackadders, so she started looking into them. At first, it all seemed unbelievable. I mean, how could something like that have been going on for years?"

"Is that why she confronted Rhodes in Bond Street last Saturday?"

"No. She didn't confront him; he came at her. One of her friends is seriously involved with the man, and Laura had decided it was her duty to tell the woman about the pregnant housemaids and abandoned babies and the poor young girls he regularly abuses on his plantation. Except of course the woman refused to believe any of it, flew into a rage, and then told Rhodes what Laura was saying about him. That's how Rhodes knew."

"Do you know the woman's name?"

The Major frowned. "Not off the top of my head, no. She's some shipbuilder's widow Laura knew from when they were at school together. Rivers or Lakes or something like that."

"Veronica Goodlakes?"

"That's it," said the Major. "Goodlakes."

Sebastian walked home through dark streets lit dimly by the murky glow of widely spaced streetlights and the oil lamps that bracketed the front doors of the stately row houses along Brook Street. The night was cool and still, the moon and most of the stars above hidden by a hazy layer of coal smoke that hung low over the city. He could hear a dog barking somewhere in the distance, but otherwise Mayfair was quiet, with only the occasional lumbering hackney or gentleman's carriage dashing past; the pungent scent of pitch from linkboys' torches lingered hot and heavy in the night.

He was aware of a profound weight of sadness settling upon him as he walked. Murder had a way of peeling back the lies and polite subterfuges of people's lives to expose the tragedies and ugly truths that all too often lay hidden beneath. The innocent, unwanted children left to suffer and die in strangers' hands. The poor and vulnerable, abused by those with power over them. The young women—and men—forced into unhappy, loveless marriages for the sake of money. Money, power, prestige, position . . .

Greed could take so many different forms.

The church bells of the city began to ring, one after the other, counting out the hour. Sebastian walked on, his attention focused now on a solitary figure he could see leaning against a lamppost some thirty or more feet ahead. The man was simply standing there, his hands in his pockets, his hat tipped forward to throw his face into shadow. He looked to be of average height, young and strong, his green coat neither fashionably cut nor rough, his buckskin breeches and top boots serviceable. Sebastian had spent enough years in the Army to recognize a former military man when he saw one.

Without altering his gait, Sebastian slipped his right hand into the pocket of his coat to close around the smooth handle of his small double-barreled pistol.

The man didn't move.

Sebastian was passing the entrance to Livery Row when he heard a sudden rush of feet as a second man, this one a big, burly ruffian in a round hat, came barreling out of the shadows to slam hard into his back. The impact threw Sebastian off-balance and shoved him forward just as Green Coat stepped away from the lamppost and brought up his right hand to smash Sebastian in the face with what felt like a lead-weighted sap.

Chapter 28

$\mathcal{S}$ebastian staggered back, the side of his face exploding in pain, his sight dimming as Round Hat seized him from behind.

"Easy there, yer lordship," he growled, holding Sebastian steady as the first man sauntered up, a hint of a malicious smile lightening his even, sun-darkened features as he leaned in close.

"You're to consider this a friendly warning," said Green Coat, his accent—unlike his partner's—that of a man of education. "What happened to Lady McInnis is none of your affair. You need to shut up and mind your own business. I trust I make myself clear?"

Swearing crudely, Sebastian threw his weight sideways and down, his coat ripping as he broke Round Hat's hold and dropped into a low crouch. Yanking the flintlock from his pocket, he came up to step forward and shove the pistol's twin barrels into Green Coat's cheek hard enough to knock against his teeth.

The man froze.

"Smart," said Sebastian, pulling back both hammers with audible clicks. "Now drop the sap or you're a dead man. I said *drop it*, damn you."

Sebastian heard the clattering thud of the sheathed lead hitting the pavement.

"And you—stay back," he warned Round Hat as the big man took a lumbering step toward them. "In case you didn't notice, this is a double-barreled pistol, which means I can put a bullet in your friend here's brain and still have one left for you."

Round Hat stopped.

"Good. Now, listen to me, gentlemen, and listen very carefully. Since you appear to enjoy playing the role of emissaries, I have a message for you to carry back to whatever bastard hired you. Tell him I don't scare easily. And if you come at me again, I'll kill you." Still holding the pistol pointed at Green Coat's face, his gaze flashing back and forth between the two men, Sebastian took a step back, then another. "That's a promise." He swiped his left fist at the blood he could feel running down the side of his face and swore again. "Now get out of here before I decide to kill you both on principle. You ripped my bloody coat."

"So who do you think hired them?" asked Hero as she watched Sebastian, stripped down to his blood-splattered shirt and breeches, lean over the washbasin in his dressing room, the water trickling back into the porcelain bowl as he carefully rinsed his face. "McInnis? The Blackadders? Basil Rhodes?"

He lifted his head and reached for his towel. "Damned if I know. But if I had to guess, I'd put my money on Rhodes."

Hero frowned as he dabbed carefully at the bruised, broken skin below his left eye. "That looks nasty."

Sebastian shrugged. "It will heal."

She muttered something under her breath and swung away, her hands cupping her elbows to hold them tight against her sides. "I keep thinking about Veronica Goodlakes deliberately sending us chasing after that chimney sweep, Hiram Dobbs, when she knew all about Laura's conflict with Rhodes. What's even worse is that *she's* the one who set Rhodes against her 'good friend' Laura in the first place."

"Charming woman," said Sebastian.

Hero turned to face him again. "I'd have said they were an unlikely pair—Veronica and Rhodes. Except they obviously have far more in common than I realized."

"They do indeed." He tossed the towel aside. "And I wouldn't put it past either one to do whatever they thought was necessary to get what they want."

Thursday, 27 July

The next day, Sebastian returned from his early-morning ride in Hyde Park to find Charles, Lord Jarvis, awaiting him in the library.

The King's powerful cousin stood beside the hearth, his hands clasped behind his back, his hat resting on a nearby table, his face stony.

"Good morning," said Sebastian, tossing aside his riding crop and stripping off his gloves as he walked into the room after a brief consultation with his majordomo, Morey. "I hope I haven't kept you waiting long. I believe Hero is—"

"I'm not here to see Hero or Simon," snapped Jarvis.

"Oh?" A tray with a pitcher of ale and two tankards, courtesy of Morey, rested on a small table near the door, and Sebastian went to pour himself a drink. At various times in the past, both men had on more than one occasion threatened to kill the other. But for Hero's sake they generally sought to maintain a facade of cold politeness. "May I offer you some ale?"

"Never mind that. What the devil do you think you're about, accusing Basil Rhodes of murder? *Basil Rhodes.* My God, are you mad?"

Sebastian poured himself a tankard of ale, then set aside the pitcher. "Well, that was fast." He raised the tankard to drink long and deeply. "Basil must have trotted over to complain to Daddy right after I saw him. And now Daddy's sent you to harangue me, has he? What about the two men who jumped me last night? Did Daddy send them, too? Or was that Basil himself?"

"What two men?"

"I didn't catch their names, and unfortunately they neglected to leave any calling cards beyond the imprint of their sap on my face."

"So you naturally leapt to the conclusion that Rhodes had something to do with it? Don't be ridiculous."

"Are you so certain he didn't? Basil Rhodes may play the amiable clown, but he's a nasty piece of work, and you know it."

"I know no such thing," said Jarvis, his voice low and lethal. "Let me make something perfectly clear: This monarchy is getting ready to celebrate the one hundred and first anniversary of their accession to the British throne, and I will not have you stirring things up by painting one of the Regent's bastards as some mad murderer."

Sebastian took another slow sip of his ale. "Afraid the people of England might see what the Hanovers are really like, are you? You think they don't know already?"

Something dangerous flashed in the Baron's cold gray eyes. "You've been warned. If you think your marriage to my daughter will protect you, you're wrong. Leave Basil Rhodes alone." He strode toward the door, then paused to turn and say, "Heed my words," before sweeping from the room.

"What was that about?" asked Hero, coming down the stairs as the front door closed behind her father.

Sebastian took another sip of his ale. "I could be wrong, but I think your father just threatened to kill me."

"Over Basil Rhodes?"

"Mm-hmm."

She went to stand by the windows overlooking the street, where one of Jarvis's footmen was holding open his carriage door. "Interesting. He must have reason to suspect Rhodes actually did kill Laura and her daughter."

Sebastian went to stand beside her as the footman closed the door and scrambled up onto his perch. The driver cracked his whip, and Jarvis's carriage pulled away from the kerb with a rattle of iron-clad wheels and the clatter of hooves. "I thought the same. And that makes me wonder why."

Chapter 29

*I*t might not be the "done thing" to call upon a lady of quality at the uncouth hour of ten in the morning, but Hero had no intention of waiting until three o'clock that afternoon to confront Mrs. Veronica Goodlakes.

The wealthy widow was settling down to a breakfast of tea and toast in her morning room when Hero arrived at the late shipbuilder's magnificent town house on St. James's Square. "I do apologize for imposing on you at such an early hour," said Hero airily when Veronica's butler ushered her into the room. "But I wanted to be certain to catch you before you went out."

"Of course, Lady Devlin," said Veronica with a wide smile. "Do please have a seat. May I offer you some tea?"

"That's very kind of you," said Hero, easing off her gloves as she settled into one of the chairs. "Thank you."

The widow reached for the nearby teapot and kept her eyes on her task as she began to pour. "Has something come up?"

"It has, actually. I've been told Laura was concerned about your plans to marry Basil Rhodes, and I was wondering if you knew what that was about."

"Sugar?" said the other woman, still not looking up.

"No, thank you."

Veronica set the teapot aside with a thump and handed Hero the cup. "It's quite simple. Laura disliked Basil because he owns plantations in Jamaica. She was passionately opposed to both the slave trade and the institution of slavery itself, and even though everyone knows that Basil is the most benevolent, indulgent owner imaginable, Laura still held it against him."

"Personally, I've never been convinced there is such a thing as a 'benevolent' slave owner."

"Oh?" Veronica reached for her own teacup and took a sip. "Have you been to the West Indies?"

"I have not."

"Nor have I, which of course makes it so difficult for one to form an educated opinion, wouldn't you say?"

"I wouldn't, no, but I have heard that argument. As I understand it, Laura was concerned about reports that not only does Rhodes make a habit of forcing himself on the young girls on his plantations, but he also raped and impregnated one of his housemaids here in London."

Veronica gave a brittle laugh. "Good heavens, wherever did you hear such a sordid, nonsensical tale? Laura disliked Basil because he's a plantation owner, pure and simple. She never said anything to me about him raping girls in Jamaica, and I don't believe a word of it— not a word. As for that sly, scheming little housemaid who seduced him and then tried to hoax him into thinking some common footman's baby was his, what did Laura expect him to do? Raise the lowborn brat as his own? What a ridiculous notion."

Hero studied the other woman's tight, determinedly smiling face.

"You knew Rhodes handed the child over to a farmer's wife named Prudence Blackadder?"

"I knew, yes. Why do you ask?"

"It doesn't bother you that the man you're planning to marry abandoned his own child to a woman who in all likelihood smothered the babe five minutes after he drove away?"

Veronica was no longer even pretending to smile. She sat rigid in her chair, her chest rising and falling with her rapid, angry breathing. "He only had the lying little hussy's word for it that the child was his; why should he care what happened to it? Under the circumstances, I'd say his offer to pay someone to look after the brat was rather magnanimous. Wouldn't you?"

"Magnanimous," repeated Hero. "I suppose that's one word for it."

Veronica picked up her teacup and took a slow, deliberate sip. "I don't understand why you're here asking all these questions about Basil anyway. Did Lord Devlin not look into that horrid chimney sweep I told you about?"

"Hiram Dobbs? He has, yes. Thank you so much for telling us about him. Have you by chance thought of anyone else who might have wished Laura harm?"

Setting aside her cup, the widow began crumbling between two fingers a piece of crust left on her plate. "No, although I have recalled the name of that lieutenant Laura once planned to marry: Finch. Lieutenant Zacchary Finch—although I see he's a major now. He was mentioned in the dispatches from Waterloo."

Hero took a slow sip of her tea. "Did Laura tell you she'd seen Finch again? That he's back in London?"

"No," said the widow with an innocent widening of her eyes. "Was she seeing him again? Are you certain? I can't believe she didn't tell me something like that."

"It is hard to believe, is it not?" said Hero dryly. "I hadn't realized until yesterday that he was still alive. I was under the impression he'd been killed long ago."

"Oh, no; only captured. He was a prisoner of war for *years*, poor man, under the most wretched conditions. One wonders how any man survives such an ordeal with his sanity intact."

The implications were blatantly obvious. Hero said, "Are you suggesting Finch might be mad? That he's the one who killed Laura?"

"I wouldn't want to think so, no," said Veronica, still all wide-eyed, earnest innocence. "But one can't help but wonder. . . ."

"Yes, I can see that," said Hero, and caught the gleam of triumph that flashed in the other woman's eyes before being quickly hidden by strategically lowered lashes.

"Beastly woman," said Hero, untying the ribbons of her hat as she walked into the library on Brook Street some time later. "I can't believe I once felt sorry for her, for being forced to marry the rich Mr. Nathan Goodlakes." She tore off the hat and cast it aside. "Now I'm wondering if she didn't smother the poor old fool in his sleep."

Sebastian looked up from where he sat behind his desk, cleaning his small double-barreled flintlock pistol. "Did she deny that she quarreled with Laura over Rhodes?"

"Not precisely. She admits Laura disliked him for owning sugar plantations but denies the stories of rape. Oh, and she thinks it magnanimous of him to have found someone to care for the footman's brat his scheming little hussy of a housemaid tried to foist onto him."

"She said that?"

"She did. She then contrived—ever so innocently, of course—to suggest that Major Zacchary Finch should be considered a suspect because he must surely have been driven mad by his years as a prisoner of war."

"So she knows we have good reason to suspect Basil Rhodes of murder and is trying to direct our attention elsewhere."

"Oh, she knows, all right."

"Do you think she suspects him herself?"

Hero met his gaze, her eyes narrowing as she thought about it for a moment. "I don't know. But I wouldn't put it beyond her to protect him even if she did think him guilty of murder."

Chapter 30

$\mathscr{B}$asil Rhodes was coming down the front steps of his Cork Street house when he saw Sebastian walking toward him and drew up abruptly.

"Good heavens," said the Regent's natural son with one of his wide, impish grins. "Whatever happened to your face?"

"It seems someone doesn't like me asking questions."

The grin widened. "Don't tell me you're here to harangue me about these dreadful murders again. And at such a godforsaken hour of the morning! I'm only up because I have an appointment with someone I must see before he leaves town."

"Fortuitous," said Sebastian, coming up to him. "As it happens, I've discovered what your fight with Laura McInnis in the middle of Bond Street last Saturday was about."

Rhodes gave an exaggerated jerk, his hair falling into his eyes as he looked sideways. "Have you now?"

"Mmm. Seems she had the effrontery to tell your betrothed about both the infant you abandoned and your habit of raping whatever women might catch your fancy if they're in no position to either fight back or retaliate. That's why you went after Lady McInnis—because you were mad as hell at her."

Rhodes stared at him a moment, then huffed a deep breath. "You think I should have allowed that bloody woman to run around making wild accusations about me without confronting her or making any attempt to defend myself, do you? Let her convince Veronica I'm some ghastly cross between Bluebeard and Henry VIII?"

"The middle of Bond Street does seem a rather strange choice for a conversation of that nature."

"Strange? It was damned awkward, that's what it was. The truth is, I encountered her unexpectedly, quite by chance, lost my temper, and lit into her. I'm not saying I'm proud of it—it was a damned stupid thing to have done."

"Yes," said Sebastian.

Rather than be offended, Rhodes rocked back on his heels and laughed. "Well, at least we can agree on that. I'll admit I'm no saint, but it's not like I ever claimed to be. And it's outside of enough, her carrying her ridiculous tales to Veronica."

"You're saying you didn't dump your child on a woman with a reputation for quietly eliminating her customers' inconvenient offspring?"

Rhodes raised one finger in the manner of a debater making a point. "Two things. First of all, I only had that blasted silly housemaid's word for it that the brat was mine—and I hope you know better than to believe that rubbish Lady McInnis was spewing about me forcing myself on the chit. I know a virgin when I have one, and believe me, Lizzy was no virgin." He put up another finger. "Secondly, I had no idea Prue Blackadder has a habit of eliminating the babes entrusted to her care. Her name was given to me by several friends who've found themselves in a similar situation. I paid through the nose to have her take the brat, and you can't deny that Pleasant Farm is a lovely place. How was I to know most of her charges don't live long enough to appreciate it?"

"How, indeed?" said Sebastian, his gaze on an ice cart rattling past them. "You're fortunate Mrs. Goodlakes appears to believe your protestations of innocence."

Rhodes's nearly lashless pale blue eyes narrowed. "What's that supposed to mean?"

"I understand she's quite wealthy."

"She is, yes. But as it happens, so am I. And I'll take leave to tell you I resent the implications of that statement."

"I assumed you would."

A muscle jumped along Rhodes's suddenly tightened jaw. "I hope you don't intend to go spreading these wild rumors about me yourself. I really don't think that would be wise, if you understand my meaning?"

"Oh?" said Sebastian. "Are you threatening me?"

"No, no, no," said Rhodes. "Only giving you a little hint. There, I've said enough. And now you must excuse me." Then he gave Sebastian a wink, flashed a wide smile, and walked away, whistling an off-key tune as he swayed back and forth in the manner of a man who hasn't a care in the world.

Chapter 31

$\mathcal{S}$ ir Henry Lovejoy stood with his hat in one hand, his head bowed, his breath a ragged tear that soughed in and out. The afternoon was warm and golden-bright, the blue sky above only faintly smudged with coal smoke, the grass between the surrounding tombs and headstones such a vivid green that it hurt his eyes. He could hear the droning of the bees buzzing at the scattered clover in the grass, smell the pungent odor of damp earth and damp stone, feel the oppressive weight of the centuries of death and sorrow that permeated this place.

How many times had he stood here like this? he wondered. One day, one year following the next, going by in a blur until here he was, fourteen years later. *Fourteen years.*

"Ah, my darlings," he whispered, his voice breaking. "I miss you so."

There had been a time when he used to come here every day. He'd stand erect and determinedly dry-eyed even as agonizing waves of howling grief coursed silently through him. Then one day, as surely as if she'd been there beside him, he'd heard his Julia say,

Enough of this, Henry. All your grief and steadfast devotion won't bring us back. You think this is what I want? For you to come here every day and torture yourself like this? You must find some other way to honor us.

And so, ever since then, he'd tried to come only every other day.

He became aware of a tall, fashionably dressed gentleman working his way toward him through the crowded tombs. "Goodness gracious, whatever happened to your face, my lord?" said Lovejoy as Devlin paused some six or seven feet away, on the far side of the granite table tomb that contained Lovejoy's wife and daughter.

"Someone sent me a message. It's not as bad as it looks."

Lovejoy suspected it was, in fact, worse, but all he said was, "How did you know where to find me?"

"A hunch."

Lovejoy nodded, his throat working as he turned his head to gaze out over the sea of gray, lichen-covered stones. "If only the dead could speak, or at least find some way to communicate with us. Tell us what happened to them. Help us find a way to see that justice is done."

"If only."

He brought his gaze back to the Viscount's face. "I've been giving more thought to what you said, about how someone might be doing this—echoing what happened to Julia and Madeline—to torment me. But if there is anyone out there with that kind of sick grudge against me, I don't know who they are." He paused, then said, "And I honestly don't think that's what we're dealing with here."

"Probably not," said Devlin.

Lovejoy moved his hands along the brim of his hat. "I can't remember if I told you that one of my constables discovered that Cato Coldfield lied. He wasn't confined to his bed too ill to move until Sunday evening; he was seen in Richmond that very morning. He claims he only went out to buy bread, but it's conceivable he could have killed Lady McInnis and her daughter. The problem is, what possible motive could he have had for killing Gilly Harper? We can't find any indication he even knew her."

"It's always possible Gilly's murder has nothing to do with what happened to Laura and Emma McInnis. The bodies weren't posed in exactly the same way."

"No. But the idea of there being two such killers is unlikely, surely? We learned this morning that Hiram Dobbs does indeed observe the Lord's Day as a day of rest. He attended church services in the morning, but has no real alibi for that afternoon. Of course, his little climbing boys swear he was with them all day, but I suspect the poor lads are too frightened of their master to dare contradict him. I don't *think* either Julia or Madeline knew him, but I could be wrong. And the man's predilection for quoting Scripture would certainly help explain why the bodies were posed in the way they were."

Lovejoy saw something flicker in the depths of Devlin's strange yellow eyes before he lowered them and said, "There is that."

Lovejoy knew what Devlin was thinking—it was the same thing his colleagues at Bow Street were thinking. That Lovejoy was distorting this investigation by refusing to concede that they could be dealing with a copyist. By constantly trying to tie the new murders back to what had happened to Madeline and Julia fourteen years ago. That he was too close to these murders, too emotionally involved. That he ought to step back and let others handle it.

He cleared his throat and nodded to the ugly wound high on the Viscount's cheek. "You've no idea who attacked you last night?"

Devlin reached up to touch the cut and darkening bruise, then let his hand fall, as if the gesture had been unconscious. "Not exactly, although I strongly suspect it was courtesy of Mr. Basil Rhodes—a warning not to look too closely into affairs he'd rather keep secret. Then again, I suppose my friends could have been sent by McInnis.

They should have been more specific when they told me to mind my own business."

"McInnis? You've learned something new?"

"It turns out Sir Ivo had a violent argument with his wife the Wednesday before she was killed, during which he accused her of having an affair. It's probably when he left those bruises on her shoulders."

"Good heavens. *Was* she involved with someone?"

"I'm not convinced she was having an affair, although I'll admit I could be wrong. I do know she was close to an old childhood playmate who recently returned to London after being wounded at Waterloo—Major Zacchary Finch is his name. He claims they were nothing more than friends, but what matters at this point is that McInnis believed they were having an affair, and the man has an ugly temper. Do we know exactly where he was last Sunday?"

"Not earlier in the afternoon, no, although we can certainly look into it—quietly, of course. Except . . . surely his daughter's murder must still preclude McInnis being considered a suspect?"

"Unless he had a reason to want to kill Emma, too."

Lovejoy found himself staring down at the tomb between them, his voice a broken whisper as he said, "I can't understand how any man could deliberately kill his own child."

"Yet it does happen."

He drew a deep breath and raised his head to meet the Viscount's steady gaze. "Yes. Yes, it does."

Chapter 32

That afternoon, Sebastian was staring thoughtfully at a map of Richmond Park and the surrounding area when he heard a door slam in the distance, followed by the pounding of running feet and Morey's annoyed hiss.

"Gov'nor! *Gov'nor!*" shouted Tom, sliding to a halt as he came through the library door, one hand flying up to catch his cap. "Wait till ye 'ear what I found out about that there fencing master yer interested in!"

Sebastian found Damion Pitcairn sitting by himself at a quiet table, drinking a tankard of porter in a public house in Soho known as the Cock.

A tidy brick inn dating to the previous century, the Cock was popular with the fading area's population of artisans, day laborers, small shop owners, and tradesmen. The atmosphere was thick with the scents of tobacco, roasting meat, spilled beer, and hardworking men's sweat; the clatter of tankards and heavy ironstone plates punctuated the roar of rough voices and laughter. When Sebastian walked up to him, the fencing master raised his tankard to his lips and took a deep swallow before saying, "I gather you're here to see me?"

Someone nearby cracked a lewd joke, and the half dozen men grouped around the table with him roared with laughter. Sebastian threw a significant glance toward the door to the street. "It might be a good idea to go for a walk."

Pitcairn stared up at him for a moment, then set aside his tankard with a dull thump and rose.

They walked down Dean Street, toward the Haymarket. This was an area of older houses and shops some two and three stories tall, interspersed with blacksmiths and stables and an extraordinary number of pubs. "You didn't tell me you're a Spencean," said Sebastian, dodging a puddle in the broken pavement.

Pitcairn's eyes narrowed, but he didn't deny it. "Why the bloody hell would I? What difference could it possibly make to anything?"

"Perhaps none," said Sebastian. "Did you know Thomas Spence?"

"I did. He was an admirable man. Spent more than twenty years in and out of prison for daring to believe—and say—that all men are created equal, slavery is an abomination, all men and women should have the right to vote, and children have a right to live free from abuse and poverty."

"Not to mention that the aristocracy should be abolished and all land held in common."

Pitcairn looked over at him and grinned. "That, too."

"I assume Sir Ivo was ignorant of your philosophical leanings when he hired you to improve his son's fencing?"

The man's smile faded and he looked away. "I don't exactly go around advertising my beliefs, if that's what you're asking. I'll be the first to admit I lack Thomas Spence's courage."

"And yet you drink at the Cock."

"So?"

Sebastian studied the other man's taut profile. He was brilliant and unbelievably talented and wise beyond his years, but he was still young—so very, very young. "Ever hear of a man named John Stafford?"

Pitcairn shook his head.

"He's a nasty, officious little clerk in Bow Street who basically functions as the domestic spymaster for the Home Office. And it just so happens that he knows all about the Spenceans' habit of frequenting places like the Mulberry Tree in Moorfields, and the Carlisle in Shoreditch, and the Cock in Soho. Thomas Spence might have thought he could evade surveillance by decentralizing his movement, with small groups of followers who meet only at inns and taverns. But the problem with that idea is that the government has the power to yank the licenses of public houses, and they learned long ago to use that threat to pressure publicans into reporting on any radicals who meet in their establishments."

Pitcairn walked along in silence for a moment, his jaw tight. Then he said, "Why are you telling me this?"

"Partially because I think you ought to know, but also because it might help you to understand how I came to hear that a Spencean named Watson has been worried about you. He knew you'd involved yourself with the sister of one of your students, and he told you last week over a couple of pints at the Cock that he was afraid you were making a dangerous mistake."

The fencing master drew up abruptly and swung to face him. "*Watson* told you that?"

"No, not Watson. But your conversation with him was overhead and reported to Bow Street. And if I know about it, then it's possible that Sir Ivo knows about it as well."

Pitcairn put a hand to his head and half turned away, swearing long and crudely.

"How did Watson know?" said Sebastian. "Did you tell him?"

Pitcairn blew out a long, harsh breath. "Not exactly. But I used to talk to him about Emma more than I should have, and he eventually guessed."

"How serious were things between you and Miss McInnis?"

"We were friends!" He paused, swallowed hard, then said, "Well, all right, maybe a bit more than friends—although that's how it started. But we both knew that what was between us could never go anywhere. I swear."

"You might have known that," said Sebastian. "But I can see a man like Sir Ivo—proud and hot-tempered and inclined to turn ugly when angry—maybe killing his own daughter if he thought she was getting too friendly with his son's handsome young Jamaican fencing master. Can you?"

Pitcairn stood very still, his chest jerking with his ragged breathing. "But why kill Emma? Why not kill *me*?"

"That I can't answer." Sebastian hesitated, then said, "Tell me more about Emma—what she was like. All anyone will say is that she was still in the schoolroom and never gave her parents any trouble."

"Who said that?"

"Her governess, Miss Braithwaite."

The young fencing master huffed a soft, disbelieving sound. "I suppose that's her version of refusing to speak what she considers 'ill of the dead.' The truth is, Emma gave both her governess and her father a great deal of trouble—simply by refusing to pretend to be the person they wanted her to be."

"Meaning?"

"You know the image of young womanhood held up as ideal by McInnis and his ilk: mindlessly obedient, submissive, self-effacing, compliant, reticent . . ."

"Emma wasn't like that?"

"Not at all. She was exactly the kind of female her father despised: independent-minded, outspoken, fiercely passionate about the things she believed in."

"Like her mother."

Pitcairn was silent for a moment, considering this. "Yes, and no. Emma shared her mother's values, her passion for social justice, her commitment to helping those less fortunate. But Emma also . . ." He paused as if searching for the right words. "I think she was determined never to find herself living her mother's life—trapped in a loveless marriage, having to fight constantly to be even a shadow of the kind of woman she wanted to be. Emma used to sneak and read books from her father's library that Miss Braithwaite considered 'unsuitable' for a girl her age. And because McInnis's library didn't exactly run to some of the more radical texts that interested her, she'd save up her pin money and use it to secretly buy books rather than hair ribbons and other trifles."

"And discuss Spencean philosophy with her brother's fencing master?"

A faint, sad smile lightened the younger man's features, then vanished, leaving him looking bleak and unexpectedly vulnerable. "That, too."

Sebastian found himself remembering something cryptic Pitcairn had once started to say. "You were secretly teaching Emma how to fence, too, weren't you?"

Pitcairn hesitated a moment, then nodded. "Malcolm went along with it—he'd even practice with her when they could. She loved it.

With time, she could have been even better at it than her brother. She was so frustrated by the limitations McInnis put on her activities."

A cloud drifted over the sun, suddenly casting the street into shadow in a way that drew Sebastian's attention to the clearing sky. "I find it surprising McInnis didn't stop his wife from doing some of the things she did."

"I don't know how much he was aware of what she was doing. I gathered from what Emma told me that they pretty much lived separate lives. Oh, he knew about her work with the Foundling Hospital, but that's something gentlewomen have been doing for years, isn't it? The other things she did—like working to improve conditions in the workhouses—she kept fairly quiet. There's a reason she asked Lady Devlin to write that article on the widespread cruelty to apprentices rather than doing it herself."

"You knew about that?"

Pitcairn nodded. "Emma talked to me about it."

"So tell me this: If Sir Ivo did find out about his daughter's increasingly serious friendship with you, how do you think he would have reacted?"

"Honestly? I don't know. There's no denying the man has an ugly temper. I've seen it myself, several times. Malcolm even told me once that his father had killed someone in the past."

"Did he say whom?"

"No, only that it happened in a duel when McInnis was younger. But I was curious enough that I asked around about it. Seems it happened when Sir Ivo was still up at Cambridge. The man—some vicar's son in his college—was in his cups when he challenged McInnis, but McInnis himself was stone-cold sober. He should have insisted the duel be put off, but he was in a rage, and when the man drunkenly insisted they fight then and there, McInnis took him up on it and killed him. The man who told me about it described it as basically murder. But what struck him more than anything was that afterward, he said McInnis showed no remorse at having taken a man's life; none at all. In fact, he spit in the dying man's face."

Chapter 33

For reasons he couldn't have entirely explained, Sebastian found himself sitting in the nave of St. Anne's, Soho, an uninspired red-brick basilica-style church dating back to the late seventeenth century.

The church was deserted, the chill, incense-scented atmosphere of the wide, barrel-vaulted nave hushed, the turmoil and noise of the surrounding city muted by thick walls. Sebastian might have lost his religious beliefs long ago on the bloody, corpse-strewn battlefields of Europe, but he could still at times find a measure of peace and perspective in the quiet, shadowy interior of a church. And at the moment he was sorely in need of peace.

He was aware of an endless wave of fury thrumming through him, fury so intense that he was close to shaking with it. Any untimely death was a tragedy. But these deaths—these deaths were deliberate, and that made them more than tragic. It made them an outrage.

Until now he had been so focused on Laura McInnis and what in the turmoil of her life could possibly have led to her death that he had been largely content to see her daughter as the simple, uncomplicated schoolgirl that had been described to him. But he knew now she was so much more than that; she was a vital, vibrant young woman on the cusp of maturity. A young woman courageously independent in her thinking, passionate in her beliefs and ideas, and determined not to resign herself to the kind of unhappy, violent marriage that had trapped her mother and made her life hell.

It seemed inevitable that she should have found herself powerfully attracted to a man like Damion Pitcairn—brilliant, handsome, virile, full of iconoclastic ideas and fiery dreams and ambitions of his own. A man who admired her for everything her father despised.

A man forbidden her by every dictate of their society.

Was that why her life had ended so soon, when it had barely begun? Why someone had so selfishly taken away all that potential, robbing Emma of the life she was meant to live? Depriving the world of everything she'd had to give?

Who had done it? Her own father? A macabre farmer's wife who'd already quietly extinguished so many lives? The spoiled, selfish natural son of a prince? Who?

Who?

Later that afternoon, Sebastian joined the Earl in the library of Hendon House in Grosvenor Square for a game of chess. Like their early-morning rides in Hyde Park, this was a tradition they'd once enjoyed regularly but had allowed to lapse in the months following the devastating series of revelations that had kept them estranged for so long.

They sat at an inlaid game table drawn up beside an open window overlooking the house's rear terrace and gardens. The afternoon was warm, the breeze lifting off the formal plantings sweet and fresh, the brandy in the glasses at their elbows French. For a time they spoke of current events—of the hordes of sightseers rushing down to Plymouth Harbor to hire boats and row out to crowd around the HMS *Bellerophon* in the hopes of catching a glimpse of Napoléon Bonaparte; of Hendon's hopes that saner heads would eventually prevail upon the Regent to agree to send the deposed Emperor into exile rather than turn him over to the Bourbons to be made a martyr. But in the end, the conversation inevitably circled around to what was, for the Earl, an endless source of frustration.

"I gather from the mess someone's made of the side of your face that you're still doing it, are you?" said Hendon as Sebastian studied his next move. "Looking into the murders out in Richmond Park, I mean."

Sebastian kept his gaze on the pieces. "I am."

Hendon grunted. "And you've found nothing to explain what happened?"

"Not really." Sebastian moved his rook. "You knew Sir Ivo's father, didn't you?"

Hendon frowned down at the realigned pieces. "Sir Winston? I did, yes. He was a good man—of far different character than his son. Why do you ask?"

"Did you ever hear talk about Ivo killing someone in a duel when he was up at Cambridge?"

Hendon looked up, his lips pressing into a thin, hard line. "I'm surprised you know about that. Sir Winston worked damn hard to keep it all quiet."

"So it did happen?"

"Oh, yes, it happened. And the circumstances were frankly disgraceful. The man Ivo killed was drunk. Ivo knew it and yet he still agreed to fight him then and there anyway. Frankly, he should by rights have been charged with murder."

"So why wasn't he?"

"Because it was late 1782, and Sir Winston was one of the King's closest companions—in fact, Ivo is George III's godson. We were in the midst of negotiating both the Peace of Paris to end the American War and the treaties at Versailles that would settle our conflicts with France and Spain. The last thing anyone wanted was to see the King's own godson taken up on murder charges. So Sir Winston paid off the dead man's father, and it was all hushed up." Hendon moved his queen to take one of Sebastian's pawns. "Don't tell me you're thinking Ivo is responsible for what happened to his wife and daughter."

"You find that hard to believe?"

Sebastian expected the Earl to dismiss the suggestion out of hand. Instead he paused for a moment, then said, "If Lady McInnis were the only one dead, then I'd probably say no, it's not outside the realm of possibility. But I can't see a man killing his own sixteen-year-old daughter—unless it was an accident, of course. And from what I'm hearing that doesn't fit."

Sebastian kept his thoughts on that aspect of the murders to himself. But as he studied Hendon's grim features, he said, "There's something else involved here that I don't know about, isn't there?"

Leaning back in his chair, Hendon reached for his pipe and to-bacco pouch. "Are you aware of a wealthy and extraordinarily attractive young widow named Mrs. Olivia Edmondson?"

"Vaguely. Why? Are you suggesting Sir Ivo is interested in her?"

"More than interested. Word has it she's been his mistress for months. I've heard it said he'd marry her if he were free. And now he is, isn't he?"

"Huh. I wonder why Aunt Henrietta didn't mention her."

"Henrietta might know every hint of scandal that's been whispered about in the drawing rooms and ballrooms of Mayfair for the last fifty-five years, but there are some things—although not many, I'll admit—that don't make it beyond the gentlemen's clubs."

Sebastian watched Hendon load his pipe, tamp down the tobacco, and reach for a tinderbox. "So is Sir Ivo in need of a rich widow?"

"Not to my knowledge. But then, one can never be entirely certain." Hendon drew hard on his pipe. "If his daughter hadn't also been killed, then I'd say Ivo could quite reasonably come under suspicion. But the girl was killed." He nodded to the chessboard, the smoke curling out of the corners of his lips. "Your move. Let's see you get out of that one."

Sebastian shifted his knight. "Checkmate."

Leaving the Earl's house some time later, Sebastian paused on the front steps, his gaze on the broad, parklike private gardens of the square that stretched out before him. Grosvenor Square was one of the largest of London's squares, its central expanse of lawn, shrubbery, and leafy trees sprawling over more than five acres. Unlike in most of London's squares, the residences here had for the most part been individually constructed and thus were not uniform in either appearance or size.

Lying on the far side of the square, Sir Ivo's town house was one of the area's larger establishments, five bays wide, with four main stories in addition to its basement and attics. Its stone-faced classical facade was well tended, the front door freshly painted black, the brass knocker, doorknob, and oil lamps polished to a high sheen. If its owner was in the kind of financial difficulties that might inspire an unscrupulous man to kill his own wife in order to marry a rich widow, it wasn't readily apparent.

Still thoughtful, Sebastian descended the steps and walked toward McInnis House, skirting the square. He could hear the voices of children playing in an open grassy area of the square beyond a nearby stand of plane trees, and for one unguarded moment the sound of their laughter sent him hurtling back in time to his own youth, when he, too, had played here as a child. And it occurred to Sebastian that eighteen or nineteen years ago, when Laura first came to her husband's town house on the square as a young bride, Sebastian himself would still have been at Eton. But if he had ever seen her here at that time, he couldn't recall it. She would have been just one of the many young mothers he would sometimes glimpse on a sunny afternoon, walking or playing here with her children.

Had she ever been happy in her marriage? he wondered. Even in those first years? Or had she realized all too soon the magnitude of the mistake she had made when, thinking her first love dead, she married her brother's best friend?

Pausing across the street from McInnis House, Sebastian let his gaze drift over the silent, black crepe–draped facade before him. Three children had been born to that ill-fated marriage: Malcolm, at eighteen the eldest and Ivo's heir; Emma, sixteen; and Thisbe, twelve. Even if Malcolm hadn't been off on a fishing trip to Scotland with his cousin, he would no doubt have scorned participating in such a tame family outing to Richmond Park. But Thisbe was only a year younger than her cousin Percy, and it bothered Sebastian that no one had ever explained why she wasn't included in Sunday's doomed expedition.

He was about to turn away, toward Brook Street, when he became aware of Sir Ivo, dressed in buckskin breeches and glossy top boots, approaching on foot from Bond Street. At the sight of

Sebastian, the Baronet paused, then shifted direction slightly to cross the street and come right up to him.

"Were you looking for me?" demanded Sir Ivo, his eyes narrowed and hard.

"Not exactly, but I'm glad you caught me. I was wondering if you'd discovered why your daughter Thisbe didn't take part in the expedition to Richmond Park. Was she ill?"

"I told you, I have no idea. I can only be thankful that she wasn't there."

"I would still be interested in speaking to her."

"And I've already explained why that's impossible," snapped McInnis, starting to turn away.

Sebastian raised his voice. "I understand you're quite friendly with a widow named Olivia Edmondson. An attractive, wealthy young widow."

Sir Ivo drew up and pivoted to face him again. "What the devil is that supposed to mean?"

"I assume you don't need me to repeat the rumors."

Sir Ivo stalked back to him, not stopping until he was less than two feet away. "You bloody son of a bitch," he hissed, pitching his voice low. "You leave Olivia out of this, you hear me? She has nothing to do with what happened, just as Laura and Emma's deaths have nothing to do with you. *Nothing.* I swear to God, if you don't quit poking into my life, I'll—" He broke off, his jaw tightening.

"You'll . . . what?" prompted Sebastian, his gaze on the older man's dark, angry face. "Hire a couple of thugs to jump me? As it happens, someone already tried that. Last night."

"Then it's a bloody shame they failed," snarled Sir Ivo, and swung abruptly away.

Chapter 34

The girl sat in a straight-backed chair, her hands folded in the lap of her plain stuff gown, her neat, light brown hair wrapped around her head in plats. Her name was Mary Paige, and she was currently apprenticed to a haberdasher in Long Acre, after having been beaten and starved by her previous mistress. It was Laura McInnis who had saved the child and who had arranged for Hero to interview her, so Hero supposed it was inevitable that she found herself thinking about her dead friend now as she settled in an armchair across from Mary in the parlor of the girl's new mistress, an older woman named Mrs. Ingles. Mrs. Ingles had fussed around them long enough to vaguely annoy Hero, but had finally retreated with her sewing to a chair in a far corner.

"How old were you when you were apprenticed to"—Hero glanced at her notes—"Mrs. Keeble, wasn't it?"

The girl nodded. She was fifteen now, small and fine-boned, with large brown eyes and a pointed chin. "I was eleven, ma'am." The haberdasher looked up from settling herself in the distant corner and hissed, and the girl quickly corrected herself. "I mean, *my lady*."

"That's quite all right, Mary," Hero said quietly with a smile. "You were apprenticed by one of the workhouses?"

"Yes, my lady. M' father was killed in the fighting in Spain the summer before, you see. Me and my mother and my brother, Wills, we did all right as long as it was still warm, selling nuts and apples and such in the streets. But then it got cold, and Wills died, and m' mother got sick and couldn't go out selling anymore. Mama tried to put it off as long as she could, but in the end there was nothing we could do but go into the workhouse."

"And which workhouse was that?"

"St. Martin's, my lady."

"They're the ones who apprenticed you to Mrs. Keeble?"

Mary hung her head. "Yes, ma'am—I mean, my lady. The girl they'd given her before had run away, so she needed somebody new."

"How long were you with her?"

A haunted look came into the girl's eyes, and she began to unconsciously rock back and forth. "Two years, my lady."

"Lady McInnis told me Mrs. Keeble used to beat you."

Mary dropped her gaze to her clenched hands, and her voice became a whisper. "Yes, my lady."

"You don't need to talk about it if you don't want to."

The girl peeped up at her. "I . . ." She paused, then swallowed. "To be honest, I don't like even thinking about that time. She used to beat me something awful, and then she'd lock me up with the rats in the coal room for *days* without anything to eat or drink. At first I used to think I'd die, from the pain and the hunger and the fear. But then . . . then I got to where I'd beg God to please take me and make it all end. Only, he never listened."

Hero reached out to rest her hand over the girl's now-clenched fists. "Let's not talk about it anymore. Tell me this: Are you happy now with Mrs. Ingles?"

The girl took a deep breath that shuddered her thin frame, then nodded. "Oh, yes, my lady. She's ever so kind. I always get enough to eat, and I have my own bed in the attic, and while she'll rap my knuckles when I do something wrong, she never *beats* me."

"It was Lady McInnis who took you away from the Keebles?"

Mary nodded. "She was in the shop one rainy day buying socks while I was workin' at scrubbing up some mud that'd been tracked onto the shop floor. I was so hungry, and Mrs. Keeble'd beat me something fierce that morning, and I . . . I guess I fainted. Lady McInnis rushed over to help me, and when she did, she saw all the bruises and sores on me. She picked me up in her arms and took me with her right then and there, with Mrs. Keeble's husband screechin' about how he was gonna call the constables on her for theft. But Lady McInnis, she told him to go right on ahead because she'd like to see *him* taken up for attempted murder. So then Mr. Keeble, he got so mad, he was all red in the face and shakin', saying if she didn't shut up and leave he was gonna kill her."

Hero looked up from scribbling her notes, her heart beginning to beat faster. "Where did you say the Keebles live?"

"They were on Castle Street, my lady. But they don't live there no more."

"No?"

"They had a fire something like six months ago, and Mrs. Keeble was burnt so bad she didn't live more'n a day or two. Then Mr. Keeble, he was taken up for deliberately startin' the fire, but he died of fever in Newgate before he could be brought to trial." Mary cast a quick look at her new mistress, who was busy sewing a shirt beside the open front window and was now paying them no heed. Then the girl leaned forward to whisper, "Mrs. Ingles says it's sinful, me

being glad they're dead. But I am, and I won't say I'm sorry for it because I'm not."

Hero met the girl's anxious brown eyes and said, her own voice
equally quiet, "I don't blame you in the slightest."

Two hours later, Hero was seated at the library table in Brook Street,
writing up her notes from that afternoon's interview, when her
cousin Victoria paid her an unexpected visit.

Small and petite and classically beautiful, with soft blue eyes,
golden hair, and an exquisitely fair complexion, Victoria was Hero's
second cousin on her mother's side and resembled the late Lady Jarvis—
physically—in many ways. But whereas Hero's mother had been gentle,
sweet, and loving, Victoria was shrewd and calculating and cunning.
She was without a doubt the most brilliant woman Hero had ever
met, although she effectively hid her intelligence—along with her
strength and her canniness—behind a gauzy, deceptive cloud of gay
frivolity and insouciance. She had married Jarvis the previous October,
which meant she was now Hero's stepmother. She was also the mother
of Hero's new little half brother, so Hero had spent the last nine months
working to overcome her instinctive dislike of the woman.

So far, Hero was not succeeding.

"Cousin Victoria," she said now, plastering on a smile as she
pushed to her feet and stepped forward to greet her stepmother.
"What a pleasant surprise. Shall we go upstairs to the drawing room
where we can be more comfortable?"

"Oh, no, this is fine," said Victoria, standing on tiptoe to kiss Hero's cheek in a way that always made Hero feel like a hulking, overgrown giant. She cast a telling glance at the notes spread across the
library table's surface. "I can see you're working, so I don't want to
disturb you *too* much. Are you writing a new article?"

"I am, on the widespread mistreatment of apprentices tolerated under our current laws. But I've almost finished with what I was doing," said Hero, drawing her father's young wife over to sit in the leather chairs beside the empty fireplace. "Shall I order some tea?"

"Oh, no; please don't bother." Victoria looked thoughtful. "Lady McInnis made the reformation of the laws on apprenticeships one of her projects, didn't she?"

"She did, yes," said Hero, wondering where Victoria was going with this.

The new Lady Jarvis gave an exaggerated shudder that was all, Hero knew, for effect. This was a woman who had lived through deadly sieges in India and hurricanes in the New World and buried two husbands in distant lands; she was not the type to be easily frightened. "These murders are beyond ghastly. I trust Devlin is close to discovering whoever was responsible?"

"He's making progress, yes."

Victoria settled back in her chair. "Oh, thank goodness for that. Hopefully, this means he's moved on from the ridiculous notion that Basil Rhodes might somehow be involved?"

Hero was silent for a moment, her gaze on her cousin's beautiful, deceptive face. But, as always, Victoria had her features under perfect control; like Jarvis, she never gave anything away. "I didn't realize you knew Rhodes."

Victoria's pretty blue eyes crinkled with her smile. "Not extraordinarily well, of course. But well enough to know he's no murderer."

"Oh?"

Victoria nodded. "Needless to say, Jarvis is beyond livid at the idea that someone might try to implicate one of the Regent's natural sons in something so utterly repulsive."

Hero had to work to keep her voice calm and level. "Are you here as Jarvis's emissary, then? Whose idea was this? Yours, or his?

Because believe me, even if Devlin were inclined to allow me to per-
suade him in such a matter—which, let me hasten to assure you, he
most definitely is not!—do you seriously think I would urge him to
allow a murderer to go free simply because he's the Regent's favorite
by-blow?"

"Except that Basil Rhodes is no murderer."

"Then he—and Jarvis—should have nothing to worry about,
wouldn't you say?"

Victoria leaned forward to touch Hero's hand where it rested on
the arm of her chair. "And now I've offended you," she said sweetly.
"I do beg your pardon; it was not my intention. But I thought I
should warn you that Jarvis will not allow anything or anyone to
harm the monarchy—especially not at such a critical moment in our
history. The transition from war footing to a peacetime economy
over the next few years is going to put a tremendous strain on the
nation. We've already seen riots in response to the new Corn Laws,
and it's inevitable that things will get worse before they get better."

"Yes," said Hero, "starvation does have a tendency to make people cranky." She rose to her feet. "Well, thank you for bringing me
your concerns, Cousin. And do be sure to give Jarvis my love. Shall I
ring for Morey to see you out?"

Hero gave the bellpull a sharper tug than she'd intended. She
pressed Victoria's hands again, smiled sweetly as she mouthed all the
polite platitudes, and waited until she heard the front door close behind her cousin. Then she slammed her fist, hard, into the back of
the leather chair beside her.

Chapter 35

$\mathcal{D}$o you think Jarvis sent her?" Sebastian asked later, when he and Hero sat at the wrought iron table on their back terrace while the boys tossed a small ball back and forth. The day was mellowing toward evening, the sky a surprisingly clear blue, the air filled with the distant clip-clop of horses' hooves, the rattle of carriage wheels, and the hum of the bees buzzing around an old red climbing rose at the base of the garden.

Hero frowned. "I was in a rage at first, thinking he must surely have done so. But then I realized . . . Jarvis knows me better than that." She was silent for a moment, watching Simon laugh as he missed the ball and ran to pick it up. "I'd like to think Victoria meant well—although I frankly find it hard to believe she could be so inept. Did she truly think I would be so frightened of what Jarvis might do that I would try to convince you to leave Rhodes alone? And even if I were such a ninny, what makes her think you would listen?"

Sebastian chose his words carefully. "Victoria is a very astute woman. If I had to guess, I'd say her purpose in coming here was something else entirely—except I'm not devious enough to figure out what that purpose is."

Hero looked over at him. "She is devious, isn't she? It's not that I'm irrationally prejudiced against her?"

Sebastian smiled and reached out to take her hand in his. "I have never known anyone less likely to fall victim to irrational prejudice."

She laughed softly. Then the amusement faded. "I don't know about that. One could certainly accuse me of being prejudiced against Sir Ivo, although I'm not convinced that in his case it's irrational."

"Laura never said anything to you that might suggest she knew he had a mistress?"

"No. But then, as I said, we didn't typically speak of such things. I considered her my friend and I had tremendous respect for her, but I don't recall our ever discussing anything that was in any way personal or private."

Hero was silent for a moment, watching Simon seize the ball and throw it awkwardly back to Patrick. "I've been thinking about trying to speak to Thisbe," she said. "I often used to meet her and Emma walking with either Laura or their governess in Grosvenor Square, so Thisbe knows me as one of her mother's friends—as does Miss Braithwaite, the governess. Unless Sir Ivo has specifically instructed the woman to keep Thisbe away from me, I don't imagine she would object if I were to contrive to run into them and stopped to speak with the child. I believe they take a walk in either Hyde Park or the square nearly every morning . . . or at least they did."

Sebastian said, "If someone had just murdered my wife and elder daughter in Richmond Park—and then attacked my wife's niece and nephew in Hyde Park—I think I'd be inclined to rule out any casual walks for my younger daughter for the foreseeable future. Not without a couple of armed footmen in tow."

"Perhaps. Except Grosvenor Square is a private garden surrounded by high iron railings, not a public park. I can see Sir Ivo perhaps thinking she would be safe there."

"Perhaps," said Sebastian, pushing to his feet as Patrick's wild throw sent the ball sailing hopelessly deep into the shrubbery, and both boys laughed. "At any rate, it's worth a try."

Friday, 28 July

The next morning dawned warm but cloudy, with a soft breeze that ruffled the leafy branches of the scattered plane trees in Grosvenor Square and carried with it the smell of coming rain. Dressed in a plain muslin gown topped by a sky blue spencer and blue kid half boots, Hero walked the square's gravel paths. The gardens had been laid out in a naturalistic style in the previous century by John Alston, with broad areas of close-cropped turf interspersed with scattered clumps of shrubbery and stands of trees. As a child, Hero had grown up playing in nearby Berkeley Square, so she supposed it was inevitable that now, as she walked the winding gravel paths looking for a little girl who had just lost her mother, Hero found her thoughts drifting to her own mother.

They had come here so often throughout Hero's growing-up years: Hero, her brother, David, and their mother, Annabelle. Those memories were a warm, happy glow that shone to Hero from out of the past, a treasure trove of cherished vignettes, of simple pleasures and wondrous discoveries, of balmy summer picnics and frosty snowball fights and endless laughter. So much laugher. It had now been nearly two years since Lady Jarvis's death, and yet Hero still found herself blinking back a sudden sting of tears. *"Oh, Mama,"* she whispered softly, then swallowed hard and kept walking.

After another half hour, she had about come to the conclusion that Sir Ivo must indeed have called a halt to Thisbe's walks, when she spotted the little girl and her governess near the mound at the square's western corner. Subtly shifting her direction, Hero walked toward them.

The governess, Miss Braithwaite, was a tall, thin woman somewhere in her thirties, with a long bony face and fading blond hair she wore pulled back in a tight bun. She had been Sir Ivo's choice, and Hero knew Laura had worried that, although gently bred and well educated, the woman was not particularly wise or kindhearted.

Walking beside the governess, Thisbe looked wan and crushed. A sturdy little girl with light brown hair and a round face, she was normally cheerful and exuberant and full of boundless energy and enthusiasm.

There was no sign of that child now.

"Good morning, Thisbe," said Hero with an encouraging smile as she came up to them. "How are you? You do remember me, don't you? And, Miss Braithwaite, I hope you are well?"

The governess smiled with shy pleasure. "Oh, yes, Lady Devlin. Thank you ever so much."

At the sound of Hero's voice, Thisbe's head came up. But her desolate expression lightened only slightly, and her voice was colorless as she answered mechanically, "Good morning, Lady Devlin. How are you?"

"All alone, as you can see. Simon's nurse thinks he might have a cold coming on, so I've left the boys at home this morning. I wonder, would you be so kind as to walk with me a ways, Thisbe?" Hero glanced over at the child's governess. "That is, if it's all right with you, Miss Braithwaite?"

"Oh, yes; of course, my lady." Bowing her head, the governess dropped back some steps, allowing Thisbe to walk on ahead beside her late mother's good friend.

The child was silent until they'd drawn away from her governess. But then Thisbe threw a quick glance over her shoulder and leaned in close to Hero to say quietly, "You know about what happened to Mama and Emma, don't you?"

"I do," said Hero, likewise keeping her voice low. "And I can't tell you how sorry I am, Thisbe. If there is anything I can ever do to help, promise me you won't hesitate to ask."

The little girl sucked in a quick breath and nodded. Then her small chin quivered, and she said, "I do so wish Malcolm were here."

"He is coming home, isn't he?"

"I don't know. I mean, I know Papa sent for him and Duncan, but it seems to be taking them ever so long to get back."

"Scotland is rather far away. But I'm sure he'll be here as soon as he can."

"I s'pose," said Thisbe bleakly, her thin chest jerking with her ragged breathing. "The house is so empty without Mama and Emma. I miss them so much, it's like this awful heavy weight pressing down on my chest and shoulders that never lets up. It keeps pressing and pressing, until I feel like it's crushing me. And when I think about never seeing them again—never, ever, for the rest of my life!—it . . ." She broke off, sucked in a shaky breath, then said, "It hurts so much, I don't know how I can bear it."

"Oh, Thisbe," said Hero, reaching out to take the child's hand in hers and hold it tight. "I do know what you mean. I've always thought that's one of the hardest parts of losing someone you love—knowing you'll never see them again."

Thisbe nodded, her lashes wet with tears she refused to let fall. "When I said that to Papa, he said I mustn't think like that. And then when I asked him what he thought would've happened if I'd gone on the picnic—if he thought whoever killed Emma and Mama would have killed me, too—he said I mustn't think like that, either. Only, how can I not think about things like that? How am I supposed to stop?"

"Were you ill?" Hero asked gently. "Is that why you didn't go?"

Thisbe shook her head. "Mama made me stay home as punishment for something she thought I'd done. But I hadn't done it, and I was so angry with her for not believing me that when they left, I refused to kiss her goodbye." Her voice broke. "And now she's gone, and I'll never, ever see her again!"

The little girl was crying openly now, great choking sobs that suspended her voice and shook her small frame. "Oh, Thisbe," said Hero, drawing the child into her arms to hug her close. Looking up, she met the governess's anxious gaze but shook her head when the woman would have come forward to help.

"I know your mother loved you, Thisbe," Hero told the sobbing girl. "She loved you so, so much, and she was so very proud of you. She would understand; I know she would. And I know that even if it only came about because of a misunderstanding that made you angry, she would still be so, so glad that she made you stay home, because it kept you alive. And nothing is more important to a mother than knowing her child is safe."

Thisbe swallowed hard and dashed the heel of one palm across her wet eyes as she cast a quick, anxious glance back at her governess, now drawn up a respectful distance away. "I've heard the servants whispering, you know," the girl said quietly. "They're saying Papa must have killed her—killed them both." The child looked up at Hero with wide, frightened eyes. "Do you think he did?"

"Oh, no, Thisbe," Hero said in a rush. "You know how servants talk."

Thisbe let out a shaky sigh and nodded. "That's what Miss Braithwaite said when I tried to talk to her about it. And then she said I mustn't even think such a thing. It's what everyone keeps saying to me, *Don't think about this. Don't think about that.* But what they really mean is, *Don't talk about it.* Nobody will talk to me about any of it, so all I can do is think about it."

They had reached the center of the square, where two wooden benches flanked a rose garden clustered around a crumbling pedestal that had once held a statue of George I on horseback but was now empty. Taking Thisbe by the hand, Hero drew the child over to sit with her on one of the benches. "I want you to know that you can talk to me about whatever is worrying you or making you sad," said Hero, keeping hold of the girl's hand. "And I mean that. Anything." When she said it, Hero wasn't thinking about the questions Thisbe might be able to answer; her entire focus was on her friend's lonely, hurting child and all the adults in her life who were failing her so very badly.

Thisbe looked up at Hero with wide, frightened eyes. "Do you think whoever killed Mama and Emma will try to kill me?"

Hero tightened her grip on the little girl's hand. "No, I don't think that at all, Thisbe. Why would they?"

"Why would anyone want to hurt Mama and Emma?"

Hero looked down into her pale, wan face. "That I don't know. But I do know that Bow Street is working very hard to try to figure it all out."

Thisbe nodded, her lips pressing tightly together. "That's what Arabella said. She's telling everyone that Major Finch must have done it, but I don't believe her."

Hero looked at her in surprise. "You know Major Finch?"

Thisbe nodded again. "He's an old friend of Mama's. I don't know how Arabella found out about him, but she's so nosy; she's

always snooping into stuff that's none of her business." It was obvious from the face she pulled that Thisbe was not fond of her cousin
Arabella.

"And what makes Arabella suspect the Major?"

"I don't know how, but she knows he and Mama had a fight.
Emma heard them and told me about it, but I can't believe she'd tell
Arabella."

Hero was careful to keep the intensity of her interest out of her
voice. "When was this? That they had the fight, I mean."

Thisbe twitched one shoulder in a shrug. "Late last week sometime. I don't know exactly."

"Do you know what the fight was about?"

Thisbe shook her head. "No, because Emma wouldn't tell me—
she said I was too young to understand such things. So I got angry
at her, too. And now I'll never see either of them again!" The words
ended on a wail, and Hero gathered the child once more into her
arms and held her small, trembling body close.

"Oh, Thisbe," she whispered, pressing a kiss to the side of the
child's hair. "I am so, so sorry."

Chapter 36

Later that morning, Sir Henry Lovejoy paid a visit to a neat brick row house on Sloane Street in Hans Town.

Lying to the south of Knightsbridge, this was a part of London that had until late in the previous century been nothing more than open fields and market gardens. It still maintained something of a rural flavor, and its comfortable, modest-sized houses were popular with professional men and moderately successful merchants. Back in the days when Julia and Madeline were alive, Lovejoy used to come here often, for this was the home of Julia's sister, Elizabeth Nelson. Even after the tragedy of fourteen years ago, Lovejoy had for some time made an effort to keep in touch with his sister-in-law and her family. But the visits between the two households had dwindled over the years.

How long has it been? Lovejoy wondered as he plied the knocker on the house's shiny green door. Two years? Three? His sister-in-law was a widow now, her children long since grown up and gone away. And as the minutes ticked past, Lovejoy found himself wondering if

Elizabeth even still lived here. Then the door was opened by a young maidservant who dropped a quick, nervous curtsy when Lovejoy introduced himself and then hurried off to discover if her mistress was at home to visitors.

Elizabeth received him without ceremony in her small rear garden, where she was supervising a workman redoing a section of plantings. She was a sturdily built woman in her late fifties, of average height, with iron gray hair, a shelflike bosom, and a no-nonsense manner.

"Henry," she exclaimed, coming forward to meet him with both hands outstretched. "It's been a long time."

"Elizabeth." He took her hands in his, awkwardly, then let her go. She looked much as she had the last time he'd seen her, which he realized now was *four* years ago, shortly after her husband's funeral. "You're looking good."

"You're very kind, Henry, but I know how I look," she said with a laugh. "Julia was always the pretty one." The amusement faded from her plain features. "And I'm not such a fool as to think you just happened to be passing through Hans Town and decided to drop in. What is it, Henry? What is it about these ghastly new murders out at Richmond Park that brings you to see me?"

"To be frank, I'm hoping you might know something—or at least remember something—that I don't," said Lovejoy as they turned to walk along the flagstone path that wound through the garden. "Do you know if there was any connection between Julia and Lady McInnis?"

"So that's what you're thinking, is it?" Elizabeth stared out over the garden for a moment, then shook her head. "No, I don't believe so—at least, not that I knew about."

"Could Julia have had anything to do with a farm woman named Prudence Blackadder? She fosters orphaned infants and foundlings for St. Martin's parish."

"No. What could Julia possibly have had to do with such a person?"

"Nothing that I can think of. What about a chimney sweep named Hiram Dobbs?"

"*A chimney sweep?* Henry, you can't be serious."

"I wish I weren't," said Lovejoy. "But they're often unsavory types. I suppose she could have quarreled with the fellow."

"She might have. But if she did, I don't recall her saying anything to me about it."

Lovejoy let out his breath in a long sigh. "I was always so pre-occupied with business. I was hoping you might have known of something—or at least remember something that I do not."

"Surely you're not thinking these new murders are the work of the same killer?"

"I see it as more than likely." He glanced over at her. "You don't?"

She shook her head. "I think they hanged the right man fourteen years ago. Whoever is doing this now is obviously copying him for some disturbing reason."

Lovejoy studied her plain, confident face and wished he could share her easy assurance. "Can you think of anyone at all that Julia or Madeline might have quarreled with in the weeks before they died? Someone we perhaps overlooked at the time?"

"Well . . ." She paused. "There was that tradesman—a butcher or some such person, wasn't there?"

"Yes; Arthur Grant was his name. But he died of a heart attack less than a week after Julia and Madeline were killed. I remember his wife accused me of setting Bow Street to harass the man to death."

"Ah, that's right; I had forgotten." She was silent for a moment, watching the gardener set to work digging a layer of manure into the newly emptied garden bed. "I don't recall anyone else at the mo-ment, but I can think on it. Something might come to me."

Lovejoy nodded and turned to go. "Thank you, Elizabeth. I know it's not easy, remembering those days."

"Henry—" She reached out her hand, stopping him. "Please don't torment yourself like this. The man who killed Julia and Madeline has been dead now for fourteen years. He was a deeply disturbed soul and he paid for what he did with his own life. But whoever is doing this now is evil. And I firmly believe the answer to who he is lies somewhere in the lives of the poor woman and her daughter he killed. Not in the past, with Julia."

Lovejoy nodded again, although he was not sure he agreed with her. "I pray to God that you are right."

Chapter 37

"One would think," grumbled the Prince Regent, his lip thrusting out as he touched one plump hand against the floral porcelain teapot that graced his breakfast table, "that a man could get a *hot* cup of tea."

"Unforgivable," said Jarvis, signalizing one of the hovering footmen to take away the offending pot and replace it with a fresh one. Jarvis himself had broken his fast hours earlier, but the Prince rarely breakfasted before midafternoon.

George took a bite of toast, chewed, and thought of another source of aggravation. "We had Liverpool at us again last night, prosing on endlessly about these bloody Spenceans. I thought you were going to do something about them."

"We've set a few things in motion," said Jarvis, making a mental note to give Liverpool a cold warning. "But these affairs do take time. One must first identify men willing and able to be used as agents provocateurs, then get them solidly in place before they can begin to make the necessary moves."

"Arrogant upstart traitors," muttered the Regent, shifting his gouty leg. "In George II's day, the bastards' heads would have been on pikes decorating London Bridge by now."

"Effective, no doubt. But also decidedly barbaric in addition to being rather malodorous, wouldn't you say?"

The Prince grumbled again. "I'm hearing from Rhodes that Devlin is still harassing him."

"Is he?" Personally, Jarvis wished the tiresome royal bastard would take himself back to Jamaica and stay there—although a convenient shipwreck would be more permanent. But all he said was, "Oh, dear; can't have that, can we?"

Chapter 38

*M*ajor Zacchary Finch, his right arm still resting in its sling, was cupping wafers at Manton's Shooting Gallery on Davies Street when Sebastian came to lean against a nearby wall. The Major glanced over at him, then took careful aim with the pistol held in his good hand and fired, striking the wafer dead center.

"You're left-handed?" said Sebastian.

"No. But I broke my right arm once as a boy, so I've been through this before." Finch handed the pistol to the attendant and said, "That will be all, thank you." Then he turned to Sebastian. "I assume you're here for a reason?"

Sebastian pushed away from the wall. "We need to talk."

They walked down Bond Street, toward Piccadilly. The wind was picking up, bunching the thickening masses of gray clouds overhead and sending loose playbills and broadsheets fluttering down the street.

Sebastian said, "I'm told you quarreled with Lady McInnis a few days before she was killed. Is that true?"

The Major was silent for a moment, his features stony as he stared out at the press of phaetons, wagons, carts, and carriages clogging the street beside them. Then a muscle flexed along the side of his tight jaw. "It is, yes. But how the devil did you find out about it?"

"What was the quarrel about?"

"Does it matter now?"

"It might."

Finch pushed out a harsh, painful breath. "She had bruises"—he touched first one shoulder, then the other, with his left hand—"here, and here. He gave them to her—McInnis, I mean."

Sebastian nodded. "They were noted in the autopsy. But if—as you claim—you weren't having an affair, I'm curious as to how you came to see them."

"I didn't see them. Well, not at first, I mean. But I chanced to put my hands on her shoulders one day, and she winced. When I asked what was the matter, she tried to pretend it was nothing, but I could tell she was lying." A ghost of a smile touched his lips and then was gone. "Laura was always such a hopeless liar. The gown she was wearing had one of those wide scooped necklines, so it was a simple enough thing to gently push the cloth aside. The bruises were clear imprints of his fingers, where he'd obviously dug them into her when he'd gripped her hard and shaken her."

"Did you know he used to hit her?"

"I didn't know before then, no. But once I saw the bruises, it made sense of some of the things she'd said to me in the past."

"And that's what you fought about? The bruises?"

"That's what started it. I was furious. Seeing how he'd hurt her like that, I . . . I lost my head. Went on a rant about how I was going to call him out and kill him." He swallowed hard. "It . . . frightened her. She was frantic—begged me not to. She was afraid I'd either kill him and be hanged for it, or be killed myself. So I said, 'Then come away with me, Laura. Please. Now.'" He paused. "That's when she started to cry. She said she wanted to be with me more than anything in the world, but she couldn't leave Emma and Thisbe." A faint line of color showed high on his cheekbones. "I'm ashamed to admit I wasn't even thinking about the girls when I said it—what her going away would mean for them. But then Laura, she swore—" His voice cracked, so that he had to pause again for a moment before he could go on. "She swore that once the girls were wed, she would leave England with me and never look back."

"Thisbe is only twelve. Were you willing to wait another six or eight years?"

"If I had to. I've loved Laura for as long as I can remember. It isn't as if my love was going away."

Sebastian studied the other man's half-averted profile. "How long were you a prisoner of war?"

"Four years."

"You were exchanged?"

"No, I escaped. I found out Laura had been told I was dead, and I was afraid of what might happen if I didn't get back to her." He hesitated, then said quietly, "But by then it was already too late."

"That was—what? Sixteen? Seventeen years ago?"

Finch looked over at him. "You find it hard to believe that I loved her from afar for so long?"

Sebastian thought of his own younger self, and of the beautiful Irish actress he'd loved for years. He shook his head. "No."

The Major was silent for a moment, his gaze on a blind street musician coaxing a lilting melody from a battered old flute at the corner. "I don't want you to get the idea that I came back to London last year planning to start something up with Laura again, because I didn't. But then I ran into her by chance one day on the Strand, and it was as if the years fell away. For both of us."

"When did McInnis find out she was seeing you?"

"I told you before, I didn't know that he had discovered it. We were always so careful. She was terrified that if he thought she was having an affair, he'd send her away from Thisbe and Emma. You know what our laws are like: Children belong to their fathers." Something cold and flinty flickered in the depths of his narrowed eyes. "The quarrel they had the day he gave her those bruises—I'm wondering if that's what it was about."

"She never said?"

"No."

"Did Laura know Sir Ivo had a mistress?"

Finch nodded. "Oh, yes, she knew."

"Do you have any idea how she found out?"

"No. I never asked." He paused. "If Emma hadn't been killed that day, too, you'd have a damned hard time convincing me that McInnis wasn't the man responsible."

"Did Laura ever talk to you about Emma?"

Finch looked over at him, but whatever he thought of the question didn't show on his face. "Some. I know Laura was worried about her. She was a brilliant girl—she read widely, everything from Plato and Marcus Aurelius to Condorcet and Mary Wollstonecraft, and she had a tendency to chafe at the restrictions imposed on her by both her sex and her social class. From a few things Laura let drop, I gathered she didn't get on well with her father."

"What about Malcolm's fencing master? Did Laura mention him?"

"The Jamaican? She did, yes. She thought him an amazingly talented young man, and I know she worried that because of his heritage he wouldn't be given the opportunities he deserved. Why do you ask? What has he to do with anything?"

Sebastian shook his head, unwilling to voice his thoughts aloud, especially not to this man. "Nothing that I know of at this point."

Sebastian found himself turning over everything he'd learned as he walked alone back up Bond Street. The various pieces of Laura McInnis's life were beginning to fall into place, and the picture they formed was disturbing.

He had no way of knowing if Laura and Major Finch were lovers or not; the truth was, reality didn't actually matter. What mattered was that Sir Ivo McInnis *believed* that his wife had taken a lover—had in fact accused her of it, no doubt digging his fingers into her shoulders and shaking her hard when she denied it. Had she then thrown his own infidelity up at him—the rich widow people were saying he'd marry if only his wife were dead?

Probably.

Was that when he'd decided to kill her? Kill both her and their freethinking daughter, who had formed a forbidden relationship with her brother's brilliant but totally ineligible Jamaican fencing master?

Perhaps.

So why choose Richmond Park as the site of the killings? Why pose his victims' bodies in a way that echoed the half-forgotten murders of fourteen years before? To deflect suspicion?

It fit. But Sebastian knew only too well that just because an answer seemed to fit didn't mean it was true.

He had almost reached Brook Street when he heard a man's voice calling his name. "Lord Devlin! I say, Lord Devlin!"

Turning, Sebastian found one of Lovejoy's constables leaping from a hackney carriage to hurry toward him. "Thank goodness I caught you," said the man, breathing heavily. "There's been another murder, my lord! In Hyde Park this time."

"Who is it? Who's been killed?"

"It's Miss Arabella Priestly's abigail. And the killer very nearly got Miss Priestly herself, too."

Chapter 39

The thick gray clouds overhead were pressing low on the city when Sebastian found Sir Henry Lovejoy with several of his constables in a wooded, naturalized area of the park to the south of the Serpentine. More men were fanning out around them, their gazes on the ground as they walked slowly back and forth, searching for something—anything—that might explain what had happened here. As Sebastian approached, he could see the ominously still body of a young woman half hidden by a clump of shrubs, with only her sturdy half boots and the flounce of her simple muslin gown visible. Standing off to one side was Lord Salinger himself, deep in a low-voiced conversation with two more constables. The Viscount wore the ravaged expression of a man who had looked into the yawning jaws of hell, and he had both arms wrapped around his daughter's slim form, hugging her close. Sebastian could see the girl's shoulders quivering with her quiet sobs as she buried her face against her father's chest.

"Lord Devlin," said Lovejoy as Sebastian walked up to him. "Thank you for coming so quickly."

"How the hell did this happen?" asked Sebastian, his stomach clenching as he drew close enough to see the dead abigail. Whoever killed her had then carefully posed the body so that she lay on her back, her feet close together, her arms crossed over her bloody, hacked chest. "What was Arabella doing out here with just her maid?"

Lovejoy looked pained. "I'm told that after Wednesday's incident, Lord Salinger forbade his children to go for walks—to go anywhere, in fact, without his explicit approval. Unfortunately, young Miss Priestly decided to ignore her father's prohibition and suborned her abigail into assisting her. It seems they crept out the area door when no one was looking, thinking it was all a great lark to sneak out and go walking in the park by themselves."

Sebastian glanced over to where Salinger still stood, clutching his daughter close. "I assume Arabella was the intended target, not her maid?"

Lovejoy nodded. "So it would seem. According to Miss Priestly, a man stepped from behind the shrubbery as they were passing and grabbed her by the arm. The abigail attempted to intervene and was stabbed, which enabled Miss Priestly to wrench free and run for help." He paused, his gaze on the dead woman laid out before them. "When the constables arrived, they found the abigail . . . like this."

His heart heavy within him, Sebastian crouched down beside the still form of the abigail. *Cassy,* he remembered Arabella had called her. The maid was young, probably no more than twenty or twenty-two, with honey-colored hair and pleasant features. She looked like a country girl, with sturdy limbs and a fresh complexion; she'd probably grown up on Salinger's own estate in Leicestershire.

Her chest was a bloody mess of slashed muslin and raw, torn flesh.

"Damn," he said softly. *Damn, damn, damn.*

For a moment he rested one forearm on his knee, his hand clenching into a fist in frustration. Then he pushed to his feet and walked over to where Salinger now stood alone with his daughter, his hands on her shoulders, her head bowed as he spoke to her quietly.

"I'd like to ask Arabella a few questions, if I may," Sebastian said to Salinger. "Just for a moment. Is that all right with you, Arabella?"

Salinger hesitated, then nodded, while Arabella kept her eyes on her feet and whispered, "Yes, sir."

In mourning for her aunt and cousin, she wore a simple muslin dress dyed black, with small puffed sleeves and a black sash that matched the ribbons on the wide-brimmed black straw hat that now hung crookedly down her back. But the image of youthful inno-cence was spoiled by a dark stain of what was probably blood across her tucked bodice and the bloody smears on her arms.

Sebastian said, "I won't ask you to go over it all again, Arabella, but I'd like you to describe for me what the man who attacked you and your abigail looked like. If you can."

Arabella sniffed, hiccupped, then sucked in a deep, ragged breath. "I can try, sir." Her voice was a broken whisper. "I think he was young—or at least he was slim and *seemed* young. He was tall—but not *too* tall. And he was dressed respectably. But I don't know what he looked like beyond that because he had a kerchief tied over his face, same as before."

"You think it was the same man who tried to grab Percy?"

"Maybe. He was very dark." She looked up, showing him a tear-swollen, wet face. "It all happened so fast. He grabbed my wrist. But then Cassy, she tried to make him let go of me, so he turned on her and kept stabbing and stabbing . . ." Her voice broke. "There was so much blood! So much . . ."

"That's enough," said Salinger hoarsely, putting one arm around his daughter's shoulders to pull her close against his side. "Come on, sweetheart. Let's go home."

Sebastian met his gaze. "I can't tell you how sorry I am this happened."

Salinger nodded, his lips pressed together as if he didn't quite trust himself to speak.

Sebastian stood for a moment, his arms crossed at his chest as he watched them walk away, Salinger's arm still around his daughter, Arabella leaning into her father, Salinger himself visibly shaken. Less than half an hour ago, after talking to Finch, Sebastian would have said he was a fair way toward understanding what had happened out at Richmond Park on that dreadful sunny day. But it was impossible to reconcile this new attack with the neat explanation he'd been building about a jealous husband and an enraged father deliberately setting out to deflect suspicion by echoing a notorious fourteen-year-old murder.

Turning, Sebastian walked slowly back to where Lovejoy still stood beside the dead abigail, although he was no longer looking at her. He was watching the constables working their way back and forth across the surrounding area. "Have they found anything?" said Sebastian.

The magistrate shook his head. "Nothing. I suspect the killer took whatever knife he used away with him, the same as he did when he killed Gilly Harper in St. James's churchyard."

Sebastian nodded, his gaze drawn again to the silent face of the dead abigail beside them. "At least this answers one question for us."

Lovejoy glanced over at him. "It does? What question?"

Sebastian raised his head to meet the magistrate's eyes. "We can now be fairly certain that Gilly's murder is somehow linked to what happened out at Richmond Park. But I'll be damned if I can fathom how it all fits together."

Chapter 40

Sebastian stood before the fireplace in his library, a glass of brandy cradled in one palm, his other hand braced against the mantelpiece as he stared down at the empty hearth. He kept trying to put everything that had happened, everything he knew about this killer and his victims, into some kind of logical pattern. But it wasn't working.

He looked up when Hero came in from taking Simon and Patrick for a walk. "Is it true?" she said, tossing aside her hat and gloves as Claire shepherded the boys upstairs. "What I'm hearing about Arabella and her abigail?"

"Has the news spread across town already?"

"I heard it from two different people. You're saying it is true—the abigail is dead?"

He nodded. "Someone tried to grab Arabella, and the abigail was killed when she tried to stop him."

"Dear God," whispered Hero. "The poor young woman. And Arabella must be beyond traumatized."

Sebastian pushed away from the mantel. "Surely the killer must realize by now that if those two children knew anything that could possibly help identify him, the information would already be in the hands of Bow Street. So why does he keep targeting them? Out of revenge, because of something he imagines Laura and all three children did to him and must be made to pay for? Because for some unknown reason he has a vendetta against the entire extended family? Or is it something else? Something I can't even begin to fathom?"

"Could Arabella describe him?"

"As much as possible, given his mask. He sounds like the same man who attacked Percy on Wednesday. Tall, slim, young, very dark."

Her lips parted as she drew a deep breath. "With that kind of a description, I'm surprised Bow Street hasn't already moved to arrest Damion Pitcairn."

"They probably would have—if they knew he was in any way involved with Emma. Although personally I can't believe it of him. Apart from anything else, it's all too clumsy by half for a man of his talents and intelligence."

"So the man in the park is a hireling?"

"Presumably. Although, if true, it's odd that the fellow is so well-dressed."

"Well, anyone who looked like a footpad wouldn't be allowed in the park, would he?"

"There is that," he acknowledged. "And one of the men who attacked me the other night was dressed respectably."

"What about Major Finch?" said Hero. "He's dark haired, of above-average height, and well-dressed. And his skin has been darkened by his years on campaign. I know he's not as young as Pitcairn, but I don't think even Percy and Arabella would describe him as 'old.'"

"As it happens, I was with Finch at the time of the attack."

"Ah. Well, that's lucky for the Major."

"And perhaps a miscalculation on the killer's part."

Hero was silent for a moment. "You think someone is deliberately trying to set up either Pitcairn or Finch to take the blame for the deaths out at Richmond Park?"

"I certainly see it as a possibility." He took a slow, deep swallow of his brandy. "But I'll be damned if I can understand how that poor little chocolatier's apprentice fits into any of this."

"Until today, I half suspected her killing had nothing to do with what happened to Laura and Emma at all. But now—" She broke off as a knock sounded at the front door.

They heard voices, and a moment later Morey appeared at the entrance to the library. "I beg your pardon, but young Master Percy Priestly is here to see you, my lord. The lad is *quite alone*," he added with emphasis.

Sebastian met his majordomo's eye and gave a slow, meaningful nod. "Show him in. You know what to do after that."

Percy came scooting into the room, his slightly crumpled hat clutched before him in both hands, one knee of his nankeens torn and dirty as if he'd taken a tumble, the expression on his face one of excitement at war with niggling apprehension. "I say, thank you awfully for agreeing to see me, my lord." His head jerked around as he became aware of Hero, who had quietly gone to stand by the open windows overlooking the street. "Oh! And your ladyship, too," he added apologetically, giving her a schoolboy's bow. "I hope you don't mind me intruding on you like this."

"Not at all, Percy," she said with a smile. "What brings you to see us today?"

The boy shifted his gaze back to Sebastian, dug the toe of one shoe into the carpet, and swallowed. "I guess I should tell you, right off, in case you're wondering, sir, that Father doesn't know I'm here."

"I did rather suspect that."

Percy's irrepressible grin peeked. "I know he's only trying to protect me, but the thing is, you see, I don't *want* to be protected. This is the most exciting thing that's ever happened to me in my life, and it's such an *amazing* opportunity. I've always been interested in murders, you know. There was a time I thought I'd like to grow up to be a Bow Street Runner. Except then my brother, Duncan—he's such a stuffed shirt!—he said viscounts' sons *can't* be runners. And while I'm not convinced that's true, I'm now thinking it would be much more grand to grow up to be like you. Jacob—he's my groom, you know—he's got a brother named Eddie who's a Bow Street Runner, and he's told me about all of your investigations, everything from the lady who was found floating out at Camlet Moat to those new Ratcliff Highway murders last year. Seems to me you get all the excitement of investigating murders but you don't have to wear scruffy clothes—unless you're going somewhere in disguise, of course—and you get to drive your curricle and that bang-up pair of chestnuts, and you don't have to do what some magistrate or Home Secretary tells you to do, or anything."

Sebastian exchanged a quick look with Hero, then was careful not to glance her way again. "Well, that certainly is one possibility for your future. But tell me this: What brings you here today?"

Percy's brows drew together in a dark frown. "After what happened to Arabella in the park today, Papa says we're not allowed to go anywhere anymore. And as soon as Aunt Laura and Emma are buried, he wants to leave for Priestly Priory and stay there until whoever's doing this is caught."

"I should think you'd enjoy the Priory at this time of year."

"Oh, the Priory is grand, sure enough. But it's nothing near as exciting as *this*."

"What happened to Arabella's abigail doesn't worry you?"

The boy bit his lower lip. "I mean, I know it's awful. But I can't help wishing I'd been there. I wouldn't have run away like Bella did."

Thank God you weren't there, Sebastian thought. Aloud, he said, "Did the man who tried to grab you on Wednesday have a knife?"

Percy thought about it a moment, then shook his head. "If he did, I didn't see it, sir. It must've been after he wasn't able to keep ahold of me that he decided to bring a knife the next time." Something flashed in the boy's eyes. "I say, do you think he's been watching the house? He must be, don't you think, to have been able to follow us like that when we went out?"

"It seems likely. Which is why you really shouldn't have come here alone, Percy."

The boy looked mulish. "But I have something I need to tell you, sir. I don't know why I didn't think of it before, when you were talking to Bella and me, but after you left it occurred to me that I should have told you about the sweep."

"You mean a chimney sweep?" said Sebastian, his voice coming out sharper than he'd intended.

Percy nodded vigorously. "I don't know what his name is, but he must've been somebody Aunt Laura had dealt with recently, because she knew him. He came right up to us when we were getting in the carriage to leave for Richmond Park and started yelling at her—telling her she was ungodly, and ranting on like a preacher about how 'aged women' should be as 'becometh holiness' in their behavior and not false accusers who blaspheme the word of God. Or something like that."

"What did your aunt do?"

"She ignored him and told Arabella and Emma to get into the carriage. So then the sweep—you should have seen him! His clothes and face were as black as a coal scuttle from all the soot—he says something about how a wise woman builds up her house while other women in their folly tear down theirs. But Aunt Laura, she keeps on ignoring him and tells me to get in the carriage, too. Then she says something to him I can't hear—something that makes him take a step back. And after that, she climbs in with us and tells her coachman to drive on."

"What was this sweep doing when you drove away?" asked Hero.

Percy glanced over at her as the jingle of harness and clatter of horses driven fast sounded in the street outside. "Just standing there on the pavement, ma'am. Staring after us."

Percy's eyes widened as they heard the carriage rattle to a halt before the house. Then quick footsteps pounded on the pavement and steps outside, and Morey moved to open the front door.

"Where is he?" they heard Salinger demand.

"In the library, my lord."

"Oh, blast," whispered Percy as his father burst into the room.

Salinger drew up abruptly inside the doorway, his chest heaving and his breath coming as hard and fast as if he'd been running. "Thank God," he said, his face ashen as he stared at his younger son. "Percy. *Why?*"

Percy hung his head. "I . . . I am sorry, Father. But I needed to talk to Lord Devlin, and I was afraid you'd stop me again, like you did before."

Salinger crossed the space between them in two swift strides and hugged the boy to him, his eyes squeezing shut for a moment. "I thought someone must have taken you," he said gruffly. Then he looked up, his gaze meeting Sebastian's. "Thank you."

Sebastian nodded. "Percy tells me you plan to leave for Priestly Priory. I think that's an excellent idea."

"Yes, as soon as the funerals are over. And I swear, if I have to lock these two up until then, I will." To Percy, he said, "Apologize to

Lord and Lady Devlin for inconveniencing them like this, and then come along."

The boy hung his head and looked sheepish. "I do beg your pardon, sir—and you, too, Lady Devlin." Then his head came up. "But you will think about what I said, won't you, my lord?"

"I will, yes. Now go home and stay there."

Percy flashed him a grin and allowed himself to be led away by his father.

Sebastian went to stand beside Hero as Salinger loaded his son into the barouche, then paused to speak to his coachman before bounding up the carriage steps himself. "Thank heavens whoever has been watching those children didn't see Percy leave the house to come here," said Hero quietly.

Sebastian reached out to take her hand in his as the carriage pulled away from the kerb. "Percy and Arabella were both extraordinarily lucky today. Hopefully, Salinger can keep the two of them safe from now on."

Hero laced her fingers with his. "Did you learn anything— anything at all—from Major Finch when you talked to him?"

"I did, actually. He claims his argument with Laura was over Sir Ivo's habit of leaving bruises on her body. He also says she knew her husband was involved with his wealthy young widow, and she had promised to leave England with Finch as soon as Emma and Thisbe were wed."

Hero looked over at him. "Suggestive—if true."

"Yes, I thought so." His gaze drifted back to the empty street. "As long as one ignores these blasted attacks on Arabella and Percy."

Chapter 41

$\mathcal{H}$iram Dobbs was coming out of a customer's tall, stately house on Harley Street, his face and clothes thickly dusted with black soot, a bundle of long-handled brushes balanced on one shoulder. Two of his little apprentices, their faces drawn with exhaustion, stumbled behind him dragging filthy bags heavy with soot; another, even smaller child stood beside the barrow drawn up at the kerb. This third boy was completely naked, for when a chimney's flues were particularly narrow, climbing boys were forced to strip bare in order to shinny up them. As he pulled on his ragged shirt, the child's ribs showed painfully against his burned, bruised, and abraded skin, and Sebastian found he had to pause, so engulfed by a tide of mingling rage and shame that he didn't trust himself to draw too near to the sweep.

With a clatter, Hiram tossed his brooms atop the bags of soot already in his barrow and turned to face Sebastian, blackened lips curling away from crooked yellow teeth in a snarl. "Wot ye want wit me now?" he demanded.

Sebastian drew a steadying breath and found his senses assaulted by a malodorous combination of soot, sweat, tobacco, and gin. "I heard an interesting tale about you today."

"Oh?" Hiram dug a clay pipe from the pocket of his filthy, ragged coat and bit down on the end of the long stem with his back teeth. "That a fact?"

"You told me you didn't go anywhere near Lady McInnis last Sunday. Except now I'm hearing that you accosted her as she and the children were about to leave for Richmond Park."

Hiram reached down to seize one of the boys' bags of soot and tossed it into his barrow. "Don't know where ye got that. Keep the Lord's Day, I do. Told ye that. Either somebody's spinnin' ye a tale or they seen somebody else. All I know is, it weren't me. It says right there in Proverbs that lying lips are an abomination t' the Lord."

Sebastian watched him heave the second bag in with the others. "I might be inclined to believe you if the description of this individual didn't fit quite so well. According to my source, the sweep's rant had a decidedly biblical flavor—he called Lady McInnis an ungodly woman and false accuser who blasphemes the word of the Lord. Rather sounds like you, wouldn't you say?"

Hiram's nostrils flared wide as he sucked in a deep, angry breath. "I told ye, I never left the court that day 'cept t' go to church. Told you, same as I told them Bow Street Runners who come at me the other mornin'."

Sebastian glanced over at the handsome brick house beside them. A maid was already kneeling on the front steps with her bucket and brush, scrubbing at the traces of soot left by the sweep and his little boys. He had no doubt that the chimney sweep Percy had seen that fatal Sunday was Hiram Dobbs; he also had no doubt that a man who could abuse and kill one of the wretched, helpless orphans so cruelly consigned to his care would have no difficulty killing a woman he'd already threatened at least twice.

The problem was, if Dobbs did commit the murders out at Richmond Park, then how to explain the attacks on Percy and Arabella here in London? No one would ever describe Hiram Dobbs as a tall, well-dressed young man, and Sebastian seriously doubted the sweep had the means to hire someone else to do his killing for him.

Of course, it was always possible that they were dealing with two different killers—one who had murdered Laura McInnis and her daughter out at Richmond Park, and another who killed Gilly Harper and attacked Percy and Arabella Priestly for reasons Sebastian couldn't begin to fathom. That struck him as an unbelievable stretch.

But that didn't mean it was inconceivable.

That evening, Sebastian donned a double-breasted black coat with covered buttons, a black silk waistcoat and knee breeches, and a chapeau bras, while Hero wore an elegantly simple evening gown of shimmering silver satin with cupped sleeves and the late Countess of Hendon's famous diamond necklace. There were two balls and several rout parties being held in Mayfair that evening, but Hero had decided they would be most likely to encounter the widowed Olivia Edmondson at Lady Farningham's musical evening.

It had rained shortly before sunset, but by now the rain had stopped, leaving the evening unusually warm and humid. "How well do you know this Mrs. Edmondson?" asked Sebastian as their carriage dashed through the still-wet streets, the golden light from the linkboys and carriage lamps swaying over scattered puddles and shuttered shops.

"Not terribly well, but well enough to ply her with a few pointed questions if I can catch her alone. I understand she's most anxious to reestablish herself as a respected member of the ton, so I doubt she will go so far as to snub me. She reminds me in some ways of Veronica Goodlakes, although the two are generally quite different." Hero was silent for a moment, her gaze on two small, ragged children huddling in the doorway of a shuttered shop. "I think perhaps it's because both were born gentlewomen but now, despite their wealth, they are seen as 'not quite the thing' by society's high sticklers, and they resent it. Of course, Olivia isn't as extraordinarily wealthy as Veronica, but at least in Olivia's case her wealth comes from land rather than from anything so vulgar as trade. She was an only child, you know, and since her father's Cornish estate was not entailed, she was his sole heir. The land is said to be honeycombed with tin mines."

"So why the need to 'reestablish' herself?"

"Ah, that's because Olivia's marriage was quite scandalous. She ran off with a fortune-hunting ne'er-do-well when she was barely sixteen, and it was weeks before her father caught up with them. At that point there was nothing to be done but let the marriage stand. Fortunately for Olivia, her father did not disinherit her, and then the ne'er-do-well died while her father was on his deathbed, so the scoundrel never had a chance to run through her money."

"Fortunate, indeed."

"Mmm. The ne'er-do-well is said to have been quite healthy before he succumbed to a fatal bout of food poisoning, which naturally gave rise to whispers. But I understand those have pretty much died down since Olivia was wise enough to wait out her two years of prescribed mourning in relative seclusion. She launched her campaign to claw her way back into Society last autumn, and she's been fairly successful. High sticklers such as the Duchess of Claiborne or Princess Lieven will probably never send the girl an invitation to one of their parties, but there are plenty of other hostesses who are more than happy to receive a slightly scandalous but very pretty, wealthy young widow who is guaranteed to lure a horde of male guests to their doors."

"Good Lord," said Sebastian, staring at her. "How on earth do you know all that?"

Hero leaned into him and laughed. "Because while you were off consorting with chimney sweeps, I went to see Aunt Henrietta."

They found the Countess of Farningham's Mount Street town house ablaze with candlelight and spilling genteel laughter and a buzz of well-bred voices out into the warm, wet night. Her ladyship's "musical evenings" had become something of an institution amongst the fashionable set, but with Parliament having closed on July twelfth, this would probably be the last such event until after Christmas.

"A castrato, is it?" said Sebastian as they worked their way into the Countess's crowded reception rooms and the full, sweet notes of a male soprano singing a piece by Bertoni washed over them.

"Mmm, Girolamo Rossini. I understand Lady Farningham is quite proud of having secured his performance, given that he returns to Rome in two days."

Sebastian paused for a moment, listening to the exquisite splendor of that clear, ethereal voice rising and falling. He took a deep, painful breath. "Beautiful, and yet also haunting and sad, I always think."

Hero nodded. "Whenever I hear one, I can't help but wonder if it was his choice or something forced upon him."

Sebastian let his gaze wander over the crowd. Some of the Countess's guests were sitting in rapt attention in the rows of chairs gathered around the Italian singer, but many others were clustered here and there in groups of two or three, quietly talking. "Any sign of the fair Olivia?"

"No," said Hero, her gaze scanning the rooms. "Although I do see Jarvis glowering at you. Try not to come to fisticuffs with him, will you, while I check the refreshment rooms?"

It didn't take Hero long to locate the wealthy young widow, who had gone in search of a glass of lemonade and was now sipping it as she headed back toward the drawing room. "Mrs. Edmondson, how *are* you?" said Hero, stepping in front of her.

Olivia Edmondson blinked up at Hero in surprise. Still in her early twenties, the widow was a small, dainty thing some ten or twelve inches shorter than Hero. She might not be as wealthy as Veronica Goodlakes, but she was both younger and prettier, with thick black hair, large dark eyes, and a winsome dimple that could peek seductively when she smiled.

"A pretty little thing, undeniably," had been the Duchess of Claiborne's caustic assessment when Hero consulted her. "But she's no better than she should be, I'm afraid. And while I'll acknowledge that sixteen-year-old girls can all too easily be led into folly by a handsome face, Olivia is one of those females who, if she hadn't been born an heiress, would doubtless have had a successful career as a courtesan. There's something about her that seems to render those of the male sex incapable of thinking of anything when they look at her except bed. And I don't exclude Claiborne from that statement. Which is rather telling, for if ever there was a dull dog, it's my son."

Hero watched now as the widow's famous dimple flashed, her full lips curving up into a smile, and thought she understood what the Duchess had been talking about. There was an inescapably sensual aura about the woman, and Hero had a feeling Olivia was very well aware of it.

"Oh, I'm quite well, thank you—although more than a trifle warm, to be honest," said the widow with a laugh as she fanned her face with the delicate confection of ivory and lace she held in her other hand. "And how are you, Lady Devlin?"

"Also quite warm. Between the sultry night, the crush of people, and the heat from the candles, it's too much to be borne. Do let's step out onto the terrace for a breath of fresh air, shall we?"

Olivia looked vaguely surprised, but was more than willing to be seen stepping out to take some air with Lord Jarvis's daughter. "Ah, that is better," said the widow, sucking in a deep breath as they passed through one of the French doors that opened onto Lady Farningham's wide bluestone terrace. "What a brilliant idea, Lady Devlin."

Hero watched Olivia go to stand beside the stone balustrade at the edge of the terrace, her pretty face lifted to the breeze as she looked out over the wet gardens. "Do you come to Lady Farningham's musical evenings often?"

"Not often, no," said the widow, smiling as she turned to face her. "I fear I am not particularly musical. But London is so thin of company these days that one must find amusement where one can, wouldn't you say?"

"Indeed. We ourselves had hoped to leave for Hampshire next week, but I doubt now that we'll be able to get away so soon." The delay was on account of the murders, of course, but Hero was careful to leave that part out. "Will you be retiring to your estate in . . . Cornwall, isn't it?"

Olivia pulled a face. "It is, yes; nearly to Penzance. But, to be honest, I'm more than half tempted to retreat to someplace both less distant and less *rustic*, if you know what I mean? I hear Leicestershire is lovely this time of year."

"Oh? Have you a hunting box there?"

The widow flushed faintly. "Not personally, no. But a dear friend keeps a lovely little place near Melton Mowbray."

"I take it you mean Sir Ivo?"

Olivia was no fool. Her pretty brown eyes narrowed and took on a steely look that reminded Hero of Veronica. "So that's why you've sought me out, is it? You've heard that Ivo and I are friends, and you thought to ascertain if there is any truth to the rumors?"

"So is there?" said Hero bluntly.

Olivia lifted her dainty little chin, her smile turning into something saucy and provocative, although the glint of steel was still in her eyes. "And if there were? You see something wrong with friendship between a man and a woman?"

"Not at all," said Hero. "So tell me this: Who do you think killed Lady McInnis?"

"Frankly, I neither know nor care." The expression on the woman's face hardened, became something considerably less winsome. "If you ask me, the woman got what she deserved."

Hero stared at her. "And why is that?"

Olivia twitched one dainty little shoulder. "It's different for men, isn't it? I mean, when they amuse themselves outside of marriage, what's the harm? But when a woman betrays her vows, she risks presenting her lord with a child not of his own begetting. And that is an abominable thing to do, wouldn't you say?"

"Are you suggesting Laura McInnis was having an affair?"

"Didn't you know?" Olivia wrinkled her dainty little nose in disgust. "What kind of woman could be so lucky as to be wed to someone like Sir Ivo and then cheat on him with a nobody in a red coat?"

"And do you think Sir Ivo's daughter Emma likewise 'got what she deserved'?" said Hero, her voice coming out husky.

The widow had the grace to look vaguely discomfited. "No, although she wasn't actually his daughter. Laura's attachment to her soldier stretched back for years—he escaped from that French prison and returned to London the very summer before Emma was born, you know. Yet even though the girl wasn't really Sir Ivo's daughter, under the terms of Laura's marriage settlement he still would have had to provide the girl with a portion of ten thousand pounds!"

"Indeed," said Hero. Olivia Edmondson might be beautiful and seductive, but she obviously wasn't as bright as Hero had at first given her credit for. The woman didn't even seem to realize she'd provided them with an excellent reason why Sir Ivo would murder both his wife *and* his daughter. "I take it Sir Ivo told you this?"

The warm, damp breeze feathered a stray curl against Olivia's cheek, and she brought up a hand to tuck it back behind her ear. "It's not exactly a secret, is it? I mean, how hard is it to count back nine months from the girl's birthday?"

Sebastian was leaning against a convenient pilaster, his arms crossed at his chest as he listened to Signor Rossini, when he noticed Jarvis working his way toward him through the milling audience.

"I take it you didn't think I was serious about Rhodes," said the King's powerful cousin, walking right up to him.

Sebastian shifted his stance to confront his father-in-law. "Has Basil been whining to Papa again?"

"Did you think he would not?"

Sebastian let his gaze wander over the glittering, wellborn crowd. "And you think I should have let that stop me?"

"You would if you were wise."

"Basil Rhodes is a damned loose screw and you know it. The Palace would be wise to cut their losses now, before the man does something that can't be denied."

Jarvis drew a pearl-studded snuffbox from his pocket, flipped it open, and raised a pinch of snuff to one nostril. "Don't attempt to force my hand. I already warned you."

"So you did." Sebastian saw Hero returning from the refreshment room, her color tellingly high. He nodded to his father-in-law, said, "Excuse me," and walked away.

"You don't think Jarvis will actually try to kill you, do you?" Hero asked later as their carriage wound its way homeward through London's lamplit streets.

Sebastian reached out to take her hand. "Honestly? I don't know. If we're lucky, maybe he'll decide to kill Rhodes instead."

Chapter 42

*T*hat night, Paul Gibson awoke to find himself lying facedown in the mud. It was the rain that roused him—rain trickling down the back of his neck and splashing in the puddle beside his head.

With a groan, Gibson opened his eyes slowly onto wet darkness. Or rather, he tried to open his eyes. The right eye worked . . . sort of. But the left one didn't seem to want to cooperate. He tried lifting his hand to touch it and see what the hell was wrong. Except he was lying on his stomach with his arms pinned beneath him, and everything hurt like hell. He could feel the rain pounding on the back of his bare head and soaking his breeches. He turned his head sideways, and the rain ran into his one open eye and into his mouth—which he realized also hurt like hell and tasted like blood.

Where the hell was he?

With another groan, he rolled over to stare up at the rain slashing down at him like cold, cutting needles hurtling out of a black sky. He could see a slope of muddy grass and a pockmarked stretch of murky water lapping against looming, ancient stone walls.

The Tower. *Why the hell was he lying beside the Tower of London in a rainstorm in the middle of the night?*

He tried to push himself up onto his elbows and felt himself slip sideways instead. If he wasn't careful, he was going to roll down into that bloody moat and drown. He drew a deep breath—or tried to—and discovered that his ribs also hurt. Then memory returned in a painful rush, and he closed his eyes again.

Bloody fool, he told himself. *Six kinds of an Irish fool, that's what you are. Wandering the streets of London in the middle of the night, thinking that if you keep walking you can somehow control the stabbing pains that make you want to scream. Control the pain and stop yourself from giving in to the deadly, seductive cravings that are eating your soul and killing you.*

Bloody, stupid fool.

He didn't need to feel for his purse to know it was gone. He knew he was lucky the men who took it hadn't killed him—although he wouldn't be surprised if they'd cracked a rib or two. He supposed they hadn't expected him to fight back—an unshaven, one-legged man driven by his own demons to walk the night.

But he had fought. Oh, he'd fought, all right.

He wondered what time it was. Wondered if Alexi had realized yet that he'd never come home. Wondered if she cared. Wondered why the hell she put up with him.

Why he didn't just swallow his pride and try her mirrored box even if he couldn't kick the bloody opium first.

He thought for a moment he heard her step, but he knew he was only dreaming. And he squeezed his eyes shut, letting his tears mingle unashamedly with the rain that coursed down his face.

Then he heard a smothered exclamation, felt the gentle touch of her hand on his face, and heard her soft voice say, *"Oh, Paul."*

Chapter 43

*T*he rain had started up again sometime after midnight, sweeping in from the North Sea, so that London awoke the next morning to an unseasonably cool and wet day, with heavy dark clouds that pressed down low on the city's clustered chimneys and slick slate rooftops.

Shortly after breakfast Sebastian drove east to Tower Hill, where he found the door to Gibson's stone outbuilding standing open and the surgeon already bent over the pallid corpse of Cassy Jones. Despite the cold and damp, he wore only breeches and a dirty, blood-stained shirt that hung open at the neck and was torn at the shoulder. His cheeks were stubbly with several days' growth of beard, his lips swollen and cut, one eye blackened and swollen shut, the other so bloodshot it practically glowed red.

"What the hell happened to you?" said Sebastian, pausing in the doorway.

"I fell."

"You fell?"

"That's right. I fell." Gibson tossed his scalpel aside with a clatter. "If you're here looking for answers, I don't have any to give you. All I can tell you is that someone stabbed this poor young woman four times with a big knife, probably something like a kitchen knife or butcher knife. No sign of bruises on her arms or wrists, so I don't think he grabbed her—or if he did, he didn't grab her very hard. Just stabbed and stabbed until he was certain she was dead. That's it. That's all she has for us."

"Bloody hell," Sebastian said softly, and turned away to stare out over Alexi's dripping-wet garden.

Gibson tilted his head, watching him out of his good eye. "You still don't have any idea who's doing this?"

"Oh, I have lots of ideas—and no proof of any of them."

"That's bad."

"Yes." Sebastian turned to look back at his friend's bruised and battered face. "Yes, it is."

The rain was still falling when Sebastian met with Sir Henry Lovejoy in a coffeehouse overlooking the sodden stalls and subdued, wet crowds of Covent Garden Market. "There's no doubt this throws an entirely different light on things," said Lovejoy after Sebastian had given him an abbreviated version of what they had learned about Sir Ivo McInnis. The magistrate was silent for a moment, his gaze on the steam rising from the cup of hot chocolate on the table before him. "And yet . . ." He paused. "I can see a man with a reputation for violence killing his wife because he suspects her of having an affair—particularly if her death will enable him to marry the seductive young widow with whom he has become involved. But for him to kill an innocent sixteen-year-old girl simply because she might not be his daughter is considerably more difficult to believe. Could any man be that monstrous? If we were talking about a boy child—an heir—whom he suspected of not being his, then that might make sense as a motive. But why kill the girl? Out of sheer rage?"

Sebastian wrapped his hands around his hot coffee. "I suppose that could have played a part, but it appears there may have been a financial incentive, as well—at least according to Mrs. Edmondson, who says that under the terms of Laura's marriage settlement, Emma was owed a portion of ten thousand pounds. Now, with the death of both mother and elder daughter, all of Laura's dowry with the exception of Thisbe's portion will remain part of the McInnis estate."

Lovejoy frowned. "I was under the impression the old Viscount was too far under the hatches to provide his daughter with much of a dowry."

"He was. The current Lord Salinger's father-in-law, Septimus Bain, put up the capital to secure a 'respectable' alliance for his daughter's sister-in-law."

"Ah." Lovejoy raised his hot chocolate to his lips and took a tentative sip. "Under the right circumstances, ten thousand pounds could certainly be construed as an ample incentive for murder."

"What do we know about Sir Ivo's movements that Sunday?"

"As it happens, he was attending a pugilistic match out at Copthall Common. There's no doubt about that; he was seen by many." Lovejoy paused. "Although obviously he could have hired a killer, and then made it a point to display himself very publicly at the crucial time."

"And now he's using the same man to try to kill his wife's niece and nephew."

Lovejoy nodded thoughtfully. "If Lady McInnis had been the only victim of what happened out at Richmond Park, then Sir Ivo might well have been seen as our most likely suspect from the very beginning. It was largely his daughter's death—combined with the strange positioning of the bodies—that seemed to rule that out." He settled the cup back in its saucer. "How very diabolical this all is. Do you think McInnis is indeed our man?"

Sebastian settled back in his chair. "I wouldn't say I'm entirely convinced of it yet, no. I can see McInnis trying to silence Percy and Arabella out of fear they might have seen or heard something that could identify him. But I'm still stumped by the role played in all this by little Gilly Harper—unless of course she was killed by someone else entirely, and then whoever McInnis hired to attack his wife's niece and nephew took advantage of the strange circumstances of the apprentice's death to pose the abigail in a similar way and throw us off."

"Perhaps. Or Gilly's death and the attacks on Lord Salinger's children could be totally unrelated." Lovejoy frowned. "Although I'll admit I still find that difficult to believe."

"Unless the murders out at Richmond Park inspired a completely unrelated killer here in London to do something similar."

The magistrate's eyes widened. "Now, there's a frightening thought."

"Yes."

Lovejoy cleared his throat. "As it happens, we do now have one other possible suspect. Young Master Percy tells us he thinks the man who attacked him in Hyde Park may have resembled a Jamaican fencing master named Damion Pitcairn. Are you familiar with the fellow?"

Sebastian felt a chill pass over him, but he was careful to keep his voice even, nonchalant. "I am, yes. And frankly, I can't believe he has anything to do with what's happened."

"Interesting. Well, we've set some of the lads to looking into him, in any case. The Home Secretary in particular is quite keen on the possibility he may be our man." Lovejoy took another slow sip of chocolate. "I'm afraid the Palace is increasing the pressure on Bow Street to have someone remanded into custody quickly. The Home Secretary tells us the Prince is outraged to discover we've been looking into Mr. Basil Rhodes, with the result that we've now been ordered to stay far, far away from the man."

"I can't say I'm surprised. Jarvis was threatening me with mayhem and murder over it again last night."

Lovejoy sighed. "My lads were trying to work quietly, but obviously they weren't quiet enough."

"Did they discover anything?"

"Well, it turns out there is a discrepancy in Mr. Rhodes's account of his movements last Sunday. He's been heard to claim he was attending a pugilistic match last Sunday at Moulsey Hurst. Except of course there was no match at Moulsey Hurst that day; it was out at Copthall Common."

Sebastian gave a soft huff of laughter. "Sounds like the kind of mistake Rhodes would make."

"He's obviously hiding something. According to his servants, Rhodes went out late Sunday morning—*walking*—without saying where he was going, and remained gone for a considerable time, not returning until the evening."

"Sounds rather ominous. Have you asked Rhodes for an explanation?"

"No. I fear it would be unwise to antagonize the Palace any further at this point." He paused, then added, "Unwise for us, that is." Then Lovejoy settled his cup in its saucer, and Sebastian saw the magistrate's eyes narrow with a hint of one of his rare smiles.

Basil Rhodes was in the elegantly appointed back room of an exclusive tailor's shop on Bond Street, looking over a selection of fine woolens spread out on a mahogany table for his inspection, when Sebastian walked up to him.

"Oh, Lord, not you again," said Rhodes, rolling his eyes.

"You weren't expecting me?"

"Is there a reason I should have been?"

"When you claim to have been attending a mill out in Moulsey Hurst at the time of a murder, and yet the Fancy was actually meeting at Copthall Common, one might anticipate provoking some puzzlement."

Rhodes gave him a broad grin. "Did I say Moulsey Hurst? I meant Copthall, of course. How silly of me."

Sebastian met the hovering tailor's anxious gaze and said, "Leave us."

"I say," bleated Rhodes as the tailor blanched, then backed away, bowing low, through the curtain and disappeared. "Of all the high-handed—"

"So tell me this," said Sebastian, cutting him off. "Exactly who was fighting on Sunday?"

The Prince's favorite natural son waved one plump, elegantly gloved hand through the air. "That Black American, obviously. And I've no doubt you know the name of the other fellow—the one everyone's always talking about. I confess I don't follow such things too closely, but I assume you do."

"Which man won?"

Rhodes tittered. "You don't seriously expect me to remember the fellow's name, do you?"

"I thought you might have some idea. But given that one man was Black and the other white, you should at least be able to remember that. So which was it?"

Rhodes blinked. "The white man, of course."

"Good guess. You had a fifty-fifty chance, after all. But as it happens, you're wrong."

Rhodes blinked again, his jaw sagging.

Sebastian said, "So where were you, in reality?"

Rhodes closed his mouth and swallowed. "I told you: I was at Copthall Common. But I left early."

"With whom?"

"What do you mean, 'with whom'?"

"You would have me believe you went by yourself? In a hired coach? When you cared so little about the fight that you didn't even bother to learn the names of the contestants—or who won?"

Rhodes straightened his shoulders and affected an air of outraged dignity. "My companions are none of your affair."

"Perhaps not. Although I suspect Bow Street might be interested in knowing the answer to that question."

Basil Rhodes threw back his head and laughed. "Do you seriously think my father would allow some upstart magistrate—appointed by a member of his own government, remember—to harass me? *Me?*"

"Probably not," said Sebastian pleasantly. "But no one appointed me. Which means no one can call me off."

Rhodes quit laughing, his face hardening as he brought up one hand to poke the air between them with a pointed finger. "You do realize I know precisely why you're doing this."

"You do?"

"I've heard about you—about your radical ideas; your sympathy for everything from republicanism to such revolting concepts as universal manhood suffrage."

"Not only manhood suffrage," said Sebastian with a quiet smile.

Rhodes's eyes bulged. "Good God."

"See? It's even worse than you thought. Although I'll be damned if I can fathom what that has to do with anything."

"It's why you're determined to persecute me—because you hate the Hanovers."

Sebastian was tempted to point out that Basil Rhodes was not, legally, a Hanover. But all he said was, "I freely admit that I loathe our current system. I am outraged by our continued toleration of the institution of slavery, and by the sight of children starving to death under bridges, and by the knowledge that the widows of the brave men who fell before Ciudad Rodrigo and Vitoria are being forced to prostitute themselves on the streets to stay alive. But the Hanovers?" He shook his head. "No; I don't *hate* them."

"The problem with you," said Rhodes, "is that you're so blinded by prejudice that you don't know where to look."

"Oh? So where do you think I should be looking? Do tell."

"How about the victim's own brother?"

"Salinger?"

The man's lips curled up in a smirk that reminded Sebastian forcibly of his royal father. "She had quite the quarrel with him, you know. Right before she died."

"Oh? And how do you happen to know this?"

Rhodes laid a finger beside his rather blobby nose and winked. "Someone told me."

Veronica Goodlakes, thought Sebastian. Although if the widow knew of such a quarrel, why the hell hadn't she mentioned it to Hero?

Rhodes's smile widened. "Do I gather from your silence that you were unaware of the siblings' rather violent disagreement?"

"You're suggesting Lord Salinger killed his own sister and niece? Because of some quarrel—which may or may not have occurred?"

"Oh, it occurred, all right. I've seen him playing the role of the grieving brother and frightened father; it's all so affecting, wouldn't you say? But there's another side to our dear Viscount, I'm afraid: a harsh, unforgiving side. After all, we're talking about a man who consigned his own wife to a lunatic asylum years ago—as soon as she gave birth to his second son—and he's kept her there ever since.

Old Septimus Bain was dead by then, of course; Salinger wouldn't have dared do it if moneybags had still been alive. But once the old man was dead and Salinger had his wife's fortune and his heir and a spare, then . . . *poof.*" Rhodes brought up both fists to burst them open in a mocking imitation of twin explosions. "Time to make the lovely lady disappear."

"Why?"

"What do you mean, *Why?* Because he was tired of her, obviously. I'm told she was a charming woman. The smell of the shop might have hung around the old man, but not her. And yet, thanks to her father's ambitious determination to see her wed to a title, she's spent all these years hidden away in an asylum while her husband lets everyone think she's dead." Rhodes ran the splayed fingers of both hands through his unruly, flyaway hair, raking it away from his forehead. Then he looked over at Sebastian and laughed. "You don't believe me, do you? You can always ask Salinger, you know. I doubt he'd lie to your face."

Sebastian studied the royal bastard's full-cheeked, self-satisfied smirk. Like most people with a flexible attitude toward the truth, Basil Rhodes was a smooth liar. But Sebastian had an uneasy feeling that this, at its core, was an assertion too bizarre, too easily disproven, to make sense as anything other than a disturbing reality.

Chapter 44

$\mathcal{C}$hrist, this rain," swore Sebastian as he pulled up in front of the Duchess of Claiborne's house on Park Lane a short time later. Water darkened the chestnuts' hides, ran swift and deep in the gutters, drummed on the leaves of the plane trees in the park across the lane. "You might as well take the curricle back to Brook Street. I'll grab a hackney when I'm finished here."

"*My lord*." Tom's wet, sharp-featured face went slack with horror. "Not a *hackney*!"

"Shocking, I know. But it's so miserable out that if I'm lucky, no one will be around to see me disgrace myself by appearing in such a humble equipage." Sebastian handed the boy the reins. "And after you've taken care of the chestnuts, I'd like you to see if you can befriend one or two of the servants at Mr. Basil Rhodes's town house in Cork Street."

The tiger's face brightened. "What ye want to know, gov'nor?"

"Mainly if it's true that no one knows where Rhodes was last

Sunday. Also if he's received any unusual visitors lately—namely someone young, dark-haired, and slim."

"Gor," breathed Tom. "You thinking Prinny's by-blow might be the killer?

Sebastian hopped down to the paving, leaping wide to avoid the rushing gutter. "Let's just say I'm not ready to discount it as a possibility."

The door was opened by the Dowager Duchess's butler, Humphrey, his normally disapproving face lightened by what looked suspiciously like a malicious smile as he eyed the rain running off the brim of Sebastian's hat and soaking the multiple capes of his greatcoat.

"Good morning, my lord. Bit wet out today, is it not? I take it you're here to see Her Grace?" Humphrey glanced toward the street, where Tom was pulling away from the kerb. "Unfortunately, Her Grace is not, at present, at home."

"Good try," said Sebastian, eyeing Humphrey's obvious glee with misgivings. "But it's barely eleven o'clock." The Duchess was famous for never leaving her bedroom before twelve or one o'clock.

"True, true. But Her Grace has indeed gone out, nonetheless." Humphrey looked pointedly at the now-empty, rain-washed street, and his smile widened enough to show a hint of teeth. "Oh, dear, I see your young groom has already departed with your curricle. Shall I send one of the footmen to procure a hackney to convey you back to Brook Street?"

The decrepit old hackney summoned by the Dowager's footman reeked of damp and rot and decay, with so much moldering straw spread on its floorboards that Sebastian was still brushing stray bits of dried vegetation from the hem of his driving coat when he was met in his entrance hall by Morey.

"A lad brought this to the door some ten minutes ago," said the majordomo, his face expressionless as he held out a silver salver upon which lay a badly folded square of cheap, grubby paper. "He said it was for 'the Viscount,' then ran off without saying more."

"Odd," said Sebastian, unfolding the dirty, crumpled page.

The message was short and crudely lettered in pencil. I got sumthin I gotta tel ye. It was signed Coldfield.

Sebastian looked up. "Describe the lad."

Morey shrugged. "Small. Thin. Filthy dark hair and dirty face. Ragged clothes. Looked as if he might be a crossing sweep or perhaps a stable boy, although I can't say I've ever seen him in the area. He's not one of the lads typically used to deliver messages around here."

Sebastian fingered the cryptic note, then turned toward the stairs. "Send a message to the stables to have my carriage brought around immed—no, better make that half an hour. I need to get out of these wet clothes."

By the time Sebastian reached the thatcher's dilapidated cottage near Richmond Park's Petersham Gate, the rain had slowed to a drizzle that pattered on the carriage roof and dimpled the puddles standing in a low ditch beside the road.

In the gloomy light of the overcast afternoon, the cottage looked deserted: The broken gate still hung open, and no smoke curled from the chimney. Sebastian stepped down to the lane's muddy verge and then paused, one hand still on the carriage door as he let his gaze roam over the ruined garden, the pile of thatching tools, the ramshackle outbuildings. The cottage door stood open perhaps a foot, but he could see no movement within, hear no trace of sound.

"I don't like that cold wind," he said, glancing up at his coachman. "Better walk them."

"Aye, my lord."

Acutely conscious of the unnatural stillness, Sebastian crossed the road. At the gate he paused again, a sense of uneasiness that he didn't like crawling up his spine. Brushing through the wet, rain-beaten tangle of basil and tansy overgrown with nettles and thistles that hung over the walkway, he stopped before the partially open door.

"Coldfield?" he called, then raised his voice. "*Coldfield.*"

Silence.

Sebastian was turning away, intending to check the outbuildings, when he heard a faint whine coming from inside the cottage. He stopped. "Bounder? Is that you?"

The whine came again, along with the soft thumping of a dog's tail.

"Bloody hell," said Sebastian under his breath. He hesitated a moment, then reached down to slip the knife from his boot and pushed the door open wide.

Of one room only, the gloomy interior of Cato Coldfield's cottage was as ill-kempt and slovenly as its exterior, with dusty cobwebs hanging from the exposed beams overhead and a hard earthen floor in need of sweeping. A rusting pot of what looked like burnt stew sat moldering on the cold hearth; a stale half loaf of bread and a scattering of food-encrusted dishes littered the surface of the nearby crude table. The air reeked of unwashed clothes, urine, and excrement heavily overlain with the unmistakable stench of blood.

"Damn," whispered Sebastian.

Cato Coldfield lay sprawled on his back not far from the opening of the large stone fireplace. His face was pale, his arms flung stiffly out, his eyes wide and dry and protuberant. The little black-and-white dog, Bounder, huddled whimpering beside his dead master's head.

"It's all right, boy," Sebastian said gently, going to crouch down beside the dead man. "Everything's going to be all right." Yanking off one glove, he touched the back of his hand to Cato's pallid cheek. The dead man was utterly cold, but his head moved: The rigor mortis that still stiffened his arms and legs was starting to go off.

Sebastian studied the pulpy mess someone had made of the man's chest. From the looks of things, he'd been both shot and stabbed. "Lovely," said Sebastian under his breath.

Bounder whined, looking up at Sebastian with hurt, pleading eyes, his tail moving feebly as Sebastian reached to run his hand down the dog's sides. "You all right there, boy?"

Bounder ducked his head, his tail thumping again.

One comforting hand still resting on the dog, Sebastian let his gaze travel around the dim, cluttered space. The room might be untidy, but it showed no visible signs of having been the scene of a struggle. Sebastian brought his gaze back to focus on the body beside him. Given Coldfield's distance from his door, Sebastian suspected the thatcher had either left the door open and been surprised by his murderer or . . .

Or he'd welcomed his killer inside.

"So which was it, Bounder? Hmm?" asked Sebastian, bringing his attention back to the dog.

But Bounder only looked up at him with dark, desperately pleading eyes.

"This makes no sense," said Sir Henry Lovejoy several hours later.

He stood with Sebastian beside what was left of Cato Coldfield, the magistrate's chin resting on his chest as he stared down at the thatcher's bloody corpse. From outside came the voices of the half dozen or so men who'd been organized to search the outbuildings and surrounding area.

"No," agreed Sebastian, his arms crossed at his chest.

Lovejoy raised his head and glanced around. "Where's the man's dog?"

"The keeper's wife is taking him."

"Ah." The magistrate blew out a long breath. "Before Gilly Harper was found, I'd come to the conclusion that Coldfield must be our killer—that Daniel O'Toole was hanged by mistake and that Coldfield must have killed Julia and Madeline the same way he'd killed Lady McInnis and her daughter. But then, after Gilly, I thought I must be wrong, that I was perhaps allowing my personal emotions to sway my thinking. And now . . ." His voice trailed away, and he swallowed hard before saying, "Now I don't know what to think."

"You said your constable discovered that Coldfield was out and about last Sunday. Perhaps he saw something, and that's why the killer decided he had to be silenced."

"Perhaps. Although if he did, then why didn't he say something?"

"Perhaps he was planning to."

Lovejoy looked over at him. "Let me see that message again." He took the crumpled, dirty sheet of paper Sebastian held out to him, his forehead creasing with thought as he studied the misspelled, crudely formed words. "Do you think Coldfield actually wrote this?"

"Do we know if he could even write?" said Sebastian.

"I've no idea."

Sebastian stared down at the dead man's pale, slack features. "That message was delivered to my house this morning. And while I could be wrong, it looks to me as if Coldfield here has been dead for at least twenty-four hours—if not longer."

Lovejoy pursed his lips. "So unless the messenger boy was shockingly tardy in delivering his note, Coldfield couldn't have sent it. Which begs the question: Who did?"

"The killer?"

Lovejoy met his gaze, his face drawn. "But *why?*"

"That I can't begin to explain."

It was some time later, when Sebastian and Lovejoy were watching a couple of men load the thatcher's body onto the bed of a cart that was to carry him to Paul Gibson's surgery in London, that one of the constables beating his way through the long wet grass beside the lane gave a shout.

Turning, Sebastian watched the man bend down to pick up something, then straighten.

"Sir Henry!" cried the man, turning to trot back toward them. "Look at this, Sir Henry! Found it lying there beside the road like somebody tossed it aside—or maybe dropped it as he was running away."

Cradling his find in both hands, the man held out a wet pistol.

Carefully wrapping one hand around the handle, Lovejoy raised the muzzle to his nostrils and sniffed. He looked over at Sebastian. "It's been fired recently."

"Let me see it."

It was a fine piece, thought Sebastian, taking it in hand; a Stanton flintlock pistol with a late eighteenth-century-style mechanism with no bridle on the flash pan. The barrel was of polished brass, as were the butt cap, escutcheon, trigger guard, and side plate; a carefully wrought, decorative silver wire inlay formed a delicate design around the barrel tang. Suddenly conscious of his pounding heart, Sebastian turned the pistol to stare down at the engraving on the butt cap.

LIEUT. Z. FINCH, 45TH REGT.

Chapter 45

$\mathcal{B}$y the time Sebastian reached Middle Temple, the sun was sinking low on the horizon and the heavy, ominous clouds that had made the last few days so dark and wet were beginning to break up.

The Middle Temple was home to one of England's Inns of Court, which were basically medieval-style guilds of law. It was in this area of centuries-old stone buildings between the Strand and the river Thames that many of the Inn's barristers lived; here that they kept chambers and trained those aspiring to the bar; here that they dined in their great medieval hall and consulted the learned tomes preserved in their ancient library.

Threading his way through clusters of barristers in old-fashioned wigs and flowing black robes, Sebastian finally located an earnest, scholarly-looking man named Michael Finch. A brief conversation with that pleasant but vaguely puzzled barrister sent Sebastian first to search the quiet old gardens that stretched along the riverbank and then, when that proved futile, to the Temple Church.

The Temple Church, like the precincts of the Middle and Inner

Temples that surrounded it, had belonged to the Knights Templar until their growing wealth and power led to their violent abolition in the fourteenth century. Like so many of the Templars' chapels, the original twelfth-century part of the structure that now served as the nave was round, with the thirteenth-century rectangular section to the east forming the chancel. As he quietly closed the weathered old door behind him, Sebastian felt the ancient church's chill atmosphere of incense, beeswax, and dank stone envelop him.

In the waning light of the overcast day, the rows of soaring Gothic arches loomed dark and deserted before him. But as his eyes adjusted to the gloom, he could see Major Zacchary Finch standing in the shadows of the round nave, his shoulders slumped, his hands grasping the iron railings that protected a row of crumbling stone effigies of long-dead medieval knights.

At the sound of Sebastian's approaching footsteps, the Major's head jerked around, his face so haggard and drawn by grief that Sebastian knew a twinge of regret for having intruded on what should have been a private, vulnerable moment of despair.

Finch turned his face away again, his chest jerking as he sucked in a ragged breath. "I've been standing here thinking about soldiers," he said hoarsely. "About honor and glory, pain and death. About what we sacrifice for king and country."

"It's an old tradition," said Sebastian, pausing beside one of the round church's worn marble pillars.

Finch nodded to the rigid, mail-clad stone knights lying before them. "Look at them. Six hundred years later and we still venerate them, still use the tales of their exploits to inspire our sons. William Marshal was my hero, you know, when I was a boy. I grew up dreaming of becoming a latter-day knight, of serving my king and winning great wealth and fame." His lips twisted into a sneer. "Funny how no one ever talks about the price we expect other people to pay for our grand and yet ultimately pitiful obsessions and ambitions. About the women we leave alone behind us to suffer . . . and die." His voice cracked, and he turned his head to look at Sebastian again. "Why the devil are you here?"

Wordlessly, Sebastian drew the Stanton pistol from the pocket of his driving coat and held it out.

"*Son of a bitch*," swore Finch, reaching for it. "Where did you get this?"

"Out near Richmond Park. About two hundred yards from the dead body of a thatcher named Cato Coldfield."

The Major's head reared back, his hand spasming around the pistol's grip. "He'd been shot?"

"And stabbed."

Finch hesitated, then raised the muzzle to his nostrils and sniffed.

"That's right," said Sebastian. "It's been recently fired."

"You can't think—" Finch began, then broke off.

"If you've an explanation, I'm willing to listen."

Leaving the church, they wound their way through Pump Court to turn down Middle Temple Lane, toward the silver ribbon of the river that beckoned in the distance. For a time Finch stared unblinkingly at the ancient, soot-stained buildings that rose up around them. Then a muscle jumped along his jaw and he said, "When I first came back to London after Waterloo, I took a room at an inn near Piccadilly. I wasn't entirely certain that Michael—that's my brother— would be willing to have me stay with him." He gave a hint of a crooked smile. "Well, I knew Michael would always welcome me, but I worried that his new wife might be a different matter. So I took a room at the Eagle. It was something like my second or third day there that I came back from visiting my brother to discover someone had gone through my room. There wasn't a lot missing—the truth is, I don't have a lot. The only important thing they took was the flintlock. It's not worth all that much on the face of it, but my grandfather gave it to me when he bought my promotion after I escaped from that wretched French prison, so it means a lot to me."

"Easy enough now to claim it was stolen," said Sebastian.

Finch looked over at him, his nostrils flaring on a quick, angry breath. "Damn you, if you don't believe me, you can ask that rascally innkeeper. I raised quite a dust over it."

"One might argue that you deliberately concocted a false accusation of theft in order to later be able to claim that the gun had been stolen."

"Why the devil would I do something like that? If I wanted to go around murdering people with it, why not clean the gun and keep it? Why throw it away at the scene of one of my supposed crimes?"

"No reason I can think of, but you know damned well that won't stop people from making the argument." Sebastian studied the Major's tight, furious face. "When you came back to England after escaping from prison, what year was that?"

Finch's brows drew together, as if he were puzzled by the shift in topic. "The summer of 'ninety-eight. Why do you ask?"

"And how long were you here, in London?"

"Five or six months. I had a wound that had festered badly, so it was a while before I was fit to return to duty."

"Did you see Laura then?"

"I already told you I did."

"And after you rejoined your regiment, how often did you see her in the years that followed?"

"I didn't—not until last summer when I was on extended leave after Boney was sent off to Elba."

"Why?"

"What do you mean, why?"

"Why didn't you see her again during all those years? You were old friends. You must have been back in England at some point."

"We decided it would be best."

They had reached the ancient Temple Gardens, once the gardens and orchards of long-dead monks, now a vast expanse of scattered, wind-tossed trees and bright green lawns that sloped steeply down to the Thames. The sky overhead was a soft pastel blue streaked with clouds touched pink and purple by the setting sun, with the river glinting silver in the slanting light. Sebastian watched as the Major went to stand at the water's edge.

"Do you know when Emma was born?"

Finch kept his face turned away. "No. Why would I?"

"It was in May. May of 1799." Sebastian paused, then said, his voice quiet, "She was your daughter, wasn't she?"

Finch jerked and started to deny it. Then he stopped, his lips pressing into a thin line as he continued to stare out over the wide, wind-ruffled expanse of the river before them. "It only happened the once, you know. We hadn't meant for it to happen at all. But we were so young—Laura was only twenty-two, and I was twenty-three. We were young, and desperately in love, and everything seemed . . . hopeless." He paused. "My love for Laura was deep and spiritual, infinite and eternal, but it wasn't passionless. She was trapped in a loveless marriage to a brutal man she'd realized all too quickly she hadn't really known, while I . . . I was about to go back to war with the very real possibility that I would be killed. We had a chance—a stolen moment out of time, and we took it. Even though we knew it was wrong, even though we both knew it could never happen again. It's why we agreed we should never see each other again—to make certain it wouldn't happen again."

"Did McInnis know?"

"That Emma wasn't his?" Finch watched as a wherryman near the far bank stopped rowing and shipped his oars. "I don't see how he could have known for certain. I mean, he was away, but only for a few weeks. I suppose he might suspect, but that's all. Even Laura said she didn't know for certain. But I knew as soon as I saw Emma last summer—she looks exactly like my sister Grace at that age. Only, McInnis never knew Grace."

He drew a deep breath, his eyes narrowing as he turned his face into the westering sun. "I stayed away from Laura for sixteen years—sixteen long, lonely years. But when by chance I saw her last summer . . ." He swallowed. "The war was over—or at least we thought it was over. I had survived. We were both older, wiser. Stronger. We thought we could control ourselves. Be friends." He brought up both hands to cover his face, and it was as if the words were torn from him. "*Oh, God.* I've loved her my entire life. I thought I'd die in that bloody war, but I didn't. I didn't! And now I'm here and she . . . she's the one who's dead. And so is Emma."

Sebastian kept his gaze on the sun-dazzled river. The air was heavy with the briny scent of the inrushing tide, and he could smell the fecund odor of soggy vegetation where the high water lapped against the grass at their feet. After a moment, he said, "When you first came back from Brussels, did you see Laura before the flintlock was taken, or only after?"

Finch raised his head to look at him. "Before. Why?"

"How long before?"

Finch turned away again, a faint suggestion of color riding high on his rugged cheekbones. "I saw her my first day in London; the pistol was taken a few days later."

"Where did you see her?"

"I knew she usually went for a walk every morning, sometimes in Grosvenor Square, sometimes in Hyde Park. So I went to the park. It was a lucky guess."

"Was she alone when you saw her?"

"No. She had Thisbe and her young nephew with her, so we spoke for only a moment."

"Did you tell her where you were staying?"

"I may have? Why?"

But Sebastian only shook his head, unwilling to put his thoughts and suspicions into words.

Late that night, Sebastian stood beside his bedroom window, his gaze on the silent, lamplit street below. He was aware of Hero sleeping peacefully in the bed behind him and was careful to move quietly, lest he wake her. Lest she somehow read the drift of his thoughts in the horror she must surely glimpse in his eyes.

He didn't like the implications of what he was learning, didn't like where his thoughts were leading him. The temptation to ignore the promptings of logic, to tell himself that he must be wrong, was damned near overwhelming. Some things . . . some things are too revolting, too horrifying, even to consider.

But that doesn't mean they aren't true.

Chapter 46

*Y*ou're up early," said Gibson the next morning, a stray lock of gray-threaded dark hair falling into his battered, still-swollen eyes as he looked up from the pallid cadaver laid out on the granite slab before him.

Sebastian paused in the open doorway. "I couldn't sleep." The morning air was cold and damp, the light still so pale and gray that Gibson had lit the lantern that hung from a chain over his slab. Its golden glow played over the naked, bloated body of Cato Coldfield, and the smell rising from the days-old corpse was so ripe, Sebastian was careful to breathe through his mouth. "Can you tell me anything yet?"

Gibson set aside his knife and reached for a rag to wipe his hands. "Probably not much you don't already know. He was shot once, from fairly close." He tossed aside the rag and pointed to a dark, round, puckered wound in Coldfield's chest. "That's what this is, obviously. As you can see, it's high enough that it wouldn't have killed him right away, although it probably knocked him over. So then your killer stabbed him." He pointed to a series of slashing wounds. "Here, and here, and here."

"Any idea what kind of knife we're talking about?"

Gibson jerked his chin toward a shelf on the far side of the door, where a blood-encrusted butcher's knife rested on a chipped enameled plate. "Bow Street sent that over this morning. I'm told they found it in the overgrown garden around the cottage, and it looks right to me."

Sebastian shifted to get a better look at the knife. It was old and worn and caked with dried blood. But beneath the blood the blade was carefully honed and polished in a way that reminded Sebastian of the diligently tended thatching tools he'd noticed stacked beside the dead man's cottage. He suspected the knife was Coldfield's own—probably seized by his panicking killer from the cluttered tabletop when that single pistol shot didn't prove fatal.

"When?" said Sebastian, bringing his gaze back to the thatcher's pallid, beard-stubbled face. "When did he die?"

"Could have been early Friday morning, but I suspect Thursday evening or night is more likely."

Sebastian nodded. "That's what I figured."

He became aware of Gibson staring at him. "Do you have any idea who's doing this?"

Sebastian met his friend's narrowed, bloodshot eyes. "Hopefully not."

"What the hell does that mean?"

Sebastian brought his gaze back to the dead man's ravaged chest. "You think he was down on the floor when he was stabbed?"

"I'd say so, yes."

"What about the angle of the shot? Can you tell me anything about that?"

Gibson looked vaguely puzzled. "Can't say I've checked. Why? You thinking this killer might be unusually tall or short?"

"Maybe. Just check, will you?"

Sebastian's next stop was Park Lane. This time there was no trace of a smile on the butler's face when he opened the Duchess of Claiborne's front door.

Humphrey groaned. "*My lord.* You can't. It's barely nine o'clock."

"Oh, good, so she hasn't gone out yet," said Sebastian, and headed for the stairs.

Aunt Henrietta was sitting up in bed, sipping a cup of hot chocolate and reading the *Times*, when Sebastian knocked on her door.

"I heard you talking to Humphrey, so you may as well come in, Devlin," she called out.

"Good heavens," he said when he saw her. "What are you doing awake at nine o'clock in the morning?"

She set aside her chocolate cup. "As it happens, I was reading about the hordes of idiots who are streaming down to Plymouth to hire every yacht, fishing vessel, and rowboat available. It's said they're clustering around the ship by the thousands, with everyone desperate to catch a glimpse of Napoléon. Did you know the sailors on the *Bellerophon* have gone so far as to set up notice boards on which they post the times when the Emperor is expected to take his walks on deck?"

"No, I didn't know. But surely you didn't wake up this early to read the latest news about Bonaparte?"

She leaned back against her pillows and gave a disgruntled huff. "I'm awake at this ungodly hour because every single one of last night's events was so wretchedly dull that I was in bed by one o'clock. If this keeps up I may be tempted to go to Bath or some such equally horrid place."

"Bath?" said Sebastian. "You can't be serious."

"It's either that or Brighton."

"Isn't Claiborne down at the Hall?"

"He is. But so is that ridiculous idiot he married, and how anyone can abide being around her for more than two hours at a stretch is beyond my imagination." She thrust aside her paper. "Enough of this. What do you want from me now?"

He went to stand at one of the velvet-hung windows, his hands clasped behind his back, his gaze on the wet, flawlessly manicured gardens below. He had a feeling he didn't want to hear what he was about to learn. "Lady Salinger, the current Viscount's wife—when did she die?"

"Oh, dear."

Sebastian turned to look at the Duchess. "So it's true, then, is it? She's not dead?"

"I suppose she may as well be."

Sebastian studied her pinched features. "Why? What happened?"

The Duchess sighed. "She was an attractive woman, you know; quite small and delicately built, with lovely pale blond hair, soft blue eyes, and a heart-shaped face. Her daughter—Arabella—looks a fair bit like her, but Georgina was much prettier."

Sebastian nodded. It sounded as if Lady Salinger had looked much like her younger son, Percy.

"Old Septimus Bain was a hopelessly crass, pushing mushroom," Aunt Henrietta was saying, "but he was wise enough to have hired a succession of superbly educated and well-bred governesses to bring up his daughter. Her manners were flawless. She had quite charming ways, as well. She was one of those people who has a knack for making almost everyone like them. Except . . ."

"Except?" prompted Sebastian when she paused.

Henrietta let out a long, pained breath. "The whispers started perhaps six months after she married Salinger. At first it was all servants' talk—you know the dreadful way they can gossip from one house to the next."

"What were they saying?"

"That Georgina had a vicious temper. That she hated to be crossed or made to feel embarrassed or slighted in any way. That she could be sweet and laughing one minute and then turn into a raging vixen. She was with child at the time, so at first her moodiness was attributed to that—and even for a while after Duncan was born because . . . well, you know how some women can become quite cast down after the birth of a child. But eventually Salinger took her off to the Priory and began spending more and more of his time there. When he did come up to London, he frequently came alone."

"What was wrong with her?"

"Who knows? I've no doubt we've all known women—and men—like that at some point: quick to anger, impulsive. Her moods would swing unpredictably from excitement and joy to something dark and reckless. At one point she had a high perch phaeton she used to drive in the park so fast and with such wild abandon that it was a miracle she didn't kill someone—or herself. There were whispers of excessive gambling, too, and crazy spending sprees. I suspect she ran through a significant chunk of her father's money before he was even dead. And then there were the rumors that she used to cut herself."

"*Cut* herself?"

"Yes, with a knife or pieces of broken glass. Not anywhere it showed, but on her . . ." Henrietta paused. "On her legs. Then one day her abigail found her cutting herself with one of Salinger's razors. The woman tried to stop her, and Georgina flew into one of her rages and killed her. Slashed her throat."

"Good God," said Sebastian. "How did they ever keep that quiet?"

Henrietta's lips flattened into a thin line. "Septimus Bain was an extraordinarily wealthy man, and as we all know, wealth brings power. He used it."

"I thought Bain was dead by then." Just one more thing, thought Sebastian, that Rhodes had obviously been lying about.

"Oh, no; he didn't have his fatal apoplexy until a year or two later, after he lost a great deal of his fortune in some bad investments. The abigail's death was declared a suicide—"

"You can't be serious."

"I wish I weren't. In exchange for the verdict, Georgina was quietly committed to a private lunatic asylum out in Bethnal Green. At first everyone was told she had retired to the countryside to recover from the distress of finding her woman with her throat slit. But after a few years, when she became worse instead of better, Salinger let it out that she had died."

Sebastian felt a heavy burden of sadness pressing down on his chest. He didn't ask how the Dowager had come to know all this, but he didn't doubt it for a moment. "Which one?" he asked hoarsely. "Which asylum?"

"Chester House. But you can't mean to go there?"

Chapter 47

*W*ith a deep sense of foreboding, Sebastian left the Dowager's house in Park Lane and turned his horses toward the depressed area on the northeastern fringes of London known as Bethnal Green.

He had never personally visited a madhouse; never had any desire to join the ranks of those who paid to be escorted through the halls of Bedlam and gawk at the public mental hospital's hordes of naked, shrieking inmates. As a private hospital, Chester House was unlikely to turn their patients into an exhibition for the entertainment of the curious. But private asylums all too often hid their own horrors, for far too many of their patients were perfectly sane men and women who were seen as problematic or inconvenient by their families: daughters locked away by their parents for being headstrong and willful; sons judged by stern fathers as hopelessly wild and immoral—or too interested in those of their own sex; wives quietly disposed of by husbands who wanted them out of the way; wealthy heirs and heiresses at the mercy of relatives scheming to control their fortunes . . . It was one of the ugliest, most disturbing secrets of their society. And while the Duchess of Claiborne seemed confident that Lady Salinger's commitment to Chester House had been warranted, Sebastian knew better than to take anything on faith—particularly when it came to murder.

At one time Bethnal Green had been the site of a number of large country homes for wealthy London merchants, back in the days when it was a simple hamlet, a place of market gardens and scattered weavers' cottages. Now the area was a wretched hellhole of breweries and foundries, of crowded, filthy tenements filled with the desperately poor, and of more than one madhouse. Sebastian tended to avoid the district as much as possible.

When he reined in before Chester House, he found himself staring at a rambling, once-grand structure that probably dated to the seventeenth century. It stood back from the lane that ran along the western edge of the old green, with a shallow, half-dead front garden thrown into deep shadow by a pair of towering, ancient yew trees that loomed menacingly over the house itself.

"Walk the horses around the green," he told Tom, handing the boy the chestnuts' reins.

The tiger scrambled forward, obviously anxious to get away from this place. "Aye, gov'nor."

Hopping down to the lane, Sebastian turned toward the house's cracked, sunken front walkway, then found himself hesitating. It was as if he could feel a sickening miasma of fear, horror, and despair emanating from the place, so that he had to force himself to walk toward that grim, forbidding front door.

He was greeted by an aged, slightly stooped matron whose stern expression relaxed as he introduced himself as Sebastian St. Cyr, Viscount Devlin. He explained his interest in seeing Lady Salinger as that of a relative—which wasn't completely a lie, since like most old families the Priestlys were connected to the St. Cyrs somewhere in the past.

"Of course, of course, my lord," exclaimed the matron, her hands coming up with their long, bony fingers entwined together as if in prayer. "Please do have a seat, my lord. I shan't be but a moment. I'll just call Dr. Palmer; I know he'll want to see to you himself."

She hurried away to reappear a few minutes later with a dark-haired, stocky gentleman somewhere in his forties who bowed and introduced himself as Dr. Samuel Palmer. "How extraordinarily kind of you, my lord, to come visit our dear Lady Salinger." He gave a sad shake of his head, his elbows spreading wide as he hooked his thumbs in the pockets of his dark, conservative waistcoat. "It's such an unfortunate case, you know. Most unfortunate. She's been here nearly as long as I have."

"So you were here when she first arrived?"

"I was, yes." He paused, a look of concern drawing his brows together and twitching his prominent nose and chin. "You're quite certain you wish to see her? She probably won't recognize you, you know."

"Yes, quite certain."

"Well, then." Palmer dropped his arms to his sides and extended a hand toward a narrow corridor that opened to their left. "This way, please. She's in the women's wing, of course."

The pungent stench of antiseptic did little to hide the underlying, pervasive odors of vomit, urine, feces, and raw fear. Sebastian walked with the physician down a long, low-ceilinged hall, trying to ignore the smells that clawed at his nostrils and seized the back of his throat. Doors lined both sides of the corridor, with each door containing a square barred opening that allowed a glimpse of the small cell-like room beyond. After one horrifying, unwitting glance at a woman chained naked to the wall, Sebastian was careful to keep his gaze fixed straight ahead. But he knew he would never forget the chorus of moans, shrieks, and mad, furtive whispers rising from those shadowy cells.

He glanced at the physician, who'd obviously long ago grown inured to the sights, sounds, and smells of the place. "In your estimation, was Lady Salinger insane when she arrived?"

"Of course she was," said Palmer. "Oh, she might not have appeared so to the casual observer. But a woman doesn't take a razor to her abigail if she's sane, now, does she?" He drew up before a door near the end of the corridor. "Here she is. Did you want to go in? Because I warn you, she's liable to become agitated if you do. She's grown quite fearful and screams if anyone tries to touch her or even come near her. It makes it difficult to take care of her bodily needs."

The room beyond was in dark shadow, for the shutters were closed over the room's single high window. Through the barred opening in the door before him Sebastian could see a skeletally thin woman dressed in a dirty, ragged gown who sat motionless on the edge of a narrow cot, staring at the wall before her. Georgina Priestly couldn't be more than thirty-nine or forty, but this woman's hair was completely white, an uncombed tangle that framed a wizened, pinched face.

"That's her?" said Sebastian, his breath catching in his throat.

"It is, yes. As I said, a sad, sad case."

The room was small, furnished with only the cot, although he had to admit it looked relatively clean. "Was she ever given any treatment?"

"Oh, yes; of course. We tried all the usual regimens, beginning with daily cold plunge baths."

Sebastian looked over at him. "Cold plunge baths?"

"Yes. The patient is repeatedly submersed in icy water. The idea is to shake them out of their insanity."

"Does it ever work?"

Palmer's broad chest expanded with his sigh. "Very rarely, unfortunately."

Sebastian had to force himself to ask, "What else?"

"As I said, the usual regimen—bleeding, blistering, emetics, purges . . . Anything and everything that might expel the melancholic humors. She fought us at first, I'm afraid. We don't like to use restraints, but with many patients it becomes necessary."

Restraints, thought Sebastian, his gaze on the small, fine-boned woman who still showed a faint, ghostly resemblance to her younger son, Percy. Were there any patients, he wondered, who calmly submitted to being stripped naked and plunged repeatedly into icy water, blistered with caustic chemicals, and dosed with noxious medicines designed to induce violent vomiting and the voiding of the bowels? Probably not at first. But if they weren't insane when they arrived, they soon would be.

"We even tried Erasmus Darwin's rotation therapy for a time," Palmer was saying.

"I don't believe I'm familiar with that," said Sebastian.

"It makes use of a chair suspended from a high ceiling by ropes. The chair is turned one way thirty to forty times, then let go to spin back around. The therapy is typically applied for one or two hours at a time, three to four times a day, for a month. The results are amazing, since it generally evacuates the bowels, bladder, and stomach simultaneously, making a profound impression on the patient's organs of sensibility."

"So I would imagine. I take it none of this worked?"

"Unfortunately, no. As I said, at first she fought us, sometimes quite violently. But the attendants soon put a stop to that. She then became fearful, cringing in the corner of her room whenever anyone came near her. After about eight months she lapsed into a deep depressive state, as you see now. She's rarely difficult these days, as long as we leave her pretty much alone."

Sebastian felt the bile rise in his throat and had to swallow. "Does her husband ever visit her?"

"Lord Salinger? Oh, yes. Time was, he used to come once a week. I fear at first he had difficulty grasping the importance of some of our treatments, which he found disturbing. But he was eventually brought to understand their necessity. Inevitably, his visits have become more and more infrequent over the years. In the beginning he would get quite distressed, for she used to cry and beg him to take her home. Now I'm not convinced she even recognizes him. But to give the man credit, he still comes. So many of our patients' families leave their relatives with us and never come back, not even when the unfortunates finally 'shuffle off this mortal coil,' as the saying goes."

Sebastian found he could take no more and turned abruptly away. "I've seen enough, thank you."

"Of course," said Palmer, turning with him. "Do feel free to come back anytime, my lord, anytime."

Sebastian found himself listening to the echo of their footsteps as they walked back down that dark, hellish corridor. How could anyone be subjected to such treatment and remain sane? he wondered. He suspected the truth was, they couldn't.

Somehow he managed to thank Dr. Palmer and the bony, stoop-shouldered matron. On the front step he paused for a moment, gratefully drawing the fresh air deep into his lungs as he heard the *snick* of the heavy door closing behind him. He stepped off the shallow porch, took one step, two.

He'd almost reached the dirt lane that ran along the green when he felt his gorge rise inexorably in his throat. Turning, he hunched over, his hands braced against his thighs, and was violently sick in the straggling, half-dead hedge of dusty hollies bordering that ancient, broken walkway.

"Ye feeling all right there, gov'nor?" asked Tom as they drove away from the green. "Yer lookin' a bit peaked."

"I'll be fine," said Sebastian, guiding his horses past the scattered, tumbledown cottages and open stretches of market gardens that lined the lane leading toward Shoreditch Road.

He couldn't have said what he'd been expecting to find at Chester House. Evidence of a hidden dark side to Laura McInnis's seemingly grief-stricken brother, perhaps? Confirmation that Georgina Priestly had been well and truly mad when locked away forever behind the grim walls of a private lunatic asylum?

But the reality of what he'd just heard and witnessed was considerably more horrifying than anything he might have imagined. And he couldn't help but wonder, Was Georgina truly insane when she struck out in fury and killed her abigail? Much as he wanted to believe it, he was no longer certain. Unstable, perhaps, but mad? How did one define madness? Where was the dividing line between what we liked to think of as sanity and the beginnings of lunacy? Was there even a line? How easy was it to slip over that indistinct, perhaps even arbitrary border? He thought about Dr. Samuel Palmer, a well-respected, widely admired physician who spent his days routinely torturing the helpless men and women consigned to his care. How could anyone define him as sane?

It was an unpleasant and ultimately unproductive line of thought, and Sebastian tried to push it away. He was aware of the warmth of the sun on his face, of the rhythmic action of the chestnuts' powerful hindquarters as they left the open fields behind to pass now between rows of workshops, all shuttered for the Sabbath.

He couldn't have said what warned him. A flicker of movement caught out of the corner of his eye? The twitching of the near gelding's ear? But he was already reining in when a familiar-looking big man on a dapple gray burst from behind the end wall of a cooperage to plow his horse straight into the chestnuts.

Swearing, Sebastian hauled on the reins as the plunging, squealing horses slewed the curricle sideways across the road. He almost had them under control when a second rider in a green coat spurred his horse from behind a nearby blacksmith's shop.

"You were warned," said the man in the green coat, calmly extending his arm to level a flintlock pistol at Sebastian's head and ease back the hammer.

Chapter 48

*R*un, Tom!" shouted Sebastian, his whip cracking as he sent the thong flashing out to cut deeply across Green Coat's upper face and eyes.

The man screamed, the pistol discharging into the air as his horse reared up, throwing him.

"You bastard," swore the man on the dapple gray, reaching awkwardly to jerk a flintlock from his waistband.

Rising up, Sebastian threw himself at the man, knocking him from the saddle. They went down together, the big oaf hitting the ground first, with Sebastian on top of him. The man's pistol went flying, the impact driving the breath from his chest with a painful *oooff* that left him gasping for air.

Rolling away from him, Sebastian snatched up the fallen pistol, thumbed back the hammer, and pivoted to shoot Green Coat in the chest as the man picked himself up from nearby and charged, blood streaming from the cut across his face.

The green-coated man spun around, took one step, and collapsed.

"Lieutenant!" shouted the man from the dapple gray, his face twisting into a snarl as he lumbered to his feet, fists clenched. Sebastian dropped the spent pistol, yanked his dagger from the sheath in his boot, and sent it whistling through the air.

The blade hit the man in the throat and sank deep.

For a moment he wavered, his eyes widening, his features going slack with shock. He sank to his knees, reaching out with one splayed hand that fluttered back to his side as he flopped forward onto his face and lay still.

"Gor," whispered Tom from where he stood holding the reins of the nervous, snorting chestnuts above their bits and making soft, soothing noises. "Are they dead?"

"I don't know yet," said Sebastian, breathing heavily as he pushed to his feet. "But I told you to run, damn it."

"I couldn't leave the horses, gov'nor!"

Sebastian grunted and went to turn over the big man. He flopped onto his back, his mouth open, his eyes empty.

Swiping one crooked forearm across his sweat-dampened face, Sebastian went to crouch down beside the green-coated man. The bullet had caught him high in the chest. He wasn't dead yet, but he soon would be.

"Who sent you?" said Sebastian, slipping an arm beneath the man's head so he wouldn't choke on his own blood.

The man reached up to grab Sebastian's coat, the hand spasming with pain.

"Tell me," said Sebastian. "For God's sake, why protect him now?"

The man looked up at him with pain-filled, anguished eyes. Sebastian saw a tear form in the corner of one eye to roll down his blood-splattered cheek, his shattered chest heaving as he struggled to get the words out. "B . . . b . . ."

Sebastian could feel the man beginning to go limp in his arms.

"Basil? Basil Rhodes? Is that it?" Or was the man trying to say *bastard*? "Who sent you?" shouted Sebastian again.

But the man stared up at him with dead, vacant eyes.

The authorities of Bethnal Green were not pleased to have their Sunday disturbed by two killings. It was a long time before Sebastian made it back to Brook Street. By then, Hero had taken the boys to visit Hendon in Berkeley Square. So he changed his dusty, torn clothes, left her a message, and had his black mare saddled to ride out to Richmond Park.

He went first to the keeper's cottage, where he found the keeper's wife, Sally Hammond, feeding the ducks down by the pond. Cato Coldfield's black-and-white dog, Bounder, lay a short distance away, his head on his paws and his ears limp.

"How's he doing?" asked Sebastian, nodding toward the dog.

"Oh, poor Bounder. It's gonna take him time to adjust, no getting around that. I'll hear him whining sometimes and know he's missing Cato." She gave a faint shake of her head. "That man was a nasty brute—no reason not to call him what he was, even if he is dead. But there's no denying he was always good to his dogs, and they loved him." She paused, then added, "Gotta give the devil his due when it's due."

Sebastian studied her plump, sad face. "Who do you think killed him?"

"Me?" She looked vaguely surprised by his question. "How would I know, my lord?"

"An irascible man like that must have made more than his fair share of enemies."

The woman stared out over the wind-ruffled gray waters of the pond, her eyes hidden by half-lowered lashes. "I can't say many people liked him." She hesitated, then added, "To be honest, I don't know if I can think of anyone who liked him. But to take a gun and shoot him? Who would do that? There aren't many people around here even own a gun."

"Did you ever see Coldfield himself with a gun?"

She nodded. "He had one a long time ago. But it's been years."

"How many years?"

"Fourteen, to be exact. I know because it was back before that first woman and her daughter were shot and killed in the park. It's one of the reasons I've always thought Cato was the one who did it—because I knew he had this big old double-barreled flintlock pistol. But then, after the murders, I never saw it again. Always figured he must've hid it someplace."

"When was the last time you saw him?"

"Cato? Why, this past Thursday, it was. He came around here looking for my Richard—said he had something he wanted to tell him. But Richard had gone into town after some wire he needed, so he never did talk to him. And then the next thing we knew, you came here with Bounder, saying the man was dead."

"Do you know if Cato could write?"

Sally Hammond stared at him blankly. "I don't think so, but I can't say I know for certain, my lord. Why?"

"Just wondering. When you saw Cato on Thursday, how was he? Did he seem agitated in any way? Worried?"

"Well, you met the man, didn't you? I mean, he was always more'n a bit agitated. That's the way he was. But he was in a rare taking that day, no denying that. Said some boy'd been askin' him all sorts of questions about the killings fourteen years ago—about the way the bodies were laid out and exactly how they'd been killed, and how Cato thought it must've been done."

Sebastian felt something twist deep in his gut. "Did he say who this boy was?"

"No. Just called him either 'the lad' or 'some nob's get.' That's all. Struck me as more'n a bit strange, seein' as how he made it sound like this had happened back *before* the second lady and her daughter were killed."

Sebastian stared across the pond toward the keeper's cottage, where a rustic bench surrounded by roses and hollyhocks and laven-der stood against one whitewashed wall. He had a vivid, painful memory of sitting there while he talked to Arabella, and of watching her bare fingers ruffle the fur of the kitten in her lap.

Aloud, he said, "Did Cato happen to mention how old this boy was? Or maybe describe him in any way?"

"No, my lord. Like I said, he didn't have much to say about the boy himself, only the questions the lad had been asking. Spooked Cato, it did. He was always a superstitious one, so lookin' back on it, I guess maybe he saw it as a bad omen." She stared at Sebastian, her features pinched with worry. "Surely you don't think that boy could've had anything to do with what happened in the park?"

Sebastian looked her in the eye and lied. "No, of course not."

He went next to the deserted, death-haunted meadow beside the quietly purling stream. The ground here was still damp from the re-cent rains, the air clean and fresh and filled with a glorious chorus of birdsong from the surrounding chestnuts and oaks.

His mare's reins held slack in one hand, Sebastian went to stand in the center of the meadow. All traces of what had happened here barely a week before were now gone. The heavy rains had washed away the blood that once stained the blades of grass and bare earth;

time, rain, and sunshine had obliterated the impression once left by a cheerful plaid picnic rug. The rug, abandoned crockery, and picnic basket had all been carried off by a man who was now dead.

The mare shook her head, jangling the bridle, and Sebastian reached out to pat the horse's neck. "Even the sense of what happened here is fading, isn't it, girl?"

Leila shook her head again.

Turning away, he tied the mare's reins to a low tree branch and started to search.

It took him the better part of an hour, but he finally found what he was looking for wadded up and thrust into the hollow of a tree: a pair of small white gloves folded together like stockings.

His mouth uncomfortably dry, Sebastian carefully unrolled the gloves. They were still faintly damp from the recent rains, but the tree's hollow had mostly sheltered them. They were expensive gloves, crafted of the finest kid, exactly what the daughter of a viscount might wear when going on a picnic to Richmond Park. The bloodstains on the fingers and palms were now old and dark. But the pattern of the stains was essentially what one would expect if their wearer had helped her brother pose the bodies of her aunt and cousin in a posture precisely calculated to echo that of an infamous murder from fourteen years before.

Sebastian's last stop was the modest manor house of Mr. Thomas Barrows, Esquire, where he found the barrister's two sons sitting side by side on the top rail of a paddock fence and watching a dapple gray mare and her pretty new foal graze peacefully nearby.

"I'm here because I need you to tell me again exactly what you heard and saw that day in Richmond Park," said Sebastian after the brothers had greeted him warily. "From the very beginning."

The brothers looked at each other, their faces drawn and tense. Then Harry sucked in a deep breath and said, "Of course, my lord."

Sebastian took them through it all—their arrival at the park; their talk and careless laughter as they drank wine beneath the clear blue sky; the shocking, unmistakable crack of first one pistol shot, then the next.

"I know you said you thought the shots were so close together that they must have come from a double-barreled pistol because there wouldn't have been time for anyone to reload. But are you quite certain the shots came from the same gun?"

Harry stared at him. "You mean, could we have heard one man firing two different guns, or maybe two men firing two guns, rather than one man firing a double-barreled pistol?"

"Yes, that's exactly what I mean."

Harry swallowed. "I suppose it is possible, my lord. Although I never thought . . . I mean, I guess I assumed . . ." His voice trailed away.

"Can you try to think back? See if you can recall what the two shots sounded like?"

Harry closed his eyes, his nostrils flaring as he fell silent for a moment. Then he opened his eyes and shook his head. "I'm sorry, sir. I can't remember clearly enough to say for certain."

Sebastian looked at the younger brother. "How about you, Ben?"

"No, sir. I'm sorry, sir."

"That's all right," said Sebastian. He was painfully aware of the stricken look on the brothers' faces, but he couldn't stop yet. "Tell me about after you found the bodies, when the children came up."

Harry cupped one hand over his nose and mouth, then let it fall. "Oh, God. I wish . . . I really wish we could have stopped them sooner than we did. I'll never forget the expression on that girl's face when she stared across the meadow and saw . . . that."

"How close did they get?"

"Close enough to see the bodies, I'm afraid, sir. And then the girl . . . She opened her mouth like she was going to scream, even though she couldn't seem to make a sound. That's when Ben and I realized we needed to keep them from getting any closer."

"So neither one came close enough to touch the bodies of their aunt or cousin?"

The boys looked shocked at the suggestion. "Oh, no, sir."

"I didn't think so," said Sebastian, "but I wanted to be certain. I know their father is very grateful that you took care of his children the way you did."

Harry dropped his gaze to the ground. "I think we could have done better, sir. I mean, if only we could have stopped them from seeing it at all."

Sebastian reached out to rest his hand on the young man's shoulder. "Don't beat yourself up. You didn't even know the children were there until they appeared, so how could you have stopped them? You did what needed to be done." He gripped Harry's shoulder, then let him go. "Thank you for taking the time to talk to me again, and I'm sorry to have had to ask you to remember a day I know you'd much rather forget."

"We're never going to be able to forget that day, my lord," said Ben softly. "Never."

Chapter 49

Sebastian was in the mews, handing the tired mare over to his groom, Giles, when Tom came skittering into the stables.

"Gov'nor! Yer back! I been talkin' to some more of Rhodes's servants, like ye asked."

Sebastian patted the mare's neck, then turned. "And did you learn anything?" he said as Giles led the Arabian away, muttering something under his breath.

Tom shook his head. "Not a blessed thing, gov'nor. None o' the ones who've been willin' t' talk t' me 'as seen 'im meetin' with any young coves in the past week or so. And nobody seems t' know where 'e took 'isself off to last Sunday. Fact is, they're in a bit of a puzzle about that themselves. You want I should keep tryin'?"

"No, never mind that for now. There's something else I need you to do."

"I don't believe it," said Hero some time later when she and Sebastian took the boys for a walk along the Thames at Millbank, the low-lying rural area to the southwest of Westminster where a new iron bridge was going up that would someday join these open fields to Vauxhall on the far bank. Out here away from the city, the air was fresh and clean, with a soft breeze that lifted the green leaves of a nearby stand of chestnuts against the clearing sky. "I simply can't believe it. Percy and Arabella are *children*. It isn't only a matter of *how* could they do such a thing; it's also *why*. Why would they want to kill anyone, let alone their own aunt and cousin—not to mention all the others?"

They paused as Simon squatted down beside Patrick to see what the older boy had spotted in the shallows where the river lapped against a sandy stretch of the bank. Watching them, Sebastian himself found it hard to believe he was suggesting that a child barely ten years older than these two boys could have done something so monstrous. "I can't begin to explain why. And the truth is, I haven't figured out all the hows, either. But the inconsistencies and coincidences have mounted to the point that I can no longer ignore it as a possibility."

"You can't think that boy broke into Major Finch's room and stole his pistol."

"I know it sounds unbelievable."

"It sounds unbelievable because it is! You also don't know that the 'nob's get' asking Cato Coldfield about the murders was Percy."

"No. Although Percy told me himself he's fascinated by murders and murderers."

"That doesn't mean he is one himself!"

"No. But it might suggest why he would kill someone: to see what it feels like. And to see if he could get away with it."

"Surely a little boy couldn't be so . . . evil."

Sebastian looked over at her. "At what age do you think it starts? That lack of caring for others, I mean."

"I don't know. But not at thirteen! Surely?"

"Actually, I suspect that fundamental lack of human feeling only makes sense if it's never there—unless it's destroyed by the kind of brutal hardships a pampered viscount's son is unlikely to have experienced."

She turned her head away, one hand coming up to hold back her windblown hair as she stared out over the choppy, sun-sparkled expanse of the river beside them. She was silent for a long moment, then said, "Even if we should somehow discover that the boy who spoke to Coldfield that day was Percy, it could still be a coincidence."

"It could be."

"And Arabella could have bloodied her gloves by cutting herself on something, and decided to hide them rather than risk a scolding. Or perhaps she shoved the gloves into the hollow of that tree intending to go back for them, then forgot. Given what happened that day, it would be totally understandable."

"Yes."

She drew a deep breath, her features composed in troubled lines as she watched Simon pick up a rock and throw it awkwardly into the water. "What about the attack on Percy in the park? If the children are the killers, then how do you explain that?"

"The only witnesses to the first supposed attack were Arabella and her abigail, remember? And the abigail is now dead."

"You're seriously suggesting the children—what? Tricked their governess into eating something that would make her so ill she wouldn't be able to accompany them on their morning walk in the park? And then fabricated the entire incident? And *that's* why the abigail was killed? Because she was threatening to tell someone the truth?"

"Yes."

"Do you know how unbelievable that sounds?"

"Yes."

"And Gilly Harper? Why kill her?"

"I've no idea. I never have been able to understand how Gilly's death fits into any of this."

Hero resolutely shook her head. "No. It can't be. They're children!"

"Think about this," said Sebastian. "Who sent us after first Pitcairn and then Finch? The children. And when I was careful not to tell Lovejoy about Pitcairn, Percy made sure he knew."

"You're suggesting they were deliberately trying to throw suspicion onto Finch and Pitcairn?"

"I am. And then, when those misdirections didn't seem to be producing an arrest, Percy evaded his father's restrictions in order to come to Brook Street and tell me about the chimney sweep Hiram Dobbs."

"Surely you don't see that as suspicious?"

"At the time I didn't, no. But now, in retrospect? I do."

"But Percy couldn't possibly have traveled all the way out to Richmond Thursday night to kill Cato Coldfield."

Sebastian was silent for a moment, his eyes narrowing as he turned to look back at the grim walls of the new penitentiary being built farther downriver, in a low marshy area that critics warned would surely turn the prison into a death trap. "That's the one part of this that makes me think I'm seeing a pattern where nothing exists except happenstance."

"That's the *only* thing that makes you suspect you might be wrong? Seriously?"

Sebastian gave her a crooked smile and reached out to take her hand. "Think about this: Thisbe was supposed to go on that picnic, but her mother made her stay home as punishment for something the girl says she didn't do. I'd like to know what that something was."

Hero watched as the two boys crouched down, laughing, with their hands tucked up under their armpits and waddled along the riverbank, quacking in imitation of a trio of ducks that had come in to land farther up the bank. "I was thinking about going for a walk in Grosvenor Square tomorrow morning in the hopes I might run into her again. I can't stop thinking about what the poor child must be going through, losing both her mother and her sister at the same time—and in such a horrible way. But . . ."

"But?" prompted Sebastian when she paused.

She swung to face him. "To be deliberately pumping an innocent, grieving child for information about her cousins under the guise of offering her my sympathy and friendship strikes me as vile."

He took both her hands in his. "Except that, as you said, you were planning on trying to see her again anyway."

"Well, that's a pathetic sop to my conscience if ever I heard one."

"Perhaps. The thing is, if there were a way to be more honest and direct with Thisbe without risking increasing her distress, then I'd take it. But there isn't. And there is still so much about that day we don't know but she very well might. Hell, I'm not entirely certain who came up with the idea for the picnic in the first place."

"I thought Arabella told you the picnic was her aunt Laura's idea—or Emma's."

"She did. But at this point I'm not inclined to take anything either of those two children tells us as the unquestioned truth. Are you?"

She met his gaze and held it. And he saw in her stricken gray eyes all the pain this was causing her, and all her doubts, along with the unwanted realization that there was too much sense in what he was saying for it to be easily dismissed. She drew a deep, ragged breath and let it out slowly. "No. No, I'm not."

Monday, 31 July

"I was hoping I'd see you again," said Thisbe the next morning as she walked with Hero along one of the gravel paths that wound through Grosvenor Square's naturalized plantings. The sun had come up bright and hot that morning, so that the wet gardens around them seemed to steam in the rising heat.

Hero tamped down an unpleasant twinge of guilt. Reaching out, she took the child's hand in her own, gave it a squeeze, and said lightly, "It's lovely to have the sun out again, isn't it?"

Thisbe nodded, although her features remained pinched and wan. "Malcolm made it home last night, you know."

"No, I didn't know. That is good news. I know you've been missing him."

Thisbe kept her gaze fixed straight ahead, but Hero saw a quiver pass over her small features. "They're going to bury Mama and Emma the day after tomorrow, on Wednesday."

Thank God, thought Hero. But all she said was, "I am so, so sorry, Thisbe."

Thisbe blinked and dashed a gloved fist across her eyes. "I keep having dreams about that picnic," she said softly. "Even though I don't want to, even though I wasn't even there, I still see it in my dreams. Miss Braithwaite says it's because I keep thinking about it."

"I don't believe anyone can control their dreams, Thisbe."

"That's what I told Miss Braithwaite. It's not like I *want* to dream about it. I never want to go on a picnic again." Her voice broke, and she swallowed before saying quietly, "Oh, how I wish Mama had never given in to Arabella and agreed to do it!"

Hero felt her breath catch. "The picnic was Arabella's idea?"

Thisbe wiped her eyes again and sniffed. "She started talking about it weeks ago. Mama wasn't particularly keen on it, but Arabella was so excited about the thought of it and kept pushing for it so hard that in the end Mama gave in. She was always telling us about how we needed to be extra kind to Arabella and Percy on account of Aunt Georgina. Whenever one or the other of them would do something nasty, Mama would sigh and say how we had to make allowances for them because they were so sad and lonely, growing up without a mother and with only governesses and nursemaids to take care of them. She said they needed to know *we* loved them, and so she was always pushing Emma to spend more time with Arabella— as if it weren't obvious to everyone that Arabella absolutely *hated* Emma."

Hero felt an unpleasant sensation crawl up her spine. "She did?"

"Malcolm always said it was because Arabella was jealous of Emma."

"Jealous? Why?"

Thisbe wrinkled her nose. "It's kinda weird. Arabella is always bragging about how her papa is a viscount, while our papa is only a baronet, and how the Priestlys go *way* back, all the way to the Conqueror. Except the McInnises are *almost* as old, and our mama was a Priestly, too, whereas Arabella's Grandpa Bain started out as a clerk." Thisbe colored faintly. "Mama always used to say it's shallow and ill-bred to talk like that. But the thing is, it's *Arabella* who's always going on and on about how grand the Priestlys are. It's like it eats at her, knowing that *both* sides of her family aren't as wellborn as she wishes they were. Not that the Priestlys don't have what Malcolm calls a *few skeletons* in their closet. Grandpapa Priestly was a horrid gambler, you know. Malcolm says that by the time he was fifty, Grandpapa Priestly had lost so much money that he almost lost the Priory, too. That's why Uncle Miles had to marry 'beneath him,' as my great-aunt

Honoria is always saying. Except then, even though Uncle Miles married Arabella's mama because her papa was so rich, before he died old Mr. Bain lost most of his money on account of what Malcolm calls 'bad investments.' So while the Priory is no longer encumbered, it isn't as though Uncle Miles is exactly *flush*, as Malcolm would say."

Hero stared at the child beside her. "Malcolm told you all this?"

"No. No one ever tells me anything. But I heard him talking to Emma about it. He said it was one of the things that drives Arabella crazy."

"Emma talked to Malcolm about your cousin?"

Thisbe nodded again. "It was after Arabella got so mad at Emma that she tried to scratch her eyes out."

"When did that happen?"

"A week or two after Waterloo. It was horrible. Malcolm had to pull Arabella off Emma, and Emma, she was so mad at Arabella that she was screaming at her, saying she was as crazy as her mother." Thisbe threw a quick glance back at her governess, then lowered her voice. "She's not really dead, you know—Aunt Georgina, I mean. She's locked up in a madhouse. No one ever talks about it because it's supposed to be this big dark secret. But Malcolm found out about it and told Emma. So then Mama got mad at Malcolm and Emma, which wasn't fair, because Arabella started it all—*and* was saying how she hated Emma and wished she was dead, on top of that."

Hero had assumed the children all believed the polite fiction given to the ton, that Lady Salinger had died. What would it do to a child like Percy, she wondered, who'd grown up believing his mother was dead, only to suddenly learn such a horrible truth?

What must it have done to Arabella, who could surely remember her mother?

Hero chose her next words carefully. "What did Arabella do after Emma said that about her mother?"

"It was really eerie. I mean, she'd been acting so wild, trying to scratch Emma's face and screaming, 'I hate you.' But then, after Emma said that about Aunt Georgina, Arabella went all still and cold-like, and said in this strange, high-pitched voice, *I could kill you.*'" Thisbe gave a little shiver, her head falling back as she watched a red squirrel scamper up the trunk of a nearby oak. "To tell the truth, in some ways I didn't mind too much being told I couldn't go on the picnic—I mean, not with Arabella going, too. I don't like being around her. She's . . . She can be scary."

Hero found she had to clear her throat before she trusted her voice enough to say, "You told me you had to stay home because you were being punished for something you didn't do?"

Thisbe set her jaw hard. "That was on account of Arabella. She wrote my name all over one of her books and then told Mama I had done it. But I didn't! I promise I didn't. Why would I? I mean, if I wanted to ruin her stupid book, why not just spill ink over it? Why write my own name so everyone would know it was me?"

Hero was aware of Laura's daughter looking up at her with tear-filled, hurting eyes. "Oh, Thisbe," she said, drawing the child into her arms and holding her close. She didn't want to believe a fifteen-year-old girl and her thirteen-year-old brother were capable of plotting and executing such a diabolical series of murders.

But she didn't like the way the facts were beginning to line up.

Chapter 50

Sebastian had only recently returned from his morning ride in the park when Hero came to stand in the doorway of his dressing room. Her cheeks were flushed from her walk in the fresh morning air and she still wore a moss green spencer over her muslin walking dress, with her broad-brimmed straw hat dangling at her side from its ribbons. But her face was solemn, her eyes wide and still.

"I think I might owe you an apology," she said.

He looked up from adjusting his cuffs. "Is what you learned from Thisbe that bad?"

"Actually," she said, walking forward to slip her arms around his waist and lay her head on his shoulder as she held him close, "it's worse."

One seemingly innocent incident or remark, followed by another and another and another. Taken all together, they formed a damning sequence. But that didn't prove anything, and Sebastian knew it.

Thinking over Thisbe's series of artless revelations, he went, first, to the Middle Temple. But Michael Finch hadn't seen his brother since breakfast, and a quick search of the gardens along the Thames and the Temple Church proved fruitless.

And so Sebastian turned toward the west, to the Haymarket.

Damion Pitcairn might teach the sons of London's wealthy elite in their own homes, but for his less exalted fencing students he often made use of a rubble-filled wasteland near Piccadilly. Once occupied mainly by aged terrace houses and shops that had been torn down in the past year, the area would someday be part of a grand scheme envisioned by the Prince Regent and his architect John Nash to clear away a section of the West End's old, fading streets and replace them with a broad, sweeping new street lined with rows of elegant, classically fronted structures. But the actual building process was slow to get underway, leaving vast stretches of dusty lots filled with piles of old timbers, used bricks and stones, and other debris.

At one end of the stalled construction site, near the propped-up relic of a stretch of old stone wall, lay the ancient courtyard of what must once have been a substantial Renaissance-era house, its cobbled surface worn smooth by the passing of the centuries. As Sebastian worked his way toward it, he could hear the familiar quick patter of stockinged feet and the ringing clang of foil meeting foil.

"Careful," he heard Pitcairn say to his student. "When used sparingly and at the proper time, the replacement is a clever means of scoring. But don't try to use it when your opponent makes a fast direct return."

Sebastian could see them now, two lithe young men dancing back and forth across the sun-soaked ancient courtyard, their foils coming together again and again in a delicate play of feint, thrust, parry, and riposte. From the distance came the familiar shouts of costermongers, the cries of street sellers, and all the racket of modern London. But the scene here was timeless: two skilled swordsmen practicing an age-old art. Sebastian leaned his shoulders against the crumbling remnant of an old chimney, crossed his arms at his chest, and watched.

Pitcairn's unknown pupil was lean and quick, with the supple grace of a dancer and the strength and agility of a born athlete. Both master and pupil had cast aside their hats, coats, and boots, stripping down to breeches, shirts, waistcoats, and fencing masks of wire and leather. But the more Sebastian watched, the more he realized the pupil's mask didn't simply protect its wearer from an opponent's sword; it also helped hide a dangerous secret.

When the lesson ended, Pitcairn pulled off his mask and paused to confer briefly with his pupil. Then he tucked the mask under one arm and turned to walk toward Sebastian.

"She's very good," said Sebastian.

A flicker of surprise passed over the fencing master's features. He glanced over to where the girl now sat perched on the steps of what looked like an old mounting block, her head bent as she tugged on her boots. "She's more than 'very good'; she could be one of the best—if she were a he."

Sebastian watched the girl push to her feet and reach for her coat and hat. Her nose was small and straight, her cheekbones high, her lips full, her skin a rich golden hue. And yet he knew that however beautiful or brilliant or talented she might be, the options open to her in their world were limited.

"But you're not here to talk about my pupil, are you?" said Pitcairn, swiping one crooked elbow across his damp forehead. "I had some bloody Bow Street Runner following me last night when I left the theater. I suppose he thought he was being clever and unobtrusive, but if so, then he failed. Am I about to be taken up for murder?"

"Not to my knowledge, no."

Pitcairn sat down and began to pull on his boots. "According to one of the bits of muslin who works the Haymarket, someone was also hanging around asking questions about me yesterday afternoon. You know anything about that?"

"No."

"In other words, your insight into the precariousness of my situation might not be exactly up-to-date, hmm?"

"Always a possibility," agreed Sebastian. "There's no denying the Palace is pushing Bow Street for an arrest—any arrest. How good is your alibi for that Sunday?"

Pitcairn's head fell back as he looked up, his face bleak. "I don't have one. I was alone, working on a concerto."

"Unfortunate. Because I've no doubt that if the Home Office can come up with an excuse to hang a Spencean, they'd be more than happy to take it."

Pitcairn stood and reached for his coat. "Since when do they need an excuse?"

"Oh, they always like to have one. Although if they can't find one, they aren't above making one up."

The fencing master shrugged into his coat, then straightened his lapels with studied care. "Exactly why are you here?"

"I'm wondering if Emma ever talked to you about her cousin Arabella."

Pitcairn turned to hunker down and stow his foil and mask in the canvas case that lay open at his feet. "Why? Why are you asking me about that?"

"Did she?"

He was silent for a moment as he fastened the straps of the case, then pushed to his feet. "She did—several times. There was no love lost between those two cousins."

"So I've been told. Do you know why?"

"You've met the girl, haven't you? Arabella, I mean."

"I have, yes. She comes across as a quiet, innocent child."

"Ah, yes; I've seen that act, too."

"You're suggesting it's an act?"

"Let's put it this way: Arabella might be only fifteen, but she's the kind of female a man like me stays far, far away from. Or at least, he does if he's wise. And while I may have made any number of stupid mistakes in my life, I'm not that stupid."

"Care to elaborate on that?"

Pitcairn glanced over to where the girl had been. She was now gone. "Not really, no."

"I take it Arabella was trying to attract your interest?"

"If you were a man in my position, would you answer that?"

Sebastian met Pitcairn's intense gaze and held it. "Probably not."

Pitcairn sucked in his cheeks and looked away again, his throat working as he swallowed. And for one brief moment, the swordsman's usual facade of rigid self-control slipped, and Sebastian could see all of his grief, all of the painful longing and desperate yearning of a man who'd just lost a woman he would never have been allowed to have but couldn't stop loving anyway. Then the fencing master gave a faint shake of his head, and that brief moment of vulnerability was gone.

"What?" said Sebastian, watching him.

Pitcairn reached for his hat and positioned it carefully. "It's just . . . the only reason Arabella was even doing it was because she was always so bloody jealous of Emma."

"Do you know why?"

"Why?" Pitcairn shrugged. "Jealousy is such a poisonous emotion, isn't it? Once it gets started, it can eat away at a person until they're so consumed by it that they lose all sense of proportion. All I know is, whatever Emma had, Arabella wanted—particularly a grandfather who wasn't 'tainted' by trade and a mother who wasn't certified insane. But it didn't stop there. She was jealous of Emma's house because it was bigger than hers and on Grosvenor Square; she was jealous because everyone talked about how pretty Emma was. Someone admired Emma's singing last Christmas, so Arabella was jealous of her voice; their dancing instructor praised Emma's dancing, so Arabella was jealous of that, too. I don't know exactly how she realized that Emma and I were . . . friends; all I know is that she decided she wanted me to find her attractive, too. And believe me, nothing is more terrifying to someone like me than the attentions of a wellborn English schoolgirl he can't afford either to spurn or encourage."

"So which did you do?" said Sebastian as they began to pick their way through the rubble, toward the street. "Spurn or encourage her?"

"What do you think? I was trying to do neither, but it wasn't easy. The way she kept finding an excuse to show up around the time of Malcolm's lessons, it had reached the point I was counting the days until he left for Scotland. Except then . . ." He blinked, his voice trailing away.

"I take it Emma told you Lady Salinger is in an asylum?"

Pitcairn pressed his lips together and nodded. "She did, yes—but only recently."

"Any particular reason?"

"It came out when she was telling me about some big argument Lady McInnis had with Salinger over his children."

Sebastian knew a flicker of surprise. Basil Rhodes had said something about a fight between Salinger and his sister, but Sebastian had dismissed it as one more of the royal bastard's lies. "When was this? The fight between Lady McInnis and her brother, I mean."

"I don't know exactly, but it was a while ago—maybe a few weeks after Waterloo?"

Rhodes had claimed the argument took place right before the murders. But then, that was exactly the kind of subtle lie Prinny's bastard would tell. Sebastian said, "Do you know precisely what about the children caused the argument?"

"I gathered Lady McInnis had been worried about Arabella and Percy for some time. But then they did something particularly awful. I can't even remember now what it was, but it was bad enough that Lady McInnis decided she couldn't put off talking to her brother any longer."

"And it didn't go well?"

"Hardly. I mean, how would you like to have your sister tell you that two of your children are on their way to being as mad as their mother?"

"That's what Lady McInnis told Salinger? That she thought Arabella and Percy were . . . unstable?"

"I don't know if she said it in so many words. But I gather it's what she thought, yes." They'd reached the street now, and Pitcairn paused to readjust his grip on the handle of his foils' case. "Why are you asking all this anyway?" said Pitcairn. "You—" He broke off. "My God; you can't think *Salinger* killed them? His own sister and niece?"

Sebastian met the other man's suddenly stricken gaze. "No, that's not what I'm thinking."

Chapter 51

$\mathcal{W}$e bury the babies in the poor hole, of course," said the Reverend Martin Shore, vicar of St. Mary's, a quaint sandstone church dominated by a sturdy Norman tower that dated all the way back to the early twelfth century. "Poor, wee things. They don't have much of a life, I'm afraid."

Sir Henry Lovejoy stood beside the vicar in the midst of St. Mary's ancient churchyard. The church had been built atop a small hill, and the wind was blowing stiffly, flattening the long grass between the crowded, lichen-covered gray headstones and worn tombs. From here, if he looked to the southeast, Lovejoy could see the tidy fields and expansive farmhouse of Pleasant Farm and, beyond that, the broad, gleaming ribbon of the river Thames.

"Precisely how many infants have you buried from Pleasant Farm?" asked Lovejoy, putting up a hand to grab his hat when a strong gust of wind threatened to carry it away.

The vicar frowned in a way that drew his dimpled chin back against his chest. He was a plump, full-faced man of medium height with pale eyes, fading sandy hair, and wind-chapped fair skin. "Too many, I'm afraid," he said, letting out a sad sigh. "Far too many."

"Are the deaths recorded?"

"Oh, yes; of course. But there's not much to be learned from that, you know. It's only 'Baby John' and 'Baby Sarah' and such."

"Any idea how the little ones die?"

The vicar shrugged. If he'd ever found the steady stream of dead infants coming from Pleasant Farm a source of alarm, it didn't show. "Not hard to tell, really. Waste away, they do."

"Do you also bury many dead infants that have been pulled from the Thames?"

"Not here, thankfully, although I understand the villages down on the river get a fair number. Sad, isn't it? The things people feel driven to do."

A knifelike shadow fell across the churchyard's tombstones and, looking up, Lovejoy spotted a hawk soaring overhead. "What can you tell me about Prudence and Joseph Blackadder?"

The question visibly shocked the vicar, as if it had only just occurred to him to wonder why this London magistrate had bothered to travel all the way out to his parish to stand here, in a fierce wind, asking questions about dead babies. "Oh, they're regular churchgoers, to be sure, to be sure, Sir Henry. Rarely miss a Sunday, they do. Quite the upstanding members of our community, they are."

"Commendable, no doubt," said Lovejoy, his lips pressing into a grim line.

So far they had found three women who had worked at Pleasant Farm at various times in the past ten years. All three insisted that they had never observed any irregularities and that Mrs. Blackadder always took care of feeding the infants herself.

"Although they never seemed to eat much," admitted one of the women, a rather slow-witted, buxom girl named Lily whom Lovejoy interviewed personally. "Slept all the time, they did. Never seen anything like it."

"Did you ever see anyone give the babies laudanum?"

"Oh, no, sir. Never."

"How long were you at Pleasant Farm?"

"Three years, sir."

"And how many babies died during that time?"

"Don't think I could rightly say, sir. Seemed like they was dying all the time. Never knew one to last more'n a month, to be honest. We was always gettin' in new ones."

"Did you ever observe either Mrs. Blackadder or her husband throwing anything into the river?"

The girl looked puzzled. "Like what, yer honor?"

"Something such as, say, a small bundle."

Lily's eyes widened. "Oh, no, yer honor." The girl might be slow-witted, but she was no fool. She knew exactly what Lovejoy was implying, just as she knew that she, too, would be held accountable if the babies' deaths were proven to be anything other than natural. "Never."

Lovejoy knew they could keep looking for a previous employee willing to tell them the truth; they could even order an extensive—and expensive—search of the farm's fields. But he doubted they'd find anything. Not with the Thames so close and handy.

Now, standing on that windblown hillside, surrounded by the timeworn stones of centuries of the dead, Lovejoy found himself at a loss. He could speak to the Home Secretary; force the parishes to remove their infants from Prudence Blackadder's care and quit sending her any more. But how could they ever hope to hold her accountable for an untold number of murders when they couldn't prove that even one had occurred?

The simple, inescapable truth was that they could not.

"Was there anything else, Sir Henry?" asked the vicar, casting a furtive glance back at his church.

"I don't think so, no. Thank you for your time, Father."

"My pleasure," said the vicar.

Still holding on to his hat, Lovejoy turned to walk down the hill to his waiting hackney. He walked slowly, buffeted by the wind and weighed down by an inescapable burden of anger and frustration and a deep, abiding sense of failure.

Chapter 52

Just because a solution seems to fit doesn't mean it's right.

Sebastian kept telling himself that as he walked the raucous, crowded streets of London, past Red Lion Square and Lincoln's Inn Fields, heading vaguely toward the river. Never had he been more desperate to be wrong about something. He kept running through his list of suspects, trying to find another explanation—any other explanation—that fit everything he knew.

He couldn't.

In the end he retreated to an ancient, low-ceilinged tavern on the Strand. He was nursing a pint of ale at an old, worn table in a dark corner, lost in thought, when someone said, "I'm told you've been looking for me."

Sebastian glanced up to find Zacchary Finch watching him. The Major had two foaming tankards in his hands and a quizzical expression on his face. "Here," said Finch, shoving one of the tankards across the scarred tabletop toward him. "I thought you looked like you could use a refresh."

"Thank you," said Sebastian, leaning back. "Have a seat."

Finch settled on the opposite bench. "So why were you looking for me?"

Sebastian took a slow sip of the ale, choosing his words carefully. "I wanted to ask if Laura McInnis had ever spoken to you about her younger nephew or his sister."

Finch's eyes widened. Whatever he'd been expecting, it obviously wasn't that. "Percy and Arabella? What about them?"

"I'm told she was worried about them. Was she?" When Finch stared down at his ale as if not quite certain how to answer, Sebastian said quietly, "I know the truth about Lady Salinger, if that helps."

"Ah." Finch looked up to meet his gaze. "It's a tragic story, isn't it? A woman so young, so gifted with what most would consider all the blessings of life—beauty, fortune, a title, a lovely home, children. And yet she was still hopelessly . . ." He paused as if searching for the right word, then finally settled on "disturbed." He wrapped both hands around his tankard. "Laura's own mother died when she was in leading strings, so she understood only too well what it's like to grow up surrounded by servants but without a mother's love. So when Salinger had to have his wife committed, Laura promised she'd do everything she could to help with the children, and she did. But lately—even as early as last spring, when I was in London before Boney busted loose and I left to rejoin my regiment—she'd been becoming increasingly worried about the two younger children. Particularly Percy."

"Why?"

Finch propped his elbows on the table and leaned forward, dropping his voice. "You've met the lad?"

"I have. He's quite captivating."

"He can be, yes. He's so bright, so full of enthusiasm for anything that catches his interest that he comes across as both charming and endearing. But . . ."

"But?" prompted Sebastian when the other man hesitated.

"After you've been around him awhile, you begin to notice that . . . well, something's a bit *off* about him. It isn't only the endless, casual lies that can take your breath away, it's . . ." Finch paused again, once more groping carefully to find the right words. "So often, his reactions to things aren't quite what they should be. He'll laugh at something that's really not funny—like a housemaid falling down the stairs, or a wherry full of passengers capsizing on the Thames when the water's so cold the chances of anyone being rescued alive are nonexistent. And while I know that can sometimes be a natural, spontaneous human reaction to shock that we've all experienced and then felt wretched about, that's not the case with Percy. He'll keep laughing. Laura told me once that she sometimes wondered if Percy had ever experienced any true compassion or fellow feeling for anyone—not a poor old blind man reduced to begging in the streets, or a skinny stray dog desperately searching for food, or even his own father when Salinger was forced to shoot his favorite hunter after it broke its leg. Salinger was devastated, and yet it was obvious that Percy didn't even care."

Sebastian took a deep breath and let it out slowly. He'd known men like that in the Army; too many. They were the ones who raped pregnant women and slit open their bellies; who collected the ears and other body parts of those they killed as souvenirs. He'd learned not to turn his back on those kinds of men. "And Arabella?" he said, his voice rough. "You say Laura was worried about her, too?"

"Not as much. Well, at least not until recently. But then Arabella flew into a rage at Emma and would have seriously hurt her if Malcolm hadn't been there to intervene, and that's when Laura decided she had to say something to Salinger."

"She told you about that? Her talk with Salinger, I mean."

"She did, yes. It was right after I came back from Belgium. I thought it was a mistake, frankly—her telling him there was something wrong with the children, I mean. But she said she'd felt she had to do it, that perhaps something could be done to help the children before it was too late."

"'Too late' meaning . . . what?"

"Before they did something unforgivable, I suppose."

Sebastian studied the other man's drawn features. "This discussion she had with Salinger—do you know where it took place?"

"I think it was at his house in Down Street. Why?"

"So the children could have overhead it."

"I suppose so," said Finch, looking puzzled. "But what difference would that make?"

"None of that proves anything," Hero said later that night as she lay in Sebastian's arms. A storm was blowing in from the northeast, and they could see the flashes of lightning reflected on the room's walls, hear the long, low rumble of distant thunder.

"No," agreed Sebastian.

She shifted so that she could look at him, her face solemn. "Could *Salinger* be the killer?"

Sebastian ran his fingers through the dark tumble of her hair, drawing it back behind her head. "Theoretically, I suppose it is possible. He could have killed his sister in a deliberate, cold rage to keep her from saying such things about his children to anyone else, and Emma because—hell, I don't know. In some sort of sick revenge because of what her mother had said? Because she was prettier than his own daughter—and sane? I suppose either one is theoretically possible. But why would he then turn around and try to kill his own children by attacking them in Hyde Park? Because he was afraid they were mad, after all, so he decided to kill them, too? Even if that weren't an unbelievably convoluted explanation, surely Arabella and Percy would have recognized their own father—apart from which, Salinger is neither young nor particularly slim. And if he were willing to personally murder his own sister and niece, I can't see him then hiring someone else to eliminate his children."

"So perhaps the children were attacked by someone else for some other reason entirely that we don't know about."

"Such as?"

"I don't know. But it is possible."

"Yes."

"There must be some other explanation. There must be. Hiram Dobbs . . . the Blackadders . . . Rhodes . . . McInnis . . . Any one of them could have done it."

"Possibly."

She studied his face, her eyes dark and luminous in the night. "But you don't think so, do you?"

He met her gaze. "I'd like to, but . . . no. No, I don't."

Chapter 53

*T*he next morning, Paul Gibson was sitting on the edge of his kitchen stoop, drinking a cup of tea and watching the bees buzz around a nearby patch of clover, when Sebastian came to sit beside him. The surgeon's eyes were bloodshot, his face unshaven, his skin—where it wasn't bruised—the color of a dead fish.

"You look like hell," said Sebastian.

Gibson grunted and took another sip of his tea. "You keep saying that."

"And you keep saying you're going to do something about it but don't."

Gibson shifted the position of his truncated leg and glanced over at him. "If you're here lookin' for the results of the postmortem on some new murder victim, Bow Street hasn't even sent over the body yet. I've been blessedly free of mangled corpses since I finished up with yon thatcher from Richmond."

"No one new—thank God. It's Coldfield I'm here about. What can you tell me about the angle of the bullet that hit him?"

"Ah, that." Gibson jerked his head toward the old stone outbuilding at the base of Alexi's garden. "The thatcher was a big man, and whoever shot him was pretty close, so you need to figure that most anyone shooting at him would've had to angle the barrel of his gun up a wee bit. Or the shooter could have been sitting down, of course."

That was a complicating possibility Sebastian hadn't considered. "So you're saying the bullet did travel upward on entering his body?"

"That it did. It's an estimate, of course, but—depending on how close they were standing—I'd say your shooter is probably around five feet tall, maybe less. Or he or she could have been sitting down, which as I said would alter everything. The impact of the bullet probably knocked Coldfield over, because the knife wounds that followed go straight down. Now, normally, they probably wouldn't tell us much, except in this instance they're of a nature that suggests your killer either isn't particularly strong, or else he wasn't trying too hard. But given that even a wounded man can be dangerous—especially when he's Cato's size—I suspect anyone trying to kill him would be more than desperate to get the job done. So I think I'd go with the idea that you're looking for someone who's short and relatively weak."

"What about the abigail, Cassy Jones? Were her stab wounds the same?"

"They were."

"You're certain?"

"Yes. Although everything was a wee bit different since she wasn't down on the ground."

"And Gilly Harper?"

Gibson scrubbed a hand down over his bruised, beard-stubbled chin and neck. "Alexi did that postmortem."

"Can you ask her about it?"

"I can. But why? What are you thinking? That an old man is do-ing this? Or a small woman?"

"Or a child," said Sebastian quietly.

Gibson slewed around to stare at him. "A *child*? You can't be se-rious."

"I wish I weren't," said Sebastian, looking up as the weathered wooden gate set into the nearby old stone wall flew open and Tom came in at a run.

"Gov'nor! Been looking fer ye everywhere, I 'ave. I been askin' 'round at both Grosvenor Square and Down Street, and I think I done found out what ye was wantin' to know. That chimney sweep ye been looking into? Seems 'e did come at Lady McInnis when she was gettin' into her carriage, only it weren't when they was on their way to Richmond Park that Sunday. According to Jem—'e's the footman I was talkin' to before, remember?—it was a couple of days *before* that."

"He's quite certain?"

"Aye. Jem says it was when 'er ladyship was gettin' ready t' take Miss Emma and Miss Arabella shoppin' on Bond Street. And as fer Master Percy, why, 'e weren't even there!"

Casual lies, Finch had called them. Except this was a casual lie with a vicious, deadly purpose, told with the ease of a habitual liar.

"Does anyone at Down Street know where Percy was last Thurs-day?"

"Sorta. Graham—'e's one o' Salinger's grooms—'e says 'e ain't sure, but 'e thinks that's the day Percy was shut up in 'is room on ac-count of somethin' er another 'e'd done. And get this: Graham says the lad 'as ways o' gettin' out of 'is room with no one being the wiser—says 'e's done it before. Graham says Percy's groom—a lad by the name o' Jacob—'as been known to 'elp 'im do all sorts o' things. I was gonna try t' talk t' him, only, get this: 'E's done loped off! Ain't nobody seen 'im since Saturday. And listen t' this: There's two knives missin' from Salinger's kitchen! The first one disappeared a week or more ago, but the second didn't go missing till Thursday. That's the day before the abigail was murdered in Hyde Park, ain't it? Graham, 'e says they're all lookin' sideways at each other, thinkin' there must be a thief on the staff, because other things've gone missin' around the house lately."

Tom paused, his face alight with excitement, but Sebastian knew such a deep sense of foreboding that he had to force himself to say, "What else is missing?"

"One of 'is lordship's flintlock pistols! It's an old double-barreled Jover 'is uncle carried in the American War, which they reckon is why 'e's in such a takin' over it being stolen."

"When did it disappear?"

"They don't rightly know since 'is lordship keeps it put away. 'E only noticed it was missin' yesterday because 'e went lookin' fer it."

"Damn," said Sebastian softly. He'd been thinking that if Finch's gun had been used to kill Laura and Emma, then the killer—or killers—would have needed a second gun. But with Salinger's old double-barreled flintlock . . .

"Damn," he said again.

Damn, damn, damn.

Lord Salinger was not an easy man to find.

Sebastian searched the gentlemen's clubs of St. James's Street, Manton's Shooting Gallery, and a host of other venues frequented by sporting men of means. It was a chance remark made by a barmaid in Limmer's that led him to the wide, soaring arches of the new Strand Bridge, still two years or more away from completion.

The new bridge rose just upstream from the eighteenth-century neoclassical government complex known as Somerset House. Once, this stretch of the riverbank had been the site of the Savoy Palace, the great medieval palace of John of Gaunt that was considered in its time the grandest nobleman's house in all of London. But over the years, riot, fire, and shifting tastes and politics had laid waste to the original buildings, reducing the palace to a hospital, a barracks, and even at times a prison. Now little remained of that once-famous structure: a crumbling Tudor chapel, some broken towers, an abandoned Lutheran burial ground, and a few stretches of shattered walls with gaping doorways and elegant arched windows that opened onto nothing. And virtually all of that would eventually be swept away when the final approach to the bridge was completed.

The bridge's wide elliptical arches were all now in place, along with most of the superstructure. As he worked his way down the rubble-strewn slope toward the water, Sebastian could see the Viscount standing at about mid-river, near one of the alcoves that topped the bridge's grand columned piers.

"It's almost all gone now," said Salinger, turning to watch him as Sebastian walked out onto the bridge toward him. He spoke so softly that his voice was barely audible above the swift rush of the river and the buffeting of the wind rising from the water to bathe their faces with the cool, sweet smell of the countryside upstream. "The old Savoy Palace, I mean. We used to come here as children, my brothers and I. We'd play amongst the old medieval ruins, pretending we were knights. Sometimes we'd drag Laura along and make her be our damsel in distress, although she always wanted to be a knight, too."

For a moment he smiled faintly at the memory. Then the smile faded. "In those days we still had the original Priestly town house, in Pall Mall." He sucked in a shaky breath. "The house I have now was a wedding gift from Septimus Bain to his daughter, Georgina. My own dear father sold the Pall Mall house to pay off some of his debts while I was up at Oxford. It only delayed the inevitable, of course, although I suppose in the end it did help save the Priory." He paused. "Did you ever meet him? My father, I mean."

"I don't believe so, no."

Salinger nodded, his eyes narrowing against the sunlight glinting off the water. "He was considered a most likable man. Charming and easygoing and cheerful, and yet so breathtakingly selfish that nothing—and I do mean *nothing*—mattered more to him than his own pleasure. Not his estates, not the family's heritage, and certainly not his children. He sold me to the rich father of a woman who was half-mad, while poor Laura ended up with a man who will no doubt remarry before she's been in her grave a month. All for *money*. Money, so that the old bastard could continue to play the horses and roll the dice and tup his whores."

"You know about McInnis and Olivia Edmondson?"

"I didn't before. But I do now—damn him all to hell. And to think I considered the son of a bitch my friend." Salinger was silent for a moment, his fists curling against the granite balustrade before him. "The funerals are tomorrow; did you know? Malcolm and Duncan finally made it home late Sunday night. Perhaps once Laura and Emma are buried we can begin to put this all behind us."

"Even if the killer has never been identified?"

Salinger's lips twisted into an odd smile. "You think I should be desperate for justice, do you?" He rolled the word "justice" around on his tongue as if it were something bitter or perhaps simply illusory. "One puts down a mad dog, shoots a horse with a broken leg, and executes a murderer; it's what we do, isn't it? Our responsibility to society. But when all is said and done, what difference would that make to Laura and Emma? My sister and her daughter would still be dead. Nothing is going to bring them back." He was silent a moment, his throat working hard as he swallowed. "I want to get my children away from"—he swept one arm through the air in a wide, violent arc that took in the river and the teeming city that stretched away to the east, north, and west—"from all of this."

Sebastian kept his gaze on the river far below, where a heavily laden coal barge was being swept downstream by the outrushing tide. "I understand Percy is fascinated by murder."

Salinger shot him a quick sideways glance. "He is, yes."

"Do you know what first attracted his interest to it?"

Salinger twitched one shoulder. "I don't recall precisely; it was one of those bizarre murders that had the city in an uproar two or three years ago. He became obsessed with reading everything he could about it, as if he could solve the murder himself by reasoning it out." He blew out a harsh breath. "If you ask me, it's shameful, the way the newspapers sensationalize these things. They do it deliberately, to stir up people's fears so they can then feed the public's appetite for shock and a strange kind of titillating, vicarious horror. And when you add in the ridiculous broadsheets they print whenever some notorious murderer is hanged, with a bunch of fabricated nonsense they pretend is the killer's 'final confession,' it . . . it's unhealthy."

"Was that what worried your sister? Percy's interest in murder?"

Salinger held himself utterly still. "What do you mean?"

"I'm told she came to see you several weeks ago because she was worried about your younger children."

Salinger stared out at the rushing turmoil of the river, his jaw tightening. "I don't know what you're talking about."

"Yes, you do."

Salinger shifted to look at him. "You think I killed her? Is that what you're saying? My own sister and niece? *Me?*"

"No," said Sebastian quietly. "Not you."

Sebastian watched as understanding dawned slowly, watched as the other man's face crumpled with revulsion before tightening with rage. "*My God.* You—you bloody, sick *bastard!*" He pushed away from the balustrade to stand facing Sebastian, his hands dangling loosely at his sides, his face flushed, his breath coming hard and fast as the wind off the river whipped around them. "There is nothing wrong with my children! Do you hear me? *Nothing.*"

Sebastian kept his voice even. "I'm told several items have gone missing from your house recently. Your cook is complaining of two knives that were stolen from her kitchen, and you yourself discovered that a double-barreled flintlock pistol that once belonged to your uncle is also missing."

Salinger was breathing so heavily now that his chest was jerking. "I don't know what you're talking about," he said again.

"I don't pretend to understand it," said Sebastian. "Least of all why they did it. Perhaps because Percy is so fascinated by murder and murderers that he wanted to see if he was clever enough to kill someone and get away with it? Because he wanted to know what it feels like to take another person's life? Because Arabella was so jealous of her cousin Emma that she wanted to kill her, or they somehow overheard what Laura said to you, and it made them angry? But for whatever reason, Percy went out of his way to learn everything he could about the old murders out at Richmond Park, and then Arabella badgered your aunt into agreeing to take them there on a picnic. One or the other of them—or perhaps both working together—stole your uncle's old double-barreled flintlock from wherever you keep it. And then, because they didn't want to kill Thisbe, too—either because they had no grudge against her or because they couldn't figure out the logistics of killing three people at once—Arabella destroyed one of her own books and blamed it on Thisbe so the child would be made to stay home."

"No," said Salinger, his head shaking back and forth, his face contorted with horror. "Do you hear me? *No.* They're children! They'd need to be mad to do such a thing."

"I don't think it's madness," Sebastian said quietly. "I suspect it's more an extreme form of selfishness and self-absorption, combined with a total lack of sympathy for the feelings of others."

"What you're describing is madness, and my children aren't mad. Do you hear me? *They are not mad!* And if you—if you *dare* to voice this disgusting theory of yours to anyone else, I swear to God I'll kill you. Do you hear me? *I'll kill you!*"

"You can try," said Sebastian evenly. "But that won't help your children. Not in the long run."

Salinger's chest shuddered as if with a suppressed sob. "God damn you. God damn you all to hell."

His face frozen in a rictus of pain, the children's father pushed away from the balustrade to brush past Sebastian and stride toward the crumbling ruins of the doomed palace on the riverbank. The wind whipped at the tails of his coat and blew hard enough that for a moment he staggered, putting up a hand to secure his hat before lowering his head and pushing on.

But Sebastian stayed where he was, his gaze on the wide sun-sparkled expanse of water and his heart so heavy within that it hurt.

Chapter 54

$\mathcal{S}$ir Henry Lovejoy stood beside the placid waters of the Serpentine in Hyde Park, watching a couple of young constables wade through the shallows of the ornamental lake in what was surely a futile search for the knife that had been used to kill Arabella Priestly's young abigail, Cassy Jones. The sun was already sinking low in the blue summer sky, for it had taken time for Lovejoy to be brought around to believing it possible that two children—two wealthy, wellborn, privileged *children*—could be guilty of murder, and more time still for Lord Devlin to convince him that the children were likely to have thrown their bloodstained weapon away someplace they assumed it would never be found, rather than carrying it off with them. Now, with evening rapidly approaching, Lovejoy found himself thinking it was a good thing the Regent's celebratory fireworks were to be set off in St. James's Park rather than here.

"My fellow magistrates at Bow Street are going to think I've gone mad, agreeing to this," he said as Devlin came to stand beside him, hands on his hips, his lordship's attention likewise fixed on the constables wading through the murky waters before them. "That we're both mad."

"I hope they're right."

Lovejoy glanced over at him. "So do I."

The two men lapsed back into silence as the minutes ticked past and the constables, stripped down to their shirts and breeches, waded back and forth, back and forth, slowly venturing out deeper and deeper, the water rising until it lapped at their groins. Lovejoy said, "Even if we find the knife and Salinger's cook identifies it as one missing from her kitchen, it doesn't prove the children took the knife."

"No."

"We couldn't possibly have them remanded into custody—not on such a flimsy string of happenstances that can each be easily explained away no matter how convincing they might seem when taken all together. The truth is, even if we had irrefutable evidence, no jury would ever convict a nobleman's thirteen-year-old son and fifteen-year-old daughter of such a heinous string of murders. We hang poor children of that age—and younger—all the time. But most people accept it as a given that the children of the lower classes are predisposed to crime."

"'Tainted,'" said Devlin wryly. He glanced toward the sinking sun. "I suspect the most we can hope for is to somehow convince Salinger that his children need help, although—" He broke off as one of the constables let out a whoop and bent over to virtually disappear into the water.

The man came up huffing air and dripping, a broad grin spreading across his wet face as he triumphantly thrust one arm in the air, his fist gripping the handle of what looked like a large cook's knife, its blade still rust-free and gleaming in the golden light of the setting sun.

Chapter 55

S ome three hours later, Sir Henry Lovejoy sat in the drawing room of Viscount Devlin's house in Brook Street, a cup of tea in his hands. He had just endured a painful, exceedingly awkward exchange with Lord Salinger and his younger son, and for the first time in many years Lovejoy found himself longing for something considerably stronger than a cup of good English tea.

"I gather things didn't go well," said Devlin from where he stood with his back to the room's open windows. Night had fallen warm and humid, with only a faint breeze that stirred the satin hangings and brought them the distant rumble of the crowds gathering for the grand fireworks display scheduled to be set off from the Parade in St. James's Park.

Lovejoy took a sip of his tea. "I suppose it could have been a good deal worse. Young Master Percy does readily admit to taking the knife from the kitchen of his father's house. Except he says he took the knife the day *after* his sister's abigail was murdered in the park and threw it in the Serpentine on a lark."

"A *lark?*"

Lovejoy sighed. "Yes, to see if he could confuse us. He appeared most contrite while admitting it. Said he understands now that it was not at all the thing to do and apologized most profusely for in any way misleading us or hampering our investigation."

"Except that according to Salinger's servants," said Lady Devlin, "the knife disappeared before the abigail was killed."

"Indeed." Lovejoy cleared his throat. He still felt uncomfortable discussing such a distressing subject as murder in the presence of a gentlewoman—particularly a gentlewoman some six months heavy with child. Although he also acknowledged that several years' acquaintance with Lady Devlin should by now have disabused him of any illusions he might once have nurtured about the nature of her sensibilities, because as far as he could tell, she had none. "A scullery maid interviewed by one of my constables told him much the same thing. Unfortunately, Lord Salinger's cook claims it truly went missing only yesterday. She insists she was mistaken when she thought it had been taken before."

"In other words, she doesn't want to be turned off by her employer without a character for implicating his son in a murder investigation."

"So one might infer." Lovejoy took another sip of his tea.

"Were you able to speak to Percy's groom, Jacob?"

"Unfortunately, no. No one has seen the lad since Saturday. From all appearances, he's taken his things and run off."

"Saturday?" said Devlin. "That's the day Coldfield's body was discovered."

Lovejoy nodded. "It could be a coincidence, of course. But it's also more than possible that the lad is bright enough to put two and two together and realized he'd inadvertently been helping his young master commit murder. Needless to say, I did not actually suggest to

Lord Salinger that we suspect his children of anything. And even though he surely realized the implications of the knife's discovery, he was never anything other than polite. Indeed, he volunteered that he'd only that day realized he'd misplaced his uncle's old double-barreled flintlock, and went so far as to show it to me."

"Had you mentioned the missing flintlock?" said Devlin.

"No, not at all. It's quite a distinctive piece, by the way—manufactured in the last century by Jover, with a lovely engraving of leaves, flowers, and grapes on the wooden grip. He even showed me a portrait of his uncle holding the weapon, so I have no doubt it is indeed the same pistol. He said it hasn't been fired in the last twenty or thirty years, although it had obviously been cleaned quite recently. When I remarked upon it, he said the first thing he'd done upon locating the pistol was clean it."

Devlin leaned back against the window frame, his hands curling around the sill at his sides. "So where do we go from here?"

Lovejoy set aside his empty cup. "To be frank, I'd say we're at point non plus. His lordship tells me the funeral for Lady McInnis and her daughter is scheduled for tomorrow evening and that he plans to depart for the Priory early the following morning."

"It's what he did before," said Lady Devlin quietly. "When he began worrying about his wife's behavior. He retreated to Leicester-shire and stayed there as much as possible."

Lovejoy rose to his feet, his knees creaking in protest. "It may be the best we can hope for—that their father's loving care and the restorative wholesomeness of country life will help the children put whatever drove them to this madness behind them."

"Perhaps," said Devlin, meeting his worried gaze. "Unless they start feeling cocky about getting away with murder and decide they can do it again."

After Lovejoy had gone, Sebastian went to stand once more at the open windows, his gaze now on the darkened street below. From the distance came an echoing boom and whizzing hiss, followed by the roar of the unseen crowds as the first salvos of the fireworks in the Prince Regent's combination anniversary and victory celebration exploded over the parks in a colorful extravaganza of cascading lights.

"You think Salinger knows the truth?" said Hero, coming to stand beside him, her gaze, like his, on the shower of sparkling green lights reflected by the windows of the houses opposite. "Even if he only acknowledges it to himself?"

"He must, to have handled Lovejoy with such adroit civility. I suspect he went home after our conversation on the bridge and instituted another search for his uncle's flintlock, only to discover that Percy had put it back. I don't know what sort of condition the pistol was in when he found it—whether it was obviously newly cleaned or had been fired and not cleaned. But either would have told him all he needed to know."

"The poor man."

"Yes," said Sebastian, watching a golden starburst mirrored in the darkened windows across the street. "I can't imagine realizing that your son and daughter had deliberately murdered your own sister and niece—along with two or three other people."

"Two or three?" said Hero.

He nodded. "I received a message from Gibson shortly before Lovejoy arrived. He talked to Alexi, and she says the stab wounds on Gilly's body were deep and obviously done by someone quite strong."

"So not by whoever killed Cassy and Cato?"

"She says there's no way to say that for certain, but the difference is real."

Hero was silent for a moment. "What if we're wrong about the children?" she said. "What if Percy has simply been trying to be clever, mucking around with the investigation and planting false clues to send you off after first one possible suspect, then another? It would still be a disturbing thing to do, but forgivable. Thirteen-year-old boys do have a well-earned reputation for behaving impulsively and making poor decisions."

"Perhaps that's what Salinger is trying to tell himself right now—unless of course his uncle's old Jover pistol had indeed been fired and not cleaned—or not cleaned well, in which case I don't see how he could continue to delude himself."

She turned to face him. "What would he do then, do you think? If he knew for certain his children were killers, I mean. He confined his wife to an asylum for murdering her abigail."

"Yes, although in that instance I doubt he was given much choice in the matter. It was either commit her or watch her stand trial for murder. And having seen what was done to his wife, I can't imagine him subjecting his children to that. Especially since in this case—"

"What?" said Hero when he broke off.

Sebastian felt his lungs empty of air. He was remembering Salinger standing at the bridge's balustrade, an expression Sebastian couldn't quite read twisting his lips as he said, *One puts down a mad dog, shoots a horse with a broken leg, and executes a murderer; it's what we do, isn't it? Our responsibility to society.*

"Oh, bloody hell," swore Sebastian as he pushed violently away from the window to turn toward the stairs. "*Morey!* Have Tom—no, there isn't time; I'll have to take a hackney. Morey, send one of the footmen to fetch a hackney—*now*. Where the bloody hell is my hat?"

"What? What is it?" said Hero, following him as he ran down the stairs to snatch up his hat and walking stick.

He jerked on his gloves as he turned to her. "He's going to kill them—Salinger, I mean. If he hasn't already, he's going to kill them both."

"Wait here for me!" Sebastian shouted to the jarvey as his hackney pulled in next to the kerb in Down Street. Salinger's house was ablaze with light, and Sebastian leapt from the carriage to take the steps to the front door in two quick strides and ring a jarring peal with the bell.

Swearing, he was about to start pounding on the panels when the door was opened by a young footman whose jaw sagged as Sebastian pushed past him into the entry hall. "Where?" demanded Sebastian, turning toward him. "Where's Salinger?"

"His lordship isn't here, my lord. He's taken the younger children to St. James's Park to watch the fireworks display. Master Percy was most keen on seeing it and—"

But Sebastian was already running back down the steps to the waiting hackney. "St. James's Park! *Go, go, go!*" he shouted at the jarvey, leaping into the hackney's musty interior as another exploding skyrocket rained down a shimmering fountain of silver-and-blue fire on the city. "And there's an extra guinea in it if you can get me there in record time."

The jarvey did his best, but the streets leading to the park were a chaos of jammed carriages and carts with nervous, head-tossing horses and swearing, whip-cracking drivers, all bathed in an eerie pulsing glow of golden lamplight and hissing torches and an endless multihued shower of bursting fireworks. Slamming his palm against the side of the hackney in exasperation, Sebastian called out, "Never mind! I'll get out here."

"Sorry, my lord!" shouted the driver as Sebastian tossed him the promised guinea and took off down St. James's Street toward the park at a run. "I did what I could."

How much time? Sebastian wondered as he shoved his way through the raucous, thickening crowds, his gut twisting into a painful knot. How much time did he have? The grounds of the park were a seething mass of humanity, drunken young bucks in top hats and glossy top boots mingling with tradesmen and shopkeepers, servants and day laborers, hawkers with trays of meat pies and gingerbread, whining beggars, sly pickpockets, and screaming children.

As he neared the parade grounds, the crowds grew ever thicker until his quest began to seem hopeless. The air was pungent with the reek of sulfur from the fireworks' gunpowder, the smoke drifting like a swirling haze. *Where?* thought Sebastian, pivoting in a frustrated circle as a skyrocket exploded overhead, lighting up the sea of sweat-sheened, laughing, uplifted faces surrounding him. Where would Salinger take his children to watch the fireworks?

And kill them.

Where, where, where?

We used to come here as children, my brothers and I.

Sebastian turned toward the Thames and started to run.

Chapter 56

By the time Sebastian reached the Strand, his bad leg was on fire, his breath coming in ragged gasps. He could hear the bells of St. Clement's tolling the hour, the slow, mournful *dong*s of the church bells nearly drowned out by the boom and crackle of the fireworks exploding overhead and the roar of the crowds. With the sulfurous smoke swirling around him, he forced himself to slow to a walk, his nostrils flaring and his chest heaving as he scanned the looming ruins of the old palace and the deserted arches of the unfinished bridge that stretched out over the dark river.

And then he saw them—or rather, he saw Salinger and Arabella, two stark silhouettes balanced perilously atop one of the stone balustrades edging the bridge. The wind rising off the river below flapped the tails of Salinger's coat and billowed the skirts of Arabella's muslin walking dress around them. The girl wore a black velvet spencer over her mourning gown, but her hat was gone, her hair a wind-whipped mess that hid her face. Beside her, her father was also bareheaded, his darker hair tumbled across his forehead. As Sebastian watched, another skyrocket exploded above them, its flickering light casting a ghostly blue hue across Salinger's sweat-slicked face and glinting on the naked blade he held pressed to his daughter's throat.

There was no sign of Percy.

His stomach again twisting into a painful knot, Sebastian stepped onto the bridge's unfinished roadway, his hands held out at his sides. "You don't need to do this, Miles," he said softly but clearly.

Salinger whipped around to stare at him, father and daughter wavering precariously on the narrow granite railing high above the rushing river. "Devlin? What are you doing here?"

"I came to stop you from doing . . . this."

Salinger sucked in a deep breath, his features contorting in a spasm of grief and horror as he shook his head. "He admitted it to me, you know. Percy, I mean. He was proud of it! Said I didn't need to worry about them ever getting caught because he'd been too clever." His body shuddered with a dry, silent sob. "*My God.* He'd been *too clever.* Planned it all so carefully. Just to show that he could."

"Let Arabella go," Sebastian said quietly.

"*I didn't do anything!*" she screamed, held fast by her father's grip on her arm, the wind blowing her tangled hair across her tear-streaked, terrified face. "Percy's the one who planned it all after talking to that old thatcher out at Richmond to find out exactly how he'd killed those other women. Percy's the one who shot Aunt Laura and Emma. He used Jacob to help him steal Major Finch's gun, and then Jacob helped him sneak back out to Richmond again so he could make sure the thatcher wouldn't tell on him. He killed Cassy, too, for the same reason, because he was afraid she might tell someone we made up the bit about being attacked in the park."

"But why?" said Salinger, staring at her with horror. "Bella, how could you?"

"Let her go," said Sebastian when Arabella simply looked up at her father and mutely shook her head. "Percy's right. He has been clever. Too clever for either of the children to ever be remanded into custody, let alone convicted of anything."

"*I didn't do anything!*" screamed Arabella again, pulling desperately against her father's hold. "I didn't! Why won't you believe me?"

Salinger tightened his grip on her arm when she would have sunk, crying, to her knees beside him, but he kept his gaze on Sebastian. "You think I should let her go? So she can spend the rest of her life in an asylum like her mother?"

"I didn't kill anyone!" sobbed Arabella, her face contorted with terror. "It was Percy's idea from the very beginning. I swear. All I said was that I'd like to kill Emma—her and Aunt Laura, too, because I was so mad at them. But then Percy, he said, 'Why don't we?' I didn't think he was serious. I thought it was like a game to him, figuring out how to do it—how we could do it and not get caught. I didn't think he was actually going to do it. But he did. He did!"

Salinger was looking at her with a wild mixture of hope and disbelief. "It didn't occur to you to tell me?"

Arabella stared up at him with wide, innocent-seeming eyes, her chest heaving with her gasping sobs. "Percy said he'd kill me if I even thought of it!"

For a moment, Salinger hesitated, desperate to believe her, desperate to salvage something good and decent from the ruins of his life.

"Let her go," said Sebastian again. He could see Salinger wavering, hear the Thames rushing swift and cold far below as a trio of fireworks exploded against the black sky above to rain down a glorious fountain of multicolored sparks that drew a roar of delight from the distant crowd. Then, before Sebastian realized what he was about, Salinger shoved his daughter away and turned the knife to plunge the blade deep into his own chest.

"No!" shouted Sebastian, lunging forward to grab Arabella as she half fell from the parapet in a scrambling rush.

For one haunting instant, Salinger's pain-filled, anguished eyes locked with Sebastian's. Then Salinger toppled backward to plummet silently toward the swirling waters of the river far below.

"*Papa!*" screamed Arabella as Salinger's body hit the water with a splash and was swept away. "Oh, God. Papa," she cried, sinking down beside the balustrade, her head bowed, her hands fisting in her wind-tangled hair as ragged sobs shuddered through her body.

"Where's Percy?" shouted Sebastian, grabbing her by her shoulders and shaking her. "Where is he?"

"*Oh, God, oh, God.*"

"Damn it, Arabella! *Where is Percy?*"

Her head fell back as she looked up at Sebastian, her wet face now blank with shock. "He's dead. Percy's dead. Papa killed him."

Chapter 57

Wednesday, 2 August

*T*he night was dying before Sebastian made it back to Brook Street; a faint bloom of light already showing in the east promised a new day. For a long time he stood beside his open bedroom window, his head bowed so that his forehead pressed against the cool glass. He sucked in a deep breath and smelled the lingering acrid tinge of last night's fireworks. He kept his eyes wide open because he knew if he closed them, his mind would conjure up visions of a moment he suspected he would never forget. The well of tormented grief and horror in a father's eyes. The fierce determination that hardened Salinger's expression as he turned his blade to thrust it deep into his own chest.

"You tried," Hero said quietly as she came to stand beside him, her hand soft and warm as it rested on Sebastian's bare hip. "At least you saved Arabella."

"I'd rather have saved Salinger—before he killed Percy. Although one wonders what sort of life the man could have lived, knowing what his children had done."

"You don't believe Arabella was as innocent as she would have us think?"

He found himself remembering that pair of small, bloodstained gloves he'd found shoved into the hollow of a tree. "Do you?"

"I'd like to, but . . ." Hero paused, then shook her head. "No. No, I don't."

Later that morning, Sir Henry Lovejoy once again sat in the drawing room of the house in Brook Street, a cup of tea in his hands. The day had dawned warm and clear, with a golden sun that shone cheerfully out of an idyllic blue sky. But deep within himself, Lovejoy felt cold, so cold he wondered if he'd ever be right again. He tried taking a sip of his tea but couldn't, and he found his hands shaking so badly that the cup rattled as he lowered it back to its saucer. "Percy's body was recovered shortly after sunrise," he told Lord and Lady Devlin. "Near Rotherhithe. But last I heard, Salinger had not yet been found."

As before, Devlin stood near the room's front windows, his arms now crossed at his chest. "Had the boy been stabbed?"

Lovejoy cast an apologetic glance at Lady Devlin, who, also as before, sat nearby. "Actually, his throat was slit."

"*My God*," whispered Devlin.

Lovejoy cleared his throat. "Two river thieves with a known propensity for violence who were picked up this morning have agreed to confess to the murders of Percy and Salinger in exchange for a promise that their death sentences for theft will be commuted to transportation."

Lovejoy suspected from the expression on the Viscount's face that he knew the thieves would never live to see Botany Bay, but all Devlin said was, "That was quick."

"Yes, the Palace is most anxious to allay the public's fears. People were already nervous as a result of the other recent murders. There was concern that if a suspect were not already in custody when it became known that a peer of the realm and his young son had been attacked and brutally murdered in the midst of the Regent's grand fireworks display, there would be widespread panic."

"And will the same two thieves be blamed for the murders of Lady McInnis and her daughter out at Richmond Park?"

"Ah, no. Those killings are to be attributed to the thatcher, Cato Coldfield."

"Convenient."

"Is it not? But the river thieves have also confessed to the murders of the two young women, Gilly Harper and Cassy Jones."

"Did Arabella ever explain why they killed Gilly?"

"She claims they did not. She says Percy posed her abigail's body in the same manner as the newspapers described Gilly to confuse things."

"Do you believe her?"

"Honestly? I don't know. The problem is, if they didn't kill Gilly, then who did?"

"I've had a note from Gibson saying he doesn't believe Gilly was stabbed by the same person who killed Cato and Cassy."

"Indeed? Well, I won't call off the search for the cheesemonger, then. If we find her, I've no doubt Sidmouth would be delighted to hang her, too."

"So who is supposed to have killed Cato?"

"I don't believe that has been decided yet, but I've no doubt Sidmouth is working on it."

"I'm confident the Home Secretary will find someone to hang for it."

"No doubt."

"What will happen to Arabella?" said Lady Devlin.

Lovejoy sighed. "I fear she may not be as innocent as she would have us believe, but one must hope she is at least telling the truth when she says her brother did the actual killings. At the moment she's in the care of her elder brother, the new Lord Salinger. But given that his lordship is still underage himself, his uncle—the late Lord Salinger's younger brother—will ultimately be appointed her guardian. He's in holy orders, with a living up in Leicestershire. Perhaps with his influence she will be able to put these unfortunate tendencies behind her."

From the frown in Lady Devlin's eyes, Lovejoy suspected that she doubted it. But all she said was, "Does the new Lord Salinger know what really happened to his father and brother?"

"He does not. Nor does he know about the, er, previous activities of his brother and sister. If it were up to me, he would have been told, but Lord Sidmouth insists that the truth must be a closely guarded secret." Lovejoy set aside his teacup and rose to his feet. "And now you must excuse me; I'm due in the Home Office again at eleven."

"I'll walk down with you," said Devlin. They'd almost reached the entry hall below when the Viscount said, "There's something else, isn't there?"

Lovejoy drew up at the foot of the stairs and turned to face him. He hesitated a moment, then said, "The authorities out at Richmond were continuing their search of Coldfield's house and outbuildings in the hopes of discovering something that might explain what happened there. I received word this morning that, late yesterday afternoon, they discovered an aged double-barreled pistol wrapped in a tattered shirt and oilcloth and hidden in the rafters of the house. The keeper's wife, Sally Hammond, identified it as the one she remembered seeing in Coldfield's possession fourteen years ago. I'm told the pistol was not cleaned before it was hidden, and both barrels had obviously been fired." He found he had to blink and look away before he could continue. "When one adds that discovery to what we've been told by Miss Priestly, it's difficult to conclude otherwise than that it was Cato Coldfield who murdered my wife and daughter fourteen years ago. Daniel O'Toole only came along and found them. Traumatized as he was by his experiences in the war, the sight of their . . ." Lovejoy's voice trembled, but he pushed on. "Of their dead bodies must have devastated him. He was a devout man, and so he set about arranging them in what he considered a more proper Christian posture for the dead." Lovejoy swallowed hard. "That's how their blood came to be on his hands. And then he unwittingly smeared it all over himself when in his anguish he touched his face and tore at his hair—exactly as he said." Lovejoy tried to swallow again, but the painful lump in his throat would not go away. "I helped hang an innocent man. And, God help me, I knew a moment of quiet satisfaction when I watched him die."

"We can't know for certain that's what happened," said Devlin.

Lovejoy shook his head. "I know." He almost said, *Julia told me,* but stopped himself in time.

"At least Cato is dead now. He might have evaded the law for fourteen years, but there is a certain kind of grim justice in his now being blamed for the murders committed by someone seeking to emulate his original crime."

"Perhaps. Except that won't bring back Daniel O'Toole. And thanks to the Palace's obsession with appearances, his innocence will never be known."

"You know he was innocent. And I know it."

"That's not enough."

Devlin met his friend's anguished gaze. "No. No, it's not. But at least it's something."

❧

That evening, Hero and Sebastian were in the drawing room after dinner when Jarvis came.

"I can't stay long," he said, refusing Sebastian's offer of a glass of wine. "I assume you've heard that arrests have been made for this dreadful string of recent murders."

"We heard," said Sebastian. His gaze met Hero's; then they both looked away.

"Just so," said Jarvis, watching them. "I'm here because I thought you might also like to know that the *Bellerophon* will be leaving Plymouth on Friday to head for Start Point, where it will rendezvous with the *Northumberland*. If all goes well, Bonaparte will be transferred to the *Northumberland* next Monday, and they will set sail that evening for St. Helena."

Hero said, "I take it wiser heads finally managed to convince the Prince that turning a former emperor over to his enemies to be hanged might not be a good idea?"

"With some difficulty, but yes. St. Helena is far enough away to discourage another escape attempt, and with only one navigable harbor it should be easy enough to guard against any rescue."

"Napoléon knows what's been decided?"

"He knows. I gather he did not take the news well. But then, that's rather to be expected, isn't it?"

"One wonders what he'll find to do there," she said. "For a man so accustomed to activity, the thought of confinement to a small, barren island in the middle of nowhere must seem unimaginable."

"I'm told he has decided to write his memoirs. With any luck, they will keep him occupied until he dies. I understand he's not well." Jarvis reached for his hat and rose to his feet. "I've no doubt word of his destination will eventually leak to the papers, but I'll ask you to keep it quiet until then."

After he had gone, Sebastian went to where Hero still sat, her hands gripping the arms of her chair, her gaze fixed absently on nothing. "You never did talk to Jarvis about that strange visit from Cousin Victoria, did you?" he said, resting his hands on her shoulders.

She looked up at him. "No. I think I finally figured out what she was up to that day. I could be wrong, but I suspect she was deliberately trying to stir up discord between Jarvis and me."

"Why would she do that?"

"I have no idea. But whatever her nasty little scheme is, I don't intend to help it along."

"You're going to need to be very careful."

She reached up to take one of his hands in hers and held it. "I know."

Friday, 4 August, shortly before dawn

Sebastian lit first one candle, then the next, the golden flames leaping up to illuminate the gilded, overwrought glories of an opulent bedchamber fit for the son of a future king.

The man in the wide, red silk-hung tester bed slept on, the pom-pom of his nightcap slipping down over his tousled auburn hair as he let out a loud, resonant snore.

Pulling up a balloon-backed Louis XVI–style chair, Sebastian straddled the seat, slipped a small flintlock pistol from his coat pocket, and settled the gun's muzzle against the end of Basil Rhodes's blobby nose.

Basil slept on, each sonorous exhalation filling the air with the stench of expensive French brandy fumes.

"*Oh, Basil,*" said Sebastian, flicking the tip of the pistol's cold barrel back and forth against that distinctive Hanoverian nose. Again. And again. "Basil?"

"Hmm?" One eye fluttered open. Closed. Then both eyes flew open wide as the Regent's favorite bastard half strangled on a swallowed snore, sucked in a rasping terrified gasp, and shrank back against his nest of pillows. "*Bloody hell!*"

Sebastian showed his teeth in a smile. "You're not an easy man to awaken, are you?"

"Devlin?" Basil's eyes darted from Sebastian, to the bunch of candles flickering on the nearby table, to the curtains billowing in the breeze from the open window. "What the devil are you doing here?"

Sebastian used the muzzle of his pistol to push back the brim of his hat. "As I've no doubt you are aware, I killed a man out at Bethnal Green last Sunday. Actually, two men were killed, but so far I've only been able to identify the one. Dean was his name; Lieutenant Francis Dean, late of the 27th Foot. And I've found someone who says Dean was hired by you, first to deliver a rather rude message, then to commit murder—my murder, to be exact."

Basil snickered. "'Someone'? What 'someone'? You can't prove any of that."

"In a court of law? Probably not. But this isn't a court of law, is it?"

Sebastian watched as the smug confidence leached out of the royal bastard's expression.

"Look," said Basil, his gaze fixed on the muzzle of Sebastian's gun, his tongue flicking out to wet his dry lips. "I was just trying to get you to quit asking awkward questions, that's all. You want to know where I was the day that blasted woman got herself killed? I'll tell you. There's this house, in Pickering Place. They specialize in—"

"I know what they specialize in," said Sebastian.

Basil swallowed hard at whatever he heard in Sebastian's voice. "Ah. Well, then you'll understand why I was most anxious to make certain that knowledge of my visits to that establishment wouldn't leak back to Veronica."

"You aren't worried that I might now tell her?"

"At this point, she wouldn't believe you."

"Probably not. And frankly, as far as I'm concerned, you two deserve each other."

Basil sniffed. "If there's supposed to be an insult hidden in there, it escapes me."

"For now," said Sebastian.

Basil frowned. "I still don't understand why you're here."

"Still?" No longer smiling, Sebastian leveled the muzzle of his pistol right between the eyes of the Regent's spoiled by-blow and pulled back the hammer with an audible click. "The thing is, you see, my tolerance for men like you was exhausted long ago. So I'm here to make certain you understand two things. First of all, send someone at me again and I'll kill not only them but you, too. And secondly, rape another one of your housemaids—or anyone, for that matter—and I'll kill you. It's as simple as that."

Basil's eyes narrowed. "I don't believe you."

Sebastian laughed out loud and pushed to his feet. "I suggest you don't put that theory to the test." He eased the flintlock's hammer back into place. "And before you go crying to Daddy again, remember this: There's six to twelve weeks of open water between here and Jamaica, and people who 'fall' overboard are rarely seen again."

"What the hell is that supposed to mean?" demanded Basil, pushing himself up on his elbows as Sebastian turned away.

"*What does that mean?*"

Monday, 7 August

On a fine summer's morning, when the sky was a deep, clear blue and drifts of yellow monkshood and purple harebell filled the open fields with color, Lovejoy took a hackney out to Richmond.

He went first to a picturesque farm that lay nestled in a hollow not far from the park. The plump, pleasant-faced farmer's wife was crossing the quadrangle with a basket of eggs on her hip when Lovejoy's hackney pulled up. She paused, one hand coming up to shade her eyes from the morning sun as she watched him step down to the yard.

"Mrs. Blackadder?" he said, touching his hand to his hat. "I'm Sir Henry Lovejoy, of Bow Street."

Her features hardened into something considerably less pleasant-looking. "What you want with me? I don't have any babies anymore. Took them all away, the parishes did."

"I know," he said, his gaze traveling around the quadrangle of lovely old stone farm buildings. It was such an idyllic-looking place, picturesquely draped with roses and jasmine and honeysuckle. Idyllic and deadly. "I'm here to let you know that we will be watching you—in case you should be thinking of taking in infants from private sources. I trust I make myself clear?"

"I'm a good foster mother, I am," she said, her heavy bosom heaving as she sucked in a deep, angry breath. "Anyone tells you differently is lying."

"Well, then, there's no reason for our closer scrutiny to worry you, is there? Because I'm not through with you, you know. You may think you've got away with the heinous crimes of the past eleven years, but I don't intend to let this go." He touched his hand once more to his hat. "We will meet again, madam."

His next stop was a certain small cottage overlooking the wide, sun-sparkled expanse of the river.

"Wait for me again," he told the jarvey, stepping down from his hackney.

He paused for a moment, one hand on the garden gate, his gaze on the simple whitewashed cottage with cheerful yellow windowsills that lay before him. Smoke rose from the house's single chimney, and someone had obviously been recently tending a bed of mint near the front step, for a trowel and pail rested beside a section of newly turned earth. The scents of roses and lavender mingled sweetly with the smell of woodsmoke carried on the river breeze. Drawing a deep, steadying breath, Lovejoy pushed open the gate to walk up the flagged path and knock on the door. He would not ask forgiveness, for what had been done to this old woman and her son was unforgivable. But he could at least admit that he knew now that he had been wrong.

He owed her that.

Later that same afternoon, Sebastian was seated at his desk in the library, reading over some long-neglected correspondence from his estate agent, when Duncan Priestly, the new Viscount Salinger, came to see him.

The young lad looked much like his father must have looked at his age, tall and strong, but with his aunt Laura's kindly gray eyes. "My lord," he said with a nervous, jerky bow as Sebastian set aside his agent's letter and rose to his feet. "My apologies for intruding on you in this manner, but I want—I need—" The youth floundered for a moment, then clenched his jaw. "I would like to ask that you tell me the truth about what happened to my father and brother." He stared at Sebastian defiantly. "All of it. Nothing held back."

Sebastian came around from behind his desk. "Are you quite certain you're ready to hear whatever I have to say?"

"Yes. At least—" The young man paused, then pushed out a hard breath. "To be honest, sir, probably not. But I need to know. I can't spend the rest of my life . . . wondering."

Sebastian walked over to where a tray of glasses and crystal decanters rested on a side table, poured a healthy measure of brandy into a glass, and held it out to the young Viscount. "Here. And you'd better have a seat."

That evening a fine mist crept up from the river Thames, swirling through the cobbled medieval streets of Tower Hill and drifting across the last vestiges of a dying moon that hung like a pale sliver in the starless sky above the ancient fortress. Sebastian stood in Alexi's darkened garden, the mist cool and damp against his face, his thoughts far, far away. Beneath the sweet perfume of roses and honeysuckle he thought for one elusive moment that he caught a faint whiff of salt from the distant sea. Or perhaps it was merely an illusion, conjured by his knowledge that some two hundred miles to the southwest, the HMS *Northumberland* was at that very moment weighing anchor and setting sail with its famous passenger for St. Helena.

"It's hard to believe it's happening, isn't it?" said Gibson, coming to stand beside him.

Sebastian was silent for a moment, his gaze on the mist-swirled darkness above. "Thank God they didn't let the Bourbons hang him."

Gibson nodded. "I wonder if Napoléon would really have done it—settled down to the quiet life of a country gentleman on a small estate somewhere in England, I mean. If they'd let him."

"I have my doubts."

Gibson looked over at him and huffed a soft laugh. "Yeah." Then he glanced back at the house, where Alexi was setting up the contraption she'd been wanting him to try for years now. It was nothing more than a simple wooden box with a mirror, an open top, and a hole cut in one side for his good leg. The reflection of Gibson's good leg in the mirror was supposed to trick his brain into thinking his missing leg was still there, so that his brain could then somehow come to terms with the leg being gone. It still didn't make sense to Gibson, and Alexi had already warned them that this would be only the first of many such sessions Gibson would need to put himself through in the days ahead. But at some point in the last week the surgeon had finally admitted to himself that, no matter how hard he tried, he was never going to kick his opium habit as long as his phantom pains had him in their grip. And if he kept eating opium at his present rate, he was going to kill himself.

"Ready?" said Sebastian.

Gibson sucked in a deep breath that shuddered his chest, his eyes narrowing as he squinted up at the sky again. But the moon had disappeared, the mist swirling thicker and thicker around them. From where they stood, even the low-slung, death-haunted stone outbuilding at the base of the garden was now no more than a lurking shadow.

For a moment, Sebastian thought his friend wavered, that he wasn't going to do it after all. Then Gibson swallowed hard, set his jaw, and summoned up a jaunty grin. "Ready."

Author's Note

The fate of Napoléon after Waterloo was essentially as described here. He really did expect to be allowed to buy a small estate somewhere in England and settle down to the quiet life of a country gentleman, much as his younger brother had done when captured some years before. There were indeed forces in the British government pushing to have him turned over to the Bourbons to be hanged; Liverpool was originally in that camp but eventually changed his opinion. Sightseers did indeed flock to the coast by the tens of thousands in the hopes of catching a glimpse of the deposed emperor. When the South Atlantic was finally chosen as his destination, the Admiralty decided to transfer Napoléon to the HMS *Northumberland* due to fears that the aging *Bellerophon* might not be able to make the long voyage to St. Helena and back. For a more detailed description of the French emperor's surrender and his days on the *Bellerophon*, see *The Billy Ruffian: The Bellerophon and the Downfall of Napoleon, the Biography of a Ship of the Line, 1782-1836,* by David Cordingly.

The English apprentice system that existed in Sebastian's time dated back centuries, to the medieval craft guilds. By enabling master craftsmen to acquire inexpensive labor in exchange for feeding, sheltering, and training young people, it was a useful system. But the potential for abuse was always there, and by the early nineteenth century it was often used as a tool of oppression. Various statutes of apprentices passed over the years granted to justices of the peace, churchwardens, and overseers the power to bind out as apprentices any children for whom they were responsible or wherever they saw it as "convenient." As the economic situation in England deteriorated and the number of poor, abandoned, and orphaned children exploded, it became a handy way for parishes to reduce their poor rates. Such children were typically sent into the most dangerous and least lucrative jobs, including mines, foundries, factories, hat making, brickmaking, etc., with little to no supervision by authorities. The exploitation and abuses that followed were inevitable. In the late eighteenth and early nineteenth century, thousands of pauper children as young as six or seven were also loaded into open carts in London and sent north to work long, dangerous hours in the textile mills.

The use of small children to clean the narrow chimneys of London was one of the more horrific practices of the day. There were places in Europe—such as Edinburgh and many parts of Germany—where the use of climbing boys was forbidden, so chimneys could be cleaned without them. A mechanical sweep had also been invented in 1803 but was little used. Various laws restricting the use of extremely young children (girls were also sometimes used) were passed in England over the years, but none were enforced. It wasn't until late in the nineteenth century that the practice of forcing small children up dirty, hot chimneys was finally stamped out.

The term "baby farm" did not come into widespread use until the Victorian age, but the practice of farming babies out to women living in the country existed long before then. Perhaps the best known of the women eventually hanged for murdering the children left in their care were Margaret Waters (1870) and Amelia Dyer (1896). But the practice of paying a fee to a woman who would then deliberately starve or quietly kill the infant left in her care was already so common in the eighteenth century that these women were popularly nicknamed "killer-nurses." A satire written in 1768 (*The Bastard Child, or a Feast for the Church-wardens*) features churchwardens who joke with a "Mother Careless" about the speed with which she eliminates her charges. Because infant mortality in those days was so high, particularly amongst the poor, intent was difficult to prove and most of the women who either purposely killed babies or deliberately let them die were never punished.

The fencing master Damion Pitcairn is a fictional character, but he is modeled on the very real Joseph Bologne, le Chevalier de Saint-Georges (1745–1799), a violinist, composer, and fencing master born to a French planter and an enslaved Black woman. Educated by his father in France, he also served as a colonel in the Légion Saint-Georges during the First Republic. In 1787, the famous London fencing master Henry Angelo arranged an exhibition fencing match between Saint-Georges and le Chevalier d'Éon at Carlton House before the Prince of Wales (d'Éon wore his trademark black dress). While in London, Saint-Georges also played one of his concertos, went foxhunting with the Prince of Wales, and met with several prominent British abolitionists. For the record, this book was already written by the time Searchlight released their biopic *Chevalier*.

The treatments described to Sebastian by the fictional Dr. Samuel Palmer were all used in the early nineteenth century (many were used on King George III when he went mad). Because there were few controls, many perfectly sane men and women were indeed locked away in "lunatic asylums" by their families for various nefarious reasons. The Erasmus Darwin who came up with "rotation therapy" (also sometimes called the "swing chair") had a considerably more famous grandson named Charles.

Thomas Spence (1750–1814) was a historical figure. The British government did spy on his followers (known as "Spenceans") when they met in pubs. John Stafford, the supervisor of the Home Office spies based at Bow Street, was also a historical figure. We will meet the Spenceans again—Jarvis has plans.

The use of what is known as mirror therapy or mirror visual feedback as a treatment for phantom limb pain was first pioneered by V. S. Ramachandran. The mirror box basically creates the illusion of two intact limbs; the idea is that when the patient moves their intact limb, the brain is tricked into believing it has "regained" control of the missing limb it thinks it sees in the mirror. This enables the easing of the phantom cramps, etc., causing the pain. The therapy has also been expanded into use by stroke patients. Although not introduced until the 1990s, the concept is so low-tech that someone such as Alexi could conceivably have come up with the idea in the early nineteenth century.

The Environs of London map reproduced on pages x–xi is from 1832 and thus includes a number of features, such as Waterloo Bridge (opened in 1817), that would not have been there in 1815.

Keep reading for a sneak peek of

WHO WILL REMEMBER

the next enthralling Sebastian St. Cyr Mystery from
USA Today bestselling author C. S. Harris

Chapter 1

The boy stood with his thin shoulders hunched against the cold, his hands shoved deep in the pockets of his ragged coat. Narrowing his eyes against the slanting rain, he studied the silent windows of a certain elegant town house on the far side of Brook Street, then shivered.

It was only midafternoon and yet already the sky was dark and gloomy, the wind icy enough to make it feel more like February or March than high summer. But then, they hadn't had anything like a summer that year. The crops in the fields were dying—or dead. People were already going hungry, and Father said he didn't know what the poor would do when winter came. Lots of folks were scared, saying the weather wasn't ever gonna get better, that the end of the world must be upon them and Jesus would be coming back soon to save the righteous and smite the wicked.

At the thought, the boy shivered again, for he sure enough knew which category he belonged to—he and Father both. Then a flicker of movement jerked his attention back across the street, and he watched as a wavering light appeared in the room that lay to one side of that shiny black front door, as if someone there were lighting a brace of candles. A tall, lean man with dark hair and a slight limp crossed in front of the room's windows. It was the nobleman the boy was here to see: Viscount Devlin, he was called.

A trickle of rain ran down the boy's cheek to tickle his bare neck, and he swiped at his wet face with the back of one hand. He was afraid that what he was about to do was a mistake. But *something* needed to be done.

Sucking in a deep breath of the foul, coal smoke–scented air, the boy leapt the rushing gutter at his feet and crossed the street's wet granite paving. But at the base of the house's steps, he faltered. He had to force himself to march up the steps and grasp the door's shiny brass knocker. He brought it down so hard that he jumped back in surprise.

The door was opened almost at once by a grim-looking major-domo with a military air and a forbidding frown that darkened as he took in the ragged, undersized lad shifting nervously from one bare foot to the other. "The service entrance is—"

"Sure then, but 'tis his lordship I'm here to see—Lord Devlin, I mean," said the boy in a rush before the man could shut the door on him. "About a body, it is; a dead man. His face is all purple, ye see, and he's hanging—hangin' upside down."

"Ah," said the majordomo, some emotion Jamie couldn't quite decipher twitching the man's thin lips as he took a step back and opened the door wider. "Then in that case, I suppose you'd better come in."

Chapter 2

Sebastian Alistair St. Cyr, Viscount Devlin, rested his hips against the edge of his desk and leaned back, taking the weight off a leg that still gave him more trouble than he liked to admit. He was a former cavalry captain in his thirties, tall and lean, with dark hair and strange, wolflike yellow eyes. He was known to the world as the only surviving son and heir of the Earl of Hendon, although he was not, in truth, Hendon's son.

The black-haired boy who stood before him, blue eyes wide with fear as he nervously twisted his wet, ragged hat between his hands, looked to be perhaps fourteen or fifteen, although seriously underfed and scrawny. His features were even and surprisingly clean, but then that might be the work of the rain.

"What's your name, lad?"

The boy had to swallow hard before he could answer, and even then his voice came out hushed and scratchy. "Gallagher, sir. Jamie Gallagher."

Jamie. It was a name that still had the power to twist at something deep inside Sebastian, even after three years, so that it was a moment before he trusted himself to speak. "Tell me about this dead man, Jamie. Where is he?"

"He's in the ruins of that old chapel, sir," said the boy in a soft Irish lilt. "Ye know the one? In the courtyard off Swallow Street where they're tearin' down everything to make way for the Regent's grand new avenue?"

"I've seen it. You say he's hanging upside down?"

Jamie nodded. "Hangin' by one foot, he is, sir. And someone done tied his hands tied behind his back, too—like this." The boy bent his arms, elbows spreading wide as he thrust both hands behind him.

So obviously not a suicide, thought Sebastian. Aloud he said, "Why come to me? Why not find a local bailiff or constable, or go to the nearest public office?"

The boy dug one mud-streaked bare big toe into the rug at his feet. "Faith, ye think they'd listen to the likes of me? Toss me in the watchhouse for making a disturbance, that's what they'd do—if they didn't go decidin' it musta been me who done for the nob and hang me."

The nob. This was a new detail. "The dead man is a gentleman?"

The boy sniffed. "Sure then, but he must be, wearin' clothes that fine."

Pushing away from the desk, Sebastian walked to the library door. He spoke for a moment with his majordomo, then glanced over at the boy. "Morey here will take you down to the kitchens for a bite to eat while the horses are put to."

At the mention of food, something leapt in the boy's eyes, something painful to see. But he wasn't about to be distracted from his original purpose. "So you'll be comin', then? You'll be lookin' into it?"

"I'll come," said Sebastian.

"It might be a trap," said Hero some minutes later as she watched Sebastian move about his dressing room. She stood in the doorway from the bedroom, the Honorable Miss Guinevere Annabelle Sophia St. Cyr, their nine-month-old daughter, balanced on one fashionably gowned hip. The baby was chewing on a chubby fist, her brilliant blue eyes narrowed with the seriousness of her task, and he paused for a moment to tousle the child's silken fair hair with a gentle hand before turning away again.

"It might be," he acknowledged, reaching for his greatcoat. "But I doubt it."

"You will be careful."

"I'm always careful."

His wife made a scoffing sound deep in her throat and shifted the baby to her other hip. "No, you're not."

"Well, more careful than I used to be," he acknowledged, looking up with a smile as he slipped a small double-barreled pistol into the pocket of his coat.

Chapter 3

The rain had eased off by the time they left, although the air was still cool and damp against their faces, the sky above a heavy gray, the city's cobblestones and granite setts glistening with wet. Sebastian had decided to take his curricle, both because the chestnuts needed exercising and because after months and months of endless rain he was sick and tired of riding in a closed carriage.

The boy, Jamie, sat hunched on the high seat beside him, his shoulders rounded and his hands clasped between his knees so tightly the knuckles showed white. He was obviously frightened. But then, reasoned Sebastian, what lad wouldn't be after stumbling upon such a gruesome corpse?

"What made you think to come to me with what you'd found?" asked Sebastian as he turned the chestnuts down Bond Street, toward Piccadilly.

Jamie cast him a quick sideways glance, then looked away again. "Heard about ye from Father, ye see. He told me about how ye solve murders, sometimes even when the other nobs don't want ye to be solvin' 'em."

"And where is your father now?"

A quiver passed over the boy's features, then was gone. "Dead. These past two years and more."

"And your mother?"

"I don't even remember her."

I'm sorry, thought Sebastian. But he didn't say it, because the rigid set of the boy's shoulders told him any expression of sympathy would not be welcome.

He was aware of the boy tensing up tighter and tighter as they threaded their way through the sodden traffic on Piccadilly and then turned into the deserted remnants of Swallow Street. Once, this had been a thriving if somewhat aged neighborhood of small shops, workshops, modest houses, livery stables, blacksmiths, and pubs. Most were now reduced to rubble, with only rain-soaked stacks of salvaged timbers or piles of old bricks and stones standing here and there. The Regent had an ambitious scheme to push a broad, architecturally consistent avenue through the western end of London, all the way from Carlton House in Pall Mall to what they were now calling Regent's Park, and the longest stretch of it was slated to run right through here. Little had as yet actually been built, largely because of the economic woes that had beset the country since the ending of the French wars. But the wholesale destruction of everything in the project's path was well underway.

"In there, he is," said Jamie, nodding to a crumbling stone archway that still stood midway up the street. As Sebastian turned into the ancient courtyard, he could see what had once been a private chapel tucked into one corner. Built of the same golden sandstone as the ancient archway, the chapel—like the arch—was the relic of a decrepit, now half-demolished Tudor-era mansion that had once stood here. The chapel's door was already gone, part of the roof appeared to have caved in, and the facade's single lancet window gaped blankly, its delicate stone tracery empty and broken. Sebastian had been here once before, although for an entirely different reason.

"Do you live around here?" asked Sebastian, reining in before the ruin.

The boy kept his gaze fixed straight ahead. "I do not."

Sebastian waited for him to say more, but he didn't. "So what were you doing here, in the chapel?"

"Ducked in there to get out of the rain, I did. If I had the doin' of it again, I reckon I'd just get wet." A quiver passed over the boy's features as he glanced at the chapel's dark, ominously yawning doorway. "I don't need t' be goin' in there again, do I?"

"Yes."

The boy's nostrils flared on a quickly indrawn breath. Then he gave a jerky nod, braced one hand on the edge of the seat, and jumped down.

For a moment, Sebastian thought he might run, but he didn't.

"Walk them out on Swallow Street," Sebastian told his young groom, Tom, as the tiger scrambled forward to take the reins. "And be ready to get out of here fast and head for Bow Street if this is a trap."

Tom glanced over to where Jamie now stood, his hands tucked up under his armpits, his solemn gaze on the black hole of a doorway before him. "Ye reckon it might be, gov'nor?"

"No." Sebastian leapt lightly down to the broken cobbles of the ancient, shattered courtyard. "But I could be wrong."

Sebastian saw the hanging body's menacing, swaying shadow first, its arms akimbo and one leg bent up so that it appeared to be dancing a bizarre pirouette over the crumbling, rain-streaked altar.

He glanced at the boy beside him. "You all right?"

Jamie nodded, his face pale and grim. Sebastian had expected him to try to hang back, but he didn't.

Due to the orientation of the old Tudor house, the door from the courtyard entered the chapel's southern wall, up near the altar, with the columned nave stretching away into shadow to their left. Debris from the partially collapsed groin-vaulted ceiling filled the dark, musty interior, so that they had to pick their way carefully over rain-soaked segments of broken, age-darkened timbers and shattered stones. Whatever pews might once have been here were long gone, doubtless carried off by the area's impoverished residents for firewood. But through the scattered rain puddles and bird droppings at his feet, Sebastian could catch glimpses of half-obliterated inscriptions on the worn paving stones. BELOVED DAUGHTER OF . . . HERE LYETH THE BODY . . . BURIED THIS DAY . . .

"You'll be findin' him just there, sir. At the back," said the boy softly.

"I see him," said Sebastian as they came abreast of one of chapel's slender columns and the dead man himself came into full view. *"Damn."*

The man had been hung by one ankle from an old wooden beam exposed by the collapsed stone vaulting above. Blood from the gory mess someone had made of his head had dripped down to pool on the worn paving stones beneath him and congealed there. A piece of white cloth Sebastian suspected was the dead man's own cravat lashed the foot of his bent right leg to his straight left knee. His elbows were also bent, his hands hidden behind his back. As the body swayed again in a gust of wind that whistled through a gaping hole in the chapel's rear wall, Sebastian could see that the same white cloth had been used to bind together the dead man's wrists.

"Ye know who he is?" whispered Jamie, taking a step back.

Sebastian studied the hanging man's blood-streaked, distorted features, now a ghastly reddish-purple thanks to what was known as the "darkening of death." He'd been in his late forties, big and stocky, with a full face and dark hair. His clothing was that of a prosperous gentleman who patronized London's best tailors without falling victim to the lures of extreme dandyism; his only jewelry was a macabre and highly distinctive gold watch that dangled from the pocket of his pantaloons, with a single fob attached to the end of its chain.

His heart beating heavily in his chest, Sebastian hunkered down to take a closer look at that watch. Exquisitely rendered in the shape of a skull decorated all around with reliefs of Adam and Eve and the Grim Reaper, the watch was hinged at the back of the cranium so that the lower jaw dropped down to reveal its elaborate dial. It was a kind of memento mori, carried by its somber-minded owner as a reminder of human mortality and the brevity of life. And even if he hadn't recognized the dead man's discolored features, Sebastian would have recognized that watch.

"I know him," said Sebastian, his voice flat.

He was aware of the rain starting up again, pounding on what was left of the roof and slanting in through the holes in the walls and ceiling. "When exactly did you find him?" Sebastian asked—or rather started to ask. Except he knew even before he twisted around to be certain that he was now alone in the chapel.

Jamie Gallagher was gone.

Photograph by Samantha Brown

C. S. Harris is the *USA Today* bestselling author of more than thirty novels, including the Sebastian St. Cyr Mysteries; as C. S. Graham, a thriller series coauthored with former intelligence officer Steven Harris; and seven award-winning historical romances written under the name Candice Proctor. A respected scholar with a PhD in nineteenth-century European history, she is also the author of a nonfiction historical study of the French Revolution. She lives in San Antonio with her husband and has two grown daughters.

VISIT C. S. HARRIS ONLINE

CSHarris.net

CSHarrisAuthor

Ready to find
your next great read?

Let us help.

Visit prh.com/nextread

Penguin
Random
House